The
Goose Girl

The Goose Girl

Shannon Hale

BLOOMSBURY

First published in Great Britain in 2003 by Bloomsbury
Publishing Plc
38 Soho Square, London, W1D 3HB

This paperback edition published in 2005

A CIP catalogue record of this book is available from the
British Library

ISBN 0 7475 7123 6

All papers used by Bloomsbury Publishing are natural, recyclable
products made from wood grown in well-managed forests.
The manufacturing processes conform to the environmental
regulations of the country of origin.

Typeset by Dorchester Typesetting Group Ltd
Printed in Great Britain by Clays Ltd, St Ives plc

1 3 5 7 9 10 8 6 4 2

www.bloomsbury.com

For Dean

Best Friend, Companion, & Squeeter Keeper
You are Home

Part One

Crown Princess

he was born Anidori-Kiladra Talianna Isilee, Crown Princess of Kildenree, and she did not open her eyes for three days.

The pacing queen directed ministers and physicians to the crib. They listened to her breathing and her hummingbird heart, felt her fierce grip and her tiny fingers soft as salamander skin. All was sound. But her eyes did not open.

For three days the grave-faced attendants came and went. They prodded her, lifted her lids, slipped thick yellow syrups down her throat.

"You are a princess," the queen whispered to her ear. "Open your eyes."

The baby cooed in her sleep.

When the third day had worn away to the lake blue of evening, a hand parted the nursery curtains. All was still for the night. The queen dozed on the bed. The baby in her crib dreamed of milk, her round, perfect lips nursing in sleep. A woman in a fern green robe

1

pulled aside the curtains and tiptoed across the carpets. She slid her callused hands under the infant's back and head, held her up, and grinned.

"Did you call me out of my house to come and tell you stories?" she said. "I will, my fat one, if you will listen."

The queen awoke to the sounds of the rocking chair creaking and a voice singing about magpies and pigeons. She stood up, ready to call to the guards, then saw that it was her own sister who sang to the baby, and that the baby was looking back at her aunt with wide eyes.

It was the aunt who shortened the crown princess's name to Ani.

On clear days she took Ani to the north edge of the palace grounds where no wall had been built. That far out, the garden was allowed to stray out of its ordered beds and rows and merge with the occasional copse of ash and pine. The aunt felt easier there, and she held her niece's small hand and named all she saw.

"You see the bird on the tallest branch there, the one with a yellow breast? She's migrating farther north now that the weather is warmer. The bluewing there is looking for twigs and says he has found himself a picky mate."

Ani began to speak sentences at one year. The aunt knew too well how Kildenreans disliked anything outside the common, and she tried to keep Ani's progress hidden. But the household staff noted it, and rumors began that perhaps the queer green-clad nurse-mary possessed unnatural methods of awakening a child's words.

The queen was uncomfortable with the talk and careful never to call the new nurse-mary "sister." But the king was too stubborn to worry much. "Why shouldn't she be a quick learner? She is our daughter, of pure of blood as are ever born in this world, and has every right to speak before her time."

But the king saw little of his firstborn, and the queen even less. Calib-Loncris was born, the first son, and then Napralina-Victery, who from birth so resembled her mother that the nurse-marys were inclined to curtsy to the crib. With the parents' attention parted, the aunt became Ani's constant companion.

In cold weather or spring rain, the aunt sat on the nursery floor and told Ani stories of fantastic and faraway things: a land where mares pawed gold nuggets from the earth and chewed them in order to breathe out music; a baker who baked birds from dough and sent them out the window in search of a treasured pot of apricot preserves; a mother who loved her baby so fiercely, she put him in a tight locket around her neck so that he might never grow up. The aunt sang songs again and again until Ani learned the words, her toddler's voice as dry and delicate as a sparrow's call.

A day in early summer when Ani was five, the two companions sat in an aspen's dappled shade on the edge of the garden swan pond. Ani loved the birds that were as big as she and begged them to eat bread out of her hands. When the bread was all gone, they shrugged their wings and skronked at her.

"What did they say?"

"They wanted to know," said the aunt, "was there more bread for the eating or should they go back to the pond."

Ani looked at the nearest swan straight in one eye. "No more bread. You may go."

The swan shrugged his wings again.

"What does that mean?"

"I don't think he speaks your language, duckling." The aunt turned her profile and one eye to the swan and made a sound like the swan spoke, not quite a honk and almost a whine. The swan padded back to the pond.

Ani watched with a solemn expression and after a moment repeated the sounds she had heard. "Was that right?"

"Perfect," said the aunt. "Say that again."

She repeated the noise and smiled. The aunt looked at her thoughtfully, the corners of her mouth tight with suppressed excitement.

"Does that make you happy?" asked the aunt.

"Yes," said Ani with little-girl certainty.

The aunt nodded and took Ani into her lap to tell her a story about beginnings. Ani leaned her head against her aunt's chest and listened to both the story and the sound of the story.

"The Creator spoke the first word, and all that lived on

the earth awoke and stretched and opened their mouths and minds to say the word. Through many patterns of stars, they all spoke to one another, the wind to the hawk, the snail to the stone, the frog to the reeds. But after many turnings and many deaths, the languages were forgotten. Yet the sun still moves up and down, and the stars still shift in the sky, and as long as there are movement and harmony, there are words."

Ani leaned her head back and, squinting, tried to look at the sun. She was young and had not yet learned that things like seeing the sun were impossible.

"Some people are born with the first word of a language resting on their tongue, though it may take some time before they can taste it. There are three kinds, three gifts. Did you know your mother has the first? The gift of people-speaking. Many rulers do. You see? And people listen to them, and believe them, and love them. I remember as children it was difficult to argue with your mother—her words confused me, and our parents always believed her over me. That can be the power of people-speaking.

"The first gift is the only reason this little land was not taken over by other kingdoms long ago. Rulers like your mother have talked themselves out of war for centuries. It can be powerful and good, and it can also be dangerous. I, unfortunately, wasn't born knowing people-speaking." The aunt laughed, and the surface of her eyes gleamed with memory.

"Do I have it, Aunt?"

"I don't know," she said. "Perhaps not. But there are other gifts. The second is the gift of animal-speaking. I've met a few who are able to learn animal languages, but like me, those people feel more comfortable near the mountains, among the trees and places where animals are not in cages. It's not always a pleasant life, sparrow. Others are suspicious of those who can speak with wild things. Once there were many of us in Kildenree, I believe, but now, so few remember.

"The third is lost or rare. I've never known one with the gift of nature-speaking, though there are tales that insist it once was. I strain my ears and my eyes and my insides"—she tapped her temple lightly—"but I don't know the tongue of fire or wind or tree. But someday, I think, someone will discover how to hear it again."

The aunt sighed and smoothed her niece's yellow hair. "Not many know the story of the three gifts, Ani. You must remember it. It's important to know stories. I felt the earth shift to make a place for you when you were born, and I came to tell you stories while you are young. And like me, you were born with a word on your tongue. I don't know what word it was. You will grow older and discover it one day without my help."

"Maybe fire or wind or tree?" said Ani.

"Maybe," said the aunt. "I don't know those tongues. I can't help you discover them."

Ani patted her aunt's cheek as though she were the elder of the two. "But you can teach me to speak with the swans."

They returned each day to the pond. When no gardener worked within sight or courtier walked near, Ani practiced the sounds she heard.

"They don't have such a complicated world as we do and need so few words," said the aunt. "Did you hear? The tall one there was greeting the one with the tail feathers missing. They are brothers. If they were sisters, the sound would go up at the end."

Ani listened. "I just heard it. Like this." She mimicked the greeting, drawing up the last sound slightly.

"Very good," said the aunt. "You know, most people wouldn't notice that. You can hear the tiny differences and imitate them—that's your talent. But it takes work, too. You have to learn what it all means, like studying any foreign language. And it's not just sounds. Watch how that one there bobs her head and moves her tail. And holds still. It all means something."

On walks, the aunt called down the little birds from ash and beech perches, but they were anxious, busy things and would not stay long from their trees. Ani learned some of what the chickens in their coops and pigeons on their ledges complained and cooed to one another. They visited the small gray falcons and gold hawks when the hunt-master was out, and the wide-eyed owls in the barn rafters.

On one walk back from their wild garden, they passed the

corrals. The warm, earthy smell drew Ani close, and she stood on a fence rail and watched the stable-master ride a graceful gray. She pointed.

"I want to speak to that one. The horse."

"What a smart girl to think to ask." She leaned behind Ani, her cheek pressed against her niece's, and watched the animal run. "I have tried to speak to so many animals, Ani. The wild ones like wolves and deer will not stay still to listen or be listened to. Lizards, toads, rats, and all the little animals—I think perhaps their language is too simple for us bigger animals to understand. The domestic creatures like dogs, cows, and cats are sleepy in their comfort and used to communicating with people on our own terms. And birds, as you have seen, are perfect for speech. Always wild and yet always listening, and the larger ones especially, for they speak more slowly.

"But the horse, ah, Ani, I will tell you a story. Several years ago, I helped a friend with his foaling mare, and the little colt fell into my arms. I heard him, just after he tumbled out, emit a mournful little sound, something like 'Yulee.' His name. Horses are born with their own name on their tongue, you see? I repeated it back to him, and he heard me, and ever since he can hear me and I can hear him. It's a horse's way to give you the key to their speech once and never repeat it. I've tried the same with a calf and a litter of kittens and a kid-goat, but only the colt has responded. What do you think of that?"

"I would like a horse friend," said Ani. "Very much." Perhaps a horse would not hit her with play swords, like her little brother, or treat her like a glass vase and then whisper behind her back, like the other palace children.

The aunt shook her head. "You're too young. Sometime, some year, when you're older and you can go to the stables and your mother will not question why. For now, you must listen to your winged friends."

Ani was eager to learn the voice of every bird that nested on the palace grounds, but the swan pond drew her return day after day. She loved to watch them swim so slowly that the water hardly rippled and watch every silent, mild movement shimmer into meaning. Soon her throat and tongue could make nearly all the sounds of the swans, and she trumpeted gleefully.

"Hush a moment, Ani," said the aunt.

The key-mistress and her daughter, Selia, passed by the pond on the walk to the gardens. The aunt waved, and the key-mistress nodded. Her little girl was pretty and poised, with hair already to her waist. She walked with hands clasped in front and eyes centered on the path ahead. As a little girl she had been prone to violent tantrums, notorious for turning all shades of pink and purple and for kicking the floor like a landed fish. But she was seven now and prim as a court lady.

"Hello, Crown Princess," said Selia. "We are going to the gardens. Come for tea sometime."

"Um, yes, thank you." Ani was not used to being addressed by other children, and besides, this strange little girl had always made her feel uneasy—at once willing to do whatever Selia asked and eager to escape her notice. The same way, in fact, that she felt around her mother. The aunt raised one eyebrow in the blue shadow of her hat and watched the pair stroll away.

"That one has the gift of people-speaking," she said. "It can be powerful. Mark me and watch her."

Ani watched the serious little girl stroll away and tried to remember. *People-speaking. That one has.*

That year, when the trees burned the fire of late summer into their leaves and the ground mist was a ghost of the river, long and wet and cold, the aunt looked from her window to the walls around her and imagined another winter inside them. She began to see the world as a bird sees bars, and she scratched her arms beneath her sleeves.

The aunt took Ani to the shore of the swan pond where the lazy-armed trees dipped themselves into their own reflections and the aspens' hard little leaves shook in the wind with a noise like snapping fingers. The aunt pointed north, where few people lived and trees grew thick and prickly green all year, and where the girl could not follow.

"I'm going home," she said. She kissed Ani's forehead, but her eyes did not leave the purple horizon. "Don't forget all you have learned. If your mother discovers what I have taught you, she will take it away. I know her. The only thing she has ever wanted is shiny and fits around her brow. Still, you are better off with her, gosling. I would not wish my solitude on you. Stay and learn to be happy."

The princess sat on a stone, rested her arm on the back of a swan, and thought how her chest felt like a gutted walnut shell, and wondered if that sensation might last forever. She watched her aunt walk away, disappearing into a tiny spot of green that the eye tricked into a shadow of a rock a long way in the distance.

The next morning, Ani was dismayed to see she had been given a new companion, a weak-hearted nurse-mary with skin like sour milk. They were not to go to the pond because "the young crown princess might fall in and drown, with her face bloated and purple like a sauced plum, would you like that?"

Despite her aunt's cautions, Ani was certain if she explained to the nurse-mary that she just wanted to speak with the swans, then it would be all right. When the woman's eyes widened, Ani mistook it for eagerness.

"I can understand what they say," Ani said. "I'll teach you how, too, if you like."

The nurse-mary rose from the garden bench, gasping, and tossed bits of grass in the air before her to shake loose the evil.

"You'll curse yourself. People don't speak to animals, and it's not such a clever game to say you do."

Ani overheard the nurse-mary report to the queen in hushed, hurried tones that made Ani feel she had done something unspeakably bad. Thereafter, outings were limited to the gardens and the nursery porch. Her mother looked at her now with a distant, disapproving frown, and Ani resolved to keep to herself until her aunt would return and carry her off into the freedom of the mountains. Long hours she spent watching the purple horizon, willing her aunt to walk back out of it with welcoming arms.

She missed the sound of bird words, and the feeling that came, like a cricket leaping inside her chest, when she heard and understood. In her world of cold marble floors and aged tutors and whispering children, only the animal-speaking felt like her own thing and the pond her own place. Once or twice when the nurse-mary was bedded with a head cold, Ani escaped the nursery porch and ran to practice with the swans. As she approached, two gardeners stepped between her and the pond.

"Can't come around here, Crown Princess," said the hard-skinned man. "Dangerous."

When she tried to slip into the mews to converse with the hawks, the hunt-master carefully escorted her out with a firm grip on her collar.

"Sorry, Crown Princess," he said. "The queen was clear that you were not to play near my birds."

She tried many times in the two years she waited for her aunt's return, and each time someone stopped her. It felt like dreams when she ran but could not move. Sometimes in secret, Ani lay on her belly and tried to mimic her puppy Lindy's whines and growls.

"Listen to me," she said. "Can you understand me, Lindy?"

The nurse-mary must have overheard, for when Ani returned from her tutor's apartment one afternoon, the puppy was gone and her mother stood in the center of the nursery, waiting.

"He is in the kennels now," said the queen. "I think it best that you no longer keep pets."

"I want Lindy back." Ani was hurt and angry, and she spoke louder than she ever had before. "You give him back."

The queen slapped Ani's mouth.

"That tone is unacceptable. This fantasy has gone unchecked for too long. If I had known that woman was teaching you those mad ideas she had when we were children, I would have sent her running from this city without her pack. It is time you learn your place, Crown Princess. You will be the next queen, and your people will not trust a queen who makes up stories and seems to talk to wild beasts."

Ani did not answer. She was holding her stinging mouth and staring at the purple horizon.

The queen turned to go, then paused before the door. "I

came to tell you. We received word today that your aunt passed away this winter. I am sorry if this hurts you."

Ani watched her mother's back walk away and felt her seven-year-old world tumble like a hatchling from a tree.

That evening her parents held a ball. The nurse-marys stood in the nursery doorway and smiled toward the music that came down the corridor like a sigh. The wet nurse held the new princess, Susena-Ofelienna, to her breast and spoke of skirts and slippers. A young, pretty nurse-mary held Napralina-Victery to her shoulder and whispered about men and secret things.

Every word they spoke seemed to empty Ani more, like buckets dipped into a shallow well. She pretended great interest in building a city of many towers with her pale wood bricks, and when the nurse-marys wandered into the corridor for a closer look, Ani slipped out the nursery porch to run away.

The light that came from behind pushed her shadow forward, a very thin giantess stretching across the lawn, her head pointing to the pond. She ran on the damp night grass and felt the breeze go right through her nightgown. It was early spring and still cold at night.

She reached the pond and looked back to where the pink marble ballroom gazed brilliantly out at the night, the glass and walls trapping the music in. The people inside looked beautiful, graceful, and completely at ease in their place. It helped her resolve to realize that she was nothing like them.

But when she turned her back to the lights, she saw that the night was so dark, the stables did not exist. She could not see the stars. The world felt as high as the depthless night sky and deeper than she could know. She understood, suddenly and keenly, that she was too small to run away, and she sat on the damp ground and cried.

The water lipped the pond's sandy side. The swans slept, blue and silver in the night. One swan roused at Ani's sob and greeted her, then nested in the sand near her feet. *I am tired*, Ani told her, *and lost from my herd.* The swan words she spoke sounded to her human ears like the mournful wail of a child. *Sleep here*, was the bird's simple reply. Ani lay down and, putting one arm over her face as though it were a wing, tried to shut out the world where she did not belong.

She awoke when two strong hands lifted her.

"Crown Princess, are you all right?"

She wondered why the world was so black, then realized her eyes were still closed. Her lids seemed too thick to open. She let her head fall against the man's shoulder and smelled the strong goat milk soap of his clothing. He was carrying her away.

"Who are you?"

"Talone, Watcher of the East Gate. You were asleep with the swans and would not rouse."

Ani creaked open one eyelid and saw that the sky above the mountains was eggshell pale. She looked at the man and was about to ask a question when she shuddered again, from her bones to her skin.

"Are you hurt, Crown Princess?"

"I'm cold."

He pulled his cloak off his shoulders and wrapped it around her, and the warmth lured her back into a fevered sleep.

It was three weeks before she was well enough that the lines on the physicians' faces relaxed into wrinkles and the youngest nurse-mary did not exclaim whenever Ani opened her eyes. Long after the fever, her name was often replaced with "that delicate child." She was kept indoors. She was never alone. She breakfasted in bed and supped on a couch and never laced her own boot. The incident with the swans was mentioned only in secret tones.

"We almost lost a future queen."

"And not just to death, but to wildness."

"What shall we do with her?" said the nursery-mistress.

The queen looked down at Ani, who lay sleepily awake, her eyes half-open, her ears pricked for the judgment that would fall from her mother's powerful mouth onto her head. Somehow by getting sick, Ani felt she had badly betrayed this woman, and remorse pricked at her with the fever chills. The queen was like some terribly beautiful bird whose language she did not yet understand, and she felt her thin body fill with the desire to understand, and to please.

The queen squinted, briefly creating spider leg–thin lines around her eyes. She laid a cool hand on Ani's forehead. The gesture was almost motherly.

"Keep her resting," said the queen, "and away from birds."

ni set down the cold remains of her peppermint tea and hoped she was still smiling. The view from the window tugged at her attention, teasing her with indistinct movements in the direction of the stables, brown spots that might have been horses running. But she kept her eyes firmly on the brown freckle on the key-mistress's upper right cheek.

"Let me express again, Crown Princess, how honored we are that you accepted our invitation this afternoon. I hope the meal was to your liking."

"Yes, thank you," said Ani.

"I have begged my daughter for some months to invite you to our apartments. You have grown as tall as your mother, save her, though not quite as pretty, and I wonder, since you seem to always be quite busy, if you have yet learned what duties are most important to your station?"

"Um, thank you, yes." Ani winced. The key-mistress had been waiting months for this afternoon because

18

Ani had taken great pains to escape it. This kind of thing was, apparently, supposed to be social and relaxing. But like every visit and tea and party Ani attended, she was aware that others expected the crown princess to act, speak, and think as queenly as her mother, a feat that for her, Ani was certain, was as likely as her blowing down the wind. "Yes," she said again, and winced again, conscious of just how dim she sounded.

Silence hovered between them like a tired moth. Clearly she was expected to say something else, but panic at having to speak stole thoughts from her head. She glanced at Selia, but her lady-in-waiting's serene demeanor gave no clues as to how to respond. Selia often reminded Ani of a cat, seemingly bored yet taking everything in with her lazy gaze. At age eighteen, Selia was two years Ani's senior, four fingers shorter, and her long hair was one pale shade darker than Ani's yellow. In appearance, they were almost as alike as sisters.

Her eyes lingered a moment on Selia, and she found herself thinking, *She would be better at playing princess than I am.* The thought stung. Ani wanted so badly to do it right, to be regal and clever and powerful. But too often her only truly happy moments were the bursts of freedom, stolen afternoons on her horse's back, brief, breathtaking rides past the stables to where the gardens turned wild, her lungs stinging with the cold, her muscles trembling with the hard ride. It had been nearly ten years since she had last thought of running away, staring out at the too big night from the shores of the swan pond. She would never try again. She was the crown princess, and she was determined to one day make a decent queen.

The key-mistress cleared her throat, and Ani looked back, thankful her hostess had taken it upon herself to crack the silence. "I hope I don't show presumption to say that you have been more than mistress to my Selia since the queen your mother chose her to be the first—and might I dare to say, most honored—member of your retinue, but you have also been her friend."

"Yes." Ani readjusted her hands in her lap and fought for something new to say. She only smiled again and said, "Thank you."

"Crown Princess, you look as though you wish to ask for something," said Selia. Ani turned to her gratefully and nodded. Selia lifted the pot. "More tea?"

"Oh, yes, um, thank you."

Selia filled her cup, and the key-mistress looked down at her own, mumbling, "Tea, yes."

"Actually," said Ani, and her heart pounded at having to speak out, "actually, if you do not mind, my father and I are to go riding today, and so, you see, I had best go soon."

"Oh." The key-mistress glanced at her daughter and gave one shake of her head.

Selia touched Ani's hand. "Crown Princess, Mother has been looking forward to this visit for a fortnight."

At once Ani felt Selia's words burn her cheeks red, and she

looked down. *I've fouled up again,* thought Ani. "I'm sorry." She sipped her tea. It was too hot, and she felt her heart beat in her burned tongue.

"Riding," said the key-mistress.

"Yes, Mother, I told you. She finds time to ride almost every day."

"Yes, rides a stallion, I believe. Do you not think, Crown Princess, that it is inappropriate for a princess to ride a stallion? Should you not ride a nice, gentle mare or gelding? Are you not afraid that you will break your crown?" The key-mistress turned to her daughter. "That was a pun, dear. Break your crown."

Selia laughed her high, lovely laugh.

Something about that exchange burned Ani's pride like her tongue. She set down her cup and stammered an awkward reply.

"Yes, well, I do ride a stallion, and if my father, the king, thinks it is inappropriate, he will tell me so. At any rate, thank you for the tea and the dinner. I must go. I'm sorry. Thank you."

She stood up. Selia looked up at her and blinked, unaccustomed, it seemed, to even that much of an outburst from her mistress. It took the key-mistress a few moments to refurbish herself with words.

"Yes, yes, off you go, Crown Princess. For the best. It is, you know, inappropriate to keep the king waiting."

They exited the key-mistress's apartments and walked

briskly down the corridor. Selia's heels made her nearly as tall as Ani, and they clicked on the tile floor like a cat's claws grown unchecked.

"Are you all right?" said Selia.

Ani let out a breath and laughed a little. "I don't know why I let myself panic like that."

"I know. But I thought it would be good for you to practice."

"You are right, Selia, I know you are. I hate the way I get so muddled and say everything wrong and take everything wrong."

"And as you are to be queen one day, you have to learn now how to converse pleasantly with people you don't care about."

"Oh, it's not that I don't care about her, or anyone else." Ani thought perhaps it was that she cared too much. She was constantly worried about what others thought of her, and how every word she spoke could condemn her further. Ani thought how to explain that to Selia and decided that she could not. Selia's ease with strangers and friends alike made Ani sure she would not understand. Besides, Ani was eager to shrug off the unpleasant feelings of another failure.

She felt herself relax a little when they passed under an arch and outside. It was an afternoon in winter, the sun bright and the air like early morning, new and wet with coming snow. When they approached the stables, Selia curtsied and walked to the gardens as she often did when Ani went riding. The lady-in-waiting was allergic to horses. Or so she said. Once, from a distance, Ani had witnessed Selia willingly entering a stable holding hands with an unknown man. But Ani had refused to inquire. She, too, had her secrets.

Ani entered the first stable. The familiar smells of warm bodies and clean hay greeted her like a friendly touch. She made her way past bowing grooms to the stall she knew best.

Falada, said Ani.

A white horse raised his head and made no audible sound.

The first time Ani had spoken that name, she had been eleven. The prime minister of Bayern, the kingdom on the other side of the mountains, had been visiting at the time, and all wary-eyed parties were so busy entertaining road-weary dignitaries that Ani had been able to steal away to the stables a few times to bring to pass a childhood wish. So it was that Ani was by the stable-master's side when an overdue mare foaled her white, long-legged colt. Ani had helped break open the birthing sac and cleared the fluids from his nostrils. She had steadied his middle as he first tried to stand, balancing his long body on stick legs and staring at the lighted world with oversize eyes. She had listened when he spoke his name, that word that had lain on his tongue while he still slept in the womb. And when she repeated it, he had heard her. After this initial connection, it was not long before she discovered they could speak to each other without other people hearing a sound.

And Ani was grateful for that. She remembered how it

had taken all her father's power just to convince the queen that Ani should be allowed to keep her horse. Certainly he would have been sent off to the provinces the moment the queen suspected Ani and Falada of having such a bond.

Falada, I am late. Tirean is gone from her stall. My father must already be riding.

The boy did not give me enough oats, said Falada.

His voice entered her mind as naturally as her own thoughts, but as distinct as the smell of citrus. Ani smiled, with sincerity now, and worked off the glumness of the lunch visit by attacking his white hide with quick brush strokes. *I wonder sometimes how much is enough.*

You give me enough.

Because I love you too much and I cannot say no. But I will for now because my father is waiting.

She saddled him, and he teased her by holding his breath when she tightened the girth. *What, you want me and the saddle to fall off your back at the first fence?* And she led him with a loose rein out of the stable and into the bright afternoon. A thin, stiff layer of snow crunched beneath their feet and reflected hard sunlight into their eyes. Ani squinted into the brilliant distance where her father rode his black mare, Tirean. He waved and rode up. He was a tall, slender man with hair so pale, Ani could not separate the natural from the graying hairs in his beard unless she was close enough to touch.

"You are late," he said.

"I was being a crown princess," said Ani.

He dismounted and gave Falada a friendly pat. "Off playing pins and balls with your siblings, no doubt. I heard them in the west hall."

"Come now, Father, you know the queen would never permit such nonsense from me. 'Anidori, a crown princess, like a queen, can succeed only by staying apart. Separation, elevation, delegation.'"

The king grimaced. He had long ago ceased to argue such points with his wife. "Tell me, then, what your business was this morning—separating, elevating, or delegating?" He clapped his hands twice as though it were a song.

"Oh, all three. I breakfasted alone while sketching a map of Kildenree from memory for my tutor, I was surrounded by my 'lessers' all morning as I received mendicants and courtiers, and then I solved all their problems by assigning them to other people. Oh, and a social visit with Selia's mother to end it all with a flourish." She nodded and curtsied.

"That is wonderful, Anidori," he said with all the force of a proud father. "And how did you do?"

"Fine." In truth it had been, from dawn until then, a horrible day full of trips, stutters, and stupidity. She felt her chin tremble a little and covered it with a hand. His assurance that she was wonderful was a stab in the soreness of her insecurity. He more than anyone knew how she tried to be what her mother was, and how often she failed. It was he who in earlier years had held her weeping at his chest and told her that she was good enough, that she was his best girl. She had not sought his comfort in years, trying as she was to grow up, to be independent and queenly enough not to hurt, but she longed for his succor now.

"Or, you know, well enough." Her voice cracked a little, and she turned away to mount Falada. But he caught her shoulders and pulled her into his embrace. The little girl in her won out, and she sobbed lightly against his chest.

"There, easy now," he said as though calming an anxious horse.

"I was terrible, Father. I'm so worried that I will say all the wrong things and that they think I'm a dim, sickly, bird-speaking girl that I actually shake, and my mind goes blank, and I just want to run away."

He stroked her hair and kissed the top of her head. "But you don't, Anidori, do you? You stay and you try. You are so much braver than I. And as you keep trying, the rest will come."

She nodded and soaked in his comfort for a moment in silence.

Falada nosed her shoulder. *I thought we were going running.*

Ani smiled and smeared the tears across her cheeks. "I think my horse is anxious for a ride."

"Yes, ride." His face brightened as he put his hands on her shoulders and kissed her brow. "And as much as I love you, my dear, I am afraid Tirean and I are going to have to teach the two of you a lesson in speed."

"Oh, really?" She laughed, knowing that the king's mare rarely outran Falada.

"Yes, yes, off we go." The king mounted and immediately began a canter that streaked into a run. He was heading for a fence that separated the ends of the training grounds from the loosely wooded wilds, and he was, indeed, riding fast. His speed made her feel uneasy. She called out to him. He waved a hand in the air and continued his assault toward the fence.

"It's too high," she shouted, but he could not hear her now. She mounted Falada and asked him to follow. They had only halved his distance when the king reached the fence. Tirean leapt.

"Father!" she said.

There was a sound like bones rubbing together as the mare's hoof just scraped the post. Tirean's balance tilted. The king looked down as his mount fell. It looked wrong to Ani, that graceful, long-legged horse and that tall man, creatures that should stand and run, instead hitting the earth like discarded things. When Tirean regained her feet, the king remained on the ground.

Ani jumped off Falada's back and ran to the fence. Other stable-hands were there before her. "Easy, easy," she heard more than one voice say. When they tried to approach the prostrate king, the mare screeched, stepped over him, and straddled his body protectively. They stepped forward slowly, and Tirean glared with one round black eye and huffed warning through wide nostrils. The stable-hands stepped back, afraid the horse would trample the king.

Ani slipped through the fence and put out her hand. "Please, Tirean, step away."

She could not speak truly to this horse or any other, just to her own Falada, who had heard her speak his name at birth. Tirean was dumb to the words and shook her head at Ani's hand. Ani reached for Tirean's halter, and the mare nodded up and down, whipping the reins against the snow. Ani felt too tired to move. Her father was facedown, one arm sprawled, one tucked beneath his chest. She could not tell if he was dead or if he slept, only that he did not open his eyes. Ani turned to Falada on the other side of the fence.

Falada, she needs to move.

Falada circled back, began a quick canter, and jumped the fence. The mare started at his leap but did not move away from the king. Falada shook his mane and walked forward to touch noses with the mare. He nudged her with his cheek and breathed on her neck. Tirean seemed to sigh, a gust of warm breath that played in Falada's mane. She stepped back carefully and huddled against a tree, her neck and mane shuddering, her head bent to the ground.

Ani rushed to him and heard his breath rattle strangely in his chest. She bade the stable-hands move the king to the stable-master's bed, where he slept for three days. The palace physicians could not wake him. The queen sat by his side, dry-eyed, sleepless. Calib, Napralina, Susena-Ofelienna, and the toddler Rianno-Hancery took turns holding his hand. Ani sat in a chair, gazing at his still face, and felt again like the little girl who had watched her aunt walk away into the purple horizon, her chest an abandoned snail shell.

On the fourth day, the king woke briefly to smile up at Susena, who was holding his hand at the time. His eyes fluttered closed, then he turned his head to one side and did not breathe in again.

The Great City was decked with white on the day of his burial. The royal family in white mourning dress walked like ghosts after the funeral wagon. Ani gripped her skirts in her fists and concentrated on the single note of the flute player and Rianno-Hancery's high, sobbing cries twisting about one another in a painful harmony. She looked up where the White Stone Palace stretched its walls like low wings and raised the head of its single high tower to the winter blue— so like a swan, the bird of mourning. She took a shred of comfort in imagining that even the palace mourned. Her mother walked at the head of her remaining family, elegant and poised in her sorrow. Ani thought, *These people watch me, their future queen. I need to seem strong.* She straightened and stopped her tears, but next to her mother, she felt only half-formed.

After the burial and ceremony, the queen stood before the tomb and spoke to the gathered people. She recalled the king's diplomatic and military successes, the alliances he had formed, and the peace Kildenree had enjoyed since his coronation. To herself, Ani remembered other things, like his smile that pulled stronger on his right side than his left, the smell of the sheep oil he kept on his beard, and how these last years he had begun to smell less of parchment wax and more of stables. That made her smile.

Then the queen said, "Do not fear that this sad day means more than the end of this king's life. We will go on. I will continue as your queen and keeper of the realm. And in that distant day when you will carry my body to this place, my noble and capable son Calib-Loncris will be ready to take up the scepter and crown."

Ani looked up, her mouth slightly agape. Selia at her side pinched her arm.

"Did you hear that, Crown Princess?"

Ani shook her head slowly. "She made a mistake. She must be . . . she is confused in her sorrow, that's all."

"Calib doesn't look confused," said Selia.

Ani caught sight of her fifteen-year-old brother standing to her mother's right. *When had he grown up so much?* she wondered. He was as tall as his very tall mother, and his face was smooth and controlled like hers.

The queen finished and descended the tomb steps. Calib looked at Ani for the first time, hesitated, then stepped close to her.

"I'm sorry," he said. His forehead creased, and his eyes filled with the concern of an uncertain boy.

"How long have you known she would do this?" said Ani.

Calib shrugged. There was a trace of smugness in his refusal to smile, before he turned and walked stately after his mother.

Selia prodded, but Ani refused to talk to her mother until after the six weeks of mourning white.

"She is your mother, and she owes you an explanation."

Ani sighed. "First, she is the queen, and she owes me nothing. Besides, I don't want to soil my father's mourning with greedy or offended thoughts." And also, Ani admitted to herself, she was afraid of the answer. Was her mother really capable of taking away everything Ani had worked and worried and studied and sweated for just on caprice? Ani took Selia's hand and they leaned back on a courtyard bench, the sides of their heads touching.

"After the six weeks, then. But I will not let you avoid it. She is fooling with your future."

"Thank you, Selia. I would feel so alone right now without you."

Selia patted her hand. Ani was thoughtful, watching the winter sky warm up into a bird's-egg blue. The brilliant pain after her father's death was subsiding into a mean ache, but Ani was not yet ready to let it go.

"Selia, why do you worry so much about what my mother said?"

It suddenly seemed to Ani that Selia's passion on the subject went beyond the feelings of a concerned friend. But Selia did not answer. They sat in silence, the question hanging between them in the chilly afternoon like a frozen breath.

At the end of six weeks, Ani stood outside the queen's study, rallying her nerve. Selia waved encouragement from down the corridor and then went into her own apartment to await the outcome.

"Enter," said the queen.

Ani took a deep breath. The queen was gifted with people-speaking, and Ani knew that arguing against her mother's powers of persuasion was difficult—almost as difficult as explaining to Selia if she did not question her.

"Mother, I ask pardon for intruding so soon after the mourning period, but I must ask you about your statement some weeks ago—"

"Yes, yes, child, about Calib-Loncris. Sit down." The queen was at her desk, looking over a parchment. She did not glance up. This was one of her tactics. Ani had been forceful and prepared, and now she was made to sit and wait at the whim of the queen.

When the queen at last set down the parchment and met her daughter's eyes, Ani was expecting an accusing stare and was surprised by the sorrow that weighed down her features.

She could not tell if the sorrow was for her father or for her. A thought buzzed in Ani's head: *I do not know this woman at all.* Her stomach turned uneasily.

The queen met her eyes with a firm blue stare. "You remember, five years ago we received a visit from Prime Minister Odaccar of Bayern." Ani nodded. It had been the year Falada was born. "It was not an idle visit. The prime minister does not journey for three months to have tea with the queen and king of Kildenree. There were issues of land."

The queen stood in front of the wall map and put her left hand, fingers spread, over the mass of Bavara Mountains and the great Forest that separated the two kingdoms. She looked at her hand a moment before speaking. "Bayern has long been a rich country, maintaining their wealth for centuries by launching successful wars.

"The current sovereign is less belligerent than his ancestors. His own father and two brothers were killed in war when he was a boy, and he has ruled differently. But war was their business, and to replace that kind of income, the king spent years financing mining in their mountains. Successfully. They are following a rich deposit of gold that brings them, each year, closer to Kildenree. At this point, five years since Odaccar visited, they must be very near indeed. There have never been roads through these mountains, so official borders have never been made."

The queen looked up at Ani, her expression forcefully smooth. "Bayern's king was becoming greedy. He claimed the bulk of the mountains for Bayern, leaving us a thin range, weak protection from a country so much larger than ours. And stronger. Your father feared intrigue. As did I. Your father did nothing but fear. I acted."

Her mother's magic with words was worming into Ani's mind. Already she was thinking, *Yes, fine, whatever you did is fine.* She pricked herself again and warned herself not to fall into the role of complacent listener.

The queen sat down and pressed her fingers against the corners of her eyes. "I have done what a queen should and what is best for Kildenree. The wide mountain range and the vastness of the Forest have kept us separated from our dangerous neighbors. In the past it would have taken an army four months at best to reach us by the Forest Road—the only road. Now, what is to defend us when the pass is cut? What will prevent that monstrous army from pouring into this valley? Nearly a generation of our men was killed in the civil war before your father and I were placed in power. Our armies are insufficient."

She seemed to be talking to herself now, and her tone was near pleading. Ani felt dread begin to prickle her skin. Her mother never pleaded.

"You are the crown princess. If it had to be one of my children, it should have been Napralina, I know. She is the third child, the second daughter, just the prize such an arrangement would require. But she was so young, and you—you were different. After the trouble with your aunt, I worried that the people would never trust you, that the rumors of your being a beast-speaker had sunk too deep."

"What did you do, Mother?" said Ani.

The queen ignored the question. Her voice twanged defensively. "A queen is never so secure that she can ignore what her people think of her, Anidori."

"What did you do?"

"Did you not pass your sixteenth birthday during the mourning period?"

Ani nodded.

The queen took an audible breath and looked back at the map. "It was fortunate, truly, that Odaccar wished for peace as much as I. In private counsel, we arranged your marriage to the king's first son. After your sixteenth birthday."

Ani stood, her chair scraping against the tile floor with a whine. The sound roused her, and she found she could argue back. "What? But, but you can't."

"I do not want you to tell me that what I did is not fair. I know it is not fair."

"But I am the crown princess. I am supposed to be the next queen. The law says I am the next queen."

"Your motivation has always seemed to come more from duty than desire. I imagined you might even be relieved."

"Do not pretend that you are doing me a favor, Mother. You can't just take away who I am. Whether or not you think I...I am good enough to be queen of Kildenree, that is what you have raised me to be, what I have worked at all my life." Ani narrowed her eyes as realization burned her blood, and her voice softened with the pain of betrayal. "Is this why you kept me away from my siblings all these years? Not because you were training me to be queen, but rather protecting them from me because you knew you would be sending me away? Separation, elevation, delegation—it was all just a ruse."

"You will still be a queen, Anidori."

Ani shook her head. "You know it's not the same. It will not be my crown. It will not be my home. I'll be a stranger, the foreigner wife of their king."

Her mother glared. "What do you want? You want me to coddle you and feel sorry for you?"

"I just—"

"I will not have you questioning me!" The queen bolted upright. Instinctively, Ani covered her mouth with a trembling hand.

"You are understandably angry, but that will not change the promises I have made, nor will it change what you will do."

Tears stung Ani's eyes, and she slowly lowered her hand from her mouth. "Did Father know?"

"No, he did not," said the queen with some contempt. "He did not want to know. I told him I arranged the marriage for Napralina, that we would tell her when she turned fifteen, and by the time he found out it was you, it would be too late for him to change it. Had he known, he would have felt he needed to protect you. Protect a future queen! You should have been strong enough not to need protection."

"I was only a little girl then."

The queen shook her head. "You should never have been only a little girl, you should have always been a crown princess."

"All right, enough," said Ani, too hurt to bear another word, and to her surprise her mother did not answer back. Her heartbeats shook her body, and she stood in silence awhile, trying to think of more things she would like to say. Battling her mother exhausted her, and hopelessness readily sucked away her anger.

The map glared at her from the wall. The Great City Valley nestled in a curve of the Bavara Mountain Range. Farmlands radiated west and south like fingers from a palm. To the north and northeast, a mass of arrowheads represented the mountains. To the east and southeast, a tight group of crossed lines indicated the Forest. Past those great barriers was a white space and, in its center in script so perfectly tiny that it looked to have been written by a cricket's claw, the word *BAYERN*.

Her eyes followed the long road that began south of the Great City and moved east, curving northeast and then north to eventually form three-quarters of a circle. It wound for weeks through the Forest and ended in that white space, that unknown. She looked down at the lines on her palm. They were all straight, not curved and long like the line of the road.

"Bayern," said Ani.

"I am sorry, Anidori," said the queen.

It was the first time she had heard her mother speak those words. They did not console. In them, she heard her mother saying, *I am sorry I had to choose such for you, and I am sorry, for I know you will do what I chose.* Ani saw herself clearly in that moment, as a face in darkness gains sudden dimensions in a flash of lightning—a young girl, a silly thing, a lapdog, a broken mare. She did as she was told. She rarely gave thought to her duties or spent deep hours or acted alone. She realized she would never have been capable of taking her mother's place. That realization did not bring relief. Instead, the thought of the journey and her unknown future chilled her skin and pricked her stomach with dread.

"I will go, but you already know that, don't you?" Ani looked at the window where the bare branches of a cherry tree crossed out the view. "I'll go."

pring shrugged off its late snows and early pollen and settled into warmness, keen for summer. For Ani, the sudden dismissal from responsibilities was bewildering. She and Selia spent days wandering around the corridors, looking for something to do. Courtiers nodded to her but did not meet the eyes of the crown princess who had been deemed unworthy to rule. Those who did address her clipped her title to "Princess" and the "Crown" was passed on to her brother. All except for Selia. Stubbornly loyal, her lady-in-waiting still insisted on using her full and original title.

Selia was, of course, wrathful to hear what the queen had done.

"You cannot just allow her to take away what is rightfully yours."

"And I cannot take it back. I have no power here, Selia."

But quickly Selia seemed to see the futility in

mourning the inevitable. At least she stopped berating Ani's passivity and even began to show eagerness for the journey.

"Just think of it, Crown Princess, you can start a new life with new possibilities. You will decide who you are."

It was little consolation at the moment, knowing that she was leaving everything she had ever known to marry a foreign prince whom no one seemed to know much about. And the betrayal still stung, as did the knowledge that had she been good enough, she would still be crown princess and Napralina would be looking forward to a long journey after her sixteenth birthday.

Selia asked to spend much of her remaining period with her mother, and Ani suddenly found time to squander in the summering world. It was a relief to be with Falada, who had never cared if Ani had a "Crown" before her name. Calib was busy with his new duties and seemed to guiltily avoid Ani's presence when he could, but Ani stole afternoons with Napralina and Susena and regretted having known them so little before. Days pushed by. The time to journey quickly arrived.

On the morning of departure, Ani woke with a gasp. The total blackness disturbed her, and she sat up quickly, .touching her eyes to see if they were still there. A little moonlight seeped through her curtains and comforted her.

It was just early.

Her nightmare still clung to her like the smell of smoke to cloth. Heralded by trumpets, serving boys had carried her into the banquet hall kneeling on a platter garnished with blue cabbage leaves and water lilies. She wore her white nightgown. Purple cherries dripping syrup had replaced her eyes. Her arms were strained backward as though she wished to fly away. They set her down before her mother, who lifted a carving knife and said, "It is your duty, daughter, for the good of the feast."

Remembering the dream made her laugh a little. "Don't be so dramatic," she told herself. "It's not as though she is sending me off to be killed." The dream, no doubt, had been inspired by the farewell banquet of last evening. The main course had been white swans roasted in their feathers.

Ani opened her curtains and breathed in the warm night air. Cricket voices battled for more night, and she wished she could grant it to them. Her brown travel dress with wide skirts hung over a chair. When the sun rose, she would go.

From her window she could not see the direction they would travel, so she sat facing north and contemplated the familiar view. No more crying, she told herself. It was not difficult. Her eyes were dry and sore. She concentrated on forming the images and sensations of her Kildenrean life into a body, and in her mind burying that body, peacefully, next to her father's tomb in the soft summer earth.

Ani was still at the window watching the sun conquer

early morning blue with hot gold light when her maid entered. She exclaimed at the late hour, helped Ani dress, and braided her hair in one long plait down her back, unadorned. Ani felt keenly unroyal, boyish, and sick to her stomach.

The escort was waiting for her at the front gates. The queen had arranged for a forty-man company, led by Talone, former watcher of the east gate, to accompany Ani on the nearly three-month journey to Bayern. One-fifth of the escort drove wagons full of supplies, as well as dresses and cloaks and gilded things that were given to Ani as last gifts. Her siblings stood before the wagons, squinting against the rising sun. Napralina and Susena cried sleepily. Calib looked distant, though when he returned her gaze she saw his eyes were full of emotion.

Ani embraced her sisters, then stood before Calib, placing her hands on his shoulders. He looked down.

"It's all right, Calib," she said. "I was upset at first, but I'm resigned to it now. The crown is yours. Enjoy it, and do it better than I would have."

His chin began to quiver, and he turned away before he could cry.

Next to Calib, Selia was smiling and mounted on her gray horse. Falada stood alone. His new saddle was a pale golden red, vibrant against his white coat. *At least he looks royal*, Ani thought. She was grateful that in this one regard her mother had respected her wishes—she would not be made to ride the endless weeks inside a carriage like a caged bird.

It is early, said Falada.

Yes, but I am late coming, said Ani. *I am not happy to leave.*

Nor I. My stall was nice and food was good. But the new place will have nice stalls and good food, too.

She imagined it would, and she wished she was as easily comforted as a horse, but the long road intimidated her, and her inability to imagine any part of her new life left it dark and daunting in her mind—a distant place, a warlike people, a shadowed husband with a face she could not imagine. Tales of naive young girls marrying murderous men performed grimly in her mind. Ani put her arms around Falada's neck and briefly hid her face in his mane. His warmth encouraged her.

"Behold, my royal daughter," said the queen.

Ani looked up. The attention of the forty-man company, royal family, and small group of well-wishers turned to the queen, who was holding aloft a beaten gold cup. A reflected glare of sunlight made Ani close her eyes and Falada lower his head. *Ah*, thought Ani, *time for the show of affection.*

"The road is long, and she will walk upon fir needles rather than velvet carpets. So let her always drink from this. The lips of our honored daughter will never touch the vulgar thing."

Ingris, the camp-master, nodded gravely and took the cup from the queen.

"And let all who see her mark her as our royal daughter and princess." At that the queen placed on Ani's head a circlet of gold with three ruby droplets pressed against her brow. The gold was cold. Her neck pricked with goose bumps.

The queen gave Ani a mother's adoring stare, and Ani returned it coldly. She was in no mood to pretend love between them. She had no more duty to these people save to leave them. The queen flinched under her gaze, and her eyes hinted at guilt and sadness. A childlike hope tickled in Ani—*Is she sad for me? Is she sorry to lose me?*

The queen pulled a neatly folded handkerchief from her sleeve and smoothed it open. It was made from a thin ivory cloth with green, rust, and yellow lace edging.

"The stitching was done by my grandmother." Her voice was soft, as though to convince Ani that the words were for her alone and not a performance for the crowd. She unfastened a horse-head brooch from her breast. "My mother used to carry it, and then she gave it to me before she died. I have always felt it held a part of her. When I wear it, I feel her eyes on me, approving, guiding, protecting. So I send with you my own protection."

The queen winced first, then stabbed her third finger with the brooch pin. She squeezed three drops of blood onto the handkerchief. Her hands were shaking.

"I have nightmares that the Forest, like a great-jawed beast, swallows the road in front of you and sucks you into its mouth. If anything should happen to you, it would break my heart." She put the stained handkerchief in Ani's hand

and held it a moment, sincerity straining her brow. "We are of one blood. I will protect you."

Ani felt overwhelmed by this sudden force of affection. Should they embrace now? Should she kiss her cheek? They stood there, the queen vehemently earnest, Ani awkward, until the queen turned back to the fifty-some watchers with an attention-calling flourish of her hand.

"The Princess Anidori-Kiladra Talianna Isilee, jewel of Kildenree. Let the road carry her lightly, for she is my daughter."

Ani felt the crowd shudder at the power in the queen's voice. *Would that her voice accompanied me*, thought Ani, *and not a stained handkerchief*. The thing felt thin and warm in her hand. She squeezed it and wished it were more than a token, wished it really could somehow carry safety and home and the love of a mother.

The escort was mounted and waiting. Ani tucked the handkerchief into her bodice and mounted Falada. She, who had never ridden through the palace front gates, would lead the way. Her mother stood beside them, straight as the stone posts. Again Ani thought, *How lovely she is*, and again she thought, *How unlike her am I*. But now, for the first time, she also felt a yearning like the beginnings of a yawn arching in her chest to have that separation and to become, finally, who she would be.

To the southwest lay the beginning of the Forest Road and the beginning of any answer she might find. She pushed her legs against Falada's sides, and he started a fast walk. She could hear the key-mistress's wailing cry, so like a mourner's song. It trailed after them until the company turned a corner, and the song snuffed out quick as a candle flame between wet fingers.

It was early. With at least two wagons full of treasures, Ani felt more like a thief sneaking away with a bounty than a princess on her way to her betrothed. And she felt exposed and sore, alone at the group head and vulnerable outside the palace walls.

Once they passed through the outer palace walls and down several blocks of the main avenue, Ani and Falada pulled back and let Talone lead the way. The guard fell into a triangle around her, and the feeling of walls their mounts made comforted Ani. Selia joined her in the center. Her horse stood three hands shorter than Falada, forcing Selia to look up to speak to her mistress.

"We will reach the borders of the city by evening, Crown Princess, and can sup and sleep at a tavern just outside the city gate. The Blue Mouse. Ungolad recommends its pork pies especially. He says we will wish for good tavern food once we're dining only on rough travel fare."

"Ungolad?"

Selia pointed to a guard riding on the heels of Talone. He had hair longer than most that he kept in two yellow braids down his back. He did not appear tall, even on horseback, but the broadness of his shoulders and the thick muscles of his arms and chest pressed through his tunic and vest and demanded he be recognized as a warrior. He turned his head as though he had heard his name spoken. Ani quickly looked away.

"Ugh, I am so glad to finally leave everything behind and just get moving, aren't you?" said Selia.

Selia was in an eager mood, and she made light observations as they rode. Once or twice she managed to get Ani to laugh. The morning almost felt pleasant. Ani looked at all the marvels of the city, the wide avenue and branches of narrow streets, the thundering of blacksmiths and calls of hawkers and click of shoed horses on cobblestones, and all the people who looked up from their work or out from windows to watch her pass. Why had she never insisted to her mother that she be allowed out in the city before? Her life locked inside palace walls seemed stunted and dull.

They arrived at the Blue Mouse just before nightfall. Ingras arranged for Ani to have a private room to sup. As Talone, Ingras, and Selia escorted her through the main room, Ani looked longingly at the huge fire, tavern singer, and crowd of unknown people. She thought about asking to eat downstairs with the rest of the escort but knew that Ingras, a man fanatically devoted to the queen, would refuse.

Selia, too, seemed to desire the excitement of the public room. Throughout supper, she watched the door and drummed her fingers to the rhythm of the tavern song that leaked through the walls.

"You may go down if you wish, Selia," said Ani.

She smiled. "Oh, I am too saddle-sore for wood benches. Anyhow, I don't want to leave you alone."

"You are a good friend."

"Mmm," she said, tapping her foot in time.

Ani noted that Selia seemed anxious that night and every night they spent in tavern lodging. During the day she was high-spirited and eager to talk, but then she seemed to begrudge the hour when they had to stop their journey.

"I would walk straight there if I could," she said once.

Ani did not understand her enthusiasm for arrival. For her, the journey was freedom and new sights, but the end of the road meant a return to both acting and failing at the part of princess, as well as a marriage to . . . to someone.

He is probably a colt with wobbly legs, said Ani, *or an old gelding who slobbers and has to be fed oats by hand.*

Falada whipped her heels with his tail in a teasing acknowledgment of what she had said but did not respond. Ani knew he did not care whom she married as long as she still brushed him and fed him and took him out for wonderful, leg-stretching rides.

Three days from the palace, the party left city dwellings behind and entered the rolling lowlands of wheat, corn, and hay fields dotted with farmhouses and small town clusters. The air was sweet and dry, and the company was in a good humor.

They stopped each night as soon as they found an inn,

and occasionally they were its only occupants. On those nights, Ingras allowed Ani to sup with the company in the public room. Yulan, Uril, and some of the others were boisterous and sang rowdy songs to satisfy the absence of a minstrel. Ingras endured it, blushing, and even let Ani try a sip of ale, which she found she did not enjoy at all. Talone, the captain of the guard, did not quiet them until, like a father with unruly children, he felt the furniture was in danger or the hour too late. Ani noticed on these nights that Selia and Ungolad often stole moments in quiet conversation. Once she saw him rub Selia's arm in a familiar way.

After two weeks of travel, the landscape began to ease upward, and scatterings of pine and fir trees gathered in with the birches. They passed no more farms. The land was wild with grasses and patches of purple heather like new bruises. A dark spot loomed on the horizon, a great green, lightless sea submerging their path. To the left, the mountains rose and the trees climbed their heights, leaving just the peaks as bare, gray rock. To the right, the open lowlands reached wide to the south. But ahead of them, in the east and north, the land was completely lost in the greatness of the Forest.

The party grew quiet as they neared the lip of the Forest. Ani took a last look behind her at the friendly lowlands, a deep breath before plunging underwater. She felt the cool shadow of the trees pass over her, and she shivered.

That first day in the woods seemed to stretch as long as the road before them, full of new noises, new smells, a feeling of closeness that was not comfortable like smooth palace walls or stone tavern rooms. Most of the company had never been inside a forest and cast uncomfortable glances into the ragged darkness, letting the sharp, sweet smell of pine mix in their heads with the tales of dark deeds and unnatural things. As the darkness slowly thickened into evening, Ani observed more and more guards instinctively gripping sword hilts.

That night was the first slept under the sky. Ingras ordered a small tent, the only private one in the camp, assembled for the princess. Even under the eaves of evergreens, he insisted on treating Ani as her mother had wished. Drinking from a gold cup in that wilderness seemed ridiculous to Ani and, she thought, to the rest of the company as well, but she was accustomed to being served and made no protest. Selia helped her undress in the privacy of the tent and then set up her own bedroll just outside.

"There is room for another," said Ani, though there scarcely was.

"No, I am fine out here, Crown Princess," said Selia.

Ani lay down in the strange solitude of her tent, closed in by walls only paper-thin. She could hear Falada move somewhere near.

Falada, the camp horse-master wanted me to tie you up with the others. I will not run away.

I know, she said. *Neither will I.*

The night was cool. The day world was summer, but the

night still dipped its ladle into the well of spring air. Even through her mat, Ani could feel the stony earth, and its chill hardened her bones. The trees made noises that she had never heard, hissing and sighing like a new kind of animal. The wind brushed through the tent flap and against her cheek, waking her with words that she did not understand.

In the first few days, Selia and most of the others seemed silenced by the forest shadows. But the Forest did not spook Falada, and Ani soon caught his mood. She liked how she felt surrounded by trees, mixing the feeling of safety in close quarters with open possibilities. Dew fed the moss and lichen, trees creaked and moaned with growing, and birds conversed in the spiny branches. Ani's ears reached for the sounds of their chatter, and she felt like smiling to discover that she understood. She did not know what birds they were, but their language was so close to the sparrows' she knew from the palace gardens that it was like hearing someone speak her same language but with a different accent. Besides the birds, other forest animals appeared—intermittent sightings of foxes, red deer, wild pigs, and, once, wolves.

Just a week into the forest, Falada woke Ani, saying, *Mad wolves. Coming toward the camp.*

"Wolves! Rabid wolves!" Ani crawled out of her tent, shouting. The night guard shook himself awake and kicked the bodies of the best archers. They rubbed their eyes and strung their bows.

"Where?" said the guard with sleepy incredulity.

Falada told her, and she pointed. Other horses were prancing and testing the ropes that held them. The commotion woke the camp, and all sat up in their bedrolls and looked into the distance that was neither near nor far in the absolute dark. Out there, something moved, shadow sliding on shadow.

It leapt. The dying fire picked out eyes and teeth. Then, with a whisk of wind, a pale shaft pierced him through the throat. He fell to the earth at the first archer's feet. His two companions were similarly downed with the hard, sharp whip sound of arrows in the dark, and in the long silence that followed, someone sighed in relief.

The next morning, Ani noticed how many of the guards now looked at her with the same wariness that marked their eyes when they contemplated the dark profundities of the forest.

I thought they would be grateful, said Ani.

Falada snorted and idly pawed a stone. In his opinion, people never made sense.

Ani scolded herself. Just because they had left Kildenree did not mean these companions would feel any better disposed to her speaking gifts than had the sour-skinned nurse-mary. A brown-speckled forest bird whistled at her passing. Ani looked down and refused to listen.

Some days later, Ani felt the tension finally ease. Spirited conversation and laughter returned, mostly centered around Selia. Many of the guards sought to ride near her, and Ungolad most of all. Ani observed that he often rode by her side and seemed to find reasons to touch her, reach out to pick a pine needle from her skirt or examine a scratch on her hand. Ani hoped a romance might make the journey worthwhile to her faithful lady-in-waiting.

Ani had been lagging behind, talking with Falada, but at the sound of wild laughter she trotted forward to join the lively group. As soon as she neared, the laughing ceased. No one looked at her.

"Did I miss a good joke?" said Ani.

"No, not really," said Selia.

One of the guards said something to Ungolad that Ani could not hear. No one else spoke.

"The days are certainly warmer now," she said.

"Yes, Princess," said the guard Uril.

"Well, that breeze is pleasant, isn't it?"

"If you say so, Princess."

"Mmm."

Ani, confused, looked at Selia. Her lady-in-waiting glanced up briefly and gave a subtle shrug that said, *What do you want from me?* Coolly, she set her gaze at the passing trees as though Ani did not exist.

Ani scowled, scraping her memory for everything she had said and done that day. Had she inadvertently offended Selia and half the members of her escort guard? They could not possibly still be upset just because she knew the wolves were coming before they did. No reasons made sense to her, and the silence became unbearable. At last she flicked Falada into a trot. Once she left the group, conversation resumed behind her and Selia's lovely laugh rang out. Emotion caught in Ani's throat, and she hummed quietly to ease the tightness.

As always, Talone rode at the front of the company, his ardent gaze sweeping about as though he expected a bandit attack any moment. Ani asked Falada to slow to a walk beside him. His silence made her wonder if what she had done to affront the others also included Talone, but soon he spoke.

"I don't know if you recall, Princess, but we have been alone before." His stoic face relaxed a little as he raised his eyebrows in an amused query.

Ani tried to remember. She had so rarely been alone.

"It was about ten years ago, I think."

"Oh," said Ani, "was that you who took me from the shore of the swan pond?"

"Well done. You were very young. It scared me how the fever chills racked your tiny body. And know, Princess, that it is not easy for a brave soldier to admit to ever being scared."

"I'll remember that of you if ever I'm in need of a brave

soldier," said Ani, teasing.

"Yes, well, if the danger can be stuck with a sword, I am your man." He smiled at her and quickly returned to watching the road.

"You are ever vigilant," she said.

"Mmm. For such a long journey, this terrain is dangerous. If there was a road cut through the Bavara Mountains, one could reach Bayern in a matter of a fortnight. But the Forest Road circumscribes the mountains. The Forest itself is striped with gorges, and the road doubles in length to avoid them. A straighter path would have to cross many bridges."

As he spoke, Ani saw the way in front of them begin to wind sharply up and left. The road cut across a long arm of mountain, and between there and the next arm the ground dropped into a deep and narrow ravine.

"Gorge to the right, mountain to the left," said Ani.

"There's much flat land in the forest, but the climbs and drops are unpredictable."

The Forest did not seem dangerous to her, just dark and brooding. She envied the permanence of the tall, thick-trunked firs that had stood in one place for generations. Her own family had always lived in Great City Valley. She was the first of her line born as crown princess, the first to leave the valley, the first to see the Forest. She wished it had been her choosing, that she had been the kind of person who would steal a horse and leave in the night to find adventure instead of one who is handed duty and numbly complies.

This road is long, said Falada. *How long until we arrive?*

Weeks yet, said Ani.

A warm breeze came up from the gorge beneath them and stirred their hair. Falada flicked his tail at it and walked a little faster.

That evening a stream passed near the road and Talone called for an early camp. It had been a week since they had found moving water. Their water barrels were low, and the company was irritable with dust, stink, and horse hair. Ingras set up a metal tub in Ani's tent and ordered water heated for her bath. While Ani soaked in the hot water in her thin privacy, the rest of the company hiked to the mountain runoff to scrub their clothes and themselves, Selia upstream and the men down. Talone assigned Ishta, a thin man with a long, tipped nose, to guard Ani. Ishta did not seem too concerned about bathing.

It was dark before the others returned. Ani dried her hair by the fire and waited. Ishta stood on the other side of the fire. The light turned his face orange, the hollows of his cheeks still in shadow. She could hear him scrape the undersides of his fingernails with a knife.

When he spoke, his voice was soft, with a lilt that seemed feminine. "How is it, Princess, to bathe in nice, warm water in your own little tent?"

"It is nice, thank you," said Ani with some unease.

"Mmm." He took a step forward. "You like being a princess?"

"I don't know. It is what I am. Do you like being a man?"

He walked to her, dead pine needles breaking like glass under his boots, and crouched beside her. He leaned in. Her pulse snapped in her throat.

"Do you like that I am a man?" He smiled. His teeth looked rotted at the roots.

"Step back," she whispered. He held his face there, and up close his expression was leering, inhuman, his face as sharp as a weapon, his breath the promise of ugly things. Ani gripped her brush in both hands and could not seem to let it go, not to push him away, not to push herself to her feet. Never had she felt this way, helpless, alone, no servant to call, no guard outside her door. No door. And a man who came too close.

"Step back, Ishta," she said again, but her voice held no more of the authority of her mother than the chattering of a magpie. He sneered.

There was a sound of bent underbrush and low laughter. Ishta stood and casually walked away as a group of guards, their faces shiny and red from bathing, entered the camp. Talone added a branch to the fire and sat beside her. Ani looked down at her shaking hands.

"Princess, is something wrong?"

She set her brush on the log and folded her hands. "I'm

all right." She had never felt before that someone could hurt her—and enjoy it. That new awareness made her look at Talone with suspicion. He had assigned Ishta to her watch. Had he known? Could she trust him? Who could guard her from her guards?

Ani made her way to her tent, feeling blindly with her slippered toes for rocks and shooting roots. Selia was readying her own bedroll beside the tent. Her wet hair was luminescent in the near dark.

Ani sat on a corner of Selia's blanket, held her knees against her chest, and hoped for conversation. *Something just happened*, she wanted to say. *There was something strange, and I wanted to tell you*, she would say, if Selia seemed in a mood to talk, like they used to do for hours on her balcony, Selia brushing oils through her long hair and relating gossip that had slipped up the stairs from the kitchen or out of the idle mouths of waiting ladies, their promises of secrecy dulled by the tedium of embroidery. Ani longed now for such an hour, the comfort of casual talk and a warm blanket around her shoulders to hold off the heavy blackness of so much space at their backs. She waited for Selia, who liked to start conversations on her own terms. Selia finished with her bedroll. She stood by her pillow and said nothing.

"How was your bath?" said Ani.

"Cold."

"Oh. I'm thoughtless, Selia. Of course you should bathe in camp in warm water."

"You mean in your used, tepid bathwater? For who is to heat water for the lady-in-waiting? No, thank you, I would rather use the stream."

"Selia, are you angry?"

Selia turned to her, and in the dark of a night before the moon and too far from the fire, all Ani could see was the pale outline of her cheek and the glint of one eye.

"No, of course not, Crown Princess," said Selia. Her voice was ordinary again, a lilting tone, pleasing and artless.

"Once we get to Bayern," said Ani, "there will, thankfully, be hot water and beds again."

"A very apt observation, Crown Princess." Her voice was still even and polite. "Yet I believe in Bayern there will be much more waiting for me than just water and goose feathers."

"What do you mean?"

Selia did not answer. Someone added wood to the fire, and in the sudden flush of light she could see Selia's face. She was looking across the camp. Ani turned. Ungolad stood by the fire. His eyes were on Ani. He smiled a closed smile, not showing any teeth.

he first four weeks of forest travel had merged into one another in the perpetual landscape of firs and pines. Despite the tension, Ani found she enjoyed the journey. A breeze moved across her face, and she fancied it was the breeze of the trees' breathing, the pines on either side inhaling and exhaling across the road.

"The tales that trees could tell, the stories wind would sing," Ani said to herself. It was a piece from a rhyme, one that as a child she had begged the nursemarys to sing. It had filled her with wonder and mystery and made her want to throw off her shoes and hat and run to meet the wildness just outside the closed panes. Her aunt had once spoken of the knowledge of speaking not with animals, but with the elements of nature. And she thought of the story of her birth, how she had not opened her eyes for three days. Her aunt had said she was born with a first word on her tongue and would not wake for trying to taste it. *What word?*

she wondered.

The stories wind would sing. Just then, she could not think of the rest of the rhyme.

Ani noticed Talone scanning the roadside for a marker and trotted up to join him.

"There will be a notched tree on the right hand to mark halfway, Princess," he said. "Or so the last trader we passed informed me. We are at a disadvantage here, none of us having ridden this road. Except Ungolad."

"Can you tell me about Ungolad?"

"He was a tradesman escort for a time, but he has not ridden the Forest Road in ten years. Still, I imagined he would be a greater asset to this trek than he has been. He volunteered, you know. They all did." Ani raised her eyebrows, and Talone nodded. "The queen did not need to command anyone to join this guard."

"But why?" said Ani. "I thought that the prospect of riding weeks through a forest would be daunting to anyone."

"Oh, not to many of us, I think. We are stout warriors, after all." He thumped his chest and smiled.

"Indeed. And I think it best that I forget how many stout warriors I saw gripping their swords and getting headaches from squinting at the trees on our first week here."

Talone cast a glance of mock terror into the depth of trees to the side. His expression made her laugh, and she realized how much she wanted to trust him.

"But what interest could a man like Ungolad have in

being in this guard?"

"I don't know. I tell you truly, Princess, I was hesitant to accept Ungolad's company when he volunteered. He has always been a little unpredictable, and traders' escorts often garner as little respect as mercenaries. But he is a member of the royal army now, and he has been to Bayern before. Look, here it is."

On their right hand, a trunk of living fir was carved with the symbol of Bayern's sun and crown.

"We are halfway," said Talone.

"That symbol—does Bayern claim this road, then?"

"Kildenree does not. Technically it is neutral territory. But if Kildenreans do not live here, what is to stop the Bayern if they so desire?" His voice grew softer. "If a country like Bayern decided they liked the looks of the Great City Valley, they could take it without much ado."

Ingras trotted to them. "Captain, time for a midday halt."

"All halt!"

As she unsaddled Falada, Ani heard the soldiers conferring pleasantly. "Midway, we have passed midway."

"Midway, not long now, lads." Ungolad's voice was encouraging, and he slapped a few on the back. He saw Ani watching and added, "Not long now, Princess."

After eating, Ani wanted a different brush for Falada and went back to the supply wagon to retrieve it. Selia stood in the third wagon. She was holding up Ani's green gown against her front.

"Selia," said Ani. Selia jumped, dropping the dress.

"Oh, hello, Crown Princess," she said, quickly casual.

Ani could not understand why Selia seemed so nervous, and she waited for Selia to speak.

"Just looking at your pretty things." Selia shook off her expression of surprise and smiled, holding up the dress again. "I know I don't have your eyes, but do you not think I would look beautiful in this gown? You are almost my size."

Ani did not respond.

Selia tipped her head to one side. "You're angry, Crown Princess. You're jealous of your treasures and don't want them sullied by a servant."

"Of course I don't mind, but Selia, you're acting so curiously. I can't believe that it's just my imagination."

"I'm sorry," said Selia.

"No, I am. Are you unhappy to be going to Bayern after all?"

"Not a whit."

"Then what? I hope I'm still your friend. . . ."

"Yes, your condescension is most entertaining, Crown Princess." Selia stepped down from the wagon. "You must congratulate yourself that you have treated me better than any servant deserves."

Selia's tone made Ani's fingers feel cold. She swallowed nervously.

"A servant," said Selia again. She looked down as her face flamed and her chin began to quiver. "All I have ever wanted is what you have. And you, you don't even care about what you are. And I have had to serve you and call you mistress and wait and wait and wait." Selia put a hand over her eyes, and her shoulders began to shake. "What a horrid title, lady-in-waiting. I have waited and waited until I thought my bones would crack and my muscles freeze and my mind shrivel like a raisin. And there you were, with horses and tutors and gowns and servants, and all you did was hide in your room."

Ani felt her lips part in amazement. How could she have been so blind all those years?

"Oh, Selia, I am so sorry I never saw." Ani placed a hand on her shoulder. Selia slapped it away.

"That is because I was careful that you would not see," Selia said. Her eyes dried up. "For years I have been waiting for my chance, and now here it is. Don't touch me and don't call for me. I am no longer your servant. You, what are you? The brat of lucky parents who were related to a childless king. There is no such thing as royal blood. I believe we are what we make ourselves, and as such, you, Crown Princess, are nothing." Selia spoke as though she had held those words inside for too long and they burned her mouth as she spoke them.

"But I—you said—I thought you wanted to come." Ani knew this was not fair but found it difficult to protest. Her thoughts spun and bumped against one another like dizzy children. Was this the effect of the gift of people-speaking?

Every word Selia spoke seemed to be the purest truth. You *are nothing. You make yourself nothing.* She took a step back, prepared to back down, as always, ready to apologize and wait for time to ease the memory.

A warm breath of wind came from the deeper trees and ran across Ani's neck. A corner of her mother's handkerchief stood out from her bodice, and the wind tapped it against her breastbone. Ani thought its touch sparked her heart to beat faster, her skin to tingle, her blood to warm her hands and feet. *A gift from my mother*, Ani thought. *Protection*, she had said.

Ani met Selia's stare and straightened her neck.

"Put down the dress, Selia," she said. Selia paused. Ani had never commanded her in anything. "Put down my dress," she repeated.

Selia tossed the dress back in the wagon. Her face was flushed, and her nostrils flared. "Go tell your guards, Crown Princess. Go stir your army. Go demand your throne and teach me a lesson—anything! I dare you."

"I am no longer a crown princess," Ani said, and her own steady tone encouraged her. "You mock me with the title. From now on, you will address me as Princess, or mistress, if you prefer, since you have never seen fit to call me by my name. My friends call me by my name."

"You don't have any friends."

"I don't want you to be my friend, Selia, or my servant, not now. I thought you were both. You have let me know I was wrong. So are you to treat me so. You are wrong."

"Oh, my dear, dear Royal Majesty, you don't know the
half of it." Selia started to smile, but she dropped her eyes
from Ani's face and walked away.

Ani did not move until she had caught her breath. Her
limbs were trembling, and the anger that had suddenly
flushed her face and steadied her voice now left her a little
worn and a little cold. But, for a moment, she had almost
sounded as confident as her mother, and she wondered
where the courage to stand up to Selia had come from.

Ani pulled the handkerchief from her bodice. The cloth
was old, the original white dimmed with age. Her mother's
blood stood out clearly, three spots of dark brown. She fingered the delicate lacing around the edges.

Maybe, she thought, *it is a thing of magic. Maybe my mother's blood
renewed its power.*

She thought of the bedside tales that spoke of mothers
and blood. A mother who nurses her baby on one breast of
milk and one breast of blood, and her child grows to be a
powerful warrior. A young girl is cursed to never become a
woman, and when the mother lies dying of old age, she cuts
her wrist and washes her daughter in the blood, and the
curse is undone. These stories had intrigued her with their
strange mix of violence and love, so unlike the distant, passionless affection of her own mother.

She thought, she hoped, that the handkerchief was something fantastic, like a piece of a tale, but real, and just for

her, a symbol of the real, hidden love of her mother. She so desperately wanted something magical, something powerful, something that meant her mother had not flung her aside but loved her as deeply as her own heart. Ani tucked the handkerchief back into her bodice, convincing herself that since the gates of the palace, the handkerchief had in some measure been protecting her.

That night, Ani set up her own bedroll. Ingras exclaimed at Selia's refusal to serve, but Ani would not have anyone ordered to be her servant, or her friend. In the privacy of her tent, Ani struggled with the laces of her bodice and called herself a fool for ever trusting anyone. Through the slit in her tent flap she could see Talone instructing the night watch. She wanted to trust him, but that dark encounter with Ingras and Selia's betrayal were both painful barbs she could not pluck out. *At least I have Falada as a true friend*, she thought, *and the handkerchief as protection*.

Two weeks after the halfway mark, a stream pregnant with summer runoff crossed their path and rose to flow over the road's bridge. Talone recommended they halt early and test the sodden wood for rotting before crossing the next day. Ungolad seemed pleased with the diversion, saying that some leagues upstream there was a waterfall.

"A sight for eyes wearied by endless trees," he said. "A

sight even royalty might deem worthy to behold." He nodded at Ani.

The main part of the company followed Ungolad up a deer trail along the river. Ani stayed behind, and Ungolad seemed disappointed. But as she brushed Falada, a breeze lifted off the river and wound its damp essence in her hair and wrapped its coolness around her face, and with it, for a moment, she thought she saw the image of a waterfall shimmer before her eyes. Her imagination, she determined, and batted the breeze away.

Still, she had never seen a waterfall, and it would be a pity to pass blindly by. While Talone and others investigated the bridge, Ani took to the deer trail.

The forest ground was spongy but pleasant footing after weeks of riding. She liked the sensation of walking on soil hollowed by deep tree roots, the noise of her steps muted echoes. The smell of pine and cool water freshened the world, and Ani felt eager.

These last days had been tense and strange, the coldness from so many of the guards, Selia's flushed face and eyes shining with anger and hate, and the burden of a handkerchief that throbbed with mystery at her heart. But now, off the road, the forest was pleasing, green like spring wheat and yet ancient and ponderous as the books of the palace library. The upper branches wrestled with the high forest wind. Below, the rumor of the river answered. Ani felt that she moved in the middle of a great conversation between sky and earth.

Soon the sound of crashing water overwhelmed all else. Ani approached the sound and ducked under the branches of a fir. There at her feet burst the white eruptions of the river, shaking the earth and breathing out a mist that wet her hair. The water fell straight for the height of three men, then continued to churn around rocks and smaller falls until the land evened farther downstream. She could see the movements of Ungolad's group above the falls and decided not to join them, enjoying the unfamiliar solitude.

Somewhere behind her she heard the dim call of a bird to its mate. *Fly away, danger.* It was a common cry among the woodland birds she had listened to as a child, and the familiar call in that foreign place made her feel as though the words were spoken to her. *Danger. Fly away.* She reached above her, gripped a branch, and began to step away from the edge.

At the same moment, something knocked the back of her ankles, and her feet slipped. Ani held to the tree and pulled her feet back onto land, and watched the stone that had struck her topple over the edge and drop into the river.

The ground beneath her was slick and wet. If she had not been holding on to a branch at that moment, she would have gone the way of the stone and possibly cracked her head on a rock or been held under by the strong current and drowned. She looked around to see what had disturbed so large a stone. No one. But perhaps, she thought, for just a moment, there had been a flash of gold. Perhaps it had been the tip of a yellow braid disappearing in the timber and shadow.

Ani ran back to camp, grimacing with each step for her sore ankles, and was brushing Falada when the hikers returned. Ungolad saw her and for a moment seemed surprised to see her alive and dry, but his expression changed again so quickly that she questioned if she had seen truly.

He passed her, patted her shoulder, and said, "You missed a fine waterfall, Princess."

She was not sure that he or anyone had thrown that stone. *But even if he did,* she thought, *I'm protected. I don't need to fear.* She patted the handkerchief at her chest and believed even more fervently that it was protecting her, that she could hear the voice of her mother's blood even as she heard the birds speak.

A week after the waterfall, the company came to a tree as thick as five men that had fallen across the road. While some of the guards and horses worked at moving the obstacle for the wagons, the rest of the company forged their own way through the forest. Ani and Falada wove through the trees a bit apart from the others.

Something is not right, said Falada.

What is it?

I do not know. His ears twisted to listen behind and to the side, but he kept on walking.

Stop a moment, said Ani. She leaned forward to pat his neck.

Suddenly Falada whined and reared. Ani clutched at his mane and gripped his middle with her legs, saying all the while, *Easy, Falada, it is nothing, easy now.*

Falada got his footing back and quieted down. His skin shivered under the saddle.

Something whipped me, he said.

Ani looked back and saw no one. Immediately to the right ran a long gorge, a fall steep enough to break a neck.

Ani and Falada caught up to the rest on the road and pulled alongside Ungolad at the end of the company. She looked the guard over. His braids hung down his back like slain prey thrown over the hunter's shoulder. He wore a long sword at his side. He was looking forward, squinting in the sun. Some bit of courage was prickling inside her, begging her for action. She considered Ungolad's horse, a bay nearly as tall as Falada.

Falada, can you tell me about this horse and what he thinks of his rider?

Falada whisked his tail and turned an eye to the horse beside him. There was a change in the rhythm of his walk, and he lowered his head. The bay shook his head and picked his hooves up higher. From long association with Falada, Ani thought she could detect the spirit of the bay's response but waited for Falada's words to make her certain. Ungolad noticed the princess's attention, and he smiled at her.

"Do you admire my beast, Princess?" he said.

She nodded. "He is a pretty horse, and you ride him well. He seems a bit meek, but I have observed that you like to be in absolute control."

Ungolad blinked in surprise. She felt surprised herself, and she smiled pleasantly.

"You are a student of men and horses, then," he said, "and I had heard that all you were fit for was to be married off and produce princelings."

Ungolad's comment would have stung, but its carelessness suggested that she had startled him, and she felt encouraged to continue.

"In my study of horses, I can say a fair bit about yours," she said as Falada silently related to her all he had learned. "He was a wild colt, caught and trained later than usual, and had to be thoroughly broken, which made him ridable, but broke his spirit as well. He has had many owners and has been beaten into obedience so often that by the time he came into your hands he was as docile as a cow. He thinks you are unpredictable, heavier than you used to be, and smell unpleasantly. And he has a stone in his right front hoof."

Ungolad laughed with obvious force. "Well, Princess, you have more game spirit in you than I thought." He smiled, and the very tips of his teeth peered through his parted lips.

"Thank you," she said, smiled graciously, and kicked Falada into a trot to the front of the company. Her hands were shaking and blood rushed into her fingertips, and she nearly laughed out loud. She fingered a corner of the hand-kerchief. *My mother's blood is protecting me,* she thought. *I have nothing to fear.*

At the next stop, she saw Ungolad, glowering, remove a small stone from his horse's right front hoof.

As they neared Bayern, the road pushed the trees farther away, and at midday there was no shade. The company was weary and sun sick. It was a bright and burning afternoon when they passed a small trading party going toward Kildenree.

"Ho there, sir," said Talone. "How many days since you left Bayern?"

"Six days'll take you to the city, if that's where you're going." He lifted his wide-brimmed sun hat as he caught sight of Ani. She smiled at his accent. He spoke his words carelessly, letting each word bleed into the next, his vowels short and consonants ringing out from his throat. She turned to see Selia, wondering if she also remembered that accent from the time the Bayern prime minister visited Kildenree five years ago, but her lady-in-waiting held back by the rear guard. The trader did not see her.

"And how many since the last town or settlement?" said Ungolad.

"Oh, two, I'd say, at a good pace."

Ani saw Ungolad and Selia exchange looks.

That night at camp, there were two fires. Dano, the cook-man, built the first, and Talone, Ingras, the wagon drivers, and some of the guards gathered around it. Ungolad built the second and drew in Selia and the majority of the guards. Ani turned from brushing down Falada to see the camp split into two parts, and she felt that something definite had been decided. She stood between them and did not know what to do.

Talone noticed her and walked to her side. "Princess, you look concerned."

His face was lined with age, his temples graying. He had been faithful to her mother for many years, but did that mean he was faithful to her?

"What is it?" he said.

Ani twisted the handkerchief between her fingers and forced herself to look at him directly in the eyes. "Talone, can I trust you?"

He blinked and looked as though she had wrenched an arrow from his side. "I have failed you if you must ask that question." He put a fist over his heart and said in his strong, solid voice, "I swear fealty to you, Princess Anidori-Kiladra, and promise to shield you to your safety and, if you wish it, will remain your personal guard until my dotage and death."

She blinked at the force of his pledge, and gratitude and relief filled her. Feeling that the oath required a sign of her acceptance, she looked about her for something to give him.

All she had on her person of value were two rings. She slipped one with a ruby droplet from her second finger and placed it in his hand. "Thank you, Talone."

Talone seemed moved, and lowering his head for a moment so she could not see his eyes, he tucked the ring into his vest pocket. "Thank you, Princess." He led her to his fire, where the conversation was bubbling with unease at the splitting of the group.

"I don't like their attitude," said Adon, Talone's second in command. He was a young man, eager for action. "Ungolad's friends make it clear they follow him and not you, Captain. I swear they grow more insubordinate the closer we get to Bayern. Smells like mutiny."

"Ungolad seemed interested to know how long it would take us to reach the first town," said Ani.

"They might have friends there," said Radal.

"Or plan to do something before we reach witnesses," said Adon.

"Or they are just eager to sleep in a bed and eat real food again," said Radal. "Aren't we all?"

"Mmm." Talone eyed the princess. "I don't know what it means. It may be they intend to stay in Bayern and not return to Kildenree next spring. But, Princess, if there is any sign of trouble, you jump on the nearest horse and ride away. Do not stop until you get to the king and safety."

Ani felt goose bumps rise on her arm. "Safety? What do you think they would do?"

"Nothing. I am just being cautious." Talone stood and approached Ungolad's group. The frivolity died down, and soon the party broke up. Talone assigned the watches that night to his most trusted men, but Ani hardly slept. She clutched the handkerchief at her breast.

The next morning dawned a bright, stinging sun. The company rode in a long line up next to the trees, hoping for a forest breeze or the occasional branch of shade. By the time they stopped to camp two hours from sundown, everyone was sick from the heat and headachy from squinting in the sun. The evening was warm and stale under the heavy-limbed canopies, and the air was sticky with the odor of pine, seemingly too thick to breathe.

There was a small clearing just off the road where the company set up camp. Ani, prodded by Falada's grumbling of thirst, tossed off her pack and walked Falada through a thicket of trees toward the sounds of a stream. She dismounted, threw off her sweat-soaked sun hat, and bent over to fill her gold cup. As she dipped the cup under, the cold water against her heated skin shocked her, and she dropped it. The gold winked green through the water before the current pulled it down and away. She thought, *One less thing to separate me from everyone else*, and lay down on her stomach, scooping the water with her hands to her lips. Her sleeves to her elbows soaked through, and she felt the cold water on her neck and on her chest. She shivered and drank.

Princess, you lost something in the river, said Falada at her side.

Yes, my cup, she said.

Princess, said Falada again.

But a shout came from the camp, and Ani stood and turned away.

Something is happening, she said.

She could still hear the echo of Falada's last word to her—*Princess*. But she walked away, toward the camp and the commotion. Embarrassed that the breast of her dress was soaked through, Ani decided to slip behind a copse of trees that separated her from the party and avoid being seen. Through a break in the leaves, she spied on the camp. Yulan was shouting. He had removed his shirt in the heat. Talone stood by. His hand rested on his side just above his sword hilt.

Trouble. Ani glanced back to Falada, who was still drinking at the river, and felt uneasy at being so far separated from him. But she reasoned there could not be any real danger or she would have a warning. She touched her chest where she kept the handkerchief and, prodded by curiosity, crept through the trees to get close enough to hear but still stay cautiously out of sight.

"While there are ladies in this camp, Yulan, you will stay dressed like a gentleman," Talone said.

"Selia does not mind, do you, lady?" said a guard by Yulan's side, and there was laughter.

"Let them be, Captain," Ani heard Selia say, though she could not see her.

"I amend my statement, then." He spoke through a clenched jaw. "While there is one lady in this camp, you will dress, and behave, like gentlemen. We are the royal guard of the princess, and we will act as such."

"Royal guard of the princess," said Terne, laughing. "She is not a princess, not here. Kildenree doesn't claim her, and we haven't reached Bayern yet."

Talone ignored Terne. "As captain of the guard, Yulan, those are my orders, and to disobey them is treason."

The pocket of men backing up Yulan shifted uneasily. Yulan looked at Ungolad, who was sitting on a log a few paces away.

"Nice and easy, lads." Ungolad stood. "This was not the way to do things, but I think at last the time has come to tell the truth."

"Not now," said Selia.

Ungolad winked at her. "Don't worry, my lady." He looked at Talone and squinted, though Ani was not sure if it was for effect or just habit from the blazing day. "We don't want a fight, but some things are going to change."

"Yes, all hail Princess Selia," said Yulan.

"Princess Selia!" Several men shouted and raised their swords above their heads.

"Hush up," said Ungolad. He spoke with genuine anger.

Talone stepped closer to Ungolad. That Ani could see, they were the only two who had not drawn their swords. Both sides were poised, waiting for action from their leaders.

"Is that what this is about, mercenary?" Talone did not seem aware that he was shaking his head. "You're aiming to dispose of a rightful princess and replace her with a fraud?"

Ani clutched at a branch to keep steady. Dispose of a princess. A fraud. They were trying to kill her. Until that moment she had never really believed it. Why would they try to kill her? So Selia could be princess. She remembered Talone's order that she run at the first sign of trouble. *But there's still no warning*, she thought. *My mother's handkerchief will protect me.*

All the same, she thought she had better get closer to Falada. She spoke his name, but he was a long way off grazing at the river and did not respond. Slowly, so that she would not cause a noise, she started to make her way to him.

"Fraud?" said Selia. "Royalty is not a right, Captain. The willingness of the people to follow a ruler is what gives her power. Here, in this place, by this people, I have been chosen. These men are tired of being told whom to follow. Now they have a choice, and they use that choice to call me Princess."

Selia's words seemed seductively convincing. Even Ani, peering through pine boughs, had to stop herself from nodding. But Adon stepped up beside Talone and challenged her.

"You mean Princess Anidori-Kiladra, don't you? You want to take not only the title, but the name—her name."

"I suppose, my little warrior pup, but it's the title that interests me most."

Ani caught a glimpse of Ungolad smiling at Selia. A couple of men near Talone chuckled at the idea of Selia being a princess, but the other half was stiffly serious, and the laugh fell like water against a stone wall.

Falada, she said again. He did not respond.

"You're mad." Talone spoke the words as though they were the final revelation.

"If we're mad," Ungolad said, "then we are mad in large numbers, at least larger than yours."

"Where is she?" said Selia. Ani covered her mouth before she gasped. They would look for her now. They would kill her as they had been trying since the waterfall. Why didn't the handkerchief protect her, whisper to her through birds or nudge her to safety?

"She's by the stream," someone said. Ani could see Terne, one of Ungolad's men, running from the group and toward the area where Falada grazed. Terne was already between her and her horse. Her cold fingers fumbled at the wet fabric at her breast where the handkerchief had been. Where it should be. Ani felt for it, patted her dress, looked at the ground around her feet. It was gone. She realized that she must have lost it in the stream. It would be far away by now. Who would protect her?

Falada, can you come to me? she said. He did not respond.

Talone shouted toward where Falada stood. "Princess, do as I told you!"

Ungolad motioned for another soldier to follow the first

toward the stream. *Do as I told you*, he had said. *Run away.*
Unable to reach Falada without being seen, Ani turned to
the dim forest and walked softly, afraid to hear fir needles
crack beneath her feet, afraid if she did run on her shaking
legs, she would fall. *Just a little farther*, she thought, *get to the next
copse, and then run.*

"There she is," said Selia.

Ani looked back. Hul left Ungolad's side and jogged
toward her. Adon shouted and started forward to rush him.
He had taken only one step when a bloody sword point burst
through the center of his chest. His face ripped in pain and
then stilled, dead standing. Ishta pulled his sword out of the
dead man's back and grinned with his animal teeth. Ani
gasped, and suddenly everything felt terribly real. She
tripped, turned, and ran.

There was the din of sword meeting sword behind her
and horses screaming and men shouting and men falling. She
ran. She tripped past a thornbush, and her hair caught in its
barbed arms. She pulled herself free. A man was close to her.
It was Ungolad, now, running after her, running faster than
she. She could hear the thumps of his boots against the hollow forest floor like an anxious heartbeat behind her. He was
getting closer.

Falada, she said, *Falada, please.* He was too far away, or perhaps he was already killed. "Falada!"

She heard Ungolad grunt and turned to see him trip
on one of the roots that ribbed their path. There was a

pounding of hooves to her right. It was Radal's dun-colored horse, riderless, cantering, and dragging his reins. A long, shallow cut marked its rump. Ani ran to him.

The horse stopped when his path was blocked by a thicket of firs and startled when Ani grabbed his reins. The reins were unknotted, and she managed to grab only one when she mounted. She leaned over his neck to grab the other rein. At once Ungolad reached her, and he growled when he sprang. Ani kicked the horse. He lurched forward as Ungolad grabbed her heel. Ani pulled tight on the reins and held to his mane to stay in the saddle. The horse reared, and Ungolad's grip loosened. She clamped her knees around his middle. When the horse's forelegs touched ground again, he bounded into a gallop.

Part Two

Goose Girl

ni rode. She did not see the trees that dashed by her and the branches that moved like executioner axes just above her ducking head. There was no purpose to the direction the horse ran—except away. For all she knew, she could be riding a circle, and suddenly she would see the campsite before her and leap the horse over slain guards and dodge the survivors' grasping hands. Whenever the horse showed signs of slowing down, Ani spurred him on with a hard heel, expecting at any moment to hear the rhythmic thuds of Ungolad's bay close behind her. Sometimes she thought she saw yellow braids in her periphery.

She rode hard, and the horse's neck was matted with sweat. At each beat of his heavy gallop, a bit of foam fell from his mouth. The reins were wet from her hands, so she clutched at his mane. The grip of her legs loosened, and when his hooves met turf she came down hard in the saddle. When a low branch struck her shoulder, she was knocked easily from the saddle and did not realize that she was on the ground until the horse had galloped away without her.

She sat still for a long time, breathing. If Ungolad was still following, he would just have to find her and kill her quickly, for she could not move. She thought she heard a twig snap as though it cracked under a foot, and she sprang to her feet to run, but her first step brought her hard back to the earth. She lay still, hugging the ground and waiting for her doom.

Ani awoke much later and realized that she was cold, that she had fir needles piercing her cheek, and that she was confused.

Falada, she said.

She bolted upright. The forest was so dark, she knew that her eyes were open only from the sensation of blinking. An owl hooted, and she jumped. It hooted again, and she wrapped her arms around her chest and tried to think. She must have been asleep, but before that? She was running. She sought to remember more and saw Adon rushing forward to protect her and a bloody sword tip parting his chest. She shivered and lay down again, covering her face with her arms, and tried to sleep away the darkness.

At dawn Ani began to walk. The forest looked the same in every direction, and she realized that she could be just a few leagues from a town and yet wander the woods for days. The canopy-dimmed sunlight gave little indication of direction, so she chose what she hoped was east and strode forward.

Her stomach ached with hunger; she had never before, in her life of white marble and breakfast trays, missed a meal. But mostly she was so thirsty that she began to contemplate digging down to the tree roots to see if she could discover what they were drinking.

Hours later, Ani heard water and thought it perhaps the loveliest noise in all creation. The sound echoed off many tree trunks and confused her senses until she finally found the stream by stepping into it. She drank from the stream until her belly warned of bursting and then walked beside it, reasoning that it must run away from the mountains and so would meet the road. The road meant direction.

Ani chased the stream for two days, only leaving its banks a short distance to search for mushrooms. She ate them tentatively, relying on dim childhood memories of her aunt's brief lessons in edible plants. Some wild onions grew in the wet black soil on the stream bank, and she bit into them raw, her mouth burning and eyes tearing from their fierce flavor.

On the third day, the stream stopped. It had thinned from waist width to a drizzle thin as a water snake and finally stopped in a green pond ringed with cattails. Ani circled the pond hoping for an outlet, then leaned against a tree and thought about crying. She did not know where she was, she had no skin to carry water in, and she had no stream to walk beside. She stayed the remainder of that day and the whole of the night beside the last bit of running stream. Thirst thrust into her dreams, coupled with the sounds of

Ungolad's heavy boots running behind her. She woke with a beating heart at every hoot of an owl.

In the morning, Ani sat awhile near the stream, playing the water through her fingers. *I wonder*, she thought, *if this creek ever touched the stream where I lost my handkerchief. If I hadn't lost that, none of this would have happened.* No sooner had she thought it than the idea was completely ridiculous, a bed-tale, a lie. She almost laughed at herself, but the laugh pulled tight in her chest and threatened to tug loose a tear before she stopped it. *I thought it was magic. I thought I was so safe. A bird warned me by the waterfall. And Falada. And my own weak reason.* She shook her head and beat her fist once against her chest. *It was I who stood up to Selia, and it was I who didn't run soon enough, not soon enough for Adon or Talone, or Falada.*

She leaned her head back to stop the tears from coming again and saw a brown owl in the pine opposite her, looking out at the morning with glassy yellow eyes.

"Are you the one that kept waking me up?" she whispered. "I don't know why your silly hooting makes me shiver at night. You look harmless enough."

She had once known the way to speak to the owls that kept watch in the stable rafters. It was long ago, and the memory awakened in her the empty confusion of homesickness. She brushed it away with an experimental hoot. The owl gave no reaction. *If only he were a swan*, she thought. Bird speech was all one language to her, yet with many different dialects, some more distinct than others, and it was swan she remembered best.

She tried her greeting again, and his head turned slightly toward her, recognizing her presence for the first time. After a few blinkless moments he greeted her, and she leaned back on her hands with tired hope. Ani followed with a question about how he was eating, a polite sort of conversation among owls, and he said nice warm mice. She wanted to ask him directions out of the forest and stumbled on how to phrase it.

Where is the place where the trees end? she said.

The owl did not know or did not understand. Perhaps he would know a place where people lived, but she had no idea how to ask about streets or buildings.

Where is the place where there is smoke?

One flight against the morning sun, he said. Then he flew from his tree to another, and then another, creating a straight line in that direction. Ani thanked him, took a long drink from the stream, and set off, praying that one flight was no farther than one day's walk.

Ani labored to keep her course straight, focusing on one tree in the distance until she reached it and then picking another farther on. The work made her eyes sore. The air was stagnant and hung close to her skin, but the ground was dry, giving no sign of spring or stream.

At first, she did not see the house. The walls were made of rough wood, and the roof was laden with branches still green with needles. Beside it stood a small garden enclosed with a stick fence. Ani noticed ripe apples on the trees and the lovely green fronds and orange tops of carrots pushing up through the earth. Her stomach made a noise. A brown goat was tied to a post outside the garden. It turned to her and said, "Neeee," in an annoyed stutter.

"What do you see, Poppo?" A woman came around the side of the house. She wore a red scarf tied on top of her head, a long tunic, and a skirt that hit above her ankles made of sturdy blue cloth. She spotted Ani and frowned.

"Well, Poppo, this isn't a badger or wolf, though it might want to eat from my garden like a common hare." The woman's short-voweled, guttural accent reminded Ani that she was in or near Bayern. Ani cleared her throat. The woman waited for her to speak.

"Hello," said Ani. She had spoken little in days, and her voice came through her throat like a fist. She cleared her throat again.

"Hmm?" said the woman.

"Hello. I'm lost."

"Yes, I see that." The woman folded her arms and looked over Ani's ragged, filthy dress. She blinked her eyes, waiting for more information. "It might help to know where you're lost from, or where you're lost to, if you see my point, and then I could push you in the right direction."

Ani opened her mouth and then closed it. *I am, or was, crown princess of Kildenree, betrothed to your king's son, what-is-his-name, I can't remember, oh mercy, and half of my escort guard attacked the other half of my escort guard and attempted to murder me and replace me with my lady-in-waiting.* It sounded absurd in her head. She began to wish for the comfort of the handkerchief in her bodice and reminded herself that she did not have it, and even if she did, it would do no good, and now she had to learn to rely on herself. That thought scared her as much as being lost in a strange forest.

"Well, child, I'm waiting," said the woman.

Ani realized that she was extremely thirsty, that it had been hours since she had left her little stream, and that she was likely to faint from panic, hunger, and exhaustion. And as she thought that, thousands of tiny black dots rushed her eyesight until, thankfully, the woman, the house, and the goat were exchanged for darkness.

Ani woke to a cottage window that looked out with a black eye on the night. She realized with a comfortable sigh that she was indoors and lying on a hay-stuffed mattress.

"You're awake, then?"

The woman had removed her headscarf, and Ani could see she wore her thick black hair cropped to her shoulders. She was sitting on a stool and knitting by the light of the hearth fire.

"You might've told me that you were thirsty and saved my boy Finn the trouble of carrying you in. I suspect you fainted on purpose just to get inside my house and onto a bed. Hmph." Ani smiled politely because she believed the woman meant it as a joke. "I guess you may as well stay the night."

She continued to knit, and Ani watched the yarn pile up in knotted lines, back and forth, with a speed she had never witnessed before. The woman nodded her head to a dish at her feet full of carrot broth and a ceramic mug of water. Ani drank quickly and then ate in silence. She could feel the water and broth go through her chest and into her belly with a warm tingle.

"So, girl," said the woman after a few minutes, "tell me what you're about."

"I was lost in the forest and need to get back to the road or on to Bayern." As she spoke, Ani was mindful of the long vowels and distinct consonants of her Kildenrean accent and wished she had thought to try to imitate the Bayern way of speaking. She thought she could learn it easily enough in the same way she had first learned to imitate the sounds of the swans, but now it was too late to try with this woman.

The woman laid her knitting down in her lap in a gesture of folding one's hands and looked carefully at Ani. "You're not from here," she said. Ani shook her head. "You're in some kind of trouble?"

"Yes, I think so."

"Well, I don't want to hear about it," she said quickly. "The less I know, the happier I'll be, I'd say. By the look of you, there's some mischief afoot. You've got yellow hair. And long, isn't it? Too long to be a wandering field-worker. Obviously not from Bayern, obviously noble, look at your soft little hands." Ani tucked her hands into each other.

"And, your accent, tsk, child, you sum up to a problem, and I've got knitting to do and pullovers to sell by marketweek. You understand?"

Ani nodded.

"Why don't you speak more?" The woman leaned forward, waiting for an answer.

"I am embarrassed about my accent," said Ani, "and I'm so confused...I don't know what to..." Ani heaved a breath but could not stop the first sob, which was followed by another and a third. Her stomach tightened, and she bent over and cried hard. Her hair closed in around her face. She felt the woman pat her shoulder.

"There, there, now. No more crying. It's all wetness and no comfort at all."

Ani thought she was right, for she felt more miserable than before, so she put her palms over her eyes and tried to stop. Her breath pulled harshly at her throat, and she sounded to herself like little Rianno-Hancery after a tantrum.

"I'm sorry," she said. "I won't cry anymore. I'm sorry."

"All right, child, all right. Now, just you tell me what I can do to set you straight, provided I don't have to get involved."

Ani nodded and then realized that the woman was asking her to make a decision. She longed for Talone, her father, Selia (no, no, not Selia), Falada, the lost handkerchief (not that either), just one of her onetime advisers. *What a child I am*, she thought. She straightened her back, placed her hands in her lap, and stared at the fire. Even from a distance, its heat burned her eyes.

Grow up. Think. What did she need? The road. But the road to where? The thought of going back to Kildenree on her own was absurd. She had no food or means, no horse, and on foot it would take her months, and the snows would arrive before then. Talone had told her to go to Bayern and find the king. It was possible that Talone and his men had defeated Ungolad, and if so, they would be with the king. Besides the king, there was the prime minister. She had met him once as a child—perhaps he would remember her face and act as her witness. And if Selia and her traitors were there waiting for the escaped princess? She could hear her heartbeat escape her ribs like the quick thuds of Ungolad's boots behind her.

Even so, were she offered a carriage back to Kildenree, passage paid, she could not go until she had found Falada and learned the fate of Talone and those faithful few. Bayern. It had to be her choice.

"How far away is the capital?"

"A day and a half in a wagon, but don't you be thinking about walking it and losing yourself again in our forest until I find you facedown in my carrot patch a week hence with no more sense than you had when you left."

"May I go with you to the city for marketweek?"

The woman considered. "Yes, that'll do, and I'll expect you'll be wanting an oufit so you don't stick out like a lightning tree. Finn'll take you come next week's end, and then we'll be done." She nodded and picked up her knitting.

A boy in late adolescence entered the house and stepped up to the hearth to kiss his mother. The firelight lit up bits of white wool that were stuck to his sleeves and the hairs of his arms. He stuck out a hand to Ani and said, "Hello."

"Hello, Finn," said Ani.

The boy smiled and disappeared into a dark corner where his bed resided.

"Go to sleep now," said the woman, rising.

"Yes, um, lady?"

"Gilsa," said the woman. "I'm no lady."

"Gilsa, when is next week's end?"

"Eight days. Hmpf, child."

Ani lay on her side, watching the black logs throb orange with the last life of the fire and thinking that she would never fall asleep. It seemed only the next moment that she opened her eyes to a room already silvery with dawn. The door opened and Gilsa came in with a handful of eggs, her hair uncombed and stuck with bits of hay and wisps of wool.

"Oh," said Ani, sitting upright, "this is your bed."

"Well, of course it is. Do you think I sleep in the shed every night?"

"I didn't think at all." Ani stood and smoothed the blankets over the pillow. She had never had to wonder where other people slept. In a palace, everyone had a place. In her ignorance, she realized, she was thoughtless and selfish.

"I'm sorry," said Ani. "Thank you. You don't have to sleep out there tonight."

"That's certain. My charity lasts about one night on thin hay and then I get tetchy."

Ani resolved that for the rest of her stay she would not be a burden. The first day, while Gilsa knit ferociously on her stool, Ani tried her hand at preparing the noon meal. After the questionable results were painfully consumed, Finn returned to the cooking and Ani, chagrined, observed carefully.

Gilsa discovered that Ani was quite good at finding the roots she needed for dyeing the yarn. Soon Ani was sent more and more on errands in the woods to keep her away, Ani suspected, from the delicate work. After one such errand, Ani made her way across the neat, dirt-swept yard with an apron full of roots when she heard the chickens croaking uncomfortably in their coop. Small feathers took flight as they left and reentered the pen again and again.

A rat, a rat, they croaked. *We will not stay, the rat stays still, there, under, under.*

"I don't know what's the matter," said Gilsa, her hand on the coop door. "They're scared, as if there's a green snake in a nest or a fox underfoot. But I've cleaned out the coop twice and can't find a thing."

"A rat," said Ani. "A dead rat, under the floor, and the hens sense him."

Ani took the roots inside and was sorting them before she

realized she might have to explain her comment. When she stepped back outside, Gilsa was directing Finn to remove the floorboard Ani had indicated. Underneath was a newly dead rat corpse.

"How did you . . . ?" Gilsa looked at her sharply.

"My parents used to raise chickens," said Ani.

After the first night, Ani spent the sleeping hours on the itchy wool and hay in the shed. She was restless at first, waking at every creak of board and whine of tree. Could Ungolad track her here? She did not know, but after her first night in the shed, Ani begged a board to lock herself in from the inside. Finn complied without asking questions.

The night before their departure, Ani sat by the fire, rolling up Gilsa's pullovers into tight bundles and fitting them into the packs. Finn prepared the travel food. Gilsa was finishing the sleeve of one last pullover, a vibrant orange with suns and birds floating on its breast and back. She hummed a tune, light and sleepy, a lullaby. It tugged at the lip of Ani's memory, and she stopped her packing and watched the singer.

"You aren't done yet," said Gilsa.

"I know that song. Does it have words here? Do you say, 'The tales that trees could tell, the stories wind would sing'?"

"'Hear the trees a-listening, feel the fire whispering. See the wind a-telling me all the forest dreams.' It's an old tune. I used to sing it to my boy."

"What does it mean?" said Ani.

Gilsa's metal needles clicked together, a sound like a strange beast feeding. "It talks about the old tales, I guess. How in faraway places there are people what talk to things not people, but to the wind and trees and such. 'The falcon hears the boar, the child speaks to spring.' And to animals, too, I gather. I've always wondered." Gilsa looked down her nose at Ani. "Is it possible? Would you know about such things, child?"

Ani continued packing. "It may be so. I . . . have heard tales about the times after creation when all the languages were known, and tales of people who still remember how to talk to the beasts. But about wind and trees and spring and all that, I thought it was just a nursery story."

"May be. But all things speak, in their way, don't they?"

"I suppose. Just not very clearly."

Gilsa looked narrowly at Ani as though at a troublesome child. "We all talk to something besides just ourselves, from time to time. I talk to my goat and my chickens and my apple tree. I don't know if I'm heard, and I don't think I've been answered back, but it can't hurt. Now, just think of this, that a person could talk to fire or to a goat and the fire and the goat could answer back. How would that be?"

"Are there such things in Bayern? Magic things?"

"Magicians, sorcerers, witches," said Finn. He rocked back on his stool, and it creaked.

"Tricks is what they do, boy," said Gilsa. "That's not what she means."

"I've seen them," Finn said softly, "in the market. A witch can look at you and say what ails you, and a sorcerer can make things into what they're not."

"Yes, yes, child." Gilsa waved a dismissive hand. "They've some kind of gift for seeing and showing, but it's all flashy and comedy and giving a coin to hear what you already know. She's talking about the old ways, aren't you, little one?"

"I think so. There are so many tales, so strange and beautiful and perfect. They are not what are real, but better. I thought I had something that was magic once, but I lost it, and now I don't think it was at all." She touched her chest where the handkerchief had been and frowned. "I wish there was magic. If all the tales were true, then maybe they could tell me what I'm doing, and what I am to do now."

"Ah, now, don't cry over lost years and forgetfulness. The tales tell what they can. The rest is for us to learn. The question is, are we smart enough to figure for ourselves? Now, that's what I'd like to know."

Ani did not respond. There was a thin wail of a wind caught in the chimney. For a moment the sound was stronger than the crackle of the fire, as sad as a broken bird.

arly the next morning, Ani was arrayed in a yellow tunic and sky blue wool skirt. She wore a pair of Finn's old boots, the soft leather laced tightly to her calves. When Gilsa told Ani that no Bayern was as fair as she, Ani requested a cloth like the one Gilsa wore to hide her long yellow hair. Disguised as a Bayern, Ani thought she had a better chance of getting to the king before being noticed by Ungolad's men. After she was safely in the king's presence, it would be simple enough to remove the headscarf and show her hair as proof of her heritage.

Gilsa finished knotting the scarf against Ani's forehead and patted her cheek as she might the goat's neck after a milking.

"These are your clothes," said Ani.

"They were," said Gilsa.

Ani slipped the remaining gold ring from her pinkie. "I would like to repay your kindness. I would like you to have the ring."

Gilsa looked down at the twinkling bit of gold.

"Now what would I do with that, pierce Poppo's nose?" She smiled, and Ani realized she had not known the woman could smile. "You may need that, my precious, before your road's won. You'll find some other way to repay me, that's certain."

Ani had little practice in arguing, and she put the ring back on, disappointed. She felt the burden of the food she had eaten and the night she had slept in Gilsa's bed.

It was still early when Finn and Ani shouldered their packs and set out, and the forest was wet and humming in the morning blueness before true dawn. Finn seemed pleased to be silent, so Ani walked for a league listening to the heartening prattle of the forest birds and to her own breath that became heavier and shorter the farther they strode. By the time Finn motioned that they stop for a rest, Ani suspected the weight of the pack had rubbed the skin from her shoulders completely off.

They halted again later that afternoon where their path merged into a green way pressed with wheel ruts. The trees there thinned into lighter woods. Ani looked back and surprised herself with a longing to stay in the true forest. Gilsa's house, small and lost in a ponderous ocean of trees, seemed more like a home than all her memories of her mother's palace. She found that she had little desire to return to that palace, except for the comfort of a bed and food and knowing her place. *But*, she reminded herself, *Kildenree is no longer my place. Nor is Gilsa's house.* She looked back to the road.

Through the whispering forest noises came the distinct sound of a horse's hooves. Finn stood up, straining his eyes down the road, and Ani backed away to a tight group of trees. Her heart quickened her breath, and she did not dare even call out to Finn. But when she listened to the clomp and rhythm of the hooves, she realized that this was a horse with a short gait, and alone, not likely one of her pursuers. When the brown nose of a cob rounded the corner, there was recognition on Finn's face.

"Hello, hello," said the driver, a boy younger than Finn. In the wagon sat another boy and a girl, her hair wrapped up in a red scarf. All their clothing was dyed in bright colors like Ani's, for which she was relieved, having felt quite loud in her bright yellow and blue among the simple green and brown of the forest. The wagon halted beside them, and the rider stood up. Ani touched her head and made certain the headscarf was pulled low over her light brows.

"Hello," said the driver. "Finn, who's she?"

"Mother sent her to help me at market," said Finn. The others looked at her, waiting. Ani had decided to use her grandmother's name until she was sure she was safe from Ungolad, but there in the woods before that weather-beaten wagon, Isilee seemed too grand.

"I'm Isi," said Ani. "It's nice to meet you."

Finn turned and looked at her. Ani had spoken with the quick vowels and smooth slurring of the Bayern accent, practiced for days while hunched over hunting for roots near Gilsa's house. Finn frowned but said nothing, and she smiled at him gratefully.

The wagon riders continued to stare.

"Well, hand me a rotten apple," said the driver.

"What's all this?" said the other boy. "She sounds like she's from around Darkpond, but she's not from around Darkpond, or we'd know her, you hear me, Finn?"

"Yeah, you'd best tell where she came from."

"Forest," said Finn.

The driver shook his head. "Well, I don't like it, and neither does Nod, and Nod's not used to pulling five, and we're not used to cozying up to strangers. We can take her pack in the wagon now, so she's useless to you, and I think she'd best be on her way."

Ani was not surprised. She waited to feel her shoulders lighten as Finn lifted the pack from her back and to be left alone in the woods that she was beginning to know.

Finn said, "All right, then," touched Ani's elbow, and began to walk down the road.

"You can go with them," Ani said softly. "I don't mind, Finn, and you can't miss marketday."

Finn shrugged and kept walking. Ani could hear the groan of the wagon as Nod pulled up beside them at a slow pace.

"Don't be stubborn, Finn," said the driver.

"Yes, get in, Gilsa-boy."

"Look now, you dolts," said the girl, "Finn's sure to be carrying a seedcake from Gilsa, and we can't get a crumb of it like this."

"Come on, Finn," said the boy, "we just want to know who she is."

Finn kept his pace. The driver reined and groaned.

"Get in, both of you, you goat brothers."

She and Finn clambered into the back of the wagon. There was little room, the large sacks taking up the floor space. Ani followed Finn's lead and sat on her sack, like children winning individual games of king-of-the-hill.

Finn reached into his pack and pulled out a small cake wrapped in a scrap of basket weave.

"Fresh yesterday," said Finn, and handed it to the girl to split. Ani smiled at her, sure she had made the protest from kindness, but the girl did not meet her eyes.

"Go on, Nod," said the driver. He looked askance at Finn and tapped the horse with the reins.

They rode at a horse walk well into night. Ani curled onto her pack of blankets and watched the clean brightness of trees in open places slowly slide by. The three neighbors chatted regularly and even managed to coax updates out of Finn. He admitted he was worried about a chick that was born with a marred foot and his mother, who often knit in too little light.

As they told stories of what had passed at home since last marketweek, Ani listened and tried to piece together what life must be like living in the Forest on the edge of Bayern—difficult, impoverished, backbreaking work and the persistent question if they would last through another winter, she guessed. But she envied their commonality.

She had no stories to share and did not speak, and the four did not speak to her. Ani curled up tighter on her pack and tried to take up as little room as possible.

The wagon stopped for the night near a blackened fire pit that was soon ablaze.

As the travelers prepared a group meal and set up their bedrolls, Ani thought to be grateful for the second half of her Forest journey when Selia had refused to help her. At least she had had some practice at setting up her own bedroll. Finn, aware of Ani's ineptitude with meals, quickly fixed hers along with his and saved her a small embarrassment. Ani thanked him in her Bayern accent.

The next morning, Ani awoke before the others. She looked at their faces in the pale hint of dawn and felt acutely alone. In sleep, even the relative familiarity of Finn's face was dulled. They seemed complete strangers, their dark hair, their work-shortened fingernails and dirty hands, their peaceful sleep noises assuring they felt at rest in this great wooded world.

She rose and stretched, pulling even tighter that tension of solitude that was strung inside her chest. The horse whinnied sleepily. The sound was like a wound awakened, and she hungered for Falada's company. The horse's brushes and fittings stood on a rock by his side, and she set to work on his dull brown coat.

Ani whispered as she brushed, hummed softly at his twitching ears, imitating the nickering of mares to their foals, and tried to sense where he most liked to be rubbed. Though she could not speak to this horse, though his words did not enter her head as Falada's had, his flesh was familiar beneath her fingers, and his movements made sense to her eyes.

"Nod seems to like you."

Ani started and turned to see the driver yawn and rub his eyes. He reached out to pat his horse's neck. "So tell, then, you're good with the beasts?"

"I think so." She did not know how the Bayern looked upon those who were able with animals, but the boy did not seem suspicious.

He patted Nod's rump. "Finish getting him ready, if you like."

The companions rose and breakfasted in sluggish silence. As the others clambered into the wagon, Ani picked up a cooled piece of charcoal from the fire pit and slipped it into her skirt pocket, reasoning it might work to darken her eyebrows and complete her disguise as a Bayern.

They traveled for most of the day. The landscape opened up ever wider. After the sun began its slide into the west, the small party rambled in the company of hundreds of wagons down a broad avenue. Ahead rose the city.

Outside the forest, Bayern was a land of surging hills and rising lowlands, and the capital was built on the grandest of hills, sloping upward gently. Surrounded by a wall five men high, it ascended into tall, narrow houses and winding streets and towers and many spires, the city a tremendous candled cake ablaze with red-tiled roofs. All the grandeur met at the peak, where stood the many-turreted palace, red-and-orange banners worried by a high wind like candle flames. Next to this, her mother's illustrious palace was a country estate.

Ani jumped and stared at the noise and colors, a sea of hatted and scarf-wrapped heads, faces marked with dark brows and lashes, soldiers bearing iron-tipped javelins and brightly painted shields.

One among them had fair hair.

She saw him before he saw her, and she quickly looked away. It was Yulan. He sat on a stone before the city wall, scanning every face carefully, his eyes squinting against the setting sun, one hand on his sword hilt.

Ani lowered herself off her bundle and sat on the floor of the wagon. Her heart beat in her ears now, and the din of wagons and people seemed small and far away. Yulan was in the city. Ungolad and Selia must be there, too. She wondered if this meant that they had defeated Talone. That they were all dead. That there was no safety. She rubbed the tightness in her neck and kept her head down.

Somehow she still had to get into the palace. In Kildenree there had been days when one of the royal family would see city supplicants, and Ani was praying for the same here. If only she could get inside the palace without being recognized by Yulan and the others, she could plead her case to the king, and if he did not believe her, then the prime minister. She hoped that more than five years after visiting Kildenree, he might still recognize her face.

The many wagons poured through the gates and lined the open expanse of the market-square. Finn's company was pushed up against the back of a three-story building facing the market. Ani set up her bedroll behind a wagon wheel and huddled there, waiting for night to hide her. Finn sat beside her and silently offered bread and cheese the others were sharing for supper.

"Finn, can one go and talk to the king or queen, or prince?"

"No queen anymore." He slowly chewed a bit of bread, unaware that her skin crept with cold while she waited for his response.

"On marketday I see people line up to talk to the king."

"That's tomorrow?"

He nodded. They ate in silence.

"You'll be wanting to leave early." He pointed to a slender street that left the market and led up.

In the gray morning, Ani awoke to a market of sleepy merchants pulling wraps and blankets and wood-carved boxes out of dewy bags. She folded her blankets, nodded farewell to Finn, and started up the street.

Not far into her walk, Ani stopped on a vacant side street and arranged the front of her head cloth at its natural place just below her hairline. She pulled the charcoal from her pocket, bent to her reflection in a curtained window, and delicately darkened her eyebrows to a dusty black. If the Kildenreans were scanning the crowds for a fair-haired girl, they might pass her over. Ani could not afford to be recognized before reaching the protection of the king. She had no doubt that, if given the chance, Ungolad would drag her off and slit her throat in private.

The farther she walked, the more people were walking with her, some in the brightly colored, simple clothing of the out-towns, others in finer stuff of the city. She arrived at the palace walls just as the sun glared its upper rim over the city wall. There was already a queue of petitioners winding its way from the high palace gates through the courtyard. She stepped in behind the last person and hoped she was blending in enough not to draw the attention of the likes of Yulan.

The line moved quickly, though it was long, and Ani soon found herself wishing she had thought to bring along a shred of breakfast from Gilsa's bag of food. The bite of hunger made her grumpy, and her thoughts grumbled, *Unfair, unfair. To have to eat out of others' foodstuff and hope for goodness and charity, to be coinless and placeless. This palace would have been my home.* She bent her neck back to stare up at the sheer height of the palace spires, each glittering with windows and a wind-nipped banner.

She glared down at herself, leaning against the wall in travel-crumpled clothing, nearly last in a line of patient peasants, hungry, with feet aching on the soft soles of Finn's boots. *This is not who I am*, she thought. *So who am I?* She did not answer her own question. Her mind was filling with thoughts of breakfast foods—molasses rolls, cooked apples, boiled eggs with cheese, nut breads, fresh sausages. She swallowed against her hollow stomach and waited. The line inched forward.

At last her end of the line reached the cool shadow of the palace doors. Ani stepped forward and felt herself nearly knocked over with royal smell. Her stomach turned about as though it would jump into her neck and choke her until she cried. Floor soap, floor wax, curtain perfume, old metal, expensive stone, drinking water, garden roses, mending paste, armor oil, skin soap, rosewater. A kingdom of smells poked at her memories of her father, and of being comfortable and clean. Just a few months had passed since she had left home, but the smells came at her as though from far away, an echo of a memory, like being reminded of a dead loved one in the face of a stranger.

She barely noticed stepping forward each time the line moved, absorbed in a reverie of memories. The man before her had just entered the king's chamber when Ani saw Selia.

elia's pale hair was striking among the dark heads, and she wore it up in a cap of curls tucked into a jeweled net. She was dressed in one of Ani's new gowns, the rust-colored one with the simple bodice. She strolled with slow confidence, so pleased with herself that she almost betrayed smugness, accompanied by two other women in attire of the Bayern fashion— long-sleeved tunics and wide skirts cut from separate cloth. They laughed.

Ani did not move. Her feet were heavy cobblestones. She bowed her head and tensed herself for discovery, listening to the soft sway of Selia's skirts, the rustling of claimants as they moved aside and guessed at bowing. When the women turned down another corridor, Ani looked up to see the chamber-mistress motioning for her to enter.

Selia is here, in the palace, in my dress.

"Come, you're next," said the chamber-mistress.

Selia is here, and that means she has killed them all—Talone,

Adon, Dano, Radal, Ingras, all.

"Step quickly, girl, as there's a line until tomorrow."

Ani held her breath and entered the chamber. It was long and narrow, with a window in the ceiling that poured hot sunlight onto the pale marble floor. Ani wanted to squint at the brilliance. The image of Selia still burned in her eyes, like looking into darkness after staring at fire, and she walked forward blindly.

She knew there were guards in the corners and beside each bright column. She did not raise her eyes to them. Ungolad would be somewhere close to Selia. His men were in the city looking for her, and here she had come to the palace, a mouse to the cheese, to announce herself before them, inviting them to simply murder her like her companions. Ani stopped, afraid that if she continued moving, she would run away.

"Come closer," said the king.

He was a wide man who seemed tall, even sitting. His hands, resting on the arms of the finely carved chair, were large and strong, and she imagined that if he had the need, he could still carry a sword to battle. He seemed tired but amused, perhaps by her reluctance to approach. Ani took a few more painful steps forward and performed her deepest curtsy, the one her tutor years ago had told her was for royalty only. No tutor could have prepared her for meeting a king no longer as Anidori-Kiladra of Kildenree, but as a forest girl in hand-me-down boy's boots, charcoal-darkened eyebrows, and an imitated accent.

"What's your petition?" said the chamber-mistress.

"I—don't know," she said, using the strong Forest accent. *Stupid, stupid,* she called herself. She could not reveal herself to the king now that she knew Selia had succeeded in penetrating the palace. What proof did she have? At her claim, the king would naturally call Selia to explain. Selia and all the guards could deny her story, and Ani would be imprisoned as an impostor or, perhaps worse, let go as a harmless nitwit and fall directly into Ungolad's hands. There was no appeal. Ani was lost.

The king sighed. "You're new to the city?"

"Yes, sire."

"You have a place to stay?"

"No," she admitted.

"What can you do?"

Thinking of finding Falada, Ani answered, hopefully, "I work with horses."

The king gestured to a counselor who stood to his right.

"No need at present for a new hand in the stables, sire." The counselor was a tall, thin-faced man who exuded awareness of his own importance. He looked over a parchment he had affixed to a thin board. "However, the goose boy finds himself alone and at odds with a gaggle of fifty."

"Good," said the king, and motioned for Ani to follow the counselor out of the room.

"Wait, uh, sire, I ask a boon. Could I speak with your

prime minister for just a moment?"

The king gestured to the waiting counselor with impatience. "As you shall."

Ani blinked, amazed that he granted her wish so readily, thanked him, and curtsied once again as a new petitioner was already waiting. When she straightened, there was a new expression on the king's face. He seemed to see her for the first time, and the lines around his mouth deepened. She felt commanded to hold still for inspection while he looked at her, and she flushed from her neck to her hair.

"Good," said the king again, and gave her a smile before the chamber-mistress called for his attention.

After the brightness of the receiving chamber, the dark wood walls and deep-toned rugs and tapestries of the corridor were a relief to her eyes. She was going to see the prime minister, and that, too, was a relief. She waited for the counselor to lead the way, but instead he called a pageboy, instructed him to take Ani to the workers' west settlement, and then turned back to the king's chamber.

"Wait, uh, sir? The king said I could speak with the prime minister."

"I am he."

"Not you. I mean, I met him once when I was younger."

The prime minister sighed annoyance. "That was someone else, then. I am Thiaddag, the prime minister of Bayern, and have been for the last four years. So sorry I can't abandon my important duties to reunite you with your old chum."

He waved her off with the back of his hand and returned to the king.

"Well, come on, then," said the boy.

Ani hesitated. Working with a goose boy was not part of her plan. But, then, her plan had been weak enough to crumble at the sight of Selia and a new prime minister. For now, she needed a way to stay in this city until she could rescue Falada.

"Yes, all right," she said, following after the page.

When they emerged into the brightness of the courtyard, the pageboy stopped to stretch back his arms and puff out his chest, and he smiled at the blazing day. He reminded Ani of a robin in his red tunic, his hair unruly like loose feathers.

"My name's Tatto. I'm the son of a captain of twenty. That's why I'm a pageboy already, and me with only twelve years."

"Oh," said Ani. "Congratulations."

He narrowed his eyes at her to see if he was catching her in a mocking tone. She shrugged, meaning she did not know if it was a good thing or not to be a pageboy at twelve. He shook his head and muttered, "Forest-born."

He was talkative as they walked down the steep city streets, informing her of his many and complicated duties as page and all about the city. At length they reached the high city wall and began to travel beside it.

"On the other side of the wall are the pastures—cows, sheep, geese, and all. That's where you'll be working."

"And where are the horses kept?" asked Ani.

"Oh, they're behind the palace, on so much land you'd have to run to get past it all before breakfast."

Behind the palace wall, Ani thought dismally. That would be a problem.

At last Tatto directed her to a long house two stories high and painted a yellow as lively as Ani's tunic. The woman inside was thin and had dull eyes that did not seem to completely take in what they saw. When she spoke, her voice dragged out of her throat reluctantly, punctuated with pauses and moans. She introduced herself as Ideca, the mistress of workers in the west settlements, and sent Tatto off with a warning not to dawdle back as he had no doubt done on the way or his captain would return him to the grease pits of the kitchen. Tatto scowled at the hall-mistress for spoiling his image and rushed out the door.

Ideca looked Ani over. "You're not to, mmm, get homesick for your Forest folks and run off at first frost."

"No, I won't," said Ani.

"Don't know why you went to the king instead of coming here direct. Suppose you think it's a grand entrance, but don't think it means you'll be treated different. We all work. That's what we do here, work."

Ani nodded and hoped that was sufficient response.

Ideca pursed her lips. "Here's where you'll take your meals, morning and night, so you may as well start off with one now, mmm." She plunked down a bowl of bean soup and a tall glass of water. Ani guzzled the glass of water immediately and then wished she had saved a few swallows to help ease down the cold soup.

Ideca took Ani upstairs to a haphazard wardrobe and gave her a spare skirt and tunic for washday, both pale orange like the rose on a peach, a long cut of birch with a bent end for herding her geese, and a hat with a low straw rim and a ribbon that tied under the chin, effectively hiding, Ani imagined, every strand of one's hair.

"You'll be living in the third house from the south, wall-side. The rest of the day's free. Be back here for breakfast tomorrow early." She sent Ani out and closed the door.

Opposite the mistress's hall squatted a row of dwellings, each with one window and a separate door. Ani found the third house and entered. The house was no more than a room—a very small room. With her arms outstretched, she could nearly touch two walls at once. It shared its wooden sidewalls with neighbors and borrowed the west wall of the city for its back wall. It smelled of the city—refuse, smoke, food, and people and animals living too close together. The house was built right on the square cobblestone of the street, and she felt as though she still stood on the street, and any moment hawkers might come through her door or children playing at catch-the-fly might crawl through her window and jump over her bed to climb the rough stones of the back wall.

A small bed, a side table, and three iron hooks on one wall

were the room's only furnishings. Ani thought of her apartments in the White Stone Palace, just the first room that could hold fifteen of these, and she imagined the walls before her pushing back and brightening, white paint pouring over the bare walls like water thickened with light, tapestries of children and birds and hills of autumn unrolling themselves, carpets growing under her feet the way a stream floods its banks, the bed expanding into a mountain of pillows and blankets the way dough explodes into bread, books on the walls, cats at her feet, food on her table, a serving girl at the door saying, "May I help you dress, Crown Princess?" Not crown princess. Not a princess anymore. The serving girl's face was just a round stone in the wall. The mean dullness came crashing back into itself, hard and bleak and small. Ani sat on the bed and stared at her soft, uncallused hands.

After wandering down, around, to dead ends and back, past the acrid smell of cows' kidneys on the street of meat shops and the dizzying emanations of the flowers in hundreds of baskets on the florists' street, Ani finally found the market-square by following the noise. The quiet wagon people from last night had transformed into brazen city peddlers, waving goods at passersby, shouting from the seats of their wagons, standing and calling, "Apples! Herbs! Jars of preserves and nuts and cones! Blankets for the cold, the cold, buy blankets against the coming cold!"

Ani found her traveling companions just as animated, with half their bags empty and a crowd of purchasers fingering Gilsa's intensely dyed yarns and tight knits. Even Finn spoke a word or two and waved a pullover in the air. She realized he was waving it at her, and she jogged to him, still feeling dazed by the noise and agitation of the square.

"Hello, Isi," he greeted her, and she reminded herself that Isi was her name, for now. The group had sold a good lot of wares, though nearly half still remained and they would have to stay on for the rest of marketweek.

"It'll be better next month," said the girl with the red scarf, "when the weather's cooling and all the world's afraid of winter."

"Finn, I've been given work here." She tried to whisper but nearly yelled to be heard above the din. "I'm to tend the king's geese." She smiled, for though it was simple labor, it sounded noble in her ears just then, as though she heard Tatto's satisfied voice swaggering the phrase.

"Good work," said Finn.

"I just wanted to tell you that, so you wouldn't wonder where I'd gone."

He patted her shoulder, then looked at her quizzically. He touched his eyebrow and smiled at her with the energy of a good, secret joke. She wondered what state they were in, hoping that the charcoal had not smeared.

"Well, I should go. Thanks for your kindness." She turned

to leave, then quickly returned and spoke near his ear.

"Finn, should anyone discover you know me, and come to you or your mother, pretending to be my friend, asking where I am, don't tell them. Please." She smiled painfully. "You two are the only friends I have in this kingdom."

He nodded. "I saved you a bit of lunch." He pulled an apple from the wagon, fat and green, smelling like the sharp, wet grasses of the forest streams. "Luck," he said, gave her the apple, and returned to his selling.

Ani threaded her way through the stands, carts and wagons, merchants, sellers from outside the city, and city dwellers come out to make a coin. There was a small crowd gathered around a man who juggled red balls. One of the balls turned into a dove, and it flew through the circle. Ani watched, openmouthed.

"Tricks."

A woman in a green headscarf waved a finger at Ani. She was seated on a blanket so covered by roots, clusters of berries, and dried bunches of leaves that she could not have moved.

"It's all tricks." The woman gestured to the juggler. "Not magic."

"Oh, of course," said Ani. The woman squinted at her and coughed or, perhaps, laughed.

"You've got something in you, don't you, now?"

Ani creased her brow.

"Words, young thing. In you. More than you think, I

think."

"Is it magic, what I have?"

"Do you know what you have?"

Ani shrugged.

"I also think you want something here." She swept a dirty hand over her gathered wares.

"Yes, actually, thornroot," said Ani, asking for a plant she had learned about in her root-gathering days at Gilsa's. "But I don't have a coin."

The woman sniffed. "For the apple." She produced from a slightly moldy mound a pinkie finger-size root. "All I've got. Not in demand."

They exchanged goods, and before Ani could question her again, the woman shooed her away.

Ani fought her way through the mayhem to the city wall and then followed the wall west, her left hand running along the stones. She had not left the market noise far behind when she caught a glimpse of long objects hanging from the wall up ahead. She blinked and tried to make them out. Before she could see them clearly, she smelled them.

The corpses emanated death under the fierce gaze of the sun. It was the biting odor of sour meat and fresh blood, and it touched the back of her throat like a finger. Her body trembled, wishing to turn inside out, and she quickly stumbled past. She stopped a few paces later. A man leaned against the wall, chewing on a sausage biscuit and staring at what hanged on the wall.

"Excuse me, sir," she said.

The man spat out a tough bit of meat and looked down at her. "I'm not a sir, Forest girl, I'm Arnout."

"Arnout, can you tell me why those, those bodies are up there?"

He shrugged. "Criminals. Probably killed somebody or stole animals or took a girl. The bad things. Not cowardice, though. Commit cowardice in the king's army and you get buried in mud, you get hidden. That's tradition." He smiled through a mouthful of chewed biscuit and patted her head. "City's not much like your little Forest, eh? You'll get used to it."

Ani walked away and did not look back. She realized that she did not know if criminals were killed in Kildenree. Perhaps they were. Perhaps they were hidden from her, as much of the world had been. Perhaps her mother had thought she was too weak to know the world.

A long walk later, Ani reached the workers' settlements. She cracked open Ideca's door to ask for a little vinegar, which she received in a loaned cup after a moaned complaint and a mild scolding.

Ani entered the third house in the row, and to avoid the gloom of gray wood and cramped space, she started right to work. The brown thornroot had been a find in that marketplace, dim and forgettable among the berries, roots, and organs used for the bright colors the Bayern sought.

With a loose rock, she cut dark, juicy strips into a hollow

in a floor stone, then bruised them in drops of vinegar. Using a little bundle of grass as a brush, she carefully covered the fair hairs of her eyebrows in the dye. Coloring her locks would take more thornroot than she imagined could be found in the entire marketplace, besides the consequence of coloring her hands to her wrists in the process. This would have to do.

She wiped off the dried dye with the underside of her skirt and curled up in bed. Even in her sleep she was aware of the wood slats pressing through the thin mattress like bruises on her back.

hen dawn creaked open its bright eye, Ani could hear both her neighbors stirring, wooden bed frames whining the truth of their age, and boots scraping across stone. She took her yellow tunic and blue skirt from the hook instead of the new rose orange, preferring familiarity to novelty on that morning. She wrapped her hair above her head in a braid and held it in place with her hat. She hoped no one would question why she wore a shade hat even though dawn was a new idea and the sun barely slipped through cracks between buildings to touch cobblestones. She tied the ribbon in a knot beneath her chin and stuffed loose hairs back into its tightness. Armed with her crook, Ani left her little room and braved Mistress Ideca's breakfast tables.

Ani opened the door to the smell of warm food mixed with the odor of cowsheds, breakfast bread, and bodies that spent too much time with animals and too little time in a bath. Ani wondered if she could eat through that smell, though the nearly three dozen workers at the table benches were eating as though half starving.

They were young, some boys nearly as young as Tatto, some girls older than Ani, all with hair shades maple-bark brown to mud black. The hall trembled with the sounds of chatter, metal spoons on ceramic dishes, the slamming of the kitchen door as Ideca's girls entered with full platters and left with dirty plates, and friends called to friends at other tables. Ani noticed that none of the other girls had their hats on. She fingered her brim nervously and looked for a place to sit and keep to herself.

It was not long before she was noticed.

"Conrad, there's your girl," someone yelled.

"There's the new one."

"Go on, Conrad, give her a kiss," said a boy. He pushed a boy in an orange cap off the end of the bench and onto the floor, and that boy promptly pulled himself to his feet and grabbed a handful of cooked eggs. Before his gooey hand reached the offending boy's face, Ideca had leaped forward, seizing his wrist with one hand and his hat and a handful of hair with the other.

"Conrad, I'll keep you cleaning eggs off the floor at bed-hour, believe I will, so meet Isi and sit down."

Conrad sniffed. He put the fistful of eggs casually on his plate, rubbed the sticky pieces onto his pant leg, and held out his hand to Ani. He had dull gray eyes, and the freckles on his face lay together as tightly as scales.

"Name's Conrad," he said. "I keep the geese."

"Kiss her," someone shouted over the din of breakfast.

Conrad jerked his head toward the yeller and yelled back, "Shut it or I'll stuff your nose holes full of breakfast, and I'll clean it and you off the floor until next morning if I have to."

He renewed his gesture of welcome, and Ani took his hand and then surreptitiously wiped off the egg goo behind her back.

"Good to meet you," she said.

"Where you from?" said a girl in the back.

"The Forest," she said.

"Of course you are, you sparrow chick," said the girl, "but which part?"

Ani realized that most of this group must have come from the Forest to work in the city and send money home to families.

"Near Darkpond," she said, repeating the place she had heard Finn's neighbors speak of.

"She talks like someone I know from Darkpond," Ani heard a girl say.

Some nodded, and she was dropped out of the general attention in favor of breakfast. Ani ate slowly, focusing on swallowing the heavy, hot food that it seemed too early to eat. She watched Conrad and his friends, amazed at the heaping plates of eggs and lumps of beans with mutton chunks and hot, greasy oat muffins they consumed with careless speed. When the dishes were empty, they wiped their mouths on the backs of their hands, their hands on their trousers, or on each other in brief, concentrated wrestling matches, and the benches emptied with rousing scrapes of wood against the stone floor.

"Get your stick," said Conrad, grabbing his own from where it stood with the others near the door. As they left, a chorus of "Conrad's got a girl, Conrad's girl," moved from mouth to mouth.

"Come on, goose girl," Conrad said testily, and they walked up a narrow street.

Ani used the base of her stick between stones to help her climb. Conrad did not wait, and she caught up to him when the steepness had ebbed out. Soon Ani could hear the mutterings of animals—sheep, pig, chicken, goat—they lost their particularity in their numbers. Conrad unlocked the door of a low structure. The jabber of housed geese greeted their entrance, and immediately Ani realized that their language was far different from swan. She found herself unable to pick out a single word.

"You kept geese before?" said Conrad. Ani shook her head, and he rolled his eyes. "Take it easy at first, all right? Just let me do it and you stand back and make sure they don't wander away. Geese don't like new people, but better a new girl than a new boy. The ganders nearly bit the knees off the last boy that came crawling from the Forest looking for a city job. He didn't last long with me. With the pigs, now."

"Thanks for the warning," she said.

"I don't care if they bite off your kneecaps, goose girl, I'm just telling you." He shrugged and opened the pen.

Geese were smaller and much less grand than the swans she knew. Though like her swans in form, the geese seemed simplified by larger heads, shorter necks, and feet and bills orange like exotic fruit.

The palace grounds in Kildenree did not have a goose pen, and Ani had seen the birds only from a distance. Sometimes from the library window she had watched a short-haired country girl with bare feet, a stick, and a hat made of thick paper rolled in on itself like a whittled bit of wood. She used to walk a dozen geese down a river-sided lane toward the free pastures on the edges of the city. It had seemed carefree enough to Ani then, and the girl had given the impression of happy complacency, the geese at her feet just pale flutterings of her thoughts.

Ani's thoughts were pulled back to the moment by a loud, unlovely honk. A broad-headed gander stepped out of the pen and knocked Ani's leg with his beak. She tumbled backward in surprise and landed on her backside. When she looked up again, his neck and head were stooped down to the ground and forward, as though his body held a ready sword. He was rushing forward, his open, hissing beak aimed at her face. She flung her arms over her head and tensed for pain, and when nothing happened, she peeked out to see Conrad's crook around the gander's neck.

"Stand up," he said. "That's a stupid thing to do."

Ani scrambled to her feet, leaning over to her dropped stick with an eye on the geese.

"I'm sorry," she said.

"Huh. Let's go."

It was several long, bruising streets to the pasture gate. Fifty geese were too many for one boy and worse for a boy and a goose-ignorant girl who more often than not found herself in the middle of the gaggle, her calves nipped emphatically. Conrad maintained his position in the rear, driving the horde with whistles and nudges from his staff. Occasionally he shouted, "Goose girl, they're drifting," and sent her scampering after a loose bunch.

Ani listened in vain to their mutterings to pick out familiar sounds. She tried some swan, and they seemed to laugh at her and nip at her legs a little harder.

At last they reached a narrow, arched gateway cut in the city wall. Beyond it lay green pastures, bordered on the near side by the outside of the city wall and on the far by tall water trees and a narrow stream. The sight of the pasture caught the geese's attention like the smell of food after a fast. Their necks straightened, and their small eyes focused on the grass and the shimmering stream beyond.

Ani slipped through the arch before them to count the bright beaks as they passed by. It was a bulky wave of white, defined by orange bills and blue eyes.

"Forty-seven," said Ani. "There should be fifty, but I'd

pledge blood we didn't let a one get away."

Conrad shrugged.

"Aren't you concerned?" she said. "Shouldn't we go back and look?"

He met her look with defiance. "They were missing before. I've been alone with this rabble for more than a week, and what can I do if three disappear when there're forty-seven off in every direction? I'd like to see you do better."

The day moved slowly with the sun, and Ani stayed in the shade of a lone beech tree in the middle of their pasture. Not distant from her feet lay the near lip of a small pond that filled with the edges of the stream. The geese wandered near the pond, moving in groups of five or so to graze where the grass was longer or digging for grubs on the muddy banks. It was not a broad pasture, but long, bordered on both ends with hedges that served as fences, beyond which Ani caught glimpses of sheep on one side and something else, maybe cows, on the other.

Ani gazed into the distance, hoping to see horses out to graze, and among them, Falada. But Tatto had told her the horses were kept in the city pastures behind the palace. To assuage her guilt, Ani reasoned that Falada was probably much better off than she, eating mountains of oats and sleeping contentedly in the royal stables. If he was not dead. That thought stung. And if he was, how could she find out without being killed herself?

Speculation was useless. There was no occasion to leave

the fields all that day. *What was I expecting,* thought Ani, *an hour off for tea?* Hours past noon, a street hawker leaned out of the pasture arch announcing hot meat-breads in a clear, practiced call. Conrad waved him away with a disappointed gesture. Neither goose girl nor goose boy had any money.

When the sharp orange of evening sun burned on the horizon, Conrad called to her that it was time to go. He had remained separate from Ani all the day, seeking his shade under the birches that grew along the stream, tossing stones upstream and lazily chasing geese to hear them honk.

The herding home was easier. The geese were worn from the day and ready to rest. Only once were the crooks employed, when a couple of ganders left the group to make sport of a broken-toothed street cat that had come too close to one of the females.

When they had locked the geese into their pen and stumbled into the dining house, Ani at last understood the concentrated devouring of breakfast. Her stomach perked up at the smell of food, muttering and tightening itself in anticipation.

Dinner with the workers was as lively as the breakfast had been, despite the fact, Ani noted, that they were fed bean and lard pies, potatoes without butter, and green beans that were cooked to mush. The group ate vigorously, and Ani felt inclined to do the same. The smell of animals on people was even more pungent, but Ani ate through it.

A noise drew her attention to the door. It slammed

behind a girl near Ani's age, red faced and huffing for breath. Her black hair was loose at her shoulders, and she had wide eyes that put Ani in mind of an owl. She leaned against the doorpost, waved her hand at a group of boys who stood nearby, and, swallowing air, pushed her voice through her throat.

"Quick. Razo, Beier. That sulky old ram . . . he beat down a hole in his pen . . . got into my chick coop . . . I tried to stop him, but I—"

Without a word, two of the boys grabbed the nearest crooks and fled the hall. The door shut, and the girl faced the hall. Immediately Ani noticed that the girl's expression changed. She no longer fought for breath, and a creeping smile pressed dimples into her cheeks. "But I couldn't stop him because I was so busy rigging a bucket of oat mush above the door."

Laughter bubbled out of the corners of the hall, building as the other workers caught on. Ani smiled, too, and shook her head as her imagination raced to the coop, where those poor boys were opening the door. The girl bobbed a curtsy and sat on Ani's bench.

"It's a payback," she said, grabbing a cold bean pie. "They put colored eggs in one of my chickens' nests for a week. I poured every medicine I knew down that poor hen's throat and laid witch-bought charms around her nest until I finally spotted a bit of paint on some hay. Devilish, they are."

The girl smiled with good humor, and Ani smiled back

until she felt shamed by the girl's prettiness and confidence and looked down.

"You're from Darkpond?" said the girl. "I'm Enna, from Sprucegrove area, you know, just down past the stream."

Ani nodded.

"Not to worry. Conrad's no festival, but he's all right enough. He takes time to warm up to new people, just like any animal."

"I've only just arrived in the city," said Ani. "My first time here, really." Enna raised her brows, and Ani nodded, grateful to have some truth to tell. "Can you tell me news? What happens here?"

A boy across the table heard her question and snorted. "Not much, not for us, you see that. Not a day off—"

"But marketday," said another.

"—but marketday, and maybe a festival or two, but won't be another festival until wintermoon, and then who knows."

No break until next marketday. Ani realized she would have to wait a month for an opportunity to find Falada. But surely he was well off, she convinced herself. *If he is alive, he must be well.*

"When's the prince married?" asked a girl one bench over.

Ani casually put her hand on her neck to hide the goose bumps pricking her skin.

"Oh, don't recall," said the boy. "Not now, anyway."

"There'll be festival then, you'll see, like the royals like to have to toot their royalness. It'll be a week long with little work and apple cakes for free."

Ani tilted her head and tried to speak as though the answer did not matter the least in the world. "Getting married, is the prince?" she said. "To whom?"

"Some yellow girl from Kildenree. A princess, I guess. Can't imagine His Royal would marry anything less."

"She's a princess," said Enna. "I laid my very own eyes on her expensive skin."

The eaters around lifted heads and quieted down.

"Why didn't you tell about it before, Enna-girl?"

"Yeah, you got secrets as dark as your mop?"

"I did tell about it to those who shut up and listened, so shut it now and I'll tell. It was two weeks or so ago, and I was heading to the apothecary near the city gate for what I *thought* was a sick chicken, and the streets were all lined with people. Everybody was talking about her. No one had known when they would come, you know, with them traveling so far, and never did send a messenger forward, I heard someone say."

"And those Kildenrees, or Kildenreans, or whatever, came marching in with their own little army, I'm guessing."

"Not really. Just twenty men or so, and more horses. The princess rode a big white horse with all the trappings."

Ani felt her heart beating in her stomach. Falada. He was alive, then. She wanted to grab Enna's arms and beg her for every detail. She sat on her hands.

"And I don't know much about horses, but I heard some

men talking by me, and they said it was a cursed good horse, and that she didn't know how to ride him right, and that she probably rode some docile puppy horse through the Forest and mounted the fine steed last minute just for show and all."

Ani smiled.

"Just like a princess," said Conrad. "But enough of horses, what'd the girl look like?"

"She's not for you, Conrad," said his neighbor, who promptly got an elbow in the ribs.

"Pretty, I guess," said Enna. "Light hair, not so much a real yellow as washed-out brown, like Conrad's bathwater. She was wearing a dress showy enough for a princess, silvery and sparkling with a neck almost this low." Enna pointed to a spot four finger widths from the hollow of her throat. One girl laughed and another sighed. Ani placed a hand on her chest and felt her cheeks warm. On her, the dress had fallen slightly lower.

A girl laughed and pointed at Ani. "I think the goose girl's dreaming she's the princess."

Enna put an arm around her shoulder and shook her amiably. "Who wants to be a snooty, lace-necked royal and miss tending the geese? Right, little sister?"

"No, that's right, I wasn't thinking that," said Ani. "Um, did you hear anything they said? The princess or her guards?"

"Mmm, no, I don't think so. There was one guard, a big

man with two braids the color of bad milk hanging down each shoulder, that rode up with her, and they leaned in close and talked, looking down at us, around at the city, passing judgment on everybody and everything they saw, I guessed. A bit boorish. I'd imagined princesses were supposed to sit up straight and look stoic, if you know what I mean."

Ani nodded.

"That's it, really. A lot of horses, a few wagons, twenty scruffy guards, and a princess in a gaudy dress showing enough bosom for a tavern girl."

A tall girl grumbled. "Tatto said that she takes one of her own guards wherever she goes, to go eat, to the gardens, like she doesn't trust the palace guards. And she's never left the palace grounds, afraid to dirty her tiny foot on our Bayern stones."

"I heard she's had ten new dresses made since she arrived," said another girl, "and that's a fact, because my aunt's friend's a seamstress in the city and she knows the palace dress-mistress."

"They say she never goes riding or into the city, but stays holed up with her Kildenrean friends and they whisper to each other in that whiny accent."

Several nodded. "That's how Kildenreans are," said one.

Ani began to nod, then stopped. *If I were where I was supposed to be, I never would have met the workers of the west settlement. I'd be the yellow girl from Kildenree, with the whiny accent and pompous manner.* Just then, that seemed a pitiable fate.

The door swung open with force, its knob thumping against the wall. Razo, a short boy with a dark, defiant head of hair and an expressive face that was grim and severe then, stood with hands in fists. Beier stood behind him, holding their unused staffs. Their hair and shoulders were dripping with a gray slop.

"Enna," said Razo, his voice trembling with warning.

Enna just laughed. "You're welcome, boys." She raised her water mug in salute. Others raised theirs, too, in a cheer heavy with laughter that did not completely break until the hour for bed.

Chapter 9

The days dawned with a frail morning chill and filled out with mild breezes. Autumn's newness hummed in the air. The geese sensed the coming change, and pairs strolled together, leaving their grown goslings solitary. Occasionally one bird interrupted its browsing to stare up at a breeze, smelling what news it brought, calling out to its brothers and sisters, *The first gust of autumn is here.*

Or so Ani imagined. She passed most of the day under her beech tree, her gaggle at a safe distance. She watched and she listened. Geese made so much more noise than swans, she wondered how she would ever be able to single out the sounds, let alone assign their meanings. This time she had no aunt to guide her. Some bird tongues were so similar that going from one to the other was like switching between her Bayern and Kildenrean accents. But goose was unlike any bird tongue she had learned. She leaned forward, cocking her head like a robin to a worm in the ground. *Prattle,*

prattle, honk, honk, hiss—the sounds were as meaningless as the rustling of dry leaves.

At night Ani felt exhausted, but often she could not sleep, not for hours, the darkness behind her eyelids promising dreams. *Adon's middle split by a sword tip. Talone yelling, yelling. Ungolad's hand on her boot.*

Lying on her bed, she could see the dark intimation of the southernmost palace spire and on certain nights a dim star of a candle flame that winked in one window. She watched it until she slept. That point of light spoke of someone else awake, someone thoughtful, someone alone. Sometimes in her dreams, her mind wandered those foreign palace halls, tripping over carpets too fine to be pressed by her dirty boot, losing herself in passages too elaborate for her goose girl brain. She was often searching for something, Falada or Selia, and when she found them, she stood there stupidly, not knowing what to do. Sometimes instead of searching, she was running. A hand seized her ankle.

In the mornings, Ani dressed her bruised, goose-bitten body and breakfasted in silence. The girl Enna sought her out from time to time, and Ani tried to respond with friend-ly attentiveness. Ani felt as dumb at conversation as she had over Gilsa's cooking pot that day she prepared the lunch, the contents turning blacker and smelling fouler despite her anx-ious attempts. She had no practice at making friends. And, she discovered, her own trust had been drained dry.

One new autumn morning, over a week after Ani had

arrived in the city, they found one of Conrad's strays. Ani saw him first, just a white mark beside the pond. She thought it might be a washed-out bit of wood pushed ashore by the night water, or a forgotten shirt, though she had yet to see a Bayern wear plain white. Ani was so absorbed with the distant figure that she was not prepared to defend herself against a particularly aggressive gander that, after passing through the pasture gate, took a moment to extend his thin neck and nip her on the rear.

"Stop it. Oh, just stop it, all of you." Ani rubbed the spot with the heel of her hand, and Conrad laughed.

"You've got a few friendly goose pals, I guess," he said.

Ani glowered. "Yes, I guess."

The lone gander did not move when the gaggle arrived at the water's edge. He squeaked a greeting, and some geese gathered around him, chattering over one another and prodding his side with their beaks.

"One of the three," said Conrad. "He's been gone two weeks."

The gander raised his head at Conrad but seemed too tired to stand. Several feathers hung loose, giving the appearance of a poorly stuffed pillow. Ani stepped forward, intending to check him for bites or scratches. A large goose turned her back on the gander and hissed at Ani, the top of her beak raised threateningly, her pink tongue trembling. Ani's bruises throbbed at the sound.

"All right," she said, "I'll stay away. Take care of your own, because I've no more good skin to give over to another bruise."

Ani sat under her tree and gazed up at the palace. The warm morning lulled her, and she rested her head against the tree and tried to imagine how to free Falada from the palace stables and, after that, how to get home again.

A rumble of hoofbeats broke her daydream apart. A group of horsemen outfitted for hunting cantered down the goose pasture. Several veered their horses to pass right through the middle of the flock and sent the geese flurrying with a cacophonous chorus of honks and a beating of wings to strike speed into their flat feet. Ani lowered her head and peered at the horsemen from under her hat brim, wary of any familiar faces or light-colored hair. There was no need. The nobles on their grand horses never turned an idle eye on the goose girl. They leaped their mounts across the goose pasture stream and entered the woods on the other side. None of their horses was white.

The beech shadow had moved, and the sun was heating Ani's cheeks. She stepped into its northern shadow. There was the gander, still in his same spot, though alone now, the others having left him when fleeing the hooves. He raised his head at her with a little more energy and opened his beak slightly. Ani was not sure if it was meant to be a hiss.

The gander slowly stood and took an awkward step. He stopped. He leaned his body forward and let the momentum pull him into a few sloppy strides.

"Are you using your last, dying strength to attack me?" she said. "Now, that would be silly."

The gander still stumbled forward and, gaining her folded leg, sat down hard by it, his body close up against her ankle. Ani held very still.

"Did you have a long journey?" She pulled up a handful of grass that was turning to seed and held it near his head. He looked at it for a moment, then lowered his beak and nibbled it out of her palm. It tickled, and Ani concentrated on not twitching her hand.

"Oh, I see, you want to be babied. Mmm. Seeing as how I'm not doing anything else, I'll oblige. But this means I've the right to name you, and your name'll be Jok, after that old tale of the wanderer that always returns."

He nibbled again but made no noises. She thought she could hear his labored breathing.

"Poor gosling. It hurts to be lost. And worse to be home with no kind of homecoming. You're my good-luck bird, Jok. I'll be lucky if I can do as well as you when all this's done, just a bit out of breath, a bit bruised and scratched, a bit wiser and sadder for it all."

He finished the last blade of grass from her palm, and when she did not immediately pull up another handful, Jok looked at her and gave a gentle honk. She had torn another fistful of grass and let him pick each blade from her palm before she realized that she had understood. He had asked for more.

That evening, Ani carried Jok home under her arm. After they locked the rest of the geese in their pen, Ani examined the animal and found three claw marks across his thigh, one of them deep, the pink flesh swollen around the wound.

"I'm taking him to Ideca to see about a salve."

"However you want," said Conrad.

Ideca had a dark and pungent balm, "good enough for anybody's scratch, goose, cow, or girl," and Ani held Jok steady while Ideca worked it under the feathers into the deepest cut. Her languid eyes brightened a little while she handled the animal.

"This should be Conrad helping you. The boy can't be coerced into lifting a finger after his geese are penned. I shouldn't say what I think around you, mmm, since you goose-keepers are no doubt tighter than knots already."

"He doesn't talk much," said Ani.

"He's probably shy of you." Ideca looked her over with similar attention that she gave the goose. "You're a pretty one. I guess you know that, since you wear that hat dawn to dusk, protecting your skin even from the weak light of the moon. Some of this Forest lot got plans to keep them in the city. Guess yours is the hope you'll marry a nobleman, mmm?"

Ani took Jok to her room, her face still burning from Ideca's comments.

Jok slept that night on Ani's bed between her feet. In the morning she jabbered at him and he jabbered back, and some

of it made sense. She fed him brown bread from the breakfast table. Razo joshed that the goose girl had found her
mate and asked Conrad if he had his eye on a particular
goose, for which Razo got a slap upside the head. The familiarity of the exchange gave Ani a smile. She brought Jok to
Ideca for more salve that night, and the next, and his cut
healed. Soon, Ani admitted to herself that she let the goose
sleep on her bed not for his own sake, but for the comfort
the creature gave her against the dark dream of running.

Ani woke to Jok squawking in her ear that the sun had risen
and it was time to eat. She imitated the sound to him, and
he repeated it again in their practiced back-and-forth game
of noises. Finally she answered him, tentatively, with what
she thought was an affirmation, that yes, it was time for eating. Ani guessed she understood more than what she could
even try to say, and when Jok gave no response, she groaned
to herself. The goose made a deep noise, which Ani thought
might be a mock of her own, and they groaned nonsensically to each other on the way to breakfast.

Herding the geese down the avenue that morning proved
to be a task fit for a battalion of goose girls. There was more
traffic than usual. A gaggle of children playing chase mixed
themselves into the gaggle of geese, and Ani left her post at
the head to round up strays. She had been trying words on

the geese and had begun to see them respond. At least, they were less inclined to bite her legs when she tried to speak their tongue.

Ani clucked and honked at the scattered geese, and Conrad rolled his eyes.

"Thinks she's a goose," he said.

"At least it works," she said.

Conrad made mock goose noises back at her until he saw something up ahead that quieted him. His expression changed, suggesting eagerness, and Ani peered ahead to see what he saw.

Two street cats, crouching, tails twitching, one perched on the rim of a wagon, the other underneath, muscles poised and eyes fixed on the nearest goose. And Ani was too far away to draw back the lead geese with her crook.

She made a noise she had heard them use before, a warning word she thought meant "dog." The geese, quick as instinct, turned their backs and huddled together, and the ganders, with strong wings raised, heads low to the ground, twenty throats hissing as one, rushed the beasts. The cats drew in their claws, hissed once in return, and loped away into the dirty streets.

Ani and Conrad flocked the geese safely through the arch and down the slope. Once the lead goose passed through the archway, Ani turned to Conrad with anger that she still felt.

"You could've warned," said Ani. "You wanted to see me fail, sacrifice a goose to see me be an imbecile."

"If you're so much better at goose-keeping, then go to." Conrad marched away, crossed the stream, and spent the day on the far side, out of sight.

Later that same day, Ani saw a single horseman. When he rode through the arch, Ani glanced up, and then, seeing that his horse was a bay, she returned her attention to the pair of geese that had approached Jok. She had to concentrate, for geese talked over one another like old men who had lost their hearing, and while they did not employ as much movement as swans did in their language, there were still neck bobbings and beak liftings and tail waggings to add to the meanings. Ani guessed they were asking Jok about his journey and he was informing them of the many adventures of a rogue goose.

After a few moments, she remembered the horseman and glanced up to the gate, but she was startled to see that he had disappeared. He was not on the far ends of the goose pasture by either of the lines of hedges, and she would have noticed had he ridden past her and crossed the stream.

The inarticulate thumping of hooves roused her to her feet, and Jok from her lap, honking resentfully. The man had jumped his horse over the hedges to the north and was racing across her field. He wrenched the reins, but the horse continued to run. The man pulled harder, and the horse bucked at the tension, his back arched, his neck bent low. The horse heaved and twisted and dumped the rider from the saddle. The horse bucked again for good measure, then trotted to a halt.

The man leaped up, grabbed the reins, and swung himself into the saddle. The bay seemed to consider bucking again but instead stood still, his body heavy, unmovable, his legs stiff. Ani recognized the stance. She had seen Falada act in like manner when a stable-hand had tried to ride him. Her breath escaped quickly through her lips in a quiet laugh.

"Mule," said the man. He swung himself off the unyielding horse. The moment his boot touched soil, the animal was wild again, rearing up on his mighty back legs, swinging his head like a banner in strong wind, ripping the reins from the man's hands. The horse knocked him aside with a sudden lurch and raced across the pasture, stopping before the line of hedges on the south side. The man tore a clump of grass and threw it back at the ground.

Ani jogged up the slope toward the bay. "Stay," she said to the man as she passed, her hand out, like an order given to a dog. He noticed her for the first time, and his face flushed.

"Oh, um, lady, I don't recommend whatever it is you have in mind."

She ignored him. The bay paced near the hedges, his ears pinned back to his neck, his steps stiff and long. When she neared, his outer ear opened to her and the muscles of his neck flinched at the new annoyance.

Ani advanced, her shoulders straight, her head high, her eyes locked on to his.

"Look at me," she said quietly. "Some riders are beneath you, aren't they? I want to be your equal. I want to meet you."

The horse pranced. He held his tail high and pounded a half circle around her, but to the side was the wall, to the back was the hedge, and on the far side sat the irritating rider. The bay seemed to find Ani more interesting and stopped near her. She smiled. He had that look Falada sometimes wore, one ear stiff and one relaxed, his back leg crooked as though he wanted her to think he did not care a thimbleful of oats about her. Ani turned her back and looked down, playing at the same game.

It was not long before she heard slow thuds behind her and felt a warm, clover-sticky huff of breath on her neck.

She turned slowly and into a rather heavy exhale that made her blink, first from the powerful smell and then again for the reminder of Falada, and she found her eyes were too wet to see straight until she could blink them dry. She put the flat of her hand on the bay's forehead and rubbed it. He rested his nose in her other hand and sniffed ponderously.

"Hello there, horse friend," she said. "Can you smell your speech on me? I knew the speech of one horse. Though I can't hear your thoughts, your touch is nearly as comforting. It's kind of you to let me touch you. It's good to be reminded how much I miss him." She spoke to him soothingly as she rubbed his neck and sides and legs, all down his right side, and then passed under his neck and rubbed his left side.

He stiffened as she approached his mounting side, so she

made nickering noises, soothing things mares murmured to their foals. The bay responded with deep sounds from his throat that were not words, akin to hums and laughter, noises that carried emotion or the basis of connection.

She continued to stroke him until her hands reached his shoulder where the knotted reins hung over one side. Holding the ends of the reins, Ani placed a boot in a stirrup and hopped onto his back. The horse rearranged his stance, but his muscles did not freeze up. Ani's skirt slid up as she mounted, but it was wide and dropped over her boot tops once arranged. She felt comfortable on a horse again, like finding a favorite childhood spot in the garden. She looked at her flock, busy and peaceful around the pond a ways down the slope, and across the stream where the trees were thicker she thought she could make out Conrad's orange cap.

"Very nice," said the rider. He had approached and was watching with an unclear expression.

She turned away and let her heels dig in. The bay sprang into a canter.

The pasture was a violent green, smoothed of shadows and imperfections by sheer speed, just one color united. The gray of the wall was constant to her right, the shimmer of the stream to her left, and she let her heart be lifted by the wind that seemed so thick as to blow through her body and make her light as itself. The horse felt glad to run, and the pressure from her legs bade him go faster, and faster. The wind fought her hat brim and filled up her ears, speaking words that she thought she could almost hear, and she rode faster, wanting to get closer to the source, to get inside the wind and see what it saw. They neared the northern hedge, and Ani crouched low to the horse's neck and gripped his sides with her knees, feeling herself become part of the thundering of hoofbeats, and then the tremendous escape from earth as he leaped. Her body lifted skyward and free.

Ani rode a short ways before, prodded by guilt, she turned the bay around and jumped the hedge again, to find the man running toward her. The wind died as the horse slowed, and she felt its words leave her skin unspoken. She stopped by the man's side and dismounted.

"What do you mean, riding away on my horse?" His breath came a little quicker from the run. "You can't . . . can't just do that."

"I'm sorry," she said. "I shouldn't have mounted him without your permission. I got carried away." But she did not feel sorry. She felt herself grinning.

The man straightened, trying to be serious in spite of her grin. "Yes, you shouldn't, I mean, he's my horse."

"That aside, I really couldn't have been expected to stand by and watch without lending a hand. It wasn't hard to see the mount didn't trust the rider."

The man opened his mouth and tried to laugh, but he just shook his head. "I could've stayed at the grounds if I'd wanted this kind of pointed abuse. I know I'm not an expert horse breaker, but I'm doing what any stable-master would do."

I should stop harassing him, she thought, but her own boldness was intoxicating, and she continued.

"Oh, come now, surely you can feel how uneasy he is when you mount. You can see him roll back his eyes as though he'd like to be everywhere he can see but here with you. He's an untrained, wild animal, and half-crazy with fright that you're leading him to predators and all kinds of uncomfortable situations. You've got to get him to commit to you before you can gallop over hedges and up and down strange pastures."

"Look now, you've overstepped yourself here, and I find this a bit of an uncomfortable situation myself and am itching to roll my own eyes, if you'd know."

"I guess I have overstepped myself, and you've every right to be angry at me, if you're angry, of which I'm not entirely certain, since you seem to be laughing at the same time, but you don't need to pretend to be innocent here. I mean, if you're as good a horse breaker as any, why did you seek out the seeming privacy of the goose pasture instead of working him on the palace grounds? You live at the palace, don't you?"

The man lifted his brows at her and nodded. *He's surprised I know that*, thought Ani, *though any fool can see the horse wears the palace insignia on his saddle blanket*. She could see he was not a nobleman's son, lacking the softness and self-assurance she remembered from her boy cousins, so the horse was probably not his. He had work-hardened hands that were broad and strong and shoulders fit for lifting. Ani decided that most likely he was a palace guard or watchman.

The man looked at the dirt on his boot tip. The pasture was suddenly quiet, and she noticed the distance-muted calls of Jok, who said, *Come back, come back.*

She looked closer at the man. He was older than she, though not by many years. He had thick black hair, cut just longer than his shoulders, that he tied back in a low pony's tail, and the kind of prominent jaw and chin that would stay prominent for all his life. His shoulders were broad, and it was not just a trick of a well-cut tunic, as his was a thin cotton, roughly made. She was thinking of how she had ordered him and insulted him and mounted his horse to ride down the pasture like a crazed thief. The anonymity of her goose girl costume and name gave leash to a freedom that she had never dared exhibit when she had been the crown princess shivering in her mother's shadow. Her throat felt dry. She coughed, and realized that she was mortified.

"So, you see, that's what I saw," said Ani. And coughed again.

The man shook his head, and then she saw that he was indeed laughing.

"Here I stand," he said, "glum as a plum because I couldn't do it by myself, and you're right, I'd run away from those blasted, overpopulated training fields to break in this beast away from the stable-master and his horde who have been laughing at my fatuous attempts all week. And to come here, for privacy, and get schooled in horse mastery by a girl."

Ani gave a vexed laugh.

"Oh, I mean," he said quickly, "not that you can't know more about horses than a man. I'm botching all from my hair to my shoes today. What I want to say is, you're better with this bay than I can ever learn to be, and you seem to enjoy riding him. When you're his mistress, he doesn't look to need any breaking at all. I can't give him to you outright as, actually, he's not mine, but I don't see why you couldn't take him to your home for as long as you like, or until I get the word that he's needed. So, yes, truly, why don't you take him so the poor beast can be ridden properly, all right?"

Ani's face flamed instantly, and she looked down and waited for him to realize his error. She shuffled her feet, wishing for a tree to lean against or behind.

"Don't be shy about it. May I remind you, lady, that you haven't been shy so far? Go on, he's yours."

Ani felt humiliation deep as her bones, and she shook her head.

"Oh, you might think that I'm trying to pawn off my job of breaking him onto you. I can pay you. I think. I'm unfamiliar with this kind of business. How much would be fair?" Ani covered her face with one hand, and the man groaned and muttered angrily at himself. "Blast, I've done something again. You don't offer to pay ladies. You've insulted her again, you daft, clumsy brute."

"No, you're very kind. You don't understand. It's just, I've no place to keep him."

The man seemed to see her dress for the first time, and his gaze fell behind her, where the gaggle waddled about and honked at the sun that was slipping into the west. It was his turn to blush.

"You're not . . . I'm sorry. I'd thought you were, you were just picnicking out here. I was thoughtless. Forgive me."

Ani laughed. "A goose girl should feel honored to be mistaken for a lady with land to put a horse on, sir."

"You didn't say 'sir' when you stole my horse. Geric. My name's Geric."

He stood expectantly after that, perhaps waiting for her name; but, her boldness spent, she just nodded and walked away. Conrad was fording the stream, and it was nearly time to herd the geese home. When she turned back, the man and his horse had gone. Ani felt disappointment slide into her body where the wind had blown her free. She shook her head at herself and tried to trick it away with forced detachment.

"You're not who you used to be," she said. "You're just a goose girl."

Chapter 10

The next day was stormy rain. Ani lay awake in her bed to the euphony of heavy water on her thin roof. The pane was a stream of moving darkness, and she watched it lighten to silver. It was the first rainfall since she had come to the city. In the dizziness of early morning and little sleep, Ani wondered what she would find outside, if the night and the water had washed it all away, the pasture, the walls, the guards, the palace, and left her with her name again standing in mud and darkness.

Soon Jok was awake, picking at the wrinkles in her wool blanket, mock grazing. Sometimes he would pull a balled bit of lint loose and let it hang from his bill. Ani greeted him, and he said, *It is raining. It is raining*, she repeated. He continued his dry graze. She asked the goose if it was morning, but he did not answer. She tried, *Is there sun in the sky?* But he still did not understand, unresponsive as though no sound had been made. *Are you hungry?* she asked. *Yes*, said the goose.

"That's no help," Ani said. "You're always hungry."

Unsure if it was night, dawn, or day, Ani dressed, steadied the bird on one shoulder, and dashed to the workers' hall.

Several workers were gathered there, and not one seemed sure of the exact time. Ideca's girls had laid out bowls of an informal breakfast, and the workers snacked casually, lounging on the benches and on the floor, talking, as though rain had scrubbed away all the work.

Ani found Conrad in a group playing at pick-up-sticks, and she asked him if they were to go to the fields.

"Maybe," he said.

"Thank you so much, Sir Helpful One," said Enna. "Isi, you'll see how it goes soon enough. The mistress only has a few rain cloaks, so we take turns seeing to our animals. We stay here, mostly, and wait for the storm to clear."

"Raindays're almost as good as marketdays," said Razo.

When two of the pig-keepers returned, Conrad and Ani took their oiled cloaks and went to the pens. Jok followed, splashing through the puddles, squawking about speed and no food, but otherwise undeterred by the rain. They brought wet clover from the animal garden and dry corn from the feed barrels, taking armloads into the clamorous stall and pulling enough water from the well to last the day. Ani left Jok there, and she and Conrad hurried back to allow others a turn at the cloaks.

The rain did not stop. The day never dawned more than the brightness of lightning shocks or the dim grayness that came from neither east nor west. Ani sat apart, gazing at the night-day, wishing to lie down on the pavement and let the water soak her, then beat down on her, through her, work her away until all that was left was her core. She wondered what that would be.

The next day would be marketday. She marveled that she had been in the city one month and she was still the goose girl. Yesterday she had been as bold as a queen with that rider, that Geric, yet she could not be bold with herself.

At the idea of Geric, her thoughts slipped to an image of his hands as he held the knotted reins, the straps seeming thin in their bigness. And the three lines that marked the corners of his eyes when he smiled. And the moment when she climbed onto his horse, when her skirt slipped up over her knee. Before she pulled it down, he must have seen her shift, or perhaps, perhaps her leg.

Ani stood to shake off the chill of embarrassment. The light of outside was wet and dull, but the hall was aflame with candles. Most of the workers were present, playing games and laughing, their holiday voices shadowed by the tenacious rainfall pounding the roof. The oiled cloaks hung on the wall, out of demand. Ani was tempted to take one and go check the geese, converse with them in their friendly, cryptic language, chattering at spiders and complaining of closeness. Or she could run back to her room, lie on her cot, and watch the rain blur the world of her window.

And hide, she realized. Always she wanted to hide. *No*

more. To approach the king again, she would need a horde of people by her side to guarantee she would not be the victim of a quick dagger in a dark corridor before ever telling her story. Where else could she meet people to help her but here? She took a breath and joined the throng.

Enna was sitting near the fire, watching cheese melt on the bread she had placed on a hearthstone. A dollop of orange cheese dripped off the crust, and Enna caught it with her finger, licking it off before she could feel the heat.

"Sit down," she said when she saw Ani. She handed her a thick slice of bread and a block of cheese with a knife, then turned her eyes to the hearth.

"Why aren't you playing?" said Ani, gesturing to the many games of cards and sticks around the room.

"Oh, the fire," said Enna. Its orange fingers waved specters on the blacks of Enna's eyes. "I get to looking and can't look away. Don't you ever feel like fire is a friendly thing? That it's signaling to you with its flames, offering something?"

Ani watched not the fire but the play of its light on Enna's face and felt comfort that there were others who listened for language in what was supposed to be mute and who sought out meaning in what was only beautiful.

"Enna, today's free. Why doesn't anyone go out into the city? Everyone huddles here as though there's nowhere else in the world."

"You know, there's not for us, all of us Forest folk. And not especially for the boys."

"Why not?"

Enna looked at Ani quizzically.

"This truly is the first time you've been out of the Forest, then? We don't really belong here, you know, if you ask anyone in the city. We still belong to our families back home and just live here. We watch their animals. We're almost, almost like animals to them." Enna looked at Razo, who sat across the room, losing at sticks.

"When these boys reach a man's age, they don't receive their rites and the javelin and shield from their chief and become a part of their community, not like the town boys. The fathers of our boys never received a javelin. There are no chiefs in the Forest, and the king doesn't think twice about his Forest men. It doesn't really matter, I guess, until poorer families like ours send their sons and daughters into a city for a little extra coin. I know my family hasn't an idea of how we're treated in the city." Enna looked back at the fire. "We're so ignorant out there in the trees, Isi. We've no idea the world's bigger than the walk to a foothill pasture."

Ani nodded.

"You belong to your family, you know, and if you marry a Forest man, you'll belong to each other, but never to a community, never to this city. I feel like we creep around the borders, stepping in to live along the west wall like spiders while we're young and unwed and then stepping out again, back into the shadow of the Forest. If you ask me, I'd rather be there. But some of these boys, they'd remove fingers to be given a javelin and belong to the city."

Ani glanced around the room. Conrad and Razo played at sticks opposite her, their boyish faces tense in the competition. *But they're nearly men,* she thought. *They should be visiting taverns and hunting and meeting daughters of butchers and tailors.* Yet every night, in clear weather or foul, all the workers left their posts and returned to the safety of the hall.

"It doesn't seem quite fair." Ani felt a moment of regret that she would not be queen of this country after all, would not have a chance to set this injustice right.

"It never did to me," said Enna. "But I don't know much. I just see how things are. And they've been so for a long time, through tales and spells. Who'm I to question the law and the king?"

"You're Enna," said Ani. "That's somebody."

Enna smiled. "So's Isi."

Is she? thought Ani. *Then I'd like to be her. I'd like to be somebody.*

"She is, you are," said Enna, as though she had heard Ani's doubt. She touched Ani's hand. "Thanks for not making fun of me about what I said about the fire. I know it was silly. Razo would've laughed."

"I do kind of the same thing, you know, but with the wind. Is that silly, then, too? I feel as if it's always tugging at my ears and speaking at me kind of desperately, but I can't hear."

"Yeah, that's it," said Enna, "that's how I feel, too."

"There's a story my aunt used to tell me that's about, well, about a lot of things, but to me it was mostly about the wind."

Enna sat squarely in front of Ani and placed her hands in her lap. "You'd better tell it now, goose girl, or I'll bother you about it till next marketday. Hey there, Bettin," said Enna, getting the attention of another girl, "come closer. Isi's telling a story."

Ani nearly blushed from the attention as the other girl joined them, but she lowered her eyes and thought about the words she would say.

"It goes like this. In a farm village far away there's a maiden with hair like the yellow apple, and she works in the fields all day with her head down and her hair dragging alongside so that the tips're black as raven beaks. Sometimes the wind catches her hair and pulls it up into the air, and the maiden looks up to where the wind is going, up to the high pastures where the wild horses run."

Razo approached, glum from losing his game, and asked Enna what they were doing.

"Isi's telling a tale," said Bettin. "Sit and listen."

"One day her mother says, 'Go to the high pastures, you lazy girl. Go and bring back dry wood for a cookfire.' So the maiden runs out of the fields she knows and up to the high pastures, and she pulls up the dead roots of a lightning-struck tree. But underneath, deep in the dark soil, you know what she finds? A nugget of gold that's growing like a potato. The maiden knows she should dig it up and take it to her mother, but she's heard of the mystery of the wild horses, and so crouches nearby and waits. The horses come."

"What horses?" said Razo. "What mystery?"

"Shut your hole, Razo, and just listen," said Enna.

Ani wished she had not started, because now the hall was quieting, and many of the workers nearby were turning toward her. Enna prodded her knee and smiled, telling her to continue. She took a deep breath and fought to remember her aunt's words, but she could remember only images. The words were her own. She let them come.

"Wild horses, white as light on water, tall as cherry trees. They love to run, so fast they think they can become the wind if they just keep running. They run by the maiden, and the wind of their running blows her hair around her.

"And then one horse sees a flash of gold, and he stops. He paws away the soil, nudges the gold from the ground, and chews it up, fast as a carrot. Gold-colored spittle drips from his chin, his eyes are brighter, he shakes his mane. Now when he breathes out, there's music. This's why she waits."

"What kind of music?" said Bettin.

"It's music more beautiful than a woman, more beautiful than a tree. It's almost as beautiful as the horses that run, so fast and so wild because they want to become the wind. The song's the sound of that wanting, of the wish for loosing of manes, and hooves that don't touch the ground, and breath that doesn't end."

Bettin smiled, and Ani raised her head and met the eyes

of those who were listening.

"The maiden returns every day to pull up roots and dig up rooted gold and hear the horses breathe out the music of flight. Every night she goes home and her mother beats her with a switch for not working the fields, and her back's bent like the snow-heavy birches, and she thinks about those horses who've never been broken, not like her. But now she's heard that song, and she disobeys her mother and returns every day. The song's so beautiful that pain doesn't hurt."

"I think I know what that means," someone whispered.

"Then one day, there's no more gold. The maiden pulls up roots until her fingers bleed, and she digs in the dirt with her fingernails, but the ground's empty. When the horses run by, they don't stop, and she puts her face on the ground and cries.

"The tears clear her thoughts, and she sits up. My hair, she thinks. I know what to do. So she goes to the snow-melt stream and washes the dirt from her hair, and it shines like a sunrise on a still pond. Then she takes a leather knife and cuts it off, all, right from her head, and puts it on the ground. She sleeps by it all night and doesn't feel cold.

"The next day the horses pass. Their running feels like earthquakes and sounds like thunder, and they don't stop for her hand-cut gold. But before her heart breaks, the last horse stops. He paws at her loose hair and looks up and sees her. Then, slowly, as though it's a handful of hay, he eats her golden mane. This time when he breathes out, the song that's on the air pierces her heart like a terrible, perfect knife. The horse shimmers and begins to run, faster and faster, and his white hide becomes whiter and whiter until it's too brilliant to see. There's a flash, and when she blinks, the horse is gone and a white-maned wind whinnies and prances and pushes around her. And the maiden mounts that wind and is borne away, up into the higher pastures, up and never seen again."

The hall was quiet. The hearth fire snapped at the silence, and the flames lowered themselves inside the glowing embers. Ani waited.

"She was never seen again," said Enna.

"What does that mean?" Beier whispered to Conrad. "Did she become wind, too?"

Conrad shrugged.

"It's true?" said Bettin.

"I don't think it's supposed to be true or false. My aunt told it to me a long time ago."

"I don't get it," said Conrad.

"Well, thanks be for that," said Enna, a protective hand on Ani's shoulder. "If you had to get every story ever told, we'd be in short supply."

Conrad's face flushed, and he turned to Ani. "Well, what's it supposed to mean? Horses eating gold and turning into wind. It doesn't make any sense."

"I don't know," said Ani. She looked at her hands. "I guess I never really knew what it meant, I just thought it was beautiful. I remember when my mother overheard my aunt tell me a story like that one, my mother was mad. But my aunt said, if we don't tell strange stories, when something strange happens we won't believe it."

"That's true," said Razo. "I haven't heard much of strange stories for years, and when Ideca served us rotten cold bean soup for the third time last week, I couldn't believe it myself."

"Isi said something *strange*, Razo," said Enna. "Ideca's cold bean soup three times is as ordinary as your boots smelling of sheep dung."

Bettin rose and yawned. "You'd best tell another story tomorrow, Isi, or I mayn't believe my dreams tonight."

A murmur of assent passed through the hall, and most nodded their heads. Tomorrow, and every night, tell a tale.

The night air was dark and heavy in after-rain when Ani left the hall for her room. The moon cleared a scrap of sky, and the moonlight turned the outside of her windowpane into a silver mirror. She stooped there a moment, examining her eyebrows to see if marketday would require another purchase of thornroot. They were dark brown, though perhaps fading from the darker color of a month before.

Ani glanced at her full face and stopped. It was the first time she had looked at herself since the morning she had left her mother's palace. Her face was emphasized by the headscarf, rounder and paler, but, she was surprised to see, not sadder. This reflection seemed more significant than the one she had often seen in the palace mirrors, staring back in simple boredom.

She looked at her face now as she might study a coin from a foreign country, deciphering what it was worth and what it could buy her. The reflection was not unkind, though it appeared raw and untested in the bleached light. She thought now it was time to be tested, to make decisions and find her own roads, to stop falling where she was told to fall and to stand only when allowed to stand.

"I would break my mother's heart," she whispered. She remembered her mother saying those words the day she left, and the memory brought a grim smile. The handkerchief, that peculiar tie to her mother's heart, was gone. It had been temporary, artificial. Her mother had never given her heart, Ani thought, just three drops of blood, blood that could be washed away, a handkerchief that could be lost. She had leaned against the idea of her mother's perfection all her childhood, as though it were the cane to her lameness. But that crutch had not served her.

She was little like her mother, though that was all she had ever longed to be. She lacked the gift of people-speaking, that power to convince and control that laced every word her mother uttered. She did not possess that grace and beauty that all in a room turned to watch. But had the queen ever told a nursery story to a room of captivated listeners? Or handled fifty head of geese? Ani smiled at the thought, and then she surprised herself by feeling proud. *I've done that much. What more can I do?*

Chapter 11

The dawn sun cut through the rain-cleaned air, and it seemed to pierce the eyes and skin, quick and impatient. Ani wore her orange rose tunic and skirt and her hat with the orange ribbon, feeling like the resplendent lizards and frogs from the south that men sold in tiny cages to rich marketgoers. Razo said if you licked the sticky flesh of the frogs, you saw colors bright as their skin. *What a strange city.* She thought about lizards and merchants and the bright, scoured air to keep from thinking about where she was going.

Into a trap, she thought. But she did not want to wait for a safe time to address the king. She must find a way to see Falada—today.

The palace sat like a ponderous beast in the shadows of morning, rising ever taller, gaining width and art and intricacies as she approached and as the sun lit out its stony features. Already a serpentine queue of marketday supplicants reached near the palace gate. Ani stopped behind the last person, just as she had on this day one month ago, but this time when the line moved forward, she slipped out to the inside of the palace wall. She passed several guards and errand boys along the cold shadow of the wall, and they nodded, greeting the goose girl as a fellow laborer. She nodded back and began to smile at the simplicity of the break-in as she neared the stables.

The horse fields were cut into the back of the palace hill, acres long and just as wide. The grandeur of the palace gardens to the east competed for attention, with autumn roses and ice blue fountains and trees hanging their leafy heads low like long-haired waiting maids drying their tresses at a fire. But to Ani's eyes, the horse grounds were more beautiful.

Ani scurried to the nearest stable and ducked in. A worker passed her by without looking up, and she jogged down the long line of stalls, searching for a white head and mane. No luck. She jogged to the next building, where there were no workers and the stalls were nearly empty. She checked each one, calling, *Falada, Falada,* in her mind. There was one sleeping white mare that made her heart leap in her chest before she saw clearly that this was not the horse she knew.

Ani had finished investigating the far side of stalls when the hushed tones of a familiar accent froze her where she stood.

"In here, you dog," he said.

Ani dropped to the straw floor and held her breath. They

were a long way down, but his voice echoed on the high roof, and she could clearly hear the Kildenrean accent.

"Now just listen to me for a moment, before it's Ungolad that is setting you straight. There is no time for pranks and pleasantries. The princess is not in yet, if you understand me."

"We are here. I don't see what all the hush-hush fuss is still about."

"You dull-witted bumble." This was the first voice, and Ani knew him now. One of her guards, one of Ungolad's men, a curly-haired soldier named Terne. "This is not over. There is still a marriage to take place. And don't forget we have the little impostor running around the forest somewhere, sure to shoot off her mouth and require all kinds of doctoring to keep our position. And did you forget that we still have a kingdom one forest away that will be sending emissaries and little sisters and such nuisances? The two masters' plan for dealing with that is still not enacted."

"Yes, but I don't see why all the sneaking still, and no travel and no fun. I feel like a chicken in a cramped coop and Ungolad checking my unders for fresh eggs."

There was a sound of a brief scuffle, and the second man quieted. "Look," said Terne, sounding as though he spoke through clenched teeth, "are you begging for a private audience with her puissantness? Is that what you want? I'm telling you to be sober for a while. You pick a side and you stay on it, you hear me, Hul?"

The conversation went quiet when she heard a third person enter the stable.

"Sirs," said a Bayern accent.

"Yes, morning," said Terne, and the two men left.

Ani sat still, feeling each heartbeat rage in her chest. If those two men had spotted her, darkened eyebrows and a wide-brimmed hat would not hide her identity. They could escort her to a nearby wood without trouble, run her through, and leave her body to be disposed of by wild beasts. The fear lodged in her throat ran to her knees, making them shake under her weight as she stood up.

The men were gone. There were five more stables to be searched. She shook herself and continued on. On the way to the third stable, Ani glanced around with a thought that Geric might be near and was stopped short by what she saw. No need to continue the search. There was her horse. In a far arena, she saw Falada. A stranger rode him, and Falada bucked.

She walked toward him. All around her were horsemen, stable-hands, guards, ladies walking with sunshades, pages. She did not meet their eyes and kept her head slightly bent to the weight of the shadow on her face. She could hear him neighing now, a savage sound she had never heard him utter before, and it made her stomach feel like a stone.

Falada, she said, *what is wrong?*

The rider held the reins tight to his mane. Falada's neck was sweating, and his head was thrown up with wild eyes open to redness. He looked at Ani.

Ani reached the fence and stood beside it, hugging the wooden rail and calling to her horse.

"That cursed thing won't break," said a stable-hand.

The rider only grunted, working on getting the horse to make a circle, but Falada lunged as though he had never seen a rider, as though wearing the saddle were torture.

Calm, Falada, calm. They might hurt you if you do not tame.

The horse kept one ear pointed at her as he pounded to the far side of the corral, but he spoke no words. Ani's head felt tight and heavy. She could not reason why he ignored her words. Or how he had forgotten how to hear them.

The rider was flung from the saddle, and he darted away from the stallion's striking hooves. Ani slid between the fence rails and approached. Falada trotted to a halt and watched. Her hand was held out, her palm up.

Falada, remember? Do you remember me?

He snorted, and his eye roved like a tormented thing. She thought he wanted to speak, but no word entered her head.

Falada, friend, all is well. Peace. All is well.

The horse sniffed at her palm, and her hand trembled under his breath. She wanted to throw her arms around his neck and cry into his mane, as she had after finding her father prostrate under his horse, as she had when the mournful cries of Rianno-Hancery stripped away her vigor until she felt small and thin and unable to take another step after the funeral wagon. Who would comfort her at the loss of

Falada? The thought broke into a sob, and she clenched her teeth and stepped closer in.

Easy, easy. She ran her hand slowly from his nose to his cheek and down his neck, hoping to awaken his old self with her touch. His skin shuddered under her hand. She held still, afraid to spook him. *Peace,* she said. *No harm.*

Falada jerked his head up, away from her hands, and rose on his hind legs and pawed the air. She jumped away as a hoof met her cheek. A pair of hands pulled her away and pushed her through a space in the fence.

"Get out of here, girl," said the rider. "You're wanting a knock on the head for acting like that."

"I thought she had him for a minute," said the stable-hand.

"What's wrong with him?" said Ani. Her head throbbed. She watched Falada dance in the corral. The morning around him seemed to dim, and the sunlight on his white coat was so bright that it pierced her eyes until she had to look down.

"He's got the animal dementia." The rider waved her away. "None of your mind, so go on."

Falada was pacing again, and foam hung from his jaw. Ani pressed her hand against her throbbing cheek. Her head felt as hollow as her chest.

Falada, she said.

"You, girl."

Ani turned, expecting to see Ungolad or Terne, but was

accosted instead by a palace attendant, who grabbed her elbow and walked her swiftly toward the palace. "Another lost supplicant? Moseying about the horse grounds like it was your own court."

"I'm just—"

"Just lost," he said. "I know, and I don't care. Not allowed." He shut his mouth and would say no more.

Ani nearly fell flat as she struggled to keep his pace and to loosen his grip on her arm. The speed and the pain made her angry. *For trying to calm my own horse I'm treated like a criminal,* she thought. Across the field, Ani spotted Hul and Terne in conference under a garden tree, and she stopped tugging at her captive arm and kept her head down.

The attendant left her in a small room and locked the door behind her. It seemed to be a cell for criminals—bare, empty, cold. A small window high on one wall threw a square of light onto the stone floor. Ani sat in that bit of sun in the middle of the room, wrapped her arms around herself, and cried silently for some time. She did not know if she shivered from the cold room or the sound of booted feet in the corridor. She jumped at every sound and waited for a guard to open the door. Her aching head did not allow her to think of Falada.

When she finally heard the noise of a key in the lock, Ani was so exhausted of being afraid that she barely made herself stand. She had followed the square of sunlight's movements closer to the wall until it had disappeared with noon.

She leaned against the wall and squinted in the half-light, waiting to make out Ungolad's form in the opening door. It was a woman.

"Come on," the woman said. Ani submitted her wrist to the attendant and was pulled up stairs and to a more decorous level. "I'd forgotten that man brought you in, it's such a busy day, marketday and all, but the king usually sits in judgment today, so let's see if we can't slip you in and out of our hair."

They waited in a wood-paneled corridor that Ani guessed ran beside the king's receiving chamber. She could hear the king's large voice and the high tones of a supplicant, and for the first time that morning, Ani thought she might leave the palace alive.

After a few minutes, the attendant signaled to the chambermistress then escorted Ani through the side entrance to stand under the noon roof window before the king.

"Not an assassin, I hope." There was tired humor in his voice.

"No, sire, a supplicant who lost her way," said the attendant, "and was found on the royal equine grounds, putting her hands to tame the princess's demented stallion."

At the word *demented*, Ani winced.

"Leave," said the king and the attendant withdrew. Ani raised her head and looked him in the face, and his countenance softened. He was not a handsome man, though the thoughts of good looks of youth remained like a reflection of a face on glass. She thought he might be as gentle as her own father with children, but more strict. He motioned for her to step forward.

"Ah, the new goose girl," he said. "With the comely curtsy. Where's that curtsy now?"

"It was difficult, sire, with one arm held at my back." Ani was not certain she had hidden the irritation and fear from her voice, but she gave a low curtsy. The king smiled.

"Hmm, now, when last you were here, you requested a post in the stables, and were denied, and now you're found there—accidentally. Was it accidentally, my girl?"

"No, sire, I never claimed it was."

"Ah." He had seemed bored when she first saw him addressing complaints, and now he leaned forward with an expression that was almost amused.

"I'm brimful of guesses," he said, "but, for time's sake, why don't you report your reason, straight and simple."

"I . . . I wanted to see the princess's horse, and when I saw him I was sorry, for he was terrorized in the spirit, and I climbed the fence because I was confident I could help him."

"And did you help him?"

"No," said Ani. She thought of Falada's eye, dim as a cow's, looking at her before his hoof struck. "I think, I think he's beyond the place where human and animal share language."

Then she forgot the image of the tormented horse and became aware of the king's critical gaze.

"Sire," said the chamber-mistress, warning him of time and of a queue that waited.

"Yes, well, young goose girl, you'll explain to me one day what precisely that means. As for now, there must be a damage of some kind for the trespass, or by next week's end we might have a city of citizens strolling the palace grounds to sightsee mad horses and trample the royal rosebushes. Do you support a family in the forest?"

"No." *My family's in Kildenree,* she wanted to say. *I'm Anidori-Kiladra, I'm the princess.* But her stomach clenched with dread and warning. *Not now. It would not be wise. He would not believe.*

"Then, the month's salary will do. Do you carry it with you?"

The workers had been paid the night before marketday. She took from her apron pocket the thin, gold coin stamped off-center with a running horse and handed it to the king.

"One steed? That's all? Well, we can't deprive you of that entire trivial sum. Counselor! Can you make change?"

A counselor approached, pouring coins from a pouch into his palm.

"It's a sad state when the king doesn't own a copper." The king plucked a silver and a copper coin from the counselor's hand and gave them to Ani. "There you are. No complaints, no return to the stables, and off you go."

"Sire," said Ani. She stood awkwardly a moment, waiting for his attention to return to her. "What's to become of the horse, the princess's horse gone wild?"

"I don't know." He spoke with sudden severity, and her head throbbed anew with the bruise Falada had given. "The king doesn't concern himself with other persons' horses. Dismissed."

Ani walked out of the palace gates and beyond sight of the guards before she stopped and sighed that she was free. She rested her shoulder against a wall and pressed her bruised cheek to the cold stones. Touch made the spot pound with her pulse as though Falada hit her again and again.

Falada had turned mad.

The realization was as real as the pain. Perhaps the cause was what he had seen in the Forest. Or after he had been used to present the false princess to Bayern, and Selia no longer had use of him, perhaps then she or Ungolad had done—something. Ani winced away from the thought. She decided she wanted to feel the pain in her head, so she left the cool wall and walked. The general movement of the people pulled her down a wide avenue, and she did not slow until she reached the first ring of the market.

The market-square was an enormous circle of noise and people that enveloped the central square and several streets beyond. She walked carefully through the fringed outer loop, a circle of beggars who sat on ragged blankets and displayed maimed limbs and sickly children like wares for sale. Some shook tin cups of coins, a noise like babies' rattles.

The next ring of the market belonged to the performers,

groups of children with their arms around shoulders singing lays of heroes or tavern songs, and men strumming lap harps and playing wood flutes, and women in tight trousers (that made Ani blush and look away) who stood on their head and on others' shoulders, and the magicians with their juggling balls and dancing wood-men.

The third loop was formed by the food vendors with their steaming pockets full of buns and women with baskets on their heads, and some, the richer ones, with wooden carts and an extra man to watch for food pinchers. Pigeons pecked at the ground and croaked warnings to each other—*My bread, my rind, my plum, stay away, stay away.* Ani saw a chunk of pork fall to the ground and was tempted to coo back at them, *My meat, stay away.* She had not yet broken her fast. Regretfully, she breathed in the smell of the sausage breads, hot cabbage salads, and syrup apples and kept walking.

And then she saw in the inner ring, surrounded by the sellers of goods, a platform where two men swung a little on their neck ropes. A man passed her waving muttonchops, and the smell twisted her stomach. She held her breath and hurried on.

Ani found Finn's group near the center of the square with their backs to the execution. She turned her back as well and came up behind them. There was an appreciable crowd bartering for Gilsa's knitted goods and the other forest wares. The day had dawned with a real autumn chill, and the people's minds turned to winter and what the Forest dwellers knew of the cold. No one seemed to mind that the goods were a bit damp from yesterday's rainstorm, and Ani imagined Finn and his neighbors camped in the drizzle around a flooded fire pit and thought to be grateful for her thin metal roof.

Finn came to her immediately. His mien betrayed concern, and she realized that it was mirroring her own.

"I'm in trouble." She pulled him apart from the others and spoke in her natural, unused voice, dropping the pretense of accent. "I need to tell someone that, and I'm so confused, and there is nothing to be done, except listen and wait, and be careful."

The boy patted her shoulder.

"They killed my friend, or near enough." She bit her lip, hard, to keep from crying. "They want to kill me. I can't go home, and I am so tired of being afraid."

Ani sobbed once and put her head on Finn's shoulder, letting herself be held a moment, be told it was all right, and imagine what it would be like to be safe and known and cared for. She did not allow herself another sob. She stood straight and laughed to disguise the sensation of crying that still hung in her throat.

"Thank you," she said. "I'm sorry."

"Two men came to the Forest," said Finn.

"Fair-haired?" she asked.

Finn nodded. "They asked after a yellow-haired girl, and Mother said she never saw one and wouldn't let one cross her gate if she did."

Ani heaved a breath and nodded.

"The way to my mother's house is the southwest Forest road called Lake, and then right toward the sign that says Spruces, and then other roads that go second on left, third on right, fifth on right, or you can ask anyone around there."

Ani repeated the way aloud several times to commit it to memory. They were looking for her. They did not think she was dead. They thought she was hiding. Fear tugged in her chest, but she pushed it down. No more. She took out the king's silver coin and gave it to Finn.

"I came here to give this to you, not to cry," she said. "For your mother, just part of all that I owe her."

Finn took the coin but handed in exchange a brown paper-wrapped package from the cart. "From Mother."

It was a deliciously thick pullover of Forest wool, in orange, brown, and blue, and on the back was the design of a yellow bird, wings out in flight. Unlike most of the other pullovers, he had somehow managed to keep it dry. She held it to her face and appreciated its warmth and the smell like a smoky fireside and the raw wool and wood floor of that safe shed where she had slept in the Forest.

"I can see that one can never pay back Gilsa for the fear that she will give again."

As she left the market, spending her copper on a warm bun and a tracked-down thornroot, Ani saw that the hanged men had been transferred from the central platform to the city wall. It was long used to bearing the dead and was marked with the thin, dark blood of past corpses like stripes on a banner of decay. She swallowed the last, hard bit of bread and hurried past.

ays later, Jok was still angry at Ani for leaving him in the pen two nights. She stood outside the pasture arch, counting the orange beaks as the geese waddled through, and she heard Jok's familiar honk on the far side of the group, letting her know that he would not be sitting on her lap again that day. He was a true goose, and Ani was lonely under her beech, passing the time picking out words of goose speech and practicing new words to the wind.

At noon, when Conrad had crossed the hedge to the sheep boys' field on his daily wanderings, Ani heard hoofbeats. It was one man on a dark horse, and he rode directly to her tree. Her muscles shook quietly, but she stayed still and watched the shadow of his hat move on his face until she recognized him.

"Goose girl," Geric called out.

She stepped out from behind the tree and leaned against its smooth gray trunk. Geric dismounted and walked the horse to her, one hand resting on the neck of his mare.

"I don't know your name," he said.

"I'm called Isi," she said.

"Isi. That suits you better than goose girl, doesn't it?"

"Yes," she said.

"Yes, sorry that I didn't know, before. Isi."

"That's all right. I didn't tell you."

"No, you didn't, did you."

"No."

"Hmm," he said. And coughed.

The conversation halted, Geric staring at a print his boot left in the still wet ground, Ani looking off toward the geese as though they might flee to the woods if not under her constant gaze. He cleared his throat and said the beginning of a word, then stopped and lowered his brow. Ani noticed that he had an expressive brow and eyes the color of warmed honey. She looked away from him to the horse.

"Not the bay," she said. At her words, he looked up gratefully.

"No," he said, "I traded him for one a mite tamer. I thought after my embarrassing display, it was clear the beast needed to be handled by a master. Did I do well?"

"Surely," she said, surprised he sought her approval.

He was quiet again, and she waited.

"I came here for two days," he said, "but you were gone, and the geese were gone, and I thought I was mistaken and it was a different pasture where we met."

"No, but it was raining, and then it was marketday, of course. Don't you go to market? And you came in the rain?"

Geric laughed a little. "I was wretched wet, and so were the flowers."

He looked at her curiously, paused, and then deluged her with explanations. "I'm such a dunce, truly I am, and I went home that night after we spoke and you rode the horse, and I made that terrible error, made you feel as though I thought you were of less worth than a stone, I'm sure. Well, you know, I felt like a kingly dolt, as I should've. I hadn't a right to come here and ride around like a fool and insult you and leave without explanation, except that I've never met a goose girl before, and you're not what I expected, though that's no explanation, I know. Still, I thought I'd better come back and bring you flowers, because I read that a gentleman gives a lady flowers, and I thought maybe I'm not a gentleman, but no reason not to treat you like a lady, isn't that so?"

He waited for her to answer.

"Yes," she said. It seemed the only answer to give. He nodded, relieved.

"Well, the rain made them a mess, the flowers, half of them bald of petals and the stems weak as noodles, and I was beginning to think that flowers were a silly idea, that you'd think, I don't know what, but I kept them all week because the last couple of days I couldn't escape to come and explain, and yesterday the flowers just flat died. So when I left today I didn't have any flowers, and wasn't sure I'd find you anyhow, so I grabbed what I could find, and it was food." He pulled a potato sack off the back of his saddle and showed the contents: apples, a loaf of potato bread, cold ham, and a leather pouch filled with custard.

"What you could find? This'd be a feast in the workers' hall. Are you a kitchen-man, then?"

"No, thanks be, or I could never escape so often as I do." He gave her half a grin as he spread out their feast on the sack. "I should confess something to you. Some of the palace guards bet me that I couldn't tame that bay, and if you had taken him for a time, I would've claimed credit for his taming."

Ani gasped and smiled. "You would not."

Geric laughed a little, bowing his head, and nodded. "Yes, yes, I probably would've. You may not know what terrible ego beatings we men give each other."

"So, you're a guard?"

"Yes, that's right."

Now why couldn't he have been one of mine? But if he were her guard, she would be a princess, and just then she wanted to be someone who sits in a pasture with another someone and eats cold ham on potato bread. So they did. After a time, he lost the halting manner of his apology, and they talked so long and easily that Ani's throat went dry and she wished for water. He wanted to know all about how she passed her time. When he learned that his picnic was the first noon dinner she had eaten as a goose girl, Geric swore he would bring her dinner every day.

"If I ruled, you'd all dine," he said.

"Would that you were king."

Jok rushed toward her, honking all the way as though he would bite her, but she honked once to stop his advance, and he turned and waddled away.

"What was all that?" asked Geric, standing.

"Jok, my little friend. He's angry that I've left him in the goose pen these past nights. He's grown used to sleeping in the crook of my knee."

"Well, I'll have none of that, some brazen bird speaking harsh words to his mistress. After all, I'm a gentleman." He stuck out his tongue in an ungentlemanly face and ran after Jok. The goose soon realized he was being pursued and fled across the field, flying in short spurts and running as fast as his flat feet could propel him. Geric slipped once on the wet grass but quickly regained his feet and grabbed Jok around the middle.

"It's time for an apology," he said, walking back to the beech with Jok in hand. "I've become an expert in apologies today, so I know, little brother, that it's time."

"Careful, Geric, you might—" said Ani as Jok turned his head and bit Geric on the arm. Geric exclaimed and dropped the goose who wasted no time in fleeing the scene. And Ani, despite her experience with goose bruises, could not hold back a laugh.

"I'm sorry, my lady," said Geric, rubbing his arm, "but I

failed to force an apology out of the offending goose."

"You're not likely to, either. He's a naughty bird. They all are."

"Poor company."

"Oh, but I like my geese. Like cats, they can't be told what to do, and like dogs, they're loyal, and like people, they talk every chance they get."

"Though they'll not deliver half so good an apology as I do."

"Not half so good," she said.

They laughed together and lay back on the grass, their heads on his rolled cloak, chuckling intermittently and claiming clouds to be ponies and dragons and large-bosomed women. Geric took his leave long after noon. He promised to return the following day if he could, hoisted himself on the mare's back, and rode away.

"Geric," she called.

He turned back around.

"What kind of flowers were they?"

"I don't rightly know," he said. He made faltering gestures with his hands, forming their size and shape from the air. "They were yellow, and smallish, and had lots of petals."

"Thank you," she said. "They were beautiful."

Ani looked toward the stream and held a branch of her beech tree as she might hold a hand. The river birches were leafing brilliant—hundreds of thin, gold coins dangling from their arms. It was perfect, as though their green leaves had been a falsehood all those months and just now the trees showed their realness, their pure autumnal yellows. Ani felt a stirring, a hope, a winged thing waking up in her chest and brushing her heart with its feathers.

Geric came back the next day, and the next, and more, and they sat in the shade of the tree or walked together along the spongy rim of the goose pond, the birds moving at their feet like incarnations of the bright white words that fell from their mouths.

"How do you get away so often?" said Ani.

"When the prince doesn't go out, I've nothing to do. I'm his guard."

"Oh. What's he like?"

Geric grinned. "Oh, he's a nice enough lad, but not half as charming as I am."

Yes, she thought, *I'm certain you're right.*

He was ignorant of goose-keeping and listened with interest as Ani explained what she knew. When she mentioned how much time she sat alone, the next day Geric brought her books on Bayern history and some tales of courtly love, evil, and justice. He was afraid at first that he had erred again and that she had never learned to read, and then he was relieved that she had.

Ani in turn wanted to know about the palace, and after

some days, she had the courage to ask after its newest members.

"The Kildenreans," he said. "A quiet lot, keep to themselves, very grave, earnest men. The senior man, the braided one, he beats the palace guards regularly at sword matches on the training grounds. I've never faced him, though I'd like a go. I've seen him beat three men consecutively, and my arm hurts just to watch." He rubbed his upper arm distractedly where Jok had bit him.

"Hmm, maybe you should challenge him to a horse-breaking match instead," she said.

"Easy, easy, my lady, for your tongue's losing its gentility from speaking too long to geese."

At that, he tossed a handful of grass blades at her, which she tossed back, until Jok appeared, snipping at the falling grass with an eager beak. The goose could not long hold a grudge.

"What of the princess? The boys here, they call her the yellow girl."

Geric smiled, amused. "Princess Anidori-Kiladra."

A cold tickle burst in her stomach at Geric speaking her own name. "You've met her, of course, being the prince's guard."

"Yes, I have. Before she came, the prince took to pacing the floor while trying to memorize her name. Princess Anidori-Kiladra Talianna Isilee. They take the names of their grandmothers there—Talianna, Isilee. Nice sentiment, though it makes for a long name."

Ani coughed, feeling self-conscious of the name Isi, and quickly said, "Shouldn't a princess have a long name, just as she should have a long life?"

"Yes, I suppose." He flung one stray blade of grass her way. She picked it up and ran her finger up its smooth side.

"She's lovely and graceful and witty and courtly, and all that a princess should be." Geric shrugged, and he no longer smiled. "But there was some darkness with her arrival. I didn't know that relations were so drawn between the two countries, but they're more tenuous than I think anyone'd thought."

Yes, thought Ani, *because Kildenree wishes to be left alone and the Bayern greedily cut through the mountains.* She wondered if her city would ever be safe. She doubted that even were she to eventually marry Bayern's prince that their alliance could bind this country to peace, this country where they hanged their dead criminals on their walls and only honored a man who carried a javelin and shield. She did not speak aloud of this to Geric. She was a goose girl and thought perhaps she should not know of such things as maps and borders and war.

One morning in midweek, Geric arrived in the pasture with not only dinner in a potato sack, but an extra horse, a chestnut gelding two hands shorter than his black mare—a lady's horse.

"They're both pretty tame. Not that I don't think you

could handle a bit more, but I didn't think I could." He grinned, and his face was a different kind of handsome from his thoughtful stare.

Ani took the chestnut's reins in silence and stood a moment before him, allowing the horse to sniff at her hands and neck and look over his rider. Geric stood by and watched. Ani waited for his approval, patted him down on both sides, then mounted. She was careful that her skirts did not rise above her ankles.

"By the way, Geric, um, did you see my shift that first day, when I rode the bay?"

Geric bowed his head. "I saw a bit of your leg."

"You saw my leg?"

"How can a man help what he sees?" he said. "And, if I could add, you possess a very fine leg."

Ani felt her face go hot and was too shocked to speak a word. Geric shook his hands in front of him in a feigned gesture of innocence.

"I'm just a gentleman and sworn to truth, and that's my defense."

"Your defense is you're an idle guard who leaves his prince to seek out maidens to spy on." She tried to still a smile, and when it threatened to push through her defenses, she nudged the horse forward.

They let their mounts canter for a bit, dashing back and forth across the pasture. From that height Ani could see Conrad's orange cap at the far end of the sheep pasture, so she dared lead Geric across the stream and into the beginning wood on the other side, as she had seen noble men and women do many times on clear autumn mornings.

They rode through the thickening evergreens, stepping over the scattered sunlight that bled through the canopy to the forest floor, windblown river birch leaves gleaming like loose coins caught in a ray of light. A cold wind came from the heart of the wood and washed over Ani's hands. She halted. The trees, the shadows, the chill, called to mind another afternoon in a forest. Talone's howled rage, Adon's sword-tipped chest, the scream of the stallion that bore a slash down his rump, the pressure of Ungolad's hand on her ankle.

"What's wrong?" asked Geric, and he leaned toward her.

The wind moved over her hand like a searching thing.

"Nothing." She flinched, and the wind left her hand like a feather blown from a palm. She shook her head and told herself that the wind was not speaking to her and that this was not the forest that was full of death and betrayal. Nothing in this wood put bodies on those thin memories and made flesh what was nightmare. In fact, she discovered, there was a comfort in the close trees. And just being on horseback again gave a confidence to her entire body. She smiled. "Nothing. This is perfect."

Geric tipped his head. "Someday you'll have to tell me what that expression on your face means when you look at these trees."

They rode on until Ani expressed concern that the geese had been too long unattended. When they returned to the stream bank, Geric halted.

"Do you dare race a man, my lady?" he said.

Ani only smiled. As one they kicked their horses into a run. Their horses splashed through the stream, wetting boots and hems, and then galloped up the pasture. The riders leaned low on their horses' necks and hollered against the wind and the sound of hooves pounding at the late autumn grass. The wall stopped them, and they gasped for breath between laughs and held their shaking stomachs.

"I won," said Geric, fighting to speak while exhaling.

"You . . . did . . . not," said Ani. "And your horse is taller."

They finished laughing and caught their breaths, and looked at each other, and Ani thought Geric looked at her too long, as though he forgot he was looking, as though he did not wish to do anything else. She looked back. Her heart took its time quieting down.

That night, Ani told the workers a story of a woman who loved a man, and when he married another, she turned into a bird and sang such sad songs to his window that his bride died of the heartbreaking sound. The hall was quiet at the tale, and when Ani left for her room, Razo just patted her shoulder and looked down.

The evening was caught in the early dark of near winter. The city was so empty and still, it seemed no creature had ever walked those stones. Ani stopped in the street outside her window. Silvery moonlight made her pane a mirror. She sought the lines and curves of her mother's face—her mother, who was beautiful. *Do others want to look at me?* she wondered. *Did he?* She put a hand to her cheek. Her face was gray, unsure, shadowed. She did not know if she was beautiful.

"Work here long enough and you can convince Ideca to give you a table mirror."

Ani straightened. Enna stood a few doors down, entering her own room.

"I didn't know you were there," said Ani. She hurried through her own door and sat on the bed beside Jok, feeling flustered and stupid. Jok made the sounds indicating he was ready to sleep, so she took off her hat and unwound her hair, scratched her head, and sighed. The weight of her hair on her back reminded her that she was not who she was. That she was a secret.

She turned at a movement. Her curtains were open, and Enna stood at the window, staring, her eyes wide like an owl's.

"Oh," said Enna.

Ani put a hand to her uncovered hair, stepped forward, and opened the door. "Please come in," she said, and closed her curtains.

Enna sat beside her on the bed.

"I'm getting pretty careless, I guess," said Ani. "I've become so used to being a goose girl, I forget to worry."

"I just came to apologize. I didn't mean to see." Enna put

out her hand and fingered an end of Ani's long yellow hair. "That's why you always wear a hat or a scarf. But your eyebrows?"

"Dyed," said Ani.

Enna ran a finger across Ani's brow and looked at her clean fingertip. She gave a little laugh and shook her head.

"If I tell you about me, can you keep it secret?"

"Yes, of course," said Enna.

So Ani whispered the story, because she knew of no other way to buy Enna's trust. She told it backward, forgetting which parts might be most important, and realized that she was better at telling imaginary tales than her own true one. The story began with the fact that she was a goose girl because the king gave her the job, because she had come to the city from the Forest, where she had been lost. She got lost when her company had mutinied, and there had been a massacre—she stumbled over that part—and her horse had witnessed it and gone mad. The reason they had rebelled against her was that her friend, her lady-in-waiting, had designs to rob her name, her title, and then kill her. And her title was, her title had been, princess.

"From Kildenree," said Ani, with true accent. "My mother was, is, the queen." She felt awkward saying it, like bragging, like saying she was something that she was not, sitting there in her goose girl boots in her room built right on the hard street against the city wall.

"Princess," Enna said quietly.

The candle had sputtered out midtale, and Enna's face was a dark shape on darkness, a faint, silvery line of cheek and chin. Ani wished to see her expression, to see if her brow lifted in surprise or her eyes tightened in doubt, or if the darkness bedded beneath her eyes and in the lines between nose and mouth, a wrinkle of deep thought, of betrayal.

"So," said Ani.

"Do you want," said Enna, still whispering, "should I bow to you? Princess?"

Ani gasped. "No. Please, no. I'm just waiting to see if you believe me."

"Believe you? Mercy, Isi."

Then Enna had questions, and they flowed in a fast current, scarcely giving Ani time to respond. About the Forest, and the kingdom, and the thornroot that could darken hair, and her horse—she could speak with him?—and how evil were those guards and how black must be their desires to spur them to murder. Ani answered every question. She felt safe there, in the absolute dark, Jok asleep in her lap, Enna's hand occasionally bridging the blackness to touch her knee, the warm conversation filling up the dark space like heat fills the air around a fire.

Enna ran out of questions, and they sat quiet again, each thinking, seeing in the dark the bright images of a white horse and red blood and green trees, and on top of it all, a high, turreted palace with blind eyes.

"It must be past midnight," said Ani.

Enna agreed.

"You've been very kind to listen," said Ani, slipping back into her Bayern accent, which she discovered felt natural to her now. "And, I'm sorry if I've ever been unkind when you sought my friendship. I'm wary of that now, I think."

"I can see why. Selia." Enna said the last word as though she might spit it. "We've got to get you your name back."

Ani nodded. "I've thought a lot about it. After the first time I met the king, I realized I couldn't go there alone and demand they take my word over Selia's and all her guards'. And I thought, maybe if I was surrounded by people who believed me, I'd be safer and have a better chance of convincing the king."

"Yes," said Enna, "let's get all the workers together and we'll be your guard and make the king listen. They can't kill all of us, right?"

Ani pressed her lips together. "Yes, that's what I think sometimes, and then I remember Adon and Talone, and Dano the cook, and the others. There were a lot of them, too, and Ungolad's friends killed them all."

"Oh," said Enna.

"For a time I thought that idea was my best hope, but the more time I spend in the workers' hall, I know that I can't risk your lives."

"Not even Conrad's?" Enna tilted her head as though it were an appealing idea.

Ani laughed quietly. "It's my trouble. Even if some of the

workers were willing to go to battle on this, I don't think it'd be right to endanger their lives just to get back my name."

"Maybe," said Enna, smothering a yawn.

"We should sleep, I guess."

"Yes, don't worry, we'll figure it out."

"Enna," said Ani as the girl rose to leave, "those guards would kill me if they knew I was here."

"I know," she said. "I won't tell anyone. You'll see that I won't. And Isi . . . can I still call you Isi? It fits you. I want to tell you how I believe you. I don't know why. I wouldn't believe Razo if he pricked his finger and told me he was bleeding, and your story's almost as crazy as your bedtime tales, but I really do believe you. And when you get tired of worrying and mourning your horse and trying not to be afraid, tell me and I'll do it for you a while so you can shut your eyes and sleep peaceful."

he next afternoon, Ani awaited Geric's visit, her ears so attuned to the distant sounds of hooves on cobbled streets that she did not hear Jok calling after her until he stood by her side. She tore grass for him and plucked loose feathers from his tail, setting aside the quills for the bundle Tatto would collect later that week. *Perhaps*, she thought, *the king or prince himself will use the quills I gather here*, and again she wondered what the prince might be like, though she found it not half so interesting as thinking about what Geric was like.

She was planning to tell Geric. Enna had believed, and so might others. Geric could help her with Falada. And if he had the prince's ear, perhaps he could convince him of her identity. She tripped on that thought. Is that what she wanted? To marry this prince and live the rest of her life with Geric standing as the silent guard at her husband's side? *No, no, there must be a better solution than that.*

When he finally came, Ani waited by the tree and

watched his approach. Geric was tall, and he rode his mare with a height and ease that made Ani feel proud. She often thought of him as a boy, the way he teased her and chased the geese and got excited over the desserts he brought with dinner. But just then he did not look silly at all—*in fact*, she thought, *in fact, quite handsome*. She smiled at him, but when he neared, she could see that his expression was troubled.

"What's wrong?"

"Nothing." Geric wiped his forehead as though trying to dismiss unpleasant thoughts. "Nothing that should disturb this autumn peace." And he tried to smile.

They walked beside the stream. Geric did not want to talk about the events that shaped his mood, saying only that there was ill gossip at the palace. He looked back to where his horse stood grazing and cursed himself, realizing that he had forgotten to bring dinner from the kitchens.

"Don't mind for me," said Ani.

But he was angry with himself and talked little, and Ani's inclination to confess secrets began to harden in the mood. Soon they sat by a hushed bit of stream, watching the yellow leaves of the autumn birches plate the surface of the water. Ani looked across the stream, contemplating fording its shallow cold to hunt out late walnuts. Conrad used to bring back pockets full, and the thought woke her stomach to mumble a complaint.

"I'm sorry," said Geric. "I came here today to escape the gloom, and I've brought it with me."

"Let's distract ourselves somehow. I heard that when the princess arrived she rode a fine mount. Can you tell me about her horse?" *My horse. Falada.* The story Enna knew was in her throat, eager.

Geric sighed. "The white stallion. Not well. I think they'll kill him."

"What?"

"So I've heard."

"But, kill him? No, surely not kill him."

"Yes, I think so. I understand the princess thinks it's best, has said from her arrival that he was a dangerous creature. And he's her horse. It's her choice."

"Oh, Geric." Ani was standing. He noticed her expression and stood beside her.

"What's the matter?" he said.

"Geric, can you save the horse?"

"Isi, the king's issued the order. It may've already been done."

Ani stared up at the baring branches, eyes wide to keep them dry. She felt powerless. Geric looked at her with sympathy, perhaps thinking she was just a sweet girl who hated to hear of the mistreatment of any animal. She shook her head, unable to explain.

"Please," she said. "Can you just ask the prince if he'll let him live? It's very important to me. That horse doesn't deserve to die."

"I'll try," he said. "If you'd like, I'll go right now and try."

"Thank you. I wouldn't ask something like this, but I feel like you're a friend, a good friend."

"Isi, I'm so glad I am. These afternoons have been, you know, so nice. More than nice. More than just getting to eat out here and know your geese and talk. It's not like—the palace—it isn't an easy place to be, especially not now, and I'm trying to say that you've been . . . no, you're so, you're—"

He stopped. Looking into his dark eyes was like gazing at a calm river, and in them she saw the reflection of the leaning trees behind her, of golden leaves, of herself crowned by autumn. She lifted her face to him and was aware of the fullness of the sun on her skin, breaking through the cold air. Geric touched her cheek, smooth as a teardrop, thrilling as a lightning storm. She felt real.

"You are," he said. His hand found hers, and he held her fingers tightly, as though he did not dare to do any more than hold her one hand, and look at her, and breathe deeply. She held his hand in both of hers.

With that touch his countenance changed. He dropped his hand and looked away.

"I should go," he said, already walking to his horse. She stayed by the stream. When he had mounted, he turned back and frowned.

"I'm sorry," he said. "I'm so sorry, Isi." He rode up the hill, through the arch, and disappeared into the stones of the city.

After the dark affirmed it was the middle night, Ani left Jok dozing on her bed, wrapped her hair into Gilsa's blue head-scarf, and slipped outside. She had recently oiled the hinge of her door, and it closed silently behind her. It was a long walk to the palace and seemed longer after dark, with nothing to watch but stray cats and closed windows. With every step the cold of the cobblestones pushed up through her boot soles and into her bones. She was wearing Gilsa's pullover. It was bright and patterned, and she felt as obvious as a goose in a murder of crows.

The night guards stopped her at the gate. Of course they would.

"I've been called to the stables," she said. Her forehead itched with cold and sweat, but she did not raise her hand to it.

The lead guard looked her over and then motioned for her to pass. She was a girl, a Forest girl by the look of her head wrap, and not possibly important enough to lie or plot. Ani knew a trusting guard might let an innocuous girl enter alone, but leading a princely, maddened horse back through was another matter. But she had to try.

There were others on the stable grounds—guards, late workers, and sleepless stable-hands. She nodded to those she walked past, and they nodded back. The stable where she had last seen Falada lay at the end of the yard, a painfully long walk that stretched on and on, the distance seemingly unchanged with every step.

When at last she ducked through the fence posts and into the long building, Ani knew it was wrong. There was an odor of stale hay and muck piles without the sharp, warm smell of animal. She ran to the end. Every stall was empty. Ani wiped her forehead with a loose end of the scarf and took a bracing breath. She would have to check every stable. Like the cold, hopelessness pricked at her skin.

She crossed the arena and ducked through the railings. Something caught—an exposed nail, a tether hook—and held a corner of her head wrap. Her fingers were numb from the cold, and she tried to feel it out blindly. Cloth, wood, metal, all felt the same.

"Ho there," said a stable-hand, "what're you doing?"

"I'm caught," she said.

"You shouldn't be here," he said.

Ani tugged harder. He spoke too loudly. Others were looking that way, and she was caught like a hooked fish breathing in cruel, dry air. And then she saw him. Across the field. He had stopped and was looking at her, wondering at the commotion.

"You'd better leave," said the stable-hand.

Two pale braids. That was all she could make out at that distance. Pale braids. Panic seized her, and she had no thought but—away. She pulled herself free, and the scarf fell, long, unraveled, on the hard ground. Her yellow hair shone like silver in the moon-lightened field. All she knew to do then was run.

Ani did not look back. She knew he was behind her. She knew he was stronger, and she was so cold. Her boots hit the ground, and the impact shook her body, but her feet could feel nothing. She was as numb as her fingers, as numb as fear had made her mind. She stumbled and ran. He would be close now. Right there, behind her. Close enough to reach out, to grab her by the neck, to bring her down like a fox on a hen, jaw tight on its throat.

There's something I can do, Ani thought. *There's something.* She could not think what. The wind from her running grabbed at her ears like a child anxious to tell secrets. She strained to understand, but it was just noise, like the chattering of the geese had been all those weeks ago.

Up ahead the guards at the side gate blocked the exit, and another hurried from his post toward the sounds of running.

"That man," she said as soon as she was close enough to speak, "he's trying to hurt me. Please."

The guards turned their attention away from her, and she continued to run, at last outside the palace and into the dark of the sleeping city. She turned back to see Ungolad at the gate and heard him yell in outrage, his pursuit stopped by the warning of javelins pointed at his chest.

Ani did not stop running until the leaning streets eased, and she looked around at unfamiliar buildings and knew she was lost. She rested against a house, her head on her trembling arm, and concentrated on breathing the cold air that stabbed at her throat and lungs like icy fingers. Ungolad knew she was there. They would search now for a Kildenrean girl with long yellow hair. There was fear again. Falada was gone, and all was wrong.

There had been something, an idea, a sensation, something she could have done, something that was stronger than the knife in his hand. Something in the wind. She could not remember, though she tried as she stumbled west on the sleepy streets, hiding behind barrels and piles of refuse when she heard footsteps behind her own, but seeing no one. She finally gained the city wall when the moon had set and followed the wall in utter darkness to her own room. At last, her own safe place.

Ani locked her door, fell on her bed, and was asleep at once. She did not wake until Conrad rapped on her door after breakfast.

Geric did not come that day. Ani waited for him to bring the news of the horse's death. She could imagine how he would look, what he would say, how his gait would be slower, despondent, each foot reluctant to take a step, his eyes slow to meet her face. But they would meet her face, and he would take her hand again, and all would be well.

He did not come.

After the sun had started its long slope into the hollow of the western sky, Tatto passed through the archway. "I've got new boots," he said, explaining why he picked his way across the grass, carefully avoiding goose droppings. Ani watched with sleepy eyes and a resigned dread.

"I've been sent by my chamber-lord to deliver to you a message." Tatto spoke officially, raising one hand, palm upright, in a stiff gesture of oration.

"Yes, go on," said Ani. He was inclined toward dramatic pauses.

"Here," he said. "A letter from someone in the palace."

The parchment was sealed with a plain pool of wax. Ani broke it and read.

> *Isi,*
>
> *Matters here are worse, and the prince needs me at present. At any rate, I think I had better not return to your pasture again. I do not know how to write this. You know, this is my fourth draft of this letter, and I am determined to finish this one even though I will sound like a right fool. So I will just say it. I cannot love you as a man loves a woman. I am so sorry if I have presumed what is not true or have taken liberties with your sentiments. I hope you can forgive me.*
>
> > *Geric*

A postscript scratched at the bottom read, "I have failed you twice. The horse you had regard for was already taken away when I arrived yesterday."

Ani folded the letter and put it in her pocket. Tatto was watching her face. Curiously, Ani did not feel like crying, or running away, or sighing. Instead, she felt anger burst open inside her, an overripe fruit. She felt like picking up the fist-size rock that lay by her foot and throwing it, hard. She did. It made an unsatisfactory thump on the ground.

"Not good news," said Tatto.

"I should be used to it. But right now I'd like all my troubles to stand in front of me in a straight line, and one by one I'd give each a black eye."

"Oh." Tatto stood by, waiting to see what she would do.

She kicked her beech tree. The trunk was as thick as two men, the smooth bark as hard as a city stone. She could not even make the branches shiver. She shouted and kicked it again as hard as she could, knowing she could not even dent the bark. She was reminded of one of her temper-prone ganders that had tried to attack a carthorse, only to get kicked by a rather large hoof.

Ani stopped and pressed her forehead on a branch in a kind of apology. The pressure of the tree on her face soothed her. She closed her eyes and thought she could hear a kind of breathing echoing all around her, from leafless branches and the thick trunk and below her feet. She opened her eyes and saw Tatto staring.

"You're angry," he said.

"I think so," she said with some satisfaction.

"I saw my ma do that once"—he pointed at the tree trunk—"but to a milk pail. Kicked and chased it clear across the yard, crushed it to a ball of metal. Really."

"Yes, well . . ." Ani looked off to where some geese paddled on the pond, though the water was near freezing. *I cannot love you as a man loves a woman.* Her heart twisted at that. *And not coming back*, she thought. *Put him away, with the others who will not come back. Aunt, father, Selia, brothers, sisters, Talone, the guards, Falada. Put Falada away.*

"Tatto, do you know where they sent the princess's horse?"

"Yes, the knacker two over east from your pens."

Ani thanked him, and when Tatto had left, she told the geese to stay put. She found the knacker's yard first by smell. The place reeked of discarded parts of animals—an odor sour and mean that lodged in her throat. Bits of coarse hair and feathers tossed around on a ground breeze and lay on the dirt thick as dust on a floor unused. A man in a heavy apron was sharpening his ax on a whetstone, even as she had imagined he would be.

"Sir," she said, "the white horse, the royal one, has he been killed?"

He looked up from his ax.

"Aye." He stepped forward. Clumps of animal hair stuck to his boots and to the dark stains on his apron.

"Yes," she said. "I thought so. Yesterday."

"A friend of yours, was he?" said the knacker, expecting her to laugh.

Ani winced. "Yes, actually. A good friend. But I've spent two months mourning and can't cry anymore."

"What are you, a misplaced stable-hand?"

"Goose girl," she said.

The knacker nodded and pumped the pedal of the whetstone.

"Sir, a favor," she said.

"Favor," he mumbled, and kept it spinning.

She removed the gold ring, the one Gilsa had refused, and held it out to him, letting the afternoon sunlight flicker on its edge like a halfhearted star.

"For payment, for a proper burial."

He looked up again and let the wheel spin down. Ani crossed the yard, conscious of the animal hair under her boots, and put it in his hand. His fingers were the dirty brown of unwashed blood. Ani swallowed at the touch. It could be Falada's blood.

"He was a noble beast and shouldn't die to be dog's meat. Give him the honorable rites due the mount of a princess."

The knacker stared at the circle of gold and shrugged. "All right." He gave the wheel another pump. "Do you want to see him?" The hand with the ring motioned to his right, and Ani noticed for the first time the hind leg of a white horse, the white hair stained all colors of brown from blood and dirt. It lay on the ground, severed from his body, being readied for dog meat. She took a step forward, her hand to her mouth. She saw the tip of another leg, the rest hidden by the hut.

"No," she said, "I've seen enough. I have to go." She turned her back and ran.

Four mornings later, Ani and Conrad herded their flock to the pasture, anxious to let them graze while the weather held clear and kept the winter rains and snows in abeyance. Ani liked to hurry into the sunshine of the pasture, not idling longer than needed in the shaded street.

That day, she stopped. Her eyes were drawn to the curve of wall above the arch. There, fastened to the stones, his neck attached to a round, polished board of dark wood, was the head of Falada. Ani grabbed at the stones in the wall to keep herself standing.

His mane was washed and combed straight down his disembodied neck. He was scrubbed clean of the blood of death and the mark of the ax. His head was imposing, bright white, nose pointed forward, like the proud carriage of a horse at a run. His eyes were glass balls, black as new moons.

"Look at him," said Conrad. He did not seem surprised.

"Why would they do that? Hang him there as they do the criminals?" She could not look away from the cold, glass eyes.

"Some favorite animal of a rich man, no wonder, though I don't know why he's hung by the goose pasture gate. You've never seen inside one of those fancy estates? Full of stuffed animals, dead pets, big deer heads."

Ani could not leave the spot. Conrad and the geese were far down by the pond, and still she stood. *Cruel, cruel,* she thought. *This is a proper burial? These are honorable rites?* She was angry and torn and heartsick and blamed herself and everyone in the world.

Falada, she said.

For a moment, the head seemed to agitate, like heat haze shimmering on a road. The dead face did not turn toward her. The dead eyes did not look. In that place in her mind where she had often heard his voice, she thought she felt a word spoken, soft as a spider's footstep. She could not understand.

Falada, look what they've done to you.

The eyes stared blindly; the stiff nose pointed forward.

inter came at last. The cold formed rain like knives that tore at the skin. Snow had topped the mountains in the west for weeks, white harbingers of the coming months, and then the first ashy flakes fell into the city streets. The geese stayed in their pens. The workers shoveled snow out of the west streets. When the snow stopped falling but stayed stubbornly on the fields, the workers stayed in the hall.

The winter Forest did not permit easy travel to visit their families. The restless ones wandered the city without coats, loitering outside taverns because they were not permitted inside, overhearing news to bring back at supper. There was talk of the wintermoon festival and the preparations for the royal wedding come spring. Tatto supped with them occasionally, full of palace news that they listened to eagerly, if with a healthy amount of incredulity.

"My da's company of soldiers doubled since harvestmoon. They don't train as much in the winter, but they're all in the city. There's going to be war."

Razo snorted. "Even if his company's bigger, that doesn't mean there'll be war."

"War in spring, that's what I've heard."

Worse was Mistress Ideca's news, some days after the first snow fell.

"This afternoon in came two of those strange warriors, what arrived with the yellow girl. They said they were looking for another yellow girl, one of their own that got lost in the coming." Ideca scowled at the thought, as though too many yellow girls could ruin anyone's day. "That's right, a second yellow girl, and said she'd have the hair and the accent and all. 'Course, I sent them on their way, said we don't keep foreigners around here."

"There's a dolt for you," said Razo. "Why'd one of the princess's girls be here? Try two places: the palace or the graveyard. That's what I say."

Razo looked to Ani for support.

"Two yellow girls," said Ani, "who would've thought?" She felt giddy suddenly, happy with her secret and her disguise. Ungolad had seen her at the palace, but she would not be going back. They had killed Falada. They could not do worse. She felt strangely free.

There was no reason now to stay in Bayern. Falada was gone. Geric was gone. Every month she collected her thin gold steed, and come spring thaw, she would have saved enough to buy supplies and her way into a company of traders going to Kildenree.

She was not looking forward to spring. Her mother and Calib would doubtless welcome her home, and it would be nice to see her sisters again, but Ani had nothing real to return to in Kildenree. Still, Ungolad was searching, and if she stayed in Bayern, he would find her sooner or later. Besides, Ani knew that the families of the slain guards needed to know of their fates, and the murders and treachery of Selia and her followers should not go unpunished. Knowing it was right did not make the decision easier. She looked around at the workers and realized she would miss them terribly.

So in the meantime, Ani meant to enjoy being the goose girl. When the others were making plans for wintermoon, Ani took part, as eager to go with them as they were eager to show off the activities to a newcomer.

"Are you sure you should?" said Enna behind a silencing hand. "Won't the guards be there, and they're looking for you now."

"I can't hide forever," said Ani. "Besides, I'm not who they're looking for. I'm Isi, the goose girl, and I'm going to wintermoon."

It was as though marketday had exploded. The festivities began in market-square and flooded outward, consuming street after street in their color and tumult. Doorways and windows burst with giant paper flowers, and colorful ropes were thrown from window to window and building to building. On top of every turret blazed a paper sun dripping ribbon rays. People wore their best clothes, dazzling with strings of glass diamonds. Improvised bands of flute, harp, and lyre played in the streets. Children lit noisy bucket bombs and strings of purple star-mirrors. Magicians drew designs in the air with the weaving pattern of their balls. Drummers sat at the feet of sorcerers, giving rhythm to the pulling of apples from their boots and the turning of pigeons into bursts of flame.

"You'll see," said Bettin, one of the sheep girls, "even Forest folk are welcome everywhere at wintermoon."

Razo walked ahead, pulling on Ani's sleeve. "Come, Isi, we'll show you the witches."

Ani had never before seen a sorcerer or heard a drum, and she lingered, mesmerized by the strokes of his hands and the beating of the drum that insisted itself into her heart's rhythm. *Is it magic?* she wondered. *Or tricks?* She watched the sorcerer transform a walnut inside his clenched fist into a scarf. She looked to the faces of the crowd around her and saw that they laughed where she had been in awe and grinned to see the rat become smoke and the child spit a coin from his mouth. *I tell strange stories,* she thought, *and they marvel, but to them a sorcerer is nothing unexpected.*

Then she saw one spectator with a face that looked as incredulous as she felt. His pale blue eyes were unblinking, afraid to miss any movement of the sorcerer's hand. He turned slightly, and Ani flinched, lowered her head, and walked away. Yulan. Standing not two persons from her side. The drum beat a faster tempo, mimicking her heart. She walked at that pace for two streets before daring to turn around, face the throng, and try to pick out his face. Yulan was not there.

Ani found her companions near the witches, dozens of women in nearly identical garb—headscarves and long skirts and heavy loop earrings—sitting on the ground and on crates at the mouth of the square. Customers knelt before them and paid a copper for the witch to shake a glass bottle of black seed oil and tell the future or prick their palms with sharpened bird bones to divine their ailments. They then prescribed which herbs to take to heal the ailments and supplied those herbs for immediate sale.

Ani asked if it was magic.

"I guess, more or less," said Razo. "Enna, get your future told."

"Not a chance," said Enna. "I've got two coppers to spare, and I want an almond cake."

"Do it, Isi," said Razo. "Don't you want to know the future?"

Ani shook her head. "Can't spare the coin. I'll just have to wait and see it for myself."

Razo stuck his hands in his pockets and leaned in to eavesdrop on a stranger's telling. Ani pulled Enna aside.

"I saw one of them," she said, "a guard named Yulan. I don't think he saw me, but keep an eye out."

Bettin and the other boys tugged on Razo's sleeves, and they continued to walk through the festival. If Enna and Ani glanced around more than before, the boys did not seem to notice.

"There're the javelin dancers," said Conrad. A circle a few paces wide had been dug three steps deep into the ground. The crowd around it was cheering and stomping their feet in unison.

"Let's see who's dancing," said Razo.

"Just see you don't try to claim kinship with those boys again, Razo," said Enna. "You're as Forest-born as any of us."

Enna led the way with her arm through Ani's. She pointed at the circle. "'Thumbprint of the Gods' is what they call this. It's supposed to be sacred, though I don't think anyone remembers why. I heard the kings used to be crowned here. Now they do it privately with nobles only and where they won't get velvet slippers dirty." Enna grinned, then remembered what Ani was. "I didn't mean to say all royals are like that. That's just how they are here, or at least, that's what I've heard."

Ani smiled and lightly knocked Enna with her shoulder.

"Do you think we should go?" said Enna. "Aren't you worried?"

Ani shrugged and stood on tiptoe to see in better. Razo shoved them from behind, and the group crammed into the crowd. The inner circle of watchers was holding javelins pointed inward, making a deadly ring of spikes. A boy of fifteen, naked but for a cloth around his hips and a strap covering his eyes, danced wildly in a space of not more than two paces. He had two shallow wounds on his back that bled freely. A drummer sat on the ground at the feet of a javelin holder, and the crowd stomped to his beat. Ani found she wanted to join the rhythm and forced her feet stay still.

"It's supposedly a mark of honor if a boy survives the dance untouched," said Enna.

"And if they don't? Can they be denied the javelin and shield?"

"Just if they die, but that's happened."

The dancer finished and was followed by another boy who also was bit by a javelin tip, and then another who blindly flung himself on a point and cried out, stopping his dance. "Keep going, Wescelo," shouted an older man from the crowd. The boy's face was lined with pain. He tipped his head back and kept dancing.

Ani pushed her way out of the crowd, and the others followed.

"That's awful," said Ani.

"Not so bad," said Razo. "If they can't stand the dance, they won't stand a war, and then why should they be given a javelin and shield?"

"I'd do it," said Conrad.

"So would I," said Razo. "If it earned me a javelin, I'd do it right now."

"Oh, look," said Enna. "It's the royals."

Ani saw a grouping of palace guards in their red-tipped yellow tunics and polished javelins. In their middle she caught a glimpse of several well-dressed, well-groomed, self-satisfied nobles. The feathers in their hats bobbed as they walked, and the lace-trimmed parasols of the ladies swayed delicately.

"They hardly ever come out in public," said Bettin. "I've never seen any of them. Must be because the new princess wanted to see the festival."

"Why don't they come out?" asked Ani.

"They're so high and mighty, is all," said Conrad.

"My ma said that in the Eastern War the king lost all his brothers and his father," said Razo, "and then he became king and there hasn't been a war since. She thinks he's being protective or something."

"The prince'll be there," said Bettin. "Isi, don't you want to see the prince?"

"The prince," said Ani. "Yes, I do, very much."

Enna nudged her. "You've never seen him?"

"Oh, don't be so high-ish, Enna," said Razo. "Neither've you."

Ani outpaced Razo to where the crowd thickened. Others had the same notion, and an ever tightening ring of onlookers hemmed in the royal party. Razo put his hands on two of his friends' shoulders and hopped up and down.

"No way through," he said. "But they've stopped to game."

He led them out of the mass and around behind the game booth. They crouched behind a wagon and peered between the backs of guards. In a moment a young boy in lavender velvet walked into their view and tossed miniature spears at a wooden boar.

"Watch it," said Enna, pushing back against Razo, "or we could get a spear in the eye."

"Which one's the king's son?" said Ani.

"The boy there in the purple," said Razo. "Tatto pointed him out once."

Ani laughed. "Truly? That's him?" He could not have been more than thirteen. His face was round and still softened with baby fat, and he grinned with boyish delight whenever one of his thrown spears hit the wooden boar.

Enna leaned to her ear and said, "Narrow escape."

"Indeed." Ani felt a surprising thrill of gratitude to Selia for having saved her from that marriage. With a low laugh, she thought of how delicious Selia's surprise must have been when she met her juvenile groom. Of course, Ani had no doubt that Selia would wed for the title but keep her Ungolad ever close.

Then another man stepped into view. Black hair, smooth as boot polish, tied back at his neck, his hat angled to his face, hands that Ani knew were broad and strong and, when they had touched her, had seemed to go through her skin and touch her blood. He walked beside the prince, his dark eyes scanning the crowd.

"Oh," Ani said softly.

The prince handed a bundle of spears to Geric and patted his arm encouragingly. Several nobles laughed at a jest Ani could not hear. Geric nodded, smiling, and stepped up to the booth. The first and second struck home in the boar's neck with a rigid thud. Some of the royal party applauded politely.

Then Selia slipped from the prince's far side and approached Geric from behind, talking with a coy smile. When his arm cocked to hurl the spear, she bumped his elbow and the spear went awry. Selia had a merry laugh. Ani could hear it lift over the noise of the crowd. Ani's fists tightened, and she hated Selia anew for teasing a poor guard in front of the nobles. He had been doing so well.

"There's the princess," said Enna.

Enna's voice sounded like a warning, and Ani started to back away, before Selia saw her. But Geric was looking toward his lost spear. It had fallen not far from where Ani crouched, and when he looked up, he saw her. *Isi*, he mouthed silently. She could not move. His gaze held her. Selia stood at his elbow, jeering and laughing, any moment sure to turn, to see what it was he saw. Yet all Ani could do was stare.

"Isi, that's the princess." Enna tugged on her sleeve.

She blinked under Geric's gaze, lowered her eyes, and moved away. They weaved their way out of the crowd and stretched to be back in open space.

"Why can't we stay and see the prince?" said Razo. Enna glared at him and kept walking away.

Geric had not seemed surprised to see her, or pleased. He had seemed sorry. Sorry to see her or sorry not to? She closed her eyes briefly and remembered that biting line from his letter—*I cannot love you as a man loves a woman.* And Selia had spoken with him in a familiar way. Ani shuddered to think how close she had come to telling him all. She had been wrong to think she could trust him.

"That yellow girl, she's not so pretty," said Razo. "I think our goose girl's prettier than the princess." Razo extended his arm with a flourish, took Ani's hand, and rested it lightly on his. "My goose lady." He was only kidding, but the attention felt good to her just then, and she placed her hand atop his.

"My sheep lord," she said.

They stopped to buy dark wheat cakes with cherry preserves. Ani, who was saving her coins for a long trip, ate the cracker bread she had brought from the hall. One of the sheep boys paid a street artist to paint an ink tattoo on his arm, a design of the Bayern sun surrounded by black blobs intended to be running sheep. The boy, proudly, asked the group if he did not look like a mercenary or a member of a rogue hundred-band.

"Guaranteed to last two months," said the artist.

"It'll wash off in your first bath," said Enna, shaking her head.

"Right, so it'll last him about two months." Razo grinned

and got socked in the arm.

The group was giddy, singing catches of Forest songs and hopping to any sorcerer's drums. Razo spun Ani around in an improvised dance, and she leaned her head back and laughed. But when she ceased spinning, her middle felt heavy again and her feet were cold. She looked back often to the game booths. A tangled mass of people separated them.

They headed toward the main avenue, where the mounted procession would pass. Conrad was intent on witnessing the costumed group of men who wore horse heads and rode horses that were dressed as men. They passed the mouth of the square and the scattered group of witches perched on their crates like wise old lizards in the sun. Ani caught the eye of one woman with stained hands and purple lips. She dropped out of her group and went to her.

"I met you," said Ani, "at an autumn marketday."

The woman nodded.

"You said I had something new in me, that I didn't know it."

She nodded again, her piled hair bobbing precariously with the movement. "It's festival. You want to know things, you give a coin."

"I can't spare it," said Ani.

The woman shrugged. "You'll figure it for yourself, then." She considered Ani a moment, as though she were a chicken she might purchase, and then dug through her mouse-eaten bag and pulled out a drying scrap of thornroot. Pointing to her eyebrows, she said, "Time again."

Ani wove her way among the crates, overhearing bits of purchased witch wisdom. "You'll find love in the out-towns." "You'll find love in the city." "You'll find gold coins buried under the cowshed." Ani pressed the thornroot with a thumbnail, wondering if there was any living juice left. Nothing dripped from the break, but her nail gleamed with a light sheen of brown. She bumped into somebody and, mumbling an apology, looked up to see where she was going.

Yulan. He stood before her, grinning, his fist resting on his hip. Ishta was beside him. Both held long, unsheathed knives.

Ani turned to run. With an easy yank, Yulan had her arm and pulled her close to him, her back pressed against his chest. Ishta stepped in, closing the circle.

"Hello, little princess," said Yulan. He pushed the long edge of his knife against her back. "Give me a coin, I will tell your future."

"Traitor," she said. Her voice responded to his accent with her natural own.

She could feel his chest shake with a chuckle. He held her wrists in his sweaty grip behind her back.

"Ishta, the bad little bird has come neatly back to her master. I nearly didn't recognize her with all her fair hair hidden. Clever little thing."

Ishta nodded. He was watching the movements around them, his body stiff and ready for action.

"Did you kill them all?" she said.

"All," said Yulan.

"Traitor!"

He laughed harder.

"If you ever return to Kildenree," Ani said with desperation, "my mother will hang you, as they do here, with your cold, dirty body on a wall for all to spit at and for dogs to gnaw on your toes and for birds to pluck out your hair for their nests."

"You have a lot more bite in you than I remember, though you still yap like a magpie." He put his face against her neck and breathed deeply. "And you smell like a magpie's nest. What, no one here offers to bathe you and drench you in scented oils? Perhaps Selia will let me do it, later."

She tried to push his face away with a knock of her head. He chuckled again, pleased with the struggle. Ani looked around her at the hundreds of people who stood near and passed them by, none glancing their way, none stopping to help.

"Later," said Ishta. "Take her to Ungolad."

Ani could not help wincing at the name, and Yulan noticed.

"You like to talk about what your mother would do, your pretty little mother who is half a year away? Let us think about our papa Ungolad, who is only up the road. Hmm, what will he do?"

Yulan pushed her forward, and the knife's edge against her

back encouraged her on. She wrapped a leg around a horse post, and Ishta kicked it free. She began to scream and was answered by Ishta's hard fist in her belly. She could not make enough breath to scream again. After a block of struggled walking, she pulled breath enough to whisper.

"It is useless," she said. "They will know. You can't keep it a secret. Visitors will come from home. They will see the impostor. You will all be hanged."

"Oh, my darling girl, you're going to give yourself a wasting disease with all this worry. Selia is a smart girl, remember? She has it all worked out. What you really should be worrying about is Ungolad."

Yulan took no care as they marched up the street, and some faces held questioning looks as to why these foreign guards laid hands on one of their laborer girls, but they passed on.

"Enna," Ani whispered. She could not shout.

Her friend stood on the corner, searching the crowd. Ani looked at her, willing her to turn her head. The girl scanned past Ani. Before she met her gaze, Enna disappeared behind the gathering crowd.

"Enna," she said again, begging all the breath from her bruised ribs. She was not loud enough.

"Hush up," said Ishta. He knocked her side with an elbow, and she doubled over, standing only by Yulan's support. They stopped.

"Keep on with that, Ishta, and you will be carrying her."

To the side, a few dozen pigeons mused over a dropped loaf of bread. Their gray heads faced down, and they cooed nervously—*Hurry, eat for winter, fill your belly with bread, hurry, hurry.*

Ani knew she would have to be loud and quick. Yulan was urging her forward again. She took several fast, deep breaths, begged memory to serve her, and called to the pigeons. *From the building, cats! Cats! Fly away! Cats!*

A rainstorm of sound erupted as the flock took to the air toward the street, their wings beating hard, ungainly flaps, louder than a crowd. The people looked up as the frenzied birds landed among them. Ani struggled anew, hoping that Enna had turned and seen, hoping to give her time. The blade pressed her back.

The street rose abruptly, and her boots slid on a wet cobblestone and out from under her.

"Walk, or I will carry you on my knife," said Yulan.

"Almost there," said Ishta.

Ani pushed her heels down between two cobblestones and resisted until her leg muscles trembled.

"Move," said Yulan. The blade felt sharper.

"Drag me. Carry me. Make a scene. I will not walk like a hooded turkey to the chopping block." Ani felt her strength enlarge as she spoke, her limbs encouraged, her will determined. Again she had the fleeting thought, the memory of an image, that there was something else she could do. A whisper too quiet to hear beyond its breath. The pain in her back flared, and it left her mind.

"Ishta, pick up her feet."

"Make her walk," said Ishta.

"She is not going to, so get her on already."

Ishta's face was close to hers. His eyes were a pale blue. Their look felt like winter.

"Walk," Ishta said.

"No."

He held one of her hands close to his mouth. "I will bite off a finger."

He opened his lips one finger width. His mouth stank of onions and mold, and his teeth were dimly brown. Her hand shook in his grasp. She closed her eyes and waited for the raw consciousness of his sinking teeth.

"You there, yellow fellows."

Ani opened her eyes to a large man in the simple dyed tunic and trousers of a laborer. With him stood a second man of the same class, and moments later two others jogged up to join their group. All carried smooth, well-worn quarterstaves. They wore plainly made patches of yellow suns stitched to their shirtfronts. Not soldiers, unless homemade soldiers. But their faces were grim and serious, and the staffs looked comfortable in their hands. Behind them stood Enna. They were the most beautiful group of people Ani had ever seen.

"Unhand the girl," said the man.

"Peace-keepers," Yulan muttered. He straightened himself,

tightening his grip on Ani's wrist. Ishta lowered her other hand from his mouth and held it casually. His touch made her shudder.

"Nothing wrong here," said Yulan. "Ease down those staffs, boys, you have been misinformed. We are friends." They did not react. "She is one of us that lost her way and committed some unruly deeds in your city that we are here to mend. We appreciate your generosity in volunteering to patrol these crowds, but no doubt your services are needed elsewhere. This girl here is under our control."

The man listened calmly to Yulan, then looked to Ani and waited for her to speak.

In her truest Bayern accent, she said, "They've a knife to my back."

The four men acted instantly. In a moment she was loosed from Yulan's and Ishta's hands and placed in the center of the peace-keepers.

"You have no right," said Yulan. His face was red, and he sheathed his dagger with an angry thrust. "This is royal business. We have fair claim here." He drew from his chest an official-looking parchment with the yellow, blue, and red Bayern symbol blazoned at the top.

"She's bleeding, Aldric," said one of the peace-keepers.

Ani pressed her hand to where she could still feel the biting sensation of the dagger and brought it back marked by blood. There was a stir among the men. Ani thought they had communicated an anger among themselves that she could feel pulsating around her, hot as walking out of summer shade.

"Since when," said one, "do Kildenrean yellow boys have the right to cut Bayern women?"

Yulan shook his document in the air. Aldric, the lead peace-keeper, knocked Yulan's hand with the tip of his staff, and the paper fell to the ground.

"Fortunately," said Aldric, "we're not royal guards. They do less to protect our women than a garbage cat. And we don't buy for tin your fine order. We're out here to keep the peace. Keep it or get knocked."

"You're done here," said another to Ani, and he touched her shoulder with a finger.

"Thank you," said Ani. She knew they heard her, but they kept their eyes on the foreigners.

Enna took Ani's hand and they ran across the street. Ani stopped to look back just to see Yulan, trembling from rage, free his long dagger and jump at Aldric. His blade never reached flesh, and his head met the quick end of a practiced quarterstaff—a deathblow. When Yulan crumpled to the ground, Ishta had already fled.

That night at the hall, the workers were hushed and eager, listening with chins in hands and bodies leaning forward. The goose girl had been seized by men at the festival and dragged up the street toward what unknown doom. The goose girl had refused to be forced, and Enna had brought help and freed her. Enna told her story, and Ani spoke as much of her version as she could, leaving out the pigeons and the reasons. They called for the story again. She gave it while holding a wet pack of herbs to the shallow cut in her back—Ideca's orders, to help speed the healing.

"No telling where that scoundrel's nasty blade had been," said Ideca. She clucked over Ani's blue dress, mending the slash with tight, quick stitches and cursing yellow foreigners with pleasant enthusiasm. Her mood came so close to cheery that the workers nearest her watched her as though she were an unpredictable animal.

"It's Enna who called the peace-keepers," said Ani.

They patted Enna's back and tossed her an extra raisin bun, but it was Ani who received a kind of awed regard for the story. A person who had been worth abducting, and been bruised and scarred, but struggled and was saved. They spoke the title of goose girl with a trace of respect.

inter days were short, spent cleaning goose pens, hauling grains, changing water, and clearing the streets of snow on days when the sky let loose its winter passion before settling into placid frigidity. Evenings, Ani roasted nuts, cheese, or pigskin by the hall fire and learned to play sticks and tell-your-neighbor. *This feels like a family*, Ani thought. The cold outside and the warm inside. The usual food on the table, the same jests repeated, and conversation as familiar as looking down at her own hands.

When Ani beat Razo at sticks for the first time, all the watchers cheered, Ani raised her hands and cheered, too, and laughed so freely that her loneliness broke and fell away as though she had never felt it.

Ani told them stories at night, of mother's blood turning children into warriors and mother's love keeping babies tight in lockets, and when she told the stories she no longer visualized her own mother, but thought of Gilsa and the mothers of the workers, and the stories gained new truth and strength.

Then, when the mood quieted into watching the flames repeat themselves along the hearth log and into singing Forest songs that made everyone wistful and hushed, Ani wandered to the window. She saw herself caught in the mirror that the candle and firelight made of the pane. She bent closer and saw the depth behind the pane, that when she shielded the indoor light with her hands and pressed her forehead against the icy glass, the world outside melted from black shadow to blue stone. Night blue cobblestones and stone houses and the high stone wall. The dark blue sky smooth as a river stone. Something was moving there.

She had begun to feel it more profoundly since winter came. The cold deadened the world—froze stones, emptied streets, buried the pasture, and iced the stream. The bare trees stood against the whiteness like rigid ink strokes reaching upward to the dimmed, gray paper sky. In all that stillness there was space to feel that something else moved, something that had eluded her in the busyness of summer and autumn. It was out there, across the stream, or deep beneath her feet, or in her chest. She could not give it a name.

One evening the feeling haunted her. She stood by the window in the hall, listening, sure that if she concentrated harder, she could understand. It was the same feeling that had told her she could do something more when she fled from Ungolad at the palace, and again when Yulan's knife drove her up the street. She wrapped her neck with a borrowed scarf and left the hall.

Ani walked quickly. There was a breeze, and it nipped at her ears and bit at the exposed skin of her wrists and face as though trying to get in. The sudden cold dulled her, and she no longer felt the pulling, but she knew where she was going.

Falada's head was a lighter shape against the dark wall. The moon was low, but its light rarely reached that sinking corner of the city. Ani looked up.

Falada, she said.

She thought of the first time she had heard that name, bleated from the small mouth of a wet, gangly, beautiful colt. He had been born with his own name on his tongue.

Falada, she said.

She remembered her aunt saying Ani had been born with the first word of a language on her own tongue and did not open her eyes for three days with the effort of trying to taste it. Her aunt had sung her a song of waiting so that she would open her eyes and be patient until the day she could learn that new tongue. Remembering that promise awoke anew the desire to discover it at last.

Falada, she said.

She remembered the last word Falada had spoken to her, in the forest, when she had lost the handkerchief and turned her back to the river. *Princess*, he had said. He had always called her Princess. She missed him sorely and strained to hear him again, not with her ears, but with that part of her inside where his voice had always come, and from where she had been able to respond.

Falada, she said.

And because she was straining, she heard the brush of that final word again.

Princess.

The resonance of Falada's voice came softly, an echo of what was once spoken, like the voice of the sea from a shell. They faced each other thus in silent conversation, the shivering once princess and the mounted head of her steed, dead speaking with dead.

A breeze wound up her skirt, touched her cheek, and chilled her where tears had left wetness. Ani wiped her cheeks and reached for a second time with her mind to hear herself named, yearning for the comfort of Falada's voice.

Falada, she said.

Princess.

Ani started. She had been expecting to hear that word, but this time the tone did not carry the distant echo of Falada. A new voice.

She struggled to hear once more.

The winter breeze still brushed against her cheek, and again she heard her name—*Princess*—and what had laid on her tongue since the morning of her birth now loosened.

Ani pulled her scarf tighter and shivered. *It is true after all. Even the wind has a language.*

The voice of the wind entered that same place inside her

where she had always heard Falada's, though its tones were unlike. It was an icy finger of thought, a rush of words that expected no response, as indifferent to her as to a tree. It was beautiful. There in the cold, blue shadow of winter night, Ani cried for Falada, and for the beauty of the language of the wind, and for the reminder of who she was.

Princess. Ani felt the wind and heard it identify her again. Then it lifted from her skin and slipped through the gate and out into the open pasture.

Ani returned every day. Conrad thought she visited that spot to check if the snow ever lifted enough from the pasture to allow grazing for the geese. But she stood before that portal and never noticed the winter world that lay on the other side. She looked up, spoke her horse's name, and strained to hear the response.

Falada.

Princess.

And when a breeze touched her skin, in place of the memory of Falada's last word, she heard the wind call her Princess.

She longed to talk to Falada in truth, to tell him that she had been lost in the Forest and that she had not meant to leave him. That she had tried. She wanted to say that the guards had seen her, chased her across the palace grounds and once at a festival, but she had begged help from strangers and birds and from a friend, and been freed. Ani smiled to herself, remembering that Falada in life would not have concerned himself much about any of the doings of people. But he would have listened. And he would have flicked her with his tail and nibbled on her hair to cheer her up.

She wanted to tell him how his last word resonated from the dead, and when all living things were dimmed by winter, she was able to hear it, and hearing it again taught her how to hear the wind.

She wanted to ask him if horses understood the wind.

His glass eyes looked at nothing. His mane was stiff, glued by the knacker to sit perfectly smooth in wind or still-ness. She knew he was gone, that what she heard was only an echo. But that echo had reminded her how to listen deeper than her bones, to listen for what no one else heard. And as the days passed, and she learned how to listen, when the wind touched her skin she began to hear much more than just her name.

It was a few weeks after wintermoon, and the days were beginning to stretch themselves out like a cat that is tired of sleeping. The sun burned holes into the frost and ice in a brief abeyance from winter, and for a few days the patches of gray winter grass livened into green. Conrad and Ani took advantage of the window of warmth and herded the geese into the pasture for the afternoon. The geese shook their feathers in the sun and ran from the arch to the pasture, waddling dangerously in their haste and honking that though winter was not over yet, at least there were green things to eat again. Ani turned to Conrad to laugh, but his expression muted her.

Conrad had been in a foul mood of late. One winter night he had told other workers, in mocking tones, how Ani believed she could speak to the geese. But instead of laughing at her, Enna and the other chicken-keepers began to ask her advice, and soon even Razo pleaded help with a naughty magpie who pestered his prize ram. Ani noticed now that whenever one of the keepers came to her with a question, Conrad sat back and watched her darkly.

"Don't mind Conrad," Enna had said. "Back home, he's the youngest of seven kids. I suspect the geese're all he's ever had of his own and he's jealous of you. He's just a boy, and fifteen, and needs to grow up. Give him time."

After the geese passed under the arch, Ani stopped and looked up. She spoke Falada's name and received her own, and the wind that came up off the stream touched her. *Stream*, it spoke. *Cold, ice, geese moving toward stream. Stones. Princess.* She was filled with the haunting, wonderful mystery of its language, and she stood enthralled, sensing the words it spoke.

"The wind. I can hear, but I can't speak."

"What?" Conrad was watching her, his lips tucked out in a cautious frown.

Ani looked away self-consciously. "I wasn't talking to you."

"Who then? The horse head?"

She shrugged and passed through the gate. Conrad followed without a word. It was not unusual for Conrad to spend a day in silence, but that day he did not visit his friends in near pastures or wander into the wood. He was always nearby, watching. When the afternoon clouded over, he stood and began to herd the geese, then stopped.

"Why do I bother? They respond to you and your little noises like you're their mother. You might as well gather your own little goslings."

He took his staff and strode off toward the city.

Conrad continued to be sullen. On the days when sufficient sun broke through the winter sky to be out of doors, Conrad always sat close enough to the beech tree to stay in Ani's view. Though she longed to listen to the wind and try to speak back, his stare stopped her.

"She's not normal," Ani heard Conrad say to Razo as she passed by his open door on the way to the hall. "She stands under that horse head like he's looking at her, and it's not that she's so good with the geese, but she actually thinks she's talking to them. Someone like that shouldn't be allowed to keep the king's geese."

"Ah, sit on it, Conrad," said Razo. "Everyone thinks you're green because she's a better goose-keeper than you."

"I am not." He sounded like a little boy on the brink of a tantrum.

The next morning dawned icy. Ani had taken her turn at the bathhouse the night before, and she woke shivering, her hair still wet on her pillow. She stayed in her room all morning, trying to comb out the coldness. When near-noon arrived with enough sun to take out the geese, Ani stuffed her damp locks into her hat and met Conrad.

She stood near her tree most of the day, walking in circles to warm her blood, listening to the wind as it spoke through the beech branches of cold that was still to come before the world brightened into spring.

Ani marveled at the words that she began to hear so clearly now. It was nothing like learning bird speech, listening to the sounds, watching the movements, and practicing again and again to get it just right. Not like horse speech, that came slowly and easily as the colt grew, words like a voice in her mind, clear as her own thoughts. The wind blew understanding. It spoke in images, repeating where it had been with each new touch. It required concentration to hear it and to untangle the images into meanings.

A breeze lifted up to the beech from the woods beyond the stream, rustling of evergreens, owls, and deer and a private spot not too distant where sunlight streaked through the trees. Ani shivered, threw a glance at Conrad, who sat on a stone glumly watching the clouds, and told the geese to stay by the pond. She hoped they would obey.

Ani hopped across a narrow waist of the stream and found the little space, a small room of warmth inside a birch copse. She sat on a rock, took off her hat, and let her hair fall loose. She scratched her head with a pleased scowl, closed her eyes, and let the sun soak up the dampness and cold, willing winter to drain out of her bones.

An errant breeze sneaked through the trees and touched her bare neck, whispering of what it had seen—a fox, a pine, a secret spring. Ani considered the breeze by her ear, then thought of her hair long and damp at her back and, with a sentiment, suggested it take that path.

Ani opened her eyes, her muscles tight in surprise and wonder. The breeze moved between her neck and her hair, wrapping itself around her locks like ivy on an oak and passing among the hairs delicately, lifting them one by one, blowing on a strand like a careful maid dusting. Ani felt the wetness loosened and taken into the air. She sat very still, afraid to think or move and lose the wonder. Somehow, she had spoken to the wind.

"Yellow girl."

She stood and whirled around. Conrad was standing between the trees. His eyes were on her hair. With a start, she put a hand to her head and felt the hairs still tossed on the breeze, though the air around her was still.

"What are you?" he said.

Ani hurriedly wrapped her dried hair around her head and secured it with her hat. She spoke silently to the breeze that still plucked at her hat ribbon, suggesting a new course for it to wander. It snaked down her arm and left the copse.

"The goose girl," she said.

Conrad laughed. "You don't come from here. You aren't natural."

"Conrad, don't say anything to anyone about my hair. If you understood—"

"It's not fair. They think you're the queen of geese or something and I'm just a dumb boy who couldn't do it by himself. But you're not even one of us."

He ran back to the pasture.

That night, a light snow fell. The mood in the hall was gloomy as the workers contemplated potatoes like warmed rocks, skimmed milk, and wrinkled, winter apples dry as cork. No cheese, no sugar for sweet breads, and no winter-moon to look forward to. The wind shook the windowpanes. Spring seemed as far away as the ocean.

The workers began to talk of home, exchanging stories of the hopelessness of pulling a livelihood out of the ever-greens and ferns and spongy soil. There had been news of sick siblings last marketday. There were widowed mothers and widower fathers and donkeys too old to keep pulling a cart to market.

"My wages are a last chance," said Razo, his head bowed as he contemplated the fleabites on his arm. "Of course, they have been now for three years."

Some chuckled, nodding their heads.

"I make more chasing sheep," said one boy, "than my da pulls in all year."

"I think the marketgoers buy my ma's weed hats out of pity."

"I know about that. You've seen our family's rugs."

Bettin pulled chicken feathers from Enna's hair. "One winter harder than this one, and they'll have to leave the house and come to the city."

All grew quiet at that. Images of the city passed as a collective thought, houses shoved in any corner, stories piled on top of wobbly stories, the whole place stinking and sweltering in the summer, children playing in the streets, splashing in downhill trickles of dirty water. Ani shuddered. The city was as beautiful as a birthday cake from afar. It was not so friendly when one was out of luck. She glanced out the window toward her little room. It had never felt like a home, but it felt safer than any place she had known.

Maybe after I return to Kildenree and all is set to right, she thought, *I'll come back here again and be queen after all.* She had no desire to wed the boy prince she had seen at wintermoon, but as queen she could do something to better the ugliness she had seen in the city. *And perhaps,* she thought wryly, *by the time I come back he might've grown up some.*

"Isi, what does your family sell?" said a girl next to Ani. Her clothes emanated clover and clean animal.

"I don't know what they're doing now," said Ani.

Conrad leaned back, put his boots on the table with two thuds, and laughed roughly.

"You don't know what they're doing now," he said. "Very good."

The attention spun to him. Ani held her breath.

"You know, Conrad," said Razo, knocking Conrad's feet off the table, "lately you've come close to being a genuine imbecile."

"What? She's fooled you all? Your beloved goose girl's not from the Forest. She's not from here at all." His voice drove higher, mocking. "Oh, you've such milky skin. Your eyes're almost green. What's wrong with my duck, goose girl? What's the matter with this pig? Go ask the stuffed horse when it's going to rain next."

"Conrad," said Ani, "this isn't going to help. Please."

He looked around as though wishing that someone would come to his side. "I can't believe no one else sees it. She's not one of us. She's been playing us all along. I've seen her out there combing her hair down to her knees like a precious little queen. She's the one those guards're looking for."

He stood up, and Ani started back.

"She's a yellow girl," he said.

The workers were silent, staring at her, the room tense as a saddled stallion.

"Isi," said someone.

Ani thought, *I'd best do something or they'll hang me on a wall like*

Falada. She stood up.

"What you're saying isn't right. I'm sorry I've come here and made you think I've taken what was yours, but you don't have to make everyone hate me for them to like you."

"Yeah, so shut it, Conrad," said Enna.

Ani winced. "Enna means that you should let this go, all right? None of us wants to choose sides in this hall."

Conrad ignored her. "You don't know, Enna. I've seen her. . . ."

"So've I," said Enna. "So just drop your ugly jealousies and eat your cold potato before I cram it in your gullet."

Conrad's face burned red, and he slammed his fist on the table. Razo and Beier stepped up beside him and gently held his arms. Conrad flinched but kept his eyes on Ani.

"Then tell me, Enna, why she's always hiding. Always with a hat or scarf. Why doesn't she just take off that scarf now and prove it?"

"Yes, Enna, you know me. Tell them." Ani looked at Enna and waited for her to speak. It felt good to take this risk and to trust another person again. But when Enna looked up, her eyes were sad and mouth drawn. *Oh no*, thought Ani, panic twisting her stomach, *I was wrong to trust her. She's going to betray me.*

"Come on, then, Enna," said Razo, "what've you got to say? Why not let Ani just take off her scarf and prove it so we can get Conrad to bed? I think it's plain that the city's getting into his head this winter."

"You sops." Enna sighed painfully, and her gaze could barely be raised to Ani's, as though weighted by shame. "I'm sorry, Isi, but I think they should know." She sighed again. "Isi's hair got burned off in a fire just before she came here. She's embarrassed, poor duck. And I'm not going to let her take off her hat just to put Conrad straight."

Ani widened her eyes and looked down, masking an unexpected desire to laugh. Enna put a protective hand on her shoulder, and the workers began to avert their eyes and poke at their cold potatoes with sudden interest.

Conrad stood still a moment, wavering between action and anger. "I'll prove it," he said. No one responded. He stomped out of the hall.

Ani touched Enna's hand on her shoulder.

"How many times'll you save me?" she whispered.

"If you were a better liar, I wouldn't have to," said Enna.

"I know, I know, I'll have to work on it. But I knew you'd be good enough for both of us." Her smile tightened. "He saw me with my hair down, Enna."

"No one'll believe him. Who's he going to tell? Let's just keep you safe until we can get you on your way come spring. Until then, I'm glad you'll let me be your guard goose."

It was sunny the next day, and the next, and Ani herded the geese to the pasture. Conrad followed from a ways behind and shouted mock encouragement.

"Nicely done, goose girl."

"Keep them together, there."

"Watch that gander, goose girl, that he doesn't bite your precious rump."

She wandered the pasture, checking for the occasional egg the geese would lay by the pond or hidden in the arc of river birch roots. Of a sudden he stood before her. She held her staff in front of her.

"You've got to leave me alone," she said. "I'm sorry I can't tell the truth to the others. I can't. I wish I could."

"Give me a strand of your hair." He stepped toward her, his hands outstretched.

"Don't touch me," she said.

A bit of wind slipped off her hat ribbon and grazed against his chin. She saw goose bumps rise on his neck.

"Leave me be, and I promise before long you won't have to see me anymore."

He shook his head but backed away.

The next afternoon, Ani looked up from reading one of Geric's books to find herself alone. Conrad was nowhere in sight. She felt calmness settle into her like rain dropped from the beech. *At last*, she thought, *he's tired of watching me and gone away.* The geese, happily paired and foraging for fresh plants, ignored her presence. A spot of sun broke through the sky and cast shadows of the branches on the ground around her, a map of forking roads.

She took off her hat and scratched her scalp and neck. She rarely uncovered her hair, even when no person was near enough to see, but she felt restlessly safe, and tired of bindings, and ready to make things happen. A breeze rapped on her forehead, and Ani encouraged it to go down, lift up the tips of her hair off the ground, and tickle them in the air.

She had not communicated with the wind in many days, conscious always of Conrad's gaze. The exercise delighted her. Tendrils of wind rose up her arms like candle smoke in still air, sought out the roots of her hair, and wound through them. She practiced sending the wind this way and that, noting that it did not always respond. Sometimes it was already set on one course and would not change. Sometimes it was too thin and slow to do more than loosen into still air, or so strong that it barely touched her skin before pushing itself away. Unlike a bird or horse, the wind was passionless; not thoughtful or playful, but often persuadable.

The shadow of the tree darkened. She saw the shadow of a hand reach toward her wind-lifted hair. Ani grouped the wind that touched her into one thought and begged it to fly away, behind her, toward the lunging shadow. She felt it leave her skin.

She turned to see Conrad chase his orange cap away from the tree. The breeze tossed the cap farther, always ahead, always a little faster. Ani watched him run and braided her wind-combed hair into a tight hoop on top of her head like a crown of gold. By the time Conrad caught his cap off the upper branches of the far pasture hedge and strode back again, Ani had replaced her hat with the ribbon firmly tied and was reading again. She could not keep her smile down.

"You're a demon, girl," he said.

"Goose girl," she said.

After that day, Conrad would not stand so near that she could put out her arm and touch him. When the workers in the hall made clear that they did not care to listen to his grumbling, he sat alone, holding sticks in the fire until they smoked and turned black.

Ani placed her raisin bun beside him. Conrad took it and ate it with a kind of acknowledged defeat, but when he glanced up, she saw that his boyish face was still disturbed by lines of anger.

wo months from wintermoon dawned brightly, and the workers, sequestered for over a week by icy rain and winds, left their rooms and stretched in the sunlight, glad for one morning to be taking their animals out to the fields again. The geese were as anxious as Ani to leave shelter and get soil beneath their feet, and they squawked cheerfully all the way.

She stopped in the shadowy corner of the wall and greeted Falada. His mane was still damp, though his hide fared well in the wild weather. His glass eyes looked indifferently at the stones of the city.

Falada, she said.

Princess.

Conrad was still disregarding her presence. Occasionally he dropped his despondency enough to tease the geese, chasing them for tail feathers or honking nonsensically. He stayed by the wall that morning, leaning against the gateway and combing his ragged, self-cut hair with his fingers.

Ani sat under the beech and listened to the wind. It sought out trees, running around their trunks and weaving through their branches, the way a cat arches under a hand, seeking a good scratch. When it touched her skin, she could feel the rumbling, wispy voice that let images of its wanderings whisper out into sound. Not speaking to her, but just speaking, its existence alone a language.

A spider's web, sang the wind, *the stream, the stream, the tattered cattails of autumn, the slender birch trunks, the wood. Men in the wood. Five men in the wood. Coming toward the stream, toward the geese and the beech and the princess.*

Ani stood up, pulling on a cool, gray branch to support her weight. Five men in the wood. No image of horses came on the wind, so they could not be nobles coming back from a predawn ride. Five was too many to be workers away from their keeps. She strained her sight toward the dark copses and light spots across the stream, looking for movement. A wild pheasant beat its wings, an agonizing sound against the tense silence. Nothing else.

Then she spotted figures, dark, crouched, moving from one shadow to the next. They stopped.

"Conrad," she said, afraid to shout. He did not look up from his musings by the pasture archway. "Conrad." She did not know if he could hear her or if he ignored her.

She looked back, and the figures were moving again, nearing the line of birches that bordered the stream banks. Again, they stopped. She saw a glint of metal winking like an ominous star.

Danger, Ani told the geese. *Danger by the stream.*

She used the word for "bear," a beast of size and fear, not "dog" or "cat," which the ganders would be tempted to turn and face. As one, the birds scurried away from the stream, making a group like a pond of milk in the middle of the pasture. Conrad looked to the noise of forty-eight geese honking and flapping their wings in ado. His eyes lifted to the stream, and when he saw, he turned into the arch and disappeared.

Ani ran to the head of the flock and placed herself between her charges and the approaching men. They wore leather of different makes and different animals, mismatched vests, jerkins, caps, and leggings, and leather-sheathed knives. Three bore poles tipped with wire loops, perfect for hooking goosenecks, and two dragged large, empty sacks. There was no temper in their miens. They met Ani's eyes and did not slow their advance.

"These geese aren't for you," said Ani.

One grunted. They were nearer.

"These're the king's geese. I won't let you take them."

One acknowledged her. "Move aside, goose girl, or we'll have to knock you aside."

Ani stood firm and held her crook with both hands. She felt as ridiculous as a gander facing a bear, but she did not move. She had decided that she would not run. The geese squawked behind her.

The first man reached her. He slammed his pole down on her and cracked her staff in two with a sound like near thunder. Her knees folded, and she fell to the ground.

Run, she told the geese.

They did not run. The ganders had circled the geese and made terrific noises of defense, their heads lowered and menacing. The men paid no mind. With their long poles they snared the birds by the necks and pulled them in like fish on a line, bagging them without a bite. Ani watched. Her face was pressed to the ground. One of the thieves stood above her and held the end of his staff to her throat. She swallowed against the pressure that made her dizzy and stomach sick. There was a creeper breeze nosing around the ground. It crawled over her arm and bare hands.

Up there, she urged, *that man, his hat, something.*

The breeze spiraled up to the man, probing his head with its brisk fingers, and slipped the cap off his head with a brief gust. The hat fell to the ground. The thief glanced down, unconcerned. The geese were honking anger and fear as nearly a fourth of their number was stuffed into the bags.

Ani concentrated on all the air that stirred on her skin, willing it to come together. Passing breezes joined, curious, wrapped together like crude wool folding into a ball. *More*, Ani pleaded. The breezes built up to a wind, flowing over her and on the grass in an ardent circle, building, like a finger-spun whirlpool in still water, like a beast pacing before attack.

"Let me go," said Ani. Her voice barely escaped the force on her throat. "These are the king's geese. They're protected."

The man did not glance at his prisoner, but he frowned slightly.

The circle of wind felt restless now, *swooshing* around her head, picking at the tiny hairs on her face and hands, waiting for an idea to lead it. She gave it a suggestion to move away a little and tear into the ground. It followed. Still making contact with her outstretched hand, the mob of wind swirled and bit at the ground, pulling loose dirt and pebbles into its body until it looked to be a short, dark creature spinning on itself. The thief heard gusting and turned his eyes, then his head, then his whole self, unbelieving and unexpectedly afraid.

"Libert, Odlef, look, will you," he said.

The men turned their backs on the geese and saw dirt-filled wind grown as tall and wide as the beech at its back.

"A trick," said one. "A sorcerer's shabby trick."

"A trick," said another. His face betrayed honest dread.

Ani's thought pushed the wind from the ground to hit the first man in the face. His eyes filled with dirt, his cheeks were pelted with small rocks, stinging like bees. He dropped his pole and threw his arms around his head.

The wind continued forward and reached the other four, rushing at their eyes, swarming around them, pushing them together as though they were the prey caught in a sack. The geese exploded into an attack, biting the thieves' ankles and calves below the isolated windstorm. The men, blinded by dust, confused the wind and the geese until it all seemed one monster, screaming in their ears, shoving them with stinging hands and biting their legs. More birds escaped from the forsaken sacks and attacked. The men, swatting at nothing like old women afraid of wasps, fled the pasture at a run. By the time they reached the stream, they had outpaced the geese and the wind had lost its ammunition and dispersed into wisps, but they still ran.

Ani sat up slowly, watching until the wood shadows swallowed sight of their retreat. Her skin tingled. Three poles and two inert sacks lay on the ground like battle corpses. The geese ran in circles and toward the stream, some posted on the near shore barking at the woods while others trumpeted victory. She rubbed her sore neck but honked happily with her geese.

The sound of running boots jerked her to her feet. Conrad raced through the arch, followed by three of the boys who worked in the field to the north. They halted when they saw Ani standing alone, dozens of angry geese running around and dozens shouting at the stream. They glanced at the broken crook that lay at her feet.

"Where are they?" said Conrad. He saw the goose-nabbing poles and bags, and relief crossed his face at the evidence that he had not fetched the other boys for nothing.

"Gone." Ani laughed deep in her chest, wondering how

she might explain.

"Your staff," said the boy named Sifrid. He picked up the two pieces and held them as testimony to the others. "You were attacked."

"Yes," she said. They waited, and she cleared her throat. "I defended myself, and then the geese chased them away."

All four boys stared at her, their mouths slightly open.

"How, how many were there?" said one.

"Five," she said.

"Uh-huh."

One of the boys grinned. "The goose girl drove off the thieves. How about that?"

Another laughed good-naturedly and gripped his shepherd's crook. "I thought I'd have to fight when Conrad came running with tales of leather-donned men prowling in the wood. Thanks for saving me a sweat." He punched her lightly on the arm.

"You're hurt," said Sifrid, pointing at her throat.

"I'm all right." She could feel her heart beating on the spot where the thief's pole had held her to the ground.

"We'd best get back in case the thieves decide to swallow their first defeat and try another keeper's flock."

"If they attack, we'll come get you."

"Yes, we'll yell, 'Help, help us, goose girl, and bring the Terrifying Legion of Warrior-Geese.'"

"How about the Bandits of a Thousand Feathers?"

The three jogged away, giddy, jawing over the event and

planning to stop briefly at the hall to recount the story to Mistress Ideca.

"Thanks for getting help, Conrad," said Ani. "I thought at first that you'd left me alone."

"I'm no coward," said Conrad.

"Of course not, that's not what I meant." Ani shook her head in frustration. She could understand the wind and speak with birds, but humans still eluded her. That was her mother's gift, after all. And Selia's.

"I would've faced them," said Conrad.

Ani nodded earnestly, hoping to convey her good faith in him. He shrugged, leaned against the archway, and inspected his boots for holes. The geese were still squawking. Ani gathered them in with words of safety and calm.

When the clouds blotted out the blue of the sky and the air shivered with an early spring chill, Ani took the geese in. As she opened the door to the hall, a cheer erupted and fists banged on the tables. Sifrid held up the pieces of her broken staff as a symbol of the battle. Mistress Ideca examined her neck and prescribed a cool pack. Though Ideca did not smile, she did not grumble, either. Ani declined to relate what had happened, so the cow and sheep boys stepped forward to relay their version, embellishing the parts they had not seen.

"And then the goose girl knocked two down with her staff, a careful blow to the head, and the second head. Bam, crack. The third was a giant man grown in the Bavara

Mountains on bear meat and raw eggs, and he crushed her staff with his fist."

The listeners responded with feigned and jovial gasps of horror. Ani laughed behind her hands. When she looked up again, she saw Conrad in a far corner. His face was serious and sad.

"So the goose girl," said Sifrid, "she tossed aside the broken weapon, and grabbed her opponent by his greasy hair and hit him with her own head right between the eyes. Bam. Down he fell, dumb as a dead tree, and shook the ground. With a word, she commanded her goose army to drive the scum from their land, and they followed their leader, trumpeting triumphantly."

There was laughter and applause, and four lads were sent to the pasture to retrieve the villains' poles and bags for more mementos. Two did not return until much later and entered the hall not with poles, but with Tatto the pageboy.

"The king's heard of the strife for the protection of his geese," said Tatto, "and he wishes to hear the story and thank those involved."

The workers cheered. Ani stayed seated. Her face felt cold.

"I, I can't go," she said.

"Oh, come on, Isi," said Sifrid, "go brag a little."

"No, no, really I can't."

Razo stomped his foot. "You're not so shy as you let us think when you first got here. You can face a king. He's just a man in a crown who eats potatoes and has gas."

"I bet he doesn't eat cold potatoes," said Bettin.

"Well, maybe not *cold* potatoes," said Razo, "but I'd bet my fist he's as gassy as Beier."

"Nobody's as gassy as Beier," said Sifrid, dodging Beier's shove.

"Guess Isi'll have to find out for herself when she goes to see the king, won't you?" said Razo.

Ani could see the workers were not going to let her sneak out of this. She spotted Conrad in the corner, pretending indifference to the commotion, and she went to him.

"Will you come?" she said.

He shrugged and stood up.

They followed Tatto out of the hall, encouraged from behind by the cheers of the workers. When they had walked a block, Ani stopped.

"I'm not going," said Ani. "I can't go. I was hoping, Conrad, that you'd go in my stead."

Tatto looked at her wide-eyed, but Conrad did not respond.

"Please," she said. "You were involved, and you would've fought them off yourself, but that you were being wise. Don't even mention me. The story's yours. Tell it how you will."

Tatto shook his head. "Aren't you the one what drove them off?"

"They don't know that. What does it matter? Besides,

Conrad deserves some credit. I can't go to the palace. I just can't."

In only two months she would have enough money and the weather would be right for a journey back to Kildenree. At this point, she knew it would be wise just to stay out of sight. Conrad shrugged and walked away with long, growing-boy strides, Tatto running after him. Ani watched their departing figures wane, two boys in a large city, and wondered if she erred in not joining them.

In her fancy she imagined being lauded before the court, and Geric admiring her bravery and looking at her as he used to, and the king insisting on knowing her history and believing her when she told it, banishing Selia and the others far away and welcoming Ani home. *That's how it would end*, she thought, *if it were a bed-tale.* But she knew it was useless to hope for such an outcome. If ever she was to walk into that palace without fearing for her life, she must first take the long road back to Kildenree and plead the aid of her mother.

If, after all that, the betrothal still stood, Ani realized she would not be sorry to return to Bayern. She did not look forward to the dim-looking boy prince as a husband and a forced marriage possibly devoid of affection, but being Bayern's queen had its appeal, and besides, the city was truly beginning to feel like home.

❧

Ani lay on her bed and read the end of the Bayern history by the evening light. She closed the book and put her cheek against it. There was still an odor of a library on it, of dust, leather, binding glue, and old paper, one book carrying the smell of hundreds. She opened the front cover and found Geric's name scratched into the first page with too watery ink, the signature of a small boy. She smiled to herself to imagine Geric at eight, with the round face of youth and impatient curiosity. She ran her fingers over the mark of his name.

Enna rapped on her door and entered. Ani shut the book guiltily.

"I thought you'd be in here. The boys've returned." She examined Ani's face. "What's the matter? You're upset?"

"Huh? Oh, no. Well, I guess, a little. I was just lovesick, a bit."

"Ah."

"But I'm recovered." She put the book down emphatically. "He's not mine, never was. Well, for a spell he brought me picnics and books to pass time, and once flowers, though they lost their petals in the rain. He even offered to give me a horse, a very nice one, really, and mistook me for a lady."

"You are a lady," said Enna.

"But that's beside the point, because I wasn't then, am not now, but he still saw me that way, as though he saw me, and not the goose girl boots, and not a princess crown. He was—he's beautiful, enough to make me sigh like a lovesick nurse-mary. He's a guard, to the prince himself, actually, and much too close to Selia for my own liking, and besides, he doesn't love me, so there it is."

Ani shrugged her shoulders with resignation and gave a quick nod as though dismissing the subject. Enna tried to smile at her, but her dark eyebrows were pinched together.

"Enna, you're worried."

Enna nodded. "I think that you should come hear what Tatto's telling the others."

When they entered the hall, Tatto was seated grandly on the end of a table, and the attention of the workers was unusually and unquestioningly his.

". . . and it's all set for spring, once the pass snows melt. It's as sure as a copper's copper, says my da."

"If it's true, peacock, why would they tell you?" said Beier.

Tatto sniffed. "Common knowledge. Rumor can't get there before the war, anyhow."

"War?" said Ani.

"With Kildenree," said Enna.

"What do you mean, Tatto? Why would Bayern attack Kildenree?"

"It's the other way 'round," said Conrad. He was looking at her shrewdly. She glanced away.

"Exactly." Tatto nodded. "Word's out they mean to attack us, have been planning it for years. But we've got the mountain pass road just about finished, and we'll be there before they can get us. I guess that princess, the yellow girl, was a decoy, sent to marry the prince to pretend all's well. But she went against those rough yellows and told the king about the war because she likes Bayern and doesn't like how evil her people are, or something like that."

"The princess," said Ani. "The news that Kildenree's attacking Bayern came from the princess. And the king believes her?"

Razo shrugged. "I heard some rumors this winter about Kildenree and their plans."

"This's her plan," Ani whispered to Enna, gripping her shoulders urgently. "This's her way of sealing her secret."

"Don't worry, Isi," said Tatto. "Da says our army'll crush them like a grape between fingers."

"Yes, he's right," said Ani. "They will."

"I say about time," said one of the sheep boys. "We haven't had a good war since my da was a boy."

"Not that we'll see any of it," said Sifrid.

"Maybe," said Razo, "if it's big enough, maybe they'll need the Forest boys, and we'll all be given javelins and shields and join the king's army and come home warrior champions to crowds of swooning city girls."

Many laughed, though there was hope in the laugh. Someone started a war song, and most of the boys and some girls joined in. "The valley quakes, the long road calls—the javelins march, the young men march, the new bloods march where kings command. The mountain shakes, the mighty falls—and warriors march, the brave men march, the bloodied march with sword in hand."

Ani watched them, and every word of the song felt like the blow of a hammer. The hall shook with their voices. Then suddenly the singers stopped, leaving the silence heavy with images of Forest boys as men and warriors. The fire in the hearth popped and flamed.

That night, Ani could not sleep, could not even lie down. She paced in her tiny room, a new plan taking uneasy form. She had told Enna once, "Even if some of the workers were willing to go to battle on this, I don't think it would be right to endanger their lives just to get back my name." But now there was war. This was no longer her battle, not just a spat between two former friends or bad blood among country-men. Now Selia was pulling all Bayern into her viciousness. The massacre in the Forest had not been one separate, bru-tal act—it was the first brawl in Selia's personal war for power. And Ani was the only person with the knowledge to stop it.

Tomorrow, she would tell the workers the truth and beg them for their aid. With a guard of friends, she had a chance of making it to the king alive, and there she would have to tell her tale. The thought of exposing herself like that was frightening. She had no evidence, just her yellow hair and her story. But Selia had a story, too, and false witnesses, and behind it all the convincing power of people-speaking.

The squeezing in her stomach would not allow her to sleep that night. She walked off restlessness by striding to the goose pens. Jok and his mate nestled near the gate, and he raised his head when she entered.

Ani greeted him and sat for a moment, wondering at the beauty of white birds in the dark. Jok nuzzled his mate sleepily, and the goose prodded his feathers with her beak.

I am alone, Ani said to Jok. *Come rest the night in my room.*

The two birds followed her, silent but for tiny, distinct flaps on the cobblestones. The walk was not far, and soon the pair nested in a disarrangement of her blanket, their stout bodies filling most of the space. Ani sat beside them awhile, a hand on the warmth of their feathers. Then she paced again. There was no room for her in the bed, and she did not care. She mumbled to herself—war, Selia, wind, the king, and war.

Her cheeks were hot from worry and movement, and she sat below her window, her back to the street, and let the crack under the door move air over her hand and up to her face.

She awoke perhaps an hour later. She was lying on the hard cobblestones of her floor, her cheek resting on her outstretched arm and her loose hair over her face. There was another noise coming from outside. The first noise had awakened her. She held perfectly still and listened.

The creak of a boot sole. A small stone freed from its mortar by a careless foot. A hushed, heavy breath. Ani, moving only her eyes, glanced up to her little table where sat the mirror Enna had given her at wintermoon. Its face tilted toward the window, toward the slit in her curtains where they never fully closed. Stooped outside was a form, one eye peering in, a bit of cheek, part of a long, pale braid.

The door opened slowly, the noise as slight as the breath of a sleeping bird. Ani did not move. Nothing seemed clear, as though she were still sleeping and seeing the strange images in a fragmented dream. The door opened wide, separating the corner where she lay from the intruder. Ani rose slowly to her feet. The rustling of her skirt was masked by his step. *His step*, she thought. *His. Ungolad.*

As the name entered her mind, fear jolted through her frame and woke her blood and widened her eyes. She could see his back now and the glint on the tip of his bare dagger. He crept toward the bed where two geese slept, indistinct pale shapes in the dark blanket. A too small draft curled around her ankle. No way out. The window was sealed. She would have to slip out the door.

Ani took a step. And another. Another. She held her skirt in her right hand, softly, to keep it from touching the door. Her toe crossed the soft line of moonlight that fell through the doorway. He was at the bed. His hand touched the blanket. Ani took another step and entered the light of night.

The two geese squawked when roused by a stranger's hand. Ani started and then ran. She heard Ungolad curse and the trumpeting calls of the geese—*attack, enemy, danger, bite, beat, protect!* Her boots pounded against the stones, and the impact beat her joints and shook her vision. The horrible thuds of boots on rock echoed behind her. She thought she heard doors opening to the right, and still, farther behind now, the honking of geese. For months she had been practicing fleeing from Ungolad in her nightmares. Now she could think of nothing but how to run.

She ran a path she knew, the easy road, past the settlements, not up to the pens but down, the street leaning toward the city wall. The west gate. Thud, thud, thud came the running behind her, always the sounds getting closer together, always the sounds getting closer. She could hear his breathing now, hard in his throat. Her muscles were trembling. She waited to feel his hand grasp her neck or spring for her legs and pull her down, a fox on a hen. The west gate rose before her, the empty socket of stone that spilled into the pasture, the wood, the Forest. Above its eye, the white blue semblance of Falada, guardian of the gateway. Ani looked up. The footsteps behind missed a beat. He leapt for her, to catch her before the city ended. A touch.

Falada, she said.

Something happened. Like lightning at her back. Like a beast tearing out her side. Like a touch of heat exploded into flame. She cried out, and her voice sounded animal in her throat, quiet and strange and frightful. It was pain. She put a word to it, and her feet stumbled.

His dagger had caught her back.

The footsteps behind her did not resume. She heard his body hit the ground with a grunt. He had leapt too far to meet her with his knife and must have fallen. *But,* she thought, *he will be there when I fall as well.* The thought was as inevitable as her stumbling feet.

Princess, said Falada.

Her feet found stones, and she kept running.

She ran from stone to grass, and the lower pitch of running startled her, and she thought he ran behind her still, so she ran still faster, down the pasture, propelled by the pain in her back as though it were her pursuer pushing her forward. She leapt over the stream and looked back to see his form racing down the hill.

There was a dry storm crackling in clouds darker than the sky. A stab of lightning briefly lit the face of the north horizon. The world seemed blacker at its departure. The pasture was restless with winds, tumbling over one another like bears at play, knocking against trees so hard that their leaves shook like knees. It swirled around her, a hundred different winds at once, pouncing on her shoulders, thumping against her back, hunching her shoulders against its force. And it stayed near, as though it sensed images of its own language like salt on her skin.

The dark figure was coming toward her. With every touch of air on her skin, with the sting in her back, with her mind that rolled over itself like the storm, she bade the wind strike. She felt the rush, and then stillness. The figure fell hard to the ground and turned over twice. He stayed down, arms over his head, crouched low as a stone, hiding from the wind that ripped at his clothes and hair. Ani turned to the woods and ran. She did not look back again.

The trees turned to wood and the wood to deeper wood, and she took no heed of where she ran, but away. To breathe was agonizing, yet she could not get enough air. She thought perhaps the running would go on the length of a forest, the length of a kingdom, the length of a world. When she came to the wall that closed in the royal woods and pastures, she climbed it without thought. It was low on her side and dropped two men's height on the far. She jumped down, hit the ground, and, stunned out of breath, lay painfully still.

The moaning noises of the woods. The buzz of a night bug's flight. An owl. No human sounds. If a guard patrolled the wall this far in the woods, he was not near. Ani told herself to stand before a guard returned, before Ungolad leaned over the wall, looked down on her, and smiled, predator at prey. A breeze that roamed the ground along the wall passed over her neck. She tried to calm her heart and clear the fear from her head enough to listen. There were no human images in its speech. She coaxed a wind to her from down the wall and sought it for news of the woods she had left. No scent of Ungolad lingered. She must have outrun him somehow or, more likely, lost him in the wood. She lay still and listened to any breeze that came near, and their stories soothed her, and her heart slowed and her eyes drooped.

She made a last effort to stand and stumbled away from the wall and farther into the woods. Afraid to fall asleep bleeding into the earth, she stayed standing as she tore strips from the hem of her tunic with an effort that awakened the pain anew. By the time she had wrapped her middle with the strips, the ground and trees and sky were tilting and spinning so that every direction seemed to be down. She put a hand over her eyes and found a darkness dimmer than the night. Her body crumpled onto the hard earth.

Part Three

Yellow Lady

ni walked for three days. Daylight revealed that her back was stained with the dark brown of dried blood, and when she touched the cut with her fingers they came back a fresh red. She kept walking.

Clear thought seemed to have left her at the pasture archway where Falada last called her Princess and where Ungolad's knife had bit her. Her hair hung long and uncovered. The sight and feel of it made her uneasy, and she avoided any person who neared her path. She remembered that there was a safe place to go, and she struggled to get there, listening to the wind for the cool murmuring of water and a path away from people.

Four nights she spent on the ground. Except for the first night, when loss of blood and exhaustion closed her eyes for her, Ani was conscious enough to feel the cold of early spring nights. Even in the deepest part of sleep, that awareness of cold pursued her, bruising her dreams and waking her often with icicle fingers on her skin. Day was an extension of the nightmare. She walked, and fell, and walked. When certain plants and mushrooms that she recognized as food crossed her vision, she dropped her left hand and harvested them in passing. But she had little thought for food, and she only sought out word of water from roaming breezes when the thirst clenched her throat. Once she awoke with a start to find her face underwater, having stopped to drink in a stream and lost consciousness.

There were people in the Forest. She did not know if they were good or bad. She never strayed far from the great road that led to the city, keeping it almost in vision off to her left. Though when breezes brought images of humans, she was forced to march farther in.

High morning after her fourth night, Ani found the familiar little path that led off one of the many twisting Forest roads. She almost fainted from relief at the sight of the places where she had wandered in search of roots and berries so many months ago, and she thanked creation for memory and luck and the hints of winds that led her.

She was startled when she first saw the cottage again, worried that she was mistaken, for its aspect was wrong, before she understood that her vision was not trustworthy and she saw two houses of shifting images. Perhaps there had not been as many trees in the woods as she had seen.

Poppo the goat bleated at her, and Gilsa raised her head from her garden.

Ani meant to call a greeting but found her voice was as questionable as her sight. The thought of rest suddenly made her giddy with fatigue. She kept walking forward until the woman caught her by her arms and held her still.

"Yes, what, child?" said Gilsa. It seemed her voice was short not from impatience but worry.

"Gilsa, I'm going to faint again."

And she did.

Ani awoke lying on her stomach on Gilsa's low cot by the fire. It was blazing cheerfully, the crackling of the wood sap accompanied by the pleasant clicking of Gilsa's knitting needles. The halfhearted light of evening peered through cracks in the shutters.

"I've slept all day," said Ani.

The clicking ceased, and with a low grunt Gilsa slid her chair closer.

"You've slept all day, night, and day again. But your fever's gone now and you're in precious little danger."

Ani winced, sure that was not completely true. Gilsa watched her, then shook her head as though dismissing sentiment.

"Heavens, child," she said, "I appreciate your warning me of the faint this time, but you might have let me know you were injured and where before tumbling to the ground. It took me time to cut the clothes off you and more time to wash you clean and find the wound. A thoughtless way to ask for hospitality."

"Oh," said Ani, "that was the blue tunic that you gave me, and I've ruined it."

Gilsa scowled. "Cry for a knife in your back, not an old blue tunic, gosling. You didn't even rouse when I washed the stab clean and tied it up tight. Finn thought you were dead."

Ani saw Finn across the room, sitting on his bed with his hands folded on his knees. He nodded once to her in greeting, then stood and brought her a large bowl of hot bean and onion stew. She ate ardently, and they watched her in silence.

"Thank you," she said.

"I told Mother," said Finn, "that somebodies—"

"Some persons," said Gilsa.

"Some persons were trying to kill you, and might come this way. She couldn't believe it."

"Yes, well, I can now, but I don't want to hear about it." Gilsa stopped and stared at her stilled knitting for a moment. She put it away and huffed. "Though, on consideration, perhaps I'd better."

Ani told them all, even of Falada's head, and learning bird tongue and the wind, telling more than needed telling, the stories clarifying and unifying themselves in her mind as she let them spill out of her mouth. When she finished, she looked from the fire to Gilsa, who scarcely hid her amazement, and Finn, who stared blankly and then nodded to her encouragingly when he noticed her gaze.

"Well," said Gilsa. "That's a story you don't hear on the eve of wintermoon, even if you do tell it with that neat little accent like you'd been grown here."

"I used to tell stories to the other workers, sometimes on rainy days, sometimes on cold nights when the only sounds were the fire and the wind outside. Tales my aunt told me, stories I'd read in books. In these last months I've told more stories than I thought I knew. And I've told lies. To hide. Now, telling you the truth, it sounds to me like just another story."

"I like that story," said Finn.

"Hush up," said Gilsa, "it's not a story that asks for liking."

"I'm not sure I like it yet," said Ani. "Maybe it's just strange to hear it aloud. I've never told it all to anyone, not even Enna, who knows some. Saying it makes me want to change it, make it sound pretty the way I do with the stories I tell the workers. I'd like it to have a beginning as grand as a ball and an ending in a whisper like a mother tucking in a child for sleep."

Gilsa huffed. "You want it all to end with you riding home on a tall horse and everyone cheering or some such like the young daydream."

Ani watched the firelight turn the hearthstones gold. "Maybe I did. Maybe I hoped I'd return home again and everyone would say, We were wrong about her. And they'd see that I'm special and beautiful and powerful and all that."

"Oh, you all wish such stuff, you and Finn like you. Right now he's probably daydreaming about getting a javelin and shield, as though such nonsense will make the chickens lay bigger eggs."

Finn looked down at his boots, his face hidden by his hair.

"We know it's all just daydreaming. In all likelihood, no one in this forest'll ever get a javelin, and I'll never see my mother's kingdom again, let alone be hailed by crowds as the jewel of Kildenree. Maybe it's vain to wish for it. But sometimes, it'd be nice just to hold something real in your hands that felt like a measure of your worth. Right, Finn?"

Finn looked up through his hair, and she saw that he smiled.

Ani was forced to stay and heal in Gilsa's house. She troubled about every passing hour and looked to the weather, wondering if the pass snows were melting, if the army had moved yet, if the prince had yet wed his false bride. She told Gilsa, "I've got to get back soon, to tell the other workers and enlist their help and go march on the palace and demand an audience and convince the king—"

"Patience," said Gilsa, and escorted her from the window

back to bed.

The cut was deep, and she had lost much blood and healing time moving through the woods. She lay on her belly day and night, fretting when she was not sleeping. After two days, Gilsa allowed her to rise awhile and follow her around the yard, though she was not to lift so much as a chicken's egg. When Ani shadowed Gilsa into the coop anyway, Gilsa slapped her hands away from the task and then asked her what the chickens were saying.

"'People are here to take the eggs' and so on. Chickens aren't the best conversationalists."

"I'm glad," said Gilsa. "Makes me feel better about eating them."

That afternoon they were visited by Gilsa's nearest neighbor, a round woman named Frigart who frequented the cottage in good weather. She sat by the hearth and complained of her husband and son while Gilsa, half listening, knitted caps. Ani, tired of lying down, was at the table, leaning forward to keep her wound from touching the chair back. The light slanted into the room from the window, and when Frigart's gesticulating hand passed through the light, it sparkled.

"That ring," said Ani. She stood and took her hand. It was a ruby in gold setting, as familiar to her as the face of its owner. Her face burned.

"Where'd you get this?"

Frigart pulled her hand away. "That's none of your affair."

"It was on a man who was murdered in these woods," said Ani. "Did you take it from his body? Did you bury him?"

"No such thing." Frigart spat with the words in agitation. "What a thing to say! It was given in payment."

"What is it, Ani?" said Gilsa.

"This was my ring." She remembered Talone that last night in the Forest, his fist at his heart swearing loyalty. "I gave it to a friend who was killed."

"Well, you can't have it back if it ever was yours," said Frigart. "I don't know how my lodger got ahold of it, but I fed him for two months before he could get out of bed to lift a finger and earn his board, so it's rightfully mine. And I'm still helping him, I'll have you know, letting him stay on and work with my husband. Says he needs to earn money to take a long journey." She frowned, and her cheeks pushed up like a little child's. "Besides, I've never had a pretty thing in all my life."

Gilsa protested enough to do any mother proud, but Ani insisted, and when Frigart left, Ani accompanied her home. Finn accompanied Ani, his arm through hers. They walked nearly an hour at a pace slow enough not to tear open the cut again and easy enough that neither Frigart nor Ani lost her breath. Ani could feel her heart beating in her back from pain and in her throat from excitement as they rounded a bend and saw the cottage. A man was chopping wood in the yard. His hair had always been dark for a Kildenrean, though now it was speckled with more gray than she remembered and grew unchecked past his shoulders.

"Talone," she said.

Talone looked up and dropped the ax. He ran forward and she tensed, afraid he would embrace her and her wound, but he stopped before her, took her hand, and fell to one knee.

"Princess," he said. He cried over her hand, his back shaking with sobs.

Frigart, with new and awkward gestures of respect, invited "Princess" indoors, where she set them up in chairs around her hearth and, with regretful looks, left them to talk alone. Finn stayed, quiet on his stool by the window.

Ani insisted that Talone tell his tale first. It was short, and she suspected that he left out many of the details of hardship. All had been slain, nearly he as well. His hand touched his side, and Ani thought it must have been a deep and mortal wound that cut him down. Talone had fainted from blood loss and awoke to the sounds of midnight grave digging. He pulled himself away unobserved and wandered through the woods, finally finding Frigart's home, where from necessity he had remained ever since.

"I knew Ungolad and his friends would be in Bayern, so my plan was to return to the queen. I . . . took . . . some time to heal, and then the winter months trapped me, and having no money or horse hindered me more." He shook his head, and his eyes lined with anger. "I thought you, too, were slain. I thought the only chance of redemption would be to stay alive and find a way back to your mother or they might never have learned of the treachery. If I had known, Princess, I would have searched for you, in the Forest, in the city. You have been unprotected all this time. I have failed unpardonably."

"Not at all, Captain. We were betrayed and outnumbered. I, like you, decided that for the time there was no remedy but perseverance. And we've both survived."

Talone smiled at her. "Your mother would be proud if she saw you now. Though she might not recognize you with your hair hid and speaking in that smart accent."

Ani covered her lips with her hand, embarrassed that she now spoke in the Bayern fashion unawares. The movement of her arm pulled the skin of her side, and she dropped it again with a shudder. He gestured to her middle and inquired.

"Ungolad," she said.

He looked mournful, an expression she guessed he had worn for many months.

"I'm sorry," he said.

"Please don't be," she said. "He was greedy and overconfident. If he'd grabbed me instead of hazarding a swipe of his dagger, I'd be much less alive."

Ani told her story to Talone, and this time it seemed more real, so much so that when she spoke of Falada's head on the wall, she had to pause with a hand over her mouth to stop a sob. Talone's eyes never left her face, his expression betraying grim wonderment. Finn leaned forward, his chin in his hands. When she forgot the detail of Conrad's chasing his hat on the wind, Finn prompted her and chuckled at the relation.

"I suppose when Conrad was invited into the presence of the king to tell of the goose thieves, he also told of me or spoke to the guards, because they found me that night. He did. Ungolad. And I ran." Ani closed her eyes briefly at the memory, but the terror was starker in darkness. She looked back at Talone and smiled. "Dear Talone, can you even know what comfort it is to find you?"

Talone breathed deeply and broke his gaze from her face to the window. The shutters were closed, and no light broke through the slits. A breeze tapped the branch of a tree on the wood in a timid knock. He seemed to study the noise and the evening as a general would look over his battlefield.

"There is a war, then," he said. "Ungolad is a clever man."

"And Selia," said Ani. "I think she's been overlooked too often. I remember years ago my aunt saying that Selia had the gift of people-speaking. She's used that gift well."

Talone nodded distractedly. He did not seem interested in the dangers of Selia or the gifts of language, only in the war.

"How long until you can safely walk back to the city?" Talone asked.

"Now," said Ani.

Talone looked at Finn.

"Mother says in a week."

"Mother's boy," said Ani with play spite.

It was decided in four days they would return. And if she could not make it by then, "I'll carry you," said Talone, "though you're a mite bigger than you were when I found you sleeping by the swan pond."

Ani and Finn slept at Frigart's house that night and returned the next day, Ani leaning on both Finn and Talone as she walked. After the excursion, she slept for a day and a night, and Gilsa assured her that she had been warned.

Talone walked to Gilsa's house daily, dragging any fallen logs he found, which he chopped into fire-size blocks with Finn's ax. After that ritual chore, he sat with Ani by the hearth or on a stool in the garden, and they planned, or talked and talked over all that happened in that Forest and all they knew of their enemies. Both agreed that returning now to Kildenree was hopeless. The Forest Road would take them months.

"There is the mountain pass," said Talone. "With war parties gathering, it would be difficult to slip through it unseen, but it may be our best option."

Ani shook her head. "Even if we succeeded, all we could do is warn the queen to ready her armies. There'd still be war. No, I think our best hope's to return to the city. I've friends there who might accompany us to act as witnesses against our murder, and with you supporting my testimony, we've more of a chance of convincing the king."

The days passed too slowly for Ani. Everything around her spoke of action—the pale blossom buds on the apple tree about to unfold, the bent green necks that poked up in Gilsa's garden ready to straighten and reveal their leafy heads, the birds that scavenged the ground for seeds and sang tunes about now, now, now. Whenever Gilsa discovered Ani pacing or leaning on the fence and looking through the trees as though looking ahead, she guided her to a chair or cot and made her sit.

"Rest while you can. Even a princess has skin that heals with time."

Gilsa was hardly impressed to learn that her refugee was royalty. She tossed around titles with a playful spirit, never really believing them. She gave Ani a simple skirt and tunic dyed beech leaf green. The first time Ani put it on, she discovered that the four thin gold coins, her savings for a way home, had been rescued from the pocket of her blue skirt and slipped into the new one.

"They're for you," said Ani. They were as light on her palm as birch leaves.

"No such thing," said Gilsa. Her tone held the tight self-awareness that a joke was imminent. "You can pay me back when you're queen."

The night before departure, Talone stayed at Gilsa's. There was much debate over who should sleep in the shed. Gilsa thought the travelers needed bed rest more than she,

Ani insisted that neither Gilsa nor Finn should be ousted from their own beds, Talone thought he and Finn would fare best in the shed, and Finn nodded to whatever plan was stated at the moment.

"Get back in my cot, girl," said Gilsa. "You're sickly."

"No, I'm not," said Ani.

"Oh, no? Well, maybe stubbornness is a sickness, did you ever think of that?"

In the end, they set up makeshift bedrolls on the floor before the hearth and slept side by side like little children sharing one bed.

They rose early and breakfasted slowly, holding too hot tea to warm their hands and staring at the morning fire. Finn was going with them, on his insistence. Gilsa was thinking of last minute cautions for her son and occasionally reminding him that she would be alone and in ignorance until he sent word. Talone cleaned his sword thoughtfully, a gift from Frigart's husband when he learned the real value of the red ring. Ani watched their faces painted an early orange from the hearth light.

Ani was stilled by the remembrance of the first time she took her leave of that place six months previous and the girl she had been then. Smiling, she thought of her blunder, thoughtlessly taking Gilsa's own bed as though she were still a princess in a palace and pleased to be waited on. And of wandering into a foreign city with a feigned accent and the naive notion of simply finding the king and telling what had happened, a plan that was easily frightened out of her by the sight of Selia wearing her dress. She had run three times since then. She would not run again. All would be set to right, or let Ungolad's dagger find its mark.

ilsa gave them each the good-luck kiss of a widow, and they took to the path. The air was clear and smelled of new, growing things. Ani listened to the breezes and all their news of spring and chose to feel confident. The men would not let her shoulder a pack, so she walked easily, if more slowly than before.

They spent two nights under the Forest canopy before they reached the thinning trees of the near-city. There Ani and Talone waited while Finn, his mind full of careful descriptions, crept ahead to scout the gate and main way for any sign of Ungolad's men. He returned some time later convinced of safety. Ani felt the city winds confirm this, their image-speech vacant of pale-haired men, and they moved on.

It was not a marketday week, and the traffic through the gate was sparse. She felt exposed entering the gate past the giant stone posts, two great sentinels on either side gazing down at her with their stony suspicion. No one hindered their course.

The wide avenue was bedecked in celebration of the impending wedding. The trunks of the tall oaks that lined the avenue were wrapped in paper—yellow, blue, orange, and white, like thick-bodied women dressed for spring. Above them, long ribbons bridged the open sky, converting the oak tops into arches. The party walked long beneath them, the straight shadows enveloping them and dismissing them again and again, a repetition steady as the beating of a sorcerer's drum. In market-square, there were more papered ornaments than people. The entire city was quiet and brilliantly colored. Ani thought it eerie and sad, like a resplendent bird that had lost its song. Everything trembled with tension and expectancy.

Ani led them through narrow streets, avoiding main ways. They reached the west city wall and followed it a distance to the workers' settlements. The low buildings crouched against the wall like a street cat hunting in the shadow. The sun was still high in the west, and the sky was full blue; the workers would still be in the pastures and stalls, gleaning the last bits of sunlight, letting their charges recover from winter and relish the green, sprouting things that were erupting from the fields. Grass burst between the cobblestones under her feet. Spring was breaking, even in the city.

When they arrived at Ideca's yellow house, Talone insisted on entering first. He paused on the threshold and said, "Princess, the room is full."

Ani stepped up beside him and saw all the workers at the benches or on the stones by the hearth.

"Isi." Enna jumped from her seat and ran to the door. Ani motioned to Talone that it was all right, and he stepped aside, sheathing his sword. Others followed Enna's lead, and soon half the hall was embracing her and congratulating her on being alive. Some touched her with a reverence and uncertainty that made Ani turn to Enna with a quizzical look.

"I told them," said Enna. "I'm sorry. It seemed right at the time. I'm just so relieved that you escaped. I saw you running away that night, and I was so scared. Your geese woke half the settlement, and we went after you. I had to tell them why you were running and who was chasing. But you both disappeared into the woods, and Isi, you don't know how crazy we've been all these days with no idea what happened."

"The geese that were in my room that night . . ."

"They're fine," said Enna. "I think that braided man kicked the gander, but he's a hardy one."

"He is," said Ani.

"So, goose girl," said Razo, shouldering past others to stand by Enna, "you're really a princess?"

"The genuine yellow girl," she said.

He smiled at her and lightly punched her arm. The rest stayed back, watching her as though she were a strange bird with large, unpredictable wings.

She introduced Talone and Finn to the workers, and they

all tried to introduce themselves back at once, shouting their names over one another. Ani cut through the commotion, asking why they were all in the hall when the weather was good.

"It's holiday week, for the prince's wedding," said Sifrid.

"When?" said Ani.

"Two days," said Ideca, speaking for the first time. She squinted at Ani. "You're that yellow girl after all? Then you'd best hurry, goose girl, because you've got until three tomorrows. Humph, imagine marrying a murderess. She'll cut his throat in their marriage bed."

"Or murder enough of Kildenree to cover up what she's done," said Enna.

"The army's marched," said Sifrid. "They left last week by the main gate. There was a celebration. The war's not a secret anymore."

Enna's expression brightened with a thought. "After you left, we had Tatto slip messages under the king's door. Anonymous. Saying that the princess was a fraud and so were the tales of Kildenrean war plans. I don't know if they got to him, or if he believed them, but we tried."

Those who had not heard of the letters to the king began to ask questions, and for a moment the hall blazed with talk. Ani looked around and saw Conrad seated in the corner, his hands in his hair. She crossed to him, loosed a strand of hair from under her scarf, and plucked it.

"Conrad, I'm sorry." He shrugged, and she sat beside him.

"You were right about who I was, and I lied because I was scared."

She handed him the long, pale hair, and he took it and rubbed it between his fingers.

"I told those foreign guards where you were." He looked up, and she saw that his chin was trembling. "I wanted them to find you. But I didn't know they would try to kill you. I swear I didn't know."

"It's all right," she said. "That part's over now."

Conrad glanced down at the hair and came close to a smile. "I really wanted to yank one of these from your head, but you got witchy on me. And now you're a princess. Who'd've thought?"

Ani stood and turned to the workers, who stood by in silence. "I don't understand something. I lied to you all before. Why do you believe me now, when I say I'm the princess?"

Enna gave a frank smile. "Because we know you."

Then everyone seemed to answer at once. "Yeah," said Bettin, "you're our goose girl."

"You're the yellow girl," said Conrad, turning to grin at the boy next to him.

"You're Isi," said Razo.

Enna touched her sleeve. "You're Ani."

Ani smiled and looked down, her eyes wet.

"Yeah, what do we call you now?" said Razo.

Ani shrugged. "Whatever you want, Razo."

Someone whispered, "Well, I'm not calling her Isi or Ani. She's a princess now."

Enna realized that they had been walking since dawn, and soon the three travelers sat to some warmed stew and nearly fresh bread. Ideca served them herself. Ani noticed that her bowl held more stew than usual. She was nervous, both to ask the workers for help and to face the Kildenreans again, but she bade her stomach be still and tried to eat quickly.

While they ate, several workers approached Finn. Some recognized him from marketweek, and they asked where he was from and what he sold. Finn answered their questions and surprised Ani by seeming pleased at the attention, particularly from Enna. He was more interested in what she had to say than in his food and did not flinch when she touched his shoulder in passing.

Before Ani had finished her bowl, she noticed that many of the workers were fetching crooks and staffs and putting on hats, while others patted their backs and spoke low things in their ears.

"What's going on?" said Ani.

"We're going with you, Isi, er, my lady." Razo pushed out his chest and held his staff in front of him with both hands. "We're your working guard, in the peace-keeper tradition, unpaid and unasked but ready with a quarterstaff, or a crook, at least."

Ani stood. "We came back here to beg your help, and before I even ask you're waiting for me at the door."

"Don't look so surprised," said Enna. "You should know by now that the Forest grows 'em loyal. Does a pine kick a bird out of its limbs or the moss off its bark?"

"Am I the moss on your bark, then?" said Ani.

Enna grabbed her around her waist and shook her affectionately. "You're the mossiest girl I know."

"Thank you, thank you for being willing. But before you come, I need you to know the danger. The group of Kildenreans and the false princess massacred over twenty of their countrymen. This isn't a game."

"Well, we're still going to play it," said Beier.

"Clearly we're going with you," said Enna. "What kind of Forest folk would we be?"

"But—" said Ani.

Enna held up her hands in defense. "Isi, I know you're worried someone'll get hurt and it'll be your fault. Don't. We know there's danger. We may be Forest folk, but we're still Bayern, and we won't back down from a fight."

A few workers stomped their staffs on the floor, and someone shouted, "For Bayern!"

Ani laughed, stuttered, and finally said, "Thank you."

Talone nodded and stepped forward. "Good, then. Listen here." The attention turned to him, and some boys straightened up and stuck out their chests as though they were regular soldiers at attention. "The impostor's guards will want to slay us before we can enter the palace. Your duty is to guard the princess. Do not fight unless they attack you, and do not leave her side. Our goal is to reach the king. It is good that we are many. With just three of us, they might have tried to pull us aside and slit our throats before the king hears our story."

"The storytelling'll be my job," said Ani. "If the king doesn't believe me, you are to come back here, and don't make a scene. I'd like you to live through this."

Enna turned to her. "I'm not going to leave you alone. I said I wouldn't."

"I'm serious, Enna. If he doesn't believe me, it'll do no good."

"We'll see," she said.

Ani opened her mouth to argue, but Talone touched her elbow. "Princess," he said.

She nodded. "For those of you willing, it's time to go."

Ani led the procession. Going before the crook- and staff-bearing mob in her leaf green clothes and leaf green headscarf, she felt more the harbinger of spring than commander or princess. The small army of skinny beast-keepers in unpolished boots gripped their crooks and looked about with anxious pride. Talone carried his sword, his eyes the color of steel, his hair flecked with gray, his figure stolid as though he had emerged from the city's stone walls. He strode beside Ani and watched the streets as cautiously as he had ever attended the east gate of the White Stone Palace. No one spoke. She felt the weight of their lives like the pressure of a wind at her back. She was neither queen nor general, but they followed her.

A wall ringed the palace, its tops fanged with iron spikes, its stones charred by ancient battles. The palace gates were open; it seemed the king did not fear invasion while his army invaded. Ten guards stood at attention when Ani's group approached, eyeing the staffs that they carried like weapons and their number, thirty youths and a man who despite his worn clothing had the gait and mien of a warrior.

"We're here to see the king," said Ani.

The guard in front shook his head. "Can't."

"This is about the war. We've discovered information that's essential before the invasion of Kildenree. We insist you let us pass, or at least send word directly to the king."

"Can't do it," said the guard. "Not the first, not the other. You're going to have to leave."

She wished, not for the first time, that she had been born with the gift of people-speaking. Ani was sure that Selia could have gotten past those guards with a few seductive words. Ani saw Talone grip the hilt of his sword. There had to be a way to get to the king without drawing weapons. She would not kill palace guards or allow the workers to risk themselves in a vain brawl.

"Please," she said, addressing all the guards that blocked the gateway. "Any of you. Just send him a message. We have to speak to the king."

"Can't be done," said the guard.

A breeze tickled Ani's ear, suggesting a way through. She

shook her head. A wind like the one that had formed on the goose pasture against Ungolad might blow down a few guards, but there would be more to take their place. After a display like that, she would find herself trapped in a cell below the palace, listening to the winds trickle through the bars to bring news of death in Kildenree.

"Then at least tell me this—"

"Can't tell you anything, either," said the guard.

"Who's that with the Forest accent and all the can'ts?" A worker stepped forward from the middle of the mob. He was Offo, one of the older sheep boys, and had never spoken a word to Ani. She had wondered why he accompanied her now and assumed his Bayern restlessness was lured by the idea of a fight. With a mild dread, she waited to hear what Offo would say.

"Is that Ratger? Look at that, Beier, it's Ratger, our pig boy of late."

Beier nodded his shaggy head and kept his expressions smooth and disinterested. "I heard his brother married a city girl and the pig boy moved in with them, got civilized and given a javelin and shield at wintermoon near three years ago. All grown up and guarding the gate now. Too high for us."

"Oh, shut it, Beier," said the guard Ratger, "I got to do my job. If some merchant-faced velvet-wearer comes down to your field and says, 'Give me a pig, please,' you'd tell him to shove coal in his mouth and swallow hard."

"And if he's an old friend and asks me real nice to give a

message to the pig, I'd do it with a smile." Offo's lips curled up in an exaggerated smile, revealing teeth large and square like a mule's. Ratger rolled his eyes and stomped his feet twice in irritation. He no longer seemed the stoic guard.

"Play along here, Ratger," said Razo. He stepped up with a straight spine and extended neck, pleading every inch out of his short frame. "You know, this's the goose girl what defended her flock from five muscle thieves—alone. You ever do anything like that? The king wanted to honor her, you know, and he won't be real pleased to hear you've stopped her at his gate as though she were the thief and you full of airs."

Ratger glanced back at Offo's mock smile and sighed. "Quit your grinning, Offo. I can't take you to the king. And I can't deliver a message. He isn't even here. They're all gone, marched with the army, off to marry the prince somewhere."

"Where?" said Ani.

"I don't know." Ratger spoke with sarcasm thick as maple sap. "Somehow the prince forgot to invite me to his wedding."

"Tatto!" Enna pointed to the far side of the palace courtyard, where the young page was ambling in the afternoon shade, swinging an empty errand basket.

"Tatto!" shouted Ani through the shoulders of the guards. He turned to see the workers' mob all staring at him through the gate of bodies and loped to them with a smile.

"Come to see me?" he said.

"To see the king, you nit," said Enna. "Where is he?"

"I don't know, but not because I'm just an apprentice page, but because no one really knows, except it's probably at some country house grand enough for a wedding and on the way to war. I guess they don't want a lot of uninvited guests showing up." He eyed them sharply, letting them know that they were uninvited as well.

"I need your help," said Ani, "so stay put for a minute."

He folded his arms and looked up at her. "Are you really what they all"—he waved a hand at the jam of workers— "say you are?"

"I am," said Ani.

"I thought so. I told my da, 'She wouldn't see the king. She's hiding something, that goose girl with her broken staff and her hat and her goose talk and her pretty hands.'" Tatto blushed suddenly and looked down.

"Ratger, are you under orders not to tell me anything?" said Ani.

Ratger glanced briefly at Offo and then back at Ani. "No, I guess not."

"Then can you tell me the name of the prime minister?"

"Thiaddag," said Ratger.

"Right. But there was one I met about six years ago when he traveled to Kildenree. Is he still alive?"

"That would be Odaccar," said one of the guards. "He's retired, got old suddenly, sick or something."

"That's right," said Ratger. "He's in the severance quarters, over the carriage houses."

"Ah," said Ani, beginning to feel some relief. "Tatto, I need you to be quick. Go to Odaccar. Tell him who I am, tell him I'm waiting here at the gate for permission to pass and see him." She turned to Ratger. "And if he calls for me, it's all right that I pass?" The guard nodded his assent, and Tatto ran off.

When he returned, the guards let Ani, Talone, Finn, and Enna through the gate. The others they insisted remain behind, to display their power as guards, Ani thought, and to get answers. She had gone only a few steps into the courtyard when she heard Ratger say, "Now, Offo, who is she?"

Tatto led the four to the inner courtyard by following the outer wall, insisting that taking them through the palace would mess up the floor polish, and then up the stairs of the carriage houses. The long white corridor was lined with unadorned pine doors, most of them opened, revealing small, clean bedrooms. In each room's one chair sat dim-faced hall-servants, hall-mistresses, and chamber-lords, retired servants of high degree, staring out the single window at the inactive courtyard. Their hair was white as mourning clothes and eyes often expressionless, watching for death. One woman turned as they passed her door, and Ani nodded. The woman turned back to her window.

Near the end of the corridor they found the former prime minister's apartment. He, too, sat in his chair and stared at his windowpane, but when he turned to the noise at his door, thoughtfulness announced itself in the lines on his brow, and his eyes were full of curiosity. She remembered first hearing the Bayern accent from his mouth, how his words had seemed stitched together, one following the other in seamless succession. She had loved the sound. She checked herself now, making sure she addressed him in her Kildenrean accent.

"Sir, I met you once when I was a girl and you had come to my mother's kingdom."

He nodded, but his brows creased together. "You're not the one I met with the prince." He shook his hand as though gesturing at everything at once. "We arranged a marriage, I remember that. But a different girl's marrying him." He shrugged. "You both look near the same to me."

Ani, waiting for his permission, sat on the edge of his bed and told the story of the designs and murders and war. The old man listened carefully, interjecting questions and receiving the answers with a deepening of wrinkles on his forehead.

"It is true, sir," said Talone. "I am the last witness of the massacre."

"And I saw the false princess's guards twice try to kill this yellow lady," said Enna.

The prime minister made a tsk, tsk sound. "War. That's what killed the old king and his other sons some years ago. That's what that lovely queen and I were trying to avoid, and look at it all come down on us like so many hunting falcons. Can't stand war. Gets in the way of order and process and all the good things. Thiaddag, now, he loves the stuff. Can't get enough of it. Eats it up like blackberry pudding. And you know what I think about Thiaddag." He squinted and stuck out his tongue.

"They have gone north," said Ani, "toward the mountain pass to invade Kildenree, and in three days the prince and Selia will wed. Do you know where they might be?"

"Oh, yes. North. Wedding. They would've gone to the estate on Lake Meginhard. The king was married there himself. I was present. It'll become a tradition, I shouldn't wonder." His eyes livened with memory, and his thin lips took shape with a smile.

Ani breathed out a sigh. "Lake Meginhard. Good. At least we know where." She twisted to look at Enna. "Can we get there in three days?"

Enna shrugged. The only place she knew outside the Forest was the city. Ani could see Talone's jaw tighten in frustration that he did not know this terrain well enough to supply the answers.

"Three days . . ." Odaccar shut his eyes tight, as though trying to see a map in his mind. "On foot you might make it in three days, maybe four."

"That is not good enough." Ani leaned forward and put her hand atop Odaccar's. "Sir, we need horses. We must get there in time to stop the wedding and the war. If we don't, people like Thiaddag get their way." Odaccar winced at that. "You once held a great deal of power in this kingdom, sir.

Do you have friends in the stables? Can you get us horses?"

"Me? No, they think I'm old and useless."

"Please," said Ani, refusing to give up. "We don't have enough coin to buy horses. If we had the time and skill, I would try to steal them. I must get to Lake Meginhard in less than three days, and the only way I see to do that is to get horses today, with your help. Can you think of a way to help?"

Odaccar rubbed his forehead and frowned. "Maybe." Then he smiled, and his wrinkles stretched into long, pleasant curves. "Maybe if they don't know it's I." He stood up by his small desk and rummaged for parchment, sending Enna to water his inkpot. The four stood by, twisting their hands with anxiety while he scrawled on the paper with the thick, scratchy strokes of a worn goose quill. He produced a stamp with a silver handle from a small drawer and shook it in the air. "Bet they don't know I kept one of these!" He inked it and stamped the bottom of the letter.

"There now, that's your passport to horses. I don't think even that tight-fingered stable-master'll think to ask which prime minister signed this letter."

Ani took his hands and thanked him.

"You have done a noble thing, sir," said Talone.

Odaccar laughed out loud and slapped his belly. "It's good to be needed, I think." The wrinkles around his lips and nose gathered together as though they existed solely to bear up his smile.

Ani sent Enna and Finn, the parchment drying in Enna's hand, to find the stable-master. She begged Tatto to escort her and Talone to Selia's quarters.

"This is good, Talone. If we can get to Lake Meginhard in time, this'll be better than meeting the king today in my goose girl clothes. I just need one of my old dresses from Selia's wardrobe, and then I think we can play Princess Napralina-Victery and her escort guard convincingly enough to get us through the doors."

"Wait, wait, Isi," said Tatto. "Do you know how wrong it'd be to break into the princess's room, and me an oathsworn page and due to receive my shield and javelin in two years?"

"I have to get a proper dress, Tatto, or they'll never believe I'm the princess's sister come to see the wedding. Anyway, it's actually my apartment, isn't it? Is it against your oath to lead the princess to her own room?"

"And if we get caught and they don't believe you're the princess—"

"Just tell them I bewitched you," said Ani. Her eyes opened wider, her closed lips turned upward teasingly, and though the room was still, Ani caught at a slight breeze and her hem and sleeves and the loose end of her headscarf rustled in the invisible current. "That shouldn't be too hard to believe."

Tatto swallowed visibly and nodded. Talone stared, and she became self-conscious and released the wind.

"I told you," she said to Talone.

"I suppose I thought you were being metaphorical." He grinned and shook his head. "If your mother saw you..."

No one questioned their errand through the palace, though the pageboy wiped his sweating palms on his tunic and tensed at every sentry's station, expecting to be pounced on and flung into a dungeon. At last he gestured to a set of doors, enjoined them to behave, and retreated down the corridor.

The doors were a double set of heavy, dark walnut, their borders engraved with climbing vines and half-opened blossoms. The brass knobs turned without stop, and they entered.

A long window breathed out over the courtyard and filled the room with light. Dark wood couches with thin velvet cushions, lamps that sparkled with dangling crystals, rugs so deep they kept the impression of her boot after she stepped away, walls painted deep orange and mahogany, tapestries of forest animals with starry eyes and horns in gold thread, curtains of curious weaving in all the natural colors that could be seen from the window, the odor of pure beeswax and rosewater. Ani felt doused by luxury, held underwater without breath. Her eyes sought out simplicity—she found a mirror and her own face.

This would have been my room, she thought.

"Would you stay here a moment, Talone?" Ani said. She left the main room for the changing room and found a wardrobe full of gowns that when rustled released the sweet, sharp scents of cloves and lavender. Not all the dresses she had brought from Kildenree were hanging from the steel hooks. Most noticeably the gold-and-white one was absent, the one the thread-mistress had intended for her bridal gown. Ani took down the pale lake green dress that had been dyed to match her eyes, held it to her chest, and looked at the long mirror. She thought, *I look like a goose girl holding up a fancy dress.*

Ani pulled loose her headscarf and let it fall to the floor. "I will not hide anymore," she said to her reflection. Two feet, one in the mirror and one in the world, kicked the scarf aside. Her hair, braided up, had loosened, and its weight pulled it out of its plait and off her head. She picked up one of Selia's—one of her—brushes, silver plated, the face of a horse a rigid knob on its handle, and broke her snarls loose. The sun was dipping low in the west and sent a lustrous orange glow from the horizon to her hair. She moved, and it flashed gold in the light. She held up the dress against her now, the ray of setting sun brightening her eyes, painting her face a yellow rose, regal as her mother.

"But different," she whispered. "Not her. Me. Ani. Isi."

She carefully folded the green dress and wrapped it up in linen she stripped from the princess's bedchamber. She took only one swift, envious glance at the mattress two hands high and let her body briefly ache at that sight, her back and legs still sensing every slat of her little bed that leaned up against the west wall.

Ani had just uncovered a pair of calfskin slippers dyed beech bark gray when she heard from the other room the sound of metal jarring against metal. She peered through the door. Talone stood in the center of the room with exposed sword, his expression deadly, and before him stood Ishta.

Ishta closed the door behind him and locked it with an unsettling click. He smiled, and Ani remembered the stink of his mouth when he'd held her hand to his lips at winter-moon, *I will bite off a finger* and his teeth, crooked and brown, giving the impression that the man was rotting from the inside.

"Alive, I see," said Ishta, his eyes on his former captain. He pulled his sword from its scabbard and shifted it against the sunlight, reflecting beams on Talone's face like pale, cancerous patches. "How lovely. I love that repeating dream where I get to kill you again and again."

"Ishta," said Ani.

He saw her and his brow raised, surprised but not displeased.

"For honor's sake, Princess," said Talone, "I ask to fight him alone." Ani understood he did not wish for a wind to push the fight in his favor, and she nodded.

"Yes, no calling for help, little princess," said Ishta. "The good captain wishes to die in private." He smiled at Talone. "I hope you are not still upset about my killing Dano that day in the forest. I seem to recall that just because all Dano had to defend himself was his cooking knife, you put up such a stink. That is, until Ungolad ran you through."

Talone's temper did not display itself on his face. He gripped the hilt and swayed a moment on his feet, as though testing the strength of the floor. Then his blade rose, slicing through the beam of sunlight and falling hard on Ishta, his own blade held out in front of him, his smile twisted into a scowl. Ishta returned the hack, and the metal rang together, a mortal bell. Neither spoke. It was not a game of young warriors testing their strength or a match of pride, but a bout of death, each warrior watching his opponent's eyes, fighting to end that life, their swords desperate vessels of their will. With each blow the other hoped to meet flesh, and each blow brought sword on sword, and the clanging was a wicked rhythm. Ani could not help the trembling in her legs, but she dared not sit. The force of Ishta's strike pushed Talone to the ground. He held him there, his sword pressing Talone's defense closer to his throat. Ishta glanced up at Ani, and for one moment the expression in his eyes said, *Next. You're next.*

Talone thrust the guard backward and against a thin-legged table that splintered and sank under his weight. Talone took the moment to gain his feet before Ishta's blade was drawn high and striking against his own. The guard had fire in his eyes, and he yelled in anger at every thrust that was countered, again, again, again, until he drove his blade with full force toward Talone's breast. Talone dodged the thrust bodily. Ishta had swung too hard, expecting to be stopped by Talone's blade. The weight of his sword and the momentum pulled him forward, and he stumbled. Talone turned, smooth as a diving hawk, and put his sword tip through Ishta's body. Through his back and into his heart, as Ishta had done in the Forest to young Adon months ago. Ishta let out a high, quick gasp, crumpled face first on the floor, and did not move again.

"Talone," said Ani.

"He was angry." Talone's breathing was heavy. "He should not have fought me angry."

Talone dragged the body behind a low couch. Where Ishta had fallen lay a small pool of blood, dark red on darker wood, like a new moon on a black sky. Talone sat on the edge of a delicate, bird-legged lounge and looked at that dark pool. *This man*, thought Ani, *should have a home and a round-cheeked grandson on his knee, not a stained blade.*

"Are you all right?"

"Better than I would be if he had got me first. I don't like killing."

Ani stood at the feet of the corpse, holding her bundle to her chest. "Should I cover him?"

"No, leave him be," said Talone.

He stood and exchanged his Forest-wrought blade for the dead man's truer steel, more like the sword he had carried as captain of the princess's guard. It occurred to Ani that it might even be the same blade.

"Time we left."

They abandoned Ishta to discovery sometime by some unlucky maid, closing the door behind them.

Chapter 19

I n the yards, the stable-master, an older man with a young man's head of hair and a distracted expression, was directing the preparation of a dozen horses, all short, skinny, or old, and at least one betrayed features of donkey heritage.

"That won't be enough, Talone," said Ani.

"Perhaps not," he said, "but I would be surprised to find a dozen in our company that know riding."

Ani and Talone approached, and the stable-master squinted his eyes at them and came forward, his gait awkward as a new colt.

"You responsible here?" he asked Talone.

"I am," said Ani.

His face swung to hers, and he eyed her uncovered hair.

"Are these all the mounts you have available?" said Ani.

"Who are you?" The stable-master had a faint whine in his voice. "What're these animals needed for?"

"Business of war," said Ani. "And that's all you need know when the prime minister orders. Now, we asked you concerning the mounts."

Ani had hoped the bold words might not seem too silly coming from her and surprised herself at how natural they sounded. Talone looked at her, his eyes smiling.

"Look here," said the stable-master, "most of the mounts've gone north, and we've got to keep a fair supply for messengers and emergencies, as the prime minister would know if he wasn't so absorbed in war, war, war, and gave a thought to animals and common sense."

"What about that one?" Ani pointed to a far stable near the one where she had seen Falada. A tall bay paced his enclosure.

"That horse's not for riding, miss. He's still wild, and doesn't respond to less experienced riders."

Ani smiled. "I've ridden him. I'll take the bay."

The stable-hands thought it would be good sport to let the yellow-haired girl saddle the bay herself, and they sat back, prepared to be amused. One called, "Watch those razor-sharp hooves now, little girl," and others laughed. A few minutes later, Ani walked the bay out of the corral, his hooves lifting high as though on parade. Ani smiled from the saddle.

"Could you shut that gate for me? Thank you kindly."

The jeering stopped, and the group of chagrined stable-hands dispersed.

Talone, Finn, and Enna all mounted, Finn the most uneasily, gripping his docile mount so tightly that the animal did not know whether to run, buck, or sit still. The four led the remaining horses out to the front gate and were greeted by an astonished and delighted cheer. Those who could ride quickly volunteered to escort the princess north.

"Please be a truer escort than my first," she said.

Among the volunteers was the palace guard Ratger.

"You'll be expelled," said one of his comrades. "You'll be labeled a traitor and a post-quitter. You'll never be allowed to enter a barrack or tavern again."

"This's the real princess," said Ratger, mounting the last horse. "And a murderer and liar's about to wed our prince and trick us into war. Tell me if my going isn't fulfilling my post more than standing by, watching the army march away and waiting like a fancy column by a gate where nothing happens."

"Welcome to the company of the true yellow girl," said Razo.

Conrad was among the riders, and he spoke up then for the first time. "She's the yellow lady, you dolt. Can't you see she's a lady?"

Ani's four gold coins bought food and blankets, packed on two of the horses, and then hats and clothings for the workers that were muted in color and could be mistaken for Kildenrean design. Ani hoped they might pass for Kildenreans long enough to get inside the gate. After that feat was accomplished, all she could do was tell her tale. At the thought, her stomach felt sick. She was certain the royal audience would not be so easy to please as weary Forest workers clamoring for a bedtime tale.

It was full night by the time the company of eleven was on the road north, the outside of the city wall just a dark border to their left. They rode for two hours, then camped by the road and slept without fire. They rose at dawn and rode all day.

Ani was immediately grateful for Ratger. The guard was the only member of their company who had ridden the road to the lake and had seen maps of this part of Bayern. Ani spent the morning by his side, learning all she could of the king and the encounter to come.

"You're so quick to answer my little queries, Ratger. At the palace gate, you clung to the suspicion and stubbornness that I'd expect from any Forest-born, but now you're as easy in talking as a magpie."

"Well, why not?" said Ratger. "We're on the same side, and there's little time to waste."

"But why'd you believe them that I'm the princess?" said Ani.

Ratger shrugged. "You look like a princess. You seem like a princess. I saw the other one a few times, and now that I've seen you, I like you better."

"Well, for whatever reason, I'm grateful," she said, though his easy loyalty disturbed her even as it gratified her. She mulled over his statement under the conversation-stifling afternoon sun.

"Sometimes it seems my identity's a matter of opinion," Ani said later as she rode with Talone at the head of the company, hoping to pull the pace faster. Talone insisted they arrive by the next day, saying that once Selia wed the prince, their job would be near impossible.

"How'll we achieve it at all?" said Ani. "She rode into town with light-colored hair wearing my dress, and they accepted her as the princess. I show up with lighter hair, and the workers, the former prime minister, and at least one palace guard vote for me. Will our fate be decided when we stand side by side and the king judges which of us looks the most like a princess?"

"You have truth on your side," said Talone.

"And on her side, the gift of people-speaking. I don't think this can be a mere matter of telling the truth."

"Nor do I," he said. "That is why you do not go alone."

They had passed sight of the walled city late that morning and rode through its sprawling villages most of the day. The road was wide, trampled hard as stone from centuries of hooves and cartwheels, and edged with houses and taverns, and people who peered curiously at the ragtag band and their unlikely leader. "Another yellow girl," Ani heard someone say. By late afternoon, the road crossed the borders of a farm and into uncultivated fields, leaving behind the smells of smoke and cows. The afternoon light picked white tree seeds out of the air, like suspended snowflakes too light to fall. The voice of the wind that came out of the wood was husky and restless. Then, from ahead, the wind brought images of men and horses.

"Could we already be near, Ratger?"

"No, tomorrow's ride, at least."

"Then we're coming up on another company."

She led them off the road and they walked their horses along its side, moving in and out of scattered spruce and aspen. At length, they saw a forest lane that converged on the main road. From it came a company of foot soldiers and some mounted men. They were many times larger than their own, each man carrying a javelin, iron points up and tipped with afternoon light like many tiny stars. Their shields were brightly painted.

"A hundred-band," said Razo. "See their shields? The spruce tree and four stars—they're the hundred-band from Urifel."

"Every village forms a hundred-band for a war, Isi," said Enna. "Usually they're made up of the younger men old enough to've received their javelin and shield, and older men who've never killed before. They're part of the community when they get a javelin, but they're men after their first kill, so they all want to kill. If you see any with beards, those are the ones who really take it seriously and won't shave, ever, until they've killed an enemy. The mounted men, those're the experienced fighters and are given command and a horse in battle. The rest fight from the ground."

"The army must be gathering at the lake," said Talone.

"One hundred from every village," said Ani. "Enna, how many villages does Bayern claim?"

"I don't know, maybe fifty, maybe two hundred."

"If that army crosses the mountain pass, they could wipe out Kildenree. My mother thinks she just made a marital alliance. Kildenree's not prepared. Even so, I know they'll fight. And all this so Selia can hide her deceit."

A few supply wagons trailed the soldiers, two carrying women—young women with babies in their arms, small children at their feet leaning out of the wagons to watch the wheels spin.

Ani looked at Enna. "They take their wives to war?"

She nodded. "It's been a tradition for centuries. All Bayern children're raised on stories of the ancient days and heroes and warriors, when gods still lived in the forest and spoke through sacred horses. It used to be that Bayern armies were aggressive, and every man was a warrior, not just a bully who carries his javelin into taverns. The peace-keepers say they're the last guardians of the old ways, but I think the old ways just meant attacking every nation that touched our lands."

"Yes." Ani had read some of that history in Geric's book. Only the immensity of the Forest and the formerly impass-able mountains had protected Kildenree all those centuries.

The last of the hundred-band and their families trailed

out of sight into the horizon of the road, and Talone motioned that it was time to mount again. They had no real reason to hide, but Ani wished to avoid having to explain themselves to anyone before they reached the estate, so the party skirted the road, out of sight, passed the slower moving hundred-band, and rejoined the road some distance in front. Talone kept a steady pace for the remainder of the day. The damp night descended, and the wood by the road trembled with voices of crickets and the hard wings of hunting birds.

They halted off the road near the line of trees. Talone made a fire. Its light sought out the faces of the company attending to their horses and feeling the ground with booted feet for smooth places without stones. Its light gathered them and kept them in its circle. They ate and talked, and sometimes were silent, the fire the only movement, each watching the flames lick the air and thinking of the next day. Enna sang a Forest song. Her voice was high and soft and simple, and she sang of a carpenter's daughter who fell in love with a tree, and of her father, who carved the tree into a man. Her voice faded, and Ani again became conscious of the croaks of night insects that came from the wood at their back and all around, surrounding them, an overwhelming army.

"Isi, tell a story," said Razo.

"Oh, you know all my stories now," said Ani. "I'd like to hear one. Do you have one, Enna?"

"There's the history or legend, I don't know which, of why our women go to war."

"Yes, that's perfect."

Enna was silent a moment, the thoughtful crease between her eyes as dark in the faint firelight as the infinite blackness of the Forest night. Her eyes were distant, and she seemed to be listening to that voice that first told her the story, a mother, sister, or aunt. Then her voice, like her singing, cut through the crickets and crackling fire.

"There was a battle between Bayern and Tira, a kingdom to the southeast. The battle was so great that all the feet and falling bodies broke the earth, and the sweat of the warriors slipped into the cracks and soaked into the soil, and to this day, that plain in the south of Bayern's a marsh where no one can farm. The leaders were killed, and the men of Bayern ran away. At the camp, the women waited for the battle to be over and victory to be bawled to the trees and hills and its echoes to ring like a bell, as had always happened. But this time their men ran back shouting, 'Vanquished! Vanquished!'"

"Vanquished," said Razo.

"Vanquished," Offo repeated. They nodded, remembering the tale.

Enna continued. "The women left their babies in their tents and came forward as one to meet their fleeing husbands. They slipped their dresses from their shoulders and let them fall to their waist, and stood there in the road, in the daylight. 'See me,' said each wife to each husband, 'see me as you first saw me, your bride in your bed when your warrior hand first touched my skin. See me as you saw me when I suckled our first baby, his eyes like your eyes looking up at mine. See me now, as the enemy'll see me when he carries me off to his dirty bed and his bastard children.'

"The men cried, and their hearts hurt more than their wounds, seeing what defeat meant, seeing what would be lost. When the enemy gained on their flight, the men turned and stood and fought the Tiran in their own camp, where wives looked on from the tents and wagons and mothers nursed their babies and watched their husbands fight to victory."

Finn sat near Ani, and she saw his face change color from merely reflecting the orange light of the fire to a flushed red. He stared down at his hands, shaking his head.

"You all right, Finn?" said Ani.

"I never understood that story," he whispered uncomfortably. "If I saw all those women—I'd want to hide."

"It's about fighting for what's most valuable," said Enna. She raised her brows in good humor. "Wouldn't you want to fight for me, Finn?"

"Yes, I would. But you wouldn't have to—show—me anything."

Enna smiled at him, and Ani saw the shadow of his hand touch Enna's fingers.

"Tomorrow," said Ani in a voice that raised all the faces

to her, and the hollows under their eyes filled with light, and their hair was flushed with the colors of dark fire, "I don't want you taking risks. If I'm not able to get to the king or to convince him, it won't do you any good to rush about looking for a head to bash." She looked from their faces to watch the flames kick the logs they burned. "I hope this works. I hope they believe I'm my sister and you my escort from Kildenree, and just let us in. And I hope the king listens and believes. No matter what happens, I want to thank you. It's a comfort to have you by my side."

Voices around the fire murmured affirmation. Talone's expression was calm and determined, the face of a soldier prepared for battle. She was relieved that at least one person knew what he was doing. She put down her bedroll and wondered if she could sleep with thoughts of tomorrow. Her plan, if it worked, would get them through the gate. After that, the only power she could depend on was that of words, and her weaknesses haunted her. Just after closing her eyes, Ani was greeted by the first images of a dream—Ungolad at her heels, and instead of running, she reached out for aid. Her fingers touched darkness.

Ani rose before first light and slipped away from the workers, just gray, still shapes under shared blankets. The winds were whispering of a stream nearby, and she searched their images for a deep place, finding it behind a tangle of wild raspberry. She walked there, stripped, and used its brambles as a bath curtain. *I'm bathing,* she told herself, *because I need to look the part of a princess, not on the chance that Geric might be there among the prince's guard.*

The water was so cold, she gasped when she surfaced and bit her lip to hold back a yelp. The stream moved softly there and was deep enough for her to submerge her chin while she balanced her toes on a slick stone somewhere under the green-blackness. She had to clamber up the slippery bank to scrub her hair and body with the hard, burnt-smelling block of dish soap, and then she leapt back in, gasping. She dried herself with Gilsa's tunic, gratefully put back on her shift, and finally donned the lake green gown and slippers she had taken from Selia's wardrobe.

When she entered camp, the morning preparations halted with a hush. For the sake of her impractical slippers, she had to weave her path around muddy spots where dishwater had been thrown and hold up the hem of her dress in one hand as a lady would do when braving stairs or stepping out of a carriage. Razo whistled through the space in his teeth.

"Yellow lady," said Offo, grinning.

"Now mark this, all honor the princess," said Ratger in serious, trained-guard tones. One by one they bowed, some falling to one knee. Enna curtsied deeply and did not meet Ani's eyes.

"Stop that," said Ani. "Oh, stand up, now, you know it's

just the dress."

"You look very lovely," said Conrad, still managing to sound perfunctory.

"I thank you, sir." She ruffled his scruffy head with her hand, and he nearly loosed a smile. "And now that I've my costume, you all need to put on yours. All but Talone make sure your hats cover your hair, and ladies, wrap your heads. Pull them as low as you can, though I don't think the charade'll take long enough to allow them a good look at your eyebrows. You don't look Kildenrean, but at least let's not make it obvious that you're Bayern."

While the others ate and packed up the camp, Enna insisted on brushing the wetness out of Ani's hair with the pilfered silver brush.

"I can do that," said Ani, still feeling self-concious in her princess garb among her worker friends. She reached up to take the brush from Enna.

"Oh, leave it," Enna said, and slapped her hand away.

"We should help pack up camp," said Ani. Enna ignored her.

"Your hair's like a streak of sunlight through a window," she said. "Like a river in the morning. I don't know, but something pretty. You're different this morning, Isi. You don't look like the goose girl anymore."

"I hope I'll always be, even if I become a princess again." Ani smoothed the fabric against her leg, soft as moss. "But I wonder if you're readying me for court or to be laid out in my coffin."

Enna rapped her lightly on her head with the brush. "Now stop that or you'll have us all in jitters."

Kit, a quiet worker with a mess of black curls, stood by watching. He timidly put a hand to Ani's hair, like a nest-building crow charmed by a shiny object.

"A warning there, pig boy," Conrad shouted from across the camp. "Don't touch her hair without leave, or keep a good hold on your hat."

Ani laughed.

Talone stomped down the breakfast fire. Hard embers crushed beneath his heel, a sound like weak bones breaking. He looked around.

"Time to ride."

Chapter 20

he party rode at a brisk pace for half a day, stopping only to water their horses and briefly allow those unused to much riding to touch their feet to steady ground and stretch out the sitting sores. The road moved past scattered farms and settlements until the occasional houses clustered into a village and the village led into a town visible from the road as orange-tipped towers and rooftops, the bells tolling absolute noon. They did not leave sight of houses again.

When the afternoon dazzled the west, the road arched down into a broad valley flanked by a wide, gray river. Over a rise, they could see where the river fattened into a lake, the waters flat as a coin in the still afternoon. The estate on its near shore was all of pale yellow stone, its many banners held up in the wind like raised hands, its many chimneys and turrets slender and high, ladies' fingers pointing straight to the sun, and the whole structure proclaiming itself and shouting, *Glory, glory.*

There were shouts from the valley. It was a broad bowl, cleared of trees and filled from rim to rim with the shining, living ocean of the army. The royal army and all the present hundred-bands from villages across the kingdom camped in a wide, open circle around the estate, each centered by a brightly colored tent for their leaders, each bearing the vivid banner of their shields. Ani felt there was no relief from the constant motion of dark heads, the glaring metal of weapons and armor, the colors of the tents, banners, and painted shields. Some bands marched in their camps, circles within circles spinning as they walked, staggered lines playing at advancing and retreating.

Out of the commotion came the notes of a song, loud and perfect. Not far from where Ani's group paused, a hundred-band stood at attention. They rested their round shields on their right shoulders, the rim pressed to their cheeks, the hollow belly of the shields turned to their mouths. Into that metal bowl the soldiers sang a war song. Soon other hundred-bands joined in. The sound rang off the iron and pushed into the air toward the estate and beyond, to the place where Ani's company stood. The song against metal was strange and loud, the notes a flock of fierce, scattered birds, the melody the sound of war.

"Oh," said Ani, as though she finally understood. "I think they must love that sound. It makes my bones feel cold."

"Indeed," said Talone.

"Talone, this is impossible. This can't be done."

Talone looked over the valley, and she thought he was estimating the numbers of soldiers and counting the banners. He squinted against the sun. "What did your horse say to you, that last word you said you heard?"

Ani thought it was an odd question but answered, "He said, he called me Princess."

Talone nodded. "Lead the way, Princess."

In the valley at her feet, the distant soldiers milled around like ants, the thousands of spear tips sparkling like sunlight on a handful of sand. She sat up straight and felt the bay tense beneath her, ready for command.

"Yes, all right, let's go."

They rode in formation like a flock of geese: Ani at the lead, followed by Talone and Ratger, then Enna and Finn, Razo and Offo, and so on. Ani sat tall in her saddle. Her stirrups were lost in the long hem of her skirts, her hands were poised with reins ready to command, her hair fell down her back, her head was up. She visualized her mother and commanded her body to feel that form—regal, imperious. The guards along the valley road watched the company's passing with wonder and apprehension. Who was this Kildenrean girl entering the camp of the army about to invade Kildenree? Because their numbers did not pose a threat, they were not stopped, though Ani could see runners taking the word of their coming to each subsequent post. When she could pick out the faces of the estate gate guard from the haze of distance, she saw they were alerted and awaiting their arrival with stern curiosity.

Ani stopped her bay short of the gate, as though expecting that it would open automatically before her. She could hear the company behind her stop quickly, the restless shifting of saddles like the creak of old wood, the whisk of a horsetail, the light thud of a quarterstaff resting on the ground. The guard stared at her with austere patience.

Ani opened her mouth to speak. Her throat felt cold, and she bade her voice not to shake. "I am Napralina-Victery Talianna Isilee, second daughter of Kildenree and granted emissary of her queen. I am arrived to be witness to the wedding of my sister, Anidori-Kiladra, the first daughter. Escort us to the king immediately."

The guards' formality slipped from their faces like drops of sweat, and they stared with open incredulity. No one addressed her. No one moved.

"Permit me to repeat myself. I said, Please allow my escort to pass and let us present ourselves to the king immediately so we may pay our respects. I expect to see the king first and no other. We have been traveling through hard weather these months to arrive in time and have suffered losses of both wagons and a small number of my guards. I take it most unkindly to be kept mounted at the gate."

"We had no word of your coming," said a slender man slightly older than the rest. Ani turned to him as the possible captain of the watch.

"I am sorry for it. After our losses, I could not spare a

guard and dared not send one of my waiting women alone. All the more reason to inform the king of our arrival immediately."

The slender man motioned to another guard and sent him running into the estate. They waited. The guards were eyeing her mount, her dress, the aspect of those who followed her, measuring her words against her appearance. She could see immediately that if she had walked up as the goose girl alone or with a couple of animal-keeper friends, these guards would have sent her out of the valley with a sword at her back. At least that much of the plan was working. They were passing for Kildenreans and just might be let through the gates. The workers wore their hats and caps, but on inspection, no one would mistake them for anything but Bayern. Ani prayed they would not be delayed enough to make time for a close look. She sat up straighter and felt the bay shift under her legs, hoping, perhaps, that her anxiety meant there would be some action.

The runner returned and whispered into his leader's ear. The slender guard nodded and gave silent commands to others.

"The king will grant an audience," he said.

Ani barely stifled a sigh of relief and readied herself to ride forward. Instead, two guards came to her side, one holding a stirrup while the other offered a hand to dismount. Disconcerted, she took the hand.

"Princess," Talone said uneasily.

The guard helped her down, took her arm, and walked her to the gate. Her company urged their steeds forward to follow.

"His Majesty the king wishes to see Princess Napralina-Victery privately and orders her escort to remain here."

Gasps escaped the mouths of her friends at her back like the fluttering of many wings.

"No," said Talone. "She requires a personal guard. We will accompany her."

Ani had two guards on either side now, holding her arms and pushing her inside the gate. She struggled, clumsily digging her slippered heels against the ground. "Wait," she said, "I will not go with you without my guard."

Talone jumped off his horse and ran after her. "Let me follow her. I tell you I will."

"Unhand me. This is a gross insult. I will not go alone."

Her captors took no heed of her protests. Four gate guards grabbed Talone. He struggled, and a guard took away his sword, pulled from its steel scabbard with a peal of metal on metal like the cry of a high voice. "Princess!" said Talone.

She looked back to see his face, wrinkled, travel stained, and worn, shut out by the closing of the iron gate. The guards held her closely, her feet barely pushing against ground to keep their pace. She struggled and protested and fought their grips. They gave no explanation. They continued their course.

Down they took her through the estate's first long corridor and then ducked into a side room and shut the door. The room was dim, but Ani could see several people standing before her, lit from behind by the light of a window.

"Welcome," said Ungolad.

Ani took in a sharp breath. A hand over her mouth stopped her scream.

All the remaining Kildenrean guards were there, lining the walls in front of dark shelves of books, their pale hair darker in the weak light. Swords at their side shivered silver in the obscurity, and each had a round shield strapped to their left arms as in preparation for battle. Selia rose from a chair against the window. The light was directly behind her. Her face was all in shadow.

"Thank you so much." Selia motioned, and the guard behind Ani dropped his hand from her mouth.

"Selia," Ani said in a whisper. "My lady-in-waiting. Won't the king be expecting me?"

"In good time." She stepped forward to place coins in the palms of the two Bayern soldiers, and they quickly left the room, shutting the door behind them.

Ani saw now that Selia wore a bright yellow tunic and skirt in the Bayern fashion. On her forehead winked the three rubies of Ani's tiara. Three points of red like the blood of the lost handkerchief, as though Selia wore the mark of the queen's approval and protection. *False*, thought Ani. *It's all show. Like the handkerchief. Like my mother's love.* But the sight of it bothered her, and she wanted to rip the circlet from her head and fling it away.

"Let me gut her right now," said Terne. His dagger rang as he ripped it from its sheath, and Ani's stomach muscles clenched. Selia held up her hand.

"Not here. My love, can you take her safely out of the estate?"

Ungolad nodded. He tickled Ani's chin with the end of one of his braids. "It will be easier if she is unable to scream."

"Don't touch me." Ani backed toward the door. A big man named Redmon was there. He put a hand on her back to stop her.

"I don't mean to kill you," said Ungolad. "I only mean to put you to sleep."

He stepped toward her. Ani felt a draft pass under the door and touch her ankle. In a panic, she spoke to it without waiting to gather more and sent it flying at Selia. A few papers rustled on the desk beside her. One piece of parchment flew off the desk and floated to the carpet like goose down on a breath of air. Her breeze died out, useless. Selia glanced back at the closed window, searching for its source.

"Stay away from me," said Ani. The guards looked unimpressed. She recalled the images that had been carried on that breeze—several guards moving down the corridor. Toward that room.

"Easy, now," said Ungolad as though speaking to an unpredictable animal.

Ani pointed at the door. "Wait. Someone is here."

There was a knock. Redmon started.

"What are you, some kind of Bayern witch?" he said.

"Who is there?" called Ungolad.

The door opened, pushing Redmon aside and admitting four soldiers with the purple slash of the king's own guard. "His Majesty has been informed that Princess Napralina-Victery arrived from Kildenree, and he calls her to his presence."

"Yes, certainly." Selia stepped into the light of the open door, an easy smile on her lips.

Ani stepped away from Ungolad's grasp and into the escort of the king's guard. The Kildenreans followed, Selia at their head. There was a hum of anticipation. Even the king's guards seemed to feel it, and they glanced from side to side with hands on sword hilts, anticipating action. Ani saw Selia lift her hand as if to calm her own mob, and her men followed quietly into the estate's small throne room.

It was a long room with a row of narrow, high windows spilling patches of light onto the stone floor. Hard sunlight fell on the dais and chair at the far end where the royal party stood waiting—the king, the young prince she had seen at wintermoon, several others in hunting clothes, the prime minister wearing court apparel and a suspicious expression, and the royal guards. And one guard in particular who watched her approach with a kind of confused concentration, as though he sought to count colors on a moving banner. *My hair,* she thought. *Geric doesn't know me for my hair.*

The guards at her side escorted her to the center of the room and withdrew. Selia and the Kildenreans gathered in a mob at the steps of the dais, facing her. Everyone was looking at her. They waited. She curtsied to the king.

"Princess Napralina-Victery," said the king. He raised one eyebrow.

"No, I am not she," she said in her careful, Kildenrean accent.

"Not Napralina?" The king's voice was a hammer that rang against the stones.

"No, I am not, but—"

The king signaled, and Ani heard the thuds of the guards' heavy boots approach from behind. Selia smirked.

"No, wait." The words broke like sobs from Ani's throat. A guard's hand was on her shoulder, and she fell to both knees and threw her hands on the ground in front of her, as though she would cling to edges of the floor stones to remain. "Please, wait, listen to me." The guards stood beside her now, close enough that she could feel the heat from their bodies on her back, but they did not pull her away. "Please."

"One moment, sire." Geric squinted against the sunlight that fell steeply through a high window and into his eyes. He took a step forward. The rays of light slipped off his shoulders and onto the ground, heavy as shadow, and his face dimmed to the light of the hall.

"Isi?" His face softened in recognition, then his mouth

widened in that wonderful smile that made lines in his
cheeks and brightened his eyes. "Isi, what's going on?"

Clearly he expected her to smile back, to laugh with him
and admit she was playing some clever joke. She wished she
were, but just a glance at Ungolad ripped away any desire to
smile. Crouched before Geric, she felt hollow and slight and
wretched, and her stomach felt light enough to float up to
her throat.

"Isi was my grandmother's name, among friends," she
said. Her voice did not sound like a princess's, rather
squeaked from her throat, narrowly escaping its tightness.
Geric's eyes darkened under a frown line. She forced her gaze
away from him and to the king, who watched her with barely controlled outrage. Slowly she stood, and the guards, for
the moment, let her be.

"Sire," she said, "I am Anidori-Kiladra Talianna Isilee,
first daughter of Kildenree. That girl"—she pointed toward
Selia without looking—"was my lady-in-waiting."

The silence of the stone hall broke then with gasps and
murmurs, but most clearly of all—a sound high and fierce
that rose above the noise like a raptor's cry—was a laugh.
The other noises died away, and the laugh remained and
became a lovely sound, dainty, artless, intelligent. Selia's pos-
ture was confident and casual, and she seemed to light up
prettily with the attention that focused on her. She smiled
and addressed the king.

"My compatriots and I stood here in silence, Your

Majesty, eagerly awaiting what word this lost bird would bear, and it has proved more entertaining than we had imagined. She is the princess!" Selia shook her head with a sympathetic expression.

"This is the little runaway I told you of, sire, the serving girl who decided in the Forest that she no longer wished to serve and slipped away in the night with one of my gowns and a bag full of coins. It would seem she still has the dress but has spent the coins—though how she managed that in just these few months might be answered only in a gambling hall or tavern. At any rate, it would seem she still does not wish to serve." Selia crossed to Ani and put a soft hand on her shoulder with a benevolent, older-sister expression. "But really, Selia, is not crying 'princess' taking one step too far?"

Ani was still. She could feel Selia's words tremble and wind around the room like a tangible breeze. They slipped from Selia's mouth and hummed in her ears. *Watch that one,* Ani thought, *she has the gift of people-speaking.* Ani had never before felt the full force of Selia's ability. Her ears filled with Selia's words, her head bowed under the weight.

"No," she said. It was all she could say.

"Come now, my dear," said Selia. Her voice was slick like running water and low enough not to echo against stone. "Being a princess is more work than a lady-in-waiting. You should know; you have watched me most of your life." Her smile was only for Ani, and it revealed traces of spite and anger. Ani winced. "You have told me how you have felt being consigned to a life of servitude. I sympathize. I know you feel trapped by your birth and have seen your talents go wasted by the narrowness of your occupation. To wait. To sit and wait and serve your mistress. I can understand it must be frustrating. But, princess?" She laughed so lightly, it seemed to be not an expression of humor, but a gift to the listener. "And as much as it is a burden at times, I'm not going to resign on your behalf. So, please, for the friendship we once shared, admit the truth."

Selia was offering her the release of all trouble, the loosening of tension, a salve for fear. It could all end peacefully. Resolution, is not that what she wanted? Ani struggled against the sound of her voice, shaking her head to free it from her ears, to shake it from her hair, where it tangled itself and whispered relentlessly, *Tell the truth, resign, and tell the truth.*

"No," said Ani. The word was like a stone on her tongue. "I mean, yes, I have told the truth. I am who I say I am."

"Enough of this." The prime minister strode down the steps of the dais. He turned to the king, his short cape lifting with a snap. "Sire, we waste time here on this runaway thief while there are pressing matters of war."

"War," said Ani. The word awoke her senses, and her head lightened. "You started all of this, Selia, in the Forest. The guards, you murdered them. She murdered them all, sire, she and Ungolad and the others. And I ran, so she could not kill me, too. I have been hiding these months as a goose girl. I have witnesses who saw these men try to kill me just as they killed my guards."

Ani spared a glance for Geric to see if he believed her, but his face was somber and unreadable, like that of a guard on duty.

"Now, dear, don't be silly," said Selia. "All my guards are right here." She gestured to the eighteen men behind her.

"No, the others. Where are Rashon, Ingras, Adon, and the others? And, and Radal, and Dano. Poor Dano, who looked up to the warriors as to older brothers and only ever carried a dinner knife in his belt, and"—her voice broke—"you killed him anyway. All of them, sire, all."

Ani looked at Selia's eyes for the first time. "Except Talone."

Selia started to shake her head, then caught herself. Ani flashed a hopeful smile.

"You did not know that, did you? That he survived your slaughter? Sire, I beg you to ask my escort Talone. He is just outside the gates. Your guards would not admit him, but he stands ready to testify to you that what I say is true. He was there. He witnessed the massacre in the Forest."

The Kildenrean guards looked at one another and murmured softly until Ungolad silenced them with one quick, slight look. Selia blinked.

"Ah, Talone, your cohort. Is he still with you?" Her voice lost its sweetness and almost betrayed real anger. Her lips curled slightly as though she would spit. "Of course, you would not be so brazen as to make these claims unless you had a false witness to improve the odds. He is so fickle, however, I would not have guessed him to stay with you since the Forest, once you lost your coin."

The prime minister rustled his cape again. "Sire, the young prince is tired from the hunt, and this Kildenrean's spy's lies are none of his concern. I recommend he be saved from this raucous tedium."

Ani looked over at the young prince. His face was pinched and white, and he tugged the bottom of his tunic with the self-consciousness of a boy who is growing too fast for his clothes. Again the thought of marrying him troubled her, but his sweet, boyish face invoked her pity as well. Knowing what she did, she could not abandon him to an unwitting marriage to the likes of Selia.

The king roughly wiped his brow. "Yes, I grow rather tired of it myself. Would that I had youth as an excuse to withdraw." He waved a hand, and two guards, neither one Geric, began to escort the young prince from the room.

"Wait," said Ani, afraid she was not being taken seriously, "shouldn't the prince stay? After all, this is the matter of his bride."

The prime minister laughed with scorn. "You see, Your Highness? She doesn't even know what she's saying." He turned to Ani with an arch in one eyebrow. "The princess, of course, is betrothed to our elder prince, Geric."

"Geric?" Ani felt as though all the wind had left her lungs, and she said his name with her last squeak of breath. "Geric is the prince?"

He met her gaze, his lips tight and thoughtful.

"You are?"

He nodded. His forehead was worried with lines, and while he stared at her, she found it hard to look away. She did not want to. She was afraid she was losing, losing the war and losing the fight for her name, and now, painfully, she realized she was also losing Geric.

"Isi, are you truly Kildenrean? Truly Anidori?"

"Yes, I am, I swear, I—"

The king grumbled. "What's all this, Geric?"

Geric addressed the king, but he kept his eyes on Ani. "I knew this girl, before, as a goose girl."

"You called her Isi," said the king.

"Yes, that's what she—that's what I thought her name was."

"And did she ever claim to you that she was the princess?"

"No, but—"

"Oh, sire," said Selia with a sigh, "clearly she was trying to use the prince to win her little game."

"Mmm," said the king. Geric looked at her again, and the new doubt in his eyes hurt her like a slap.

"Sire, there are other matters that beg your attention," said the prime minister.

"The war," said Ani. She felt a new urgency to convince them, and she watched Geric's face anxiously as she spoke. "It is her idea, the war. Kildenree is not plotting. There is no conspiracy. She invented it all to hide her bloody deeds."

"Sire," said the prime minister.

"Please listen to me. Geric, you know me. You must believe that what I'm saying is true."

The prime minister huffed. "This is obviously a Kildenrean spy sent to thwart our endeavors."

"She is a fraud," said Ani. "All she says is a lie."

"Sire, don't let this yellow-haired wench craft doubt on our war."

"Enough!" said the king. His face was red, and his eyes were on Ani.

"Sire," said Geric, putting a hand on his arm, "we should listen to her."

At Geric's words, Selia frowned.

"We have listened enough." The king shook off his son. "This girl announces herself as Napralina, then she says she's Anidori, then you call her Isi, then she's Selia. It appears that she's also that goose girl who curtsies so prettily and was found spying around the royal stables last winter. Whoever she is, she'd better decide quickly so we know what to engrave on her tombstone. I smell treason." The king stomped down the stairs and stood before Ani, his eyes searching her face for answers. "Anidori, my dear."

Ani opened her mouth to answer.

"Yes, my lord," said Selia.

"What's the punishment for treason in Kildenree?"

Banishment, thought Ani, *but Selia will not say that*, and she noted that Selia's eyes sparkled while she thought.

"My lord," said Selia, "it is a grave crime and thus a public castigation. To be placed naked in a barrel full of nails and dragged through the streets by four white horses, I believe."

A phantom pain prickled down Ani's skin. She could not speak.

"You believe?" said the king. "Be sure. We've heard enough. She's not our citizen or our concern. I'm seriously considering leaving her in the dungeon here until this war is through and I've a free moment to deal with such nonsense."

"Oh, there's no need for that, Father," said Geric. "No one has proved she's done anything criminal."

"It's wartime, Geric," said the king. "I don't need proof." He stood up and gestured to the guards to carry her away.

"A moment," said Geric with a staying hand. "As you said, she isn't your citizen or your concern. Leave the girl here with her compatriots, and together they can arrive at a suitable resolution. Maybe the reminder of what her punishment might be will encourage her to tell the truth."

"Fine." The king looked at Selia. "Send for my chief guard in an hour. If you haven't convinced her to tell the truth, we'll lock her up until we've time for this."

Ani looked at the Kildenrean guards. They were all smiling.

"No, Geric, you don't understand them," Ani said. "Please don't leave me." She followed the king and Geric to the door.

The guards held her back.

"It's for the best, Isi," said Geric. He studied the room a moment, his eyes scanning the faces of the Kildenreans, before frowning and turning away.

"No," she said as Geric and the king exited the room. "Don't leave me here with them. They are murderers." She tried to pull away from the two guards holding her arms and let her shouts chase down the corridor after Geric. "Come back, please!"

All the king's guard were gone but her two captors. She turned to them, clinging to their tunics.

"Don't leave me," she said, sobbing, panic wretching her gut. "Please. Just you two stay."

Ani would not let go, so one pushed her to the ground. She scrambled to her feet as they exited, closed, and locked the door behind them. She ran to the door and banged with her fists, calling after the guards, begging them to come back, to just ask the king and he would give them permission to guard her, ask the prince and come back. After a while she stopped banging and tried to hear over the sound of her own heaving breath if there was anyone on the other side of the door. Nothing. Silence.

She stood against it for a few moments, her forehead pressed on the polished grain, breathing against its closeness, feeling her breath touch the wood and bounce back to her face, hot and quick. A cold chill raced down her back. Behind her, the room was still.

he one door was closed, the few high windows shut out any wind. Ani closed her eyes. There was no air stirring the tiny hairs on the back of her hand or passing across her neck. She felt no movement of any kind, save her heartbeat in her fingertips pressed against the door—a fast beat, the kind drummers played for their sorcerers when the trick reached its climax. At last she turned around.

They were all watching her, carrion crows perched on a fence, Selia the wild hunting cat in yellow. Selia stretched out a finger and motioned Ani forward.

"Away from the door," she said softly. "I would rather no one heard us just now."

Ani turned and leaned her back fully against the hard wall, letting her body soak in that last feeling of safety. Selia spoke a word, and Redmon and Uril grabbed her elbows and carried her to the far end of the room. Ani cried out but doubted anyone in the corridor heard or cared. They dumped her on the dais steps.

Selia stood over her. Ani stared at the hem of Selia's dress where the slant of light from a high window slashed it. The yellow was almost too bright to see, and she squinted, filtering the light through her lashes. She wondered if Selia would speak again and tangle her mind in words. She heard whispering and looked up. Ungolad stood close to Selia, his arm tight around her waist, his lips on hers.

"We have won," Selia said, and kissed him again. Ungolad caught Ani's eyes and leaned over her. One of his braids slapped her cheek.

"Little bird," said Ungolad, "the king sounded convinced, hmm? Aren't you proud of our Selia for thinking of such a diverting execution for you so quickly?"

"It seems you need the king's army to kill me, as you were so easily overwhelmed by two sleeping geese."

Ungolad pulled her arms and forced her to stand, and a thorny pain tore at her half-healed wound. She would not look at his eyes. She could feel the heat of his breath and of his anger on her cheeks.

"Why do you not crawl, little princess? Why do you not beg?"

"I hear you have been hiding as a goose girl all these months," said Selia. "A shame you had to stoop so low only to be killed now."

"Not so low," Ani said. "Where is Yulan?" She felt bitterness like a hot wind prickle the skin of her face, and she wanted to hurt Selia somehow, see her composure fail.

"Where is Yulan?" said Selia in a mocking voice. "You think to surprise me? We heard of your little stunt from Ishta."

"Ishta," said Ani. "Last I saw, Ishta was bleeding on your bedroom carpets, though perhaps his body has already been found."

Selia seemed to see Ani's dress for the first time and recognize it from her wardrobe. She covered her mouth and muffled a scream of frustration. Her face flashed and reminded Ani of the tantrums she threw as a little girl. *She has not grown up*, thought Ani, *after all this time*. But the girl calmed herself with eerie speed. She dropped her hands to lift Ani's chin and look in her eyes, speaking softly.

"These months have been really, really wonderful for me, Crown Princess. They truly have. I want you to know that. I have always known what I wanted, since I was a little girl, and you helped me to achieve it." She kissed Ani's forehead and caressed her cheek with her thumb. "Thank you. And thank you for coming back. My one last wish, even when I thought you were dead in the woods, was to let you see me being you and doing it better."

Ungolad watched Selia, her every word fascinating him. He caressed her arm and murmured something low. Selia's attention did not waver from Ani.

"But unfortunately you did cause one little bother. The king is unquestioning, but my betrothed, my prince, seemed to have some doubts because of your convenient acquaintance. He seemed to resolve them there at the end, but I want to be sure. I spent months working to own his heart, and I don't wish to go through that process again. So, dearest, here is the plan. When they return, you will confess to the king that you made it all up and in fact are my serving girl, and in turn, I will talk him down from the crime of treason. You will live. If you like, I will even let you return to your little goose herd. Agreed?"

Ani bit her lip hard. The temptation to give in seemed to squeeze her ribs against her lungs. She spoke through clenched teeth. "Do you know why you have such trouble persuading Geric to love you? He fell in love with me as the goose girl in my pasture months ago." *At least, I hoped he had,* she thought, but stared defiantly at Selia as though she had no doubts.

Selia slapped Ani's cheek. Ani stumbled backward and found herself in Ungolad's arms. He held both her hands behind her back and raised a knife to her throat.

"Listen to me, little bird," he said. "When they come back, you will say what my Princess Anidori-Kiladra tells you to."

The edge of his dagger was so close, she did not dare to swallow. The blade felt as sharp as fear. "You will not kill me here," she said.

"No?" said Ungolad. "And if I claim you went mad and attacked me? As mad as that poor white horse?"

"We had to take care of that animal of yours, of course,"

said Selia. "If you had appeared and all the world witnessed that oh-so-magical bond you had with my mount? It was not difficult. He was already half-mad from the Forest, and Ungolad knows ways of making an animal a little madder."

Ani struggled, and Ungolad kneed the raw scar on her back. She cried out, and he released her wrists and put a hand over her mouth. "Was I right? Is this the spot where I tickled you?" He kneed her there again, her scream muffled by his hand, a tear dropping on his first finger. She grabbed his arms and thought she might as well tug against metal bars.

"I'm telling you again," said Ungolad, "you will agree with your new mistress or you will die here."

"Enough, enough, my love." Selia stroked his chin with her finger, the expression in her eyes as soft and distant as a cat's. "She will not speak. Can you not see that she's in love with the prince?"

"But, Talone," said Ungolad.

"He does not concern me. I don't know how he escaped our notice, but he can't have proof beyond scars and a questionable testimony. It is the prince's doubt that troubles me. Ungolad, I want you to cut me."

Ani could feel him shake his head.

"Release her and cut me. I will scream, we will claim she attacked me, and the worst will be over."

"Selia, love," said Ungolad. It was the first time Ani had detected fear in his voice. "I can't cut you, I can't cut your skin."

"I'll do it," said Terne.

"Shut it, you piece of meat," said Ungolad. "You think I'd let you touch her?"

Selia pressed herself close to Ungolad, her lips at his ear. His hands began to shake. Ani could hear Selia whisper, "I'm not afraid. Be brave, my love, and our labors will be over." She kissed his neck.

Ungolad took two panicked breaths. "All right," he said with a growl. "I will, if we can kill her first. Then we can claim she attacked, and I was defending you."

"Stop! Don't touch her!"

All turned to look in the direction of the voice, toward the dais and the throne. It was empty. Ungolad's hand pressed harder against Ani's mouth. Selia took a step forward. The voice had come from behind them. No one was there.

An enormous tapestry behind the throne covered the far wall of the room. It had the appearance of age, of colors once vibrant that had dimmed from candle smoke and sunlight. It was unremarkable—a traditional scene of some dead king at the hunt on a once dark steed, the white, slender-antlered hart fleeing, hounds with long snouts and gold collars fast at its hooves—unremarkable, but that its center was fluttering like the breast of a bird.

Its edge lifted and Geric burst forth. The king followed, and then the king's guard. Ani heard Ungolad curse and Selia gasp. Ani felt like gasping herself.

Geric's eyes searched the room wildly, stopping when he saw Ani, Ungolad's hand over her mouth and knife at her throat. He shouted in rage, drew his sword, and rushed forward.

"Get back!" Ungolad pulled Ani tighter and turned the dagger threateningly.

Geric halted and took a step back to show he would not provoke Ungolad, but he did not sheathe his sword. The king's guard stood around him with ready swords. The Kildenreans drew theirs as well.

"Don't be fools," said Geric. "You hurt her and your lives are forfeit."

The door at the head of the room opened and soldiers with the royal insignia on their shields filed into the chamber and took position. Ani knew there were more waiting in the corridor, though she could not see them. She did not stop to realize how she knew.

"Let her go," said Geric. "Isi, are you all right?"

She looked at him beseechingly and felt Ungolad squeeze his hand as though he could crack her jaw. A small note of pain escaped her throat.

"Easy, Ungolad," said Geric, raising his shield arm in peace. "Let's talk. What do you want to let the princess go?"

"You are mistaken," said Selia, her voice shaking. "She is my lady-in-waiting. This is all a joke. I'm the princess."

The king shook his head sadly and descended the steps closer to Selia. "We heard your entire conversation, I'm afraid, so let's skip the declarations of innocence and move on to bargaining, shall we?" She stared at him with wide, frightened eyes. He smiled back and motioned to the tapestry behind him.

"Clever opening back there, is it not, my girl? Years ago, before this estate was generously and unwillingly turned over to the crown, the lord here was a genuine dimwit. He had a minister stashed behind his throne to whisper clever things to say. I'd forgotten about it until now, but Geric used to play there as a boy and he brought it to my attention as soon as we left you."

The king glanced at his son. Geric kept his eyes on Ungolad and tightened the grip on his sword.

"He is a good boy, always was a better judge of character than me. It was his idea to make you think you were alone and employ the listening portal. I guess he thought I was too stubborn to believe this girl's story unless he arranged for me to hear you all admit it yourselves, and I suppose he was right."

The king smiled fondly at Selia and reached out a hand to her. She took a step back.

"I think you know I never wish to harm a lady," said the king. "Your own hands have spilt no blood, I think. Tell your lover there to release the princess and we'll judge you all fairly."

For several moments no one spoke. The tension was as tight as the stones in the walls, as stifling as the heat and closeness. Ungolad's hand was sweating against Ani's skin. His shield on his left arm pressed against her back. His sword hung at his side. She knew he yearned to feel his blade break her skin, to stop her breathing and her heart that beat through her back against his own chest, but that her life was the only coin in his hand.

Geric glanced at the king, at the soldiers around him, at the Kildenreans. No one moved. He reached out his hand to Ani. Ungolad took half a step backward.

"Easy there, sir," said Geric as though he spoke to a wild horse. "Just lower your knife and let her come to me."

"Ungolad," said Selia. Her voice was raw with fear, and Ungolad stiffened at her command.

"Come here," he said, "all of you!"

There was an echo of boot steps that made Ani's skin shiver as Selia and the Kildenreans took position behind Ungolad and his hostage. Geric and some of the guards stepped forward.

"I will kill her," said Ungolad. "Believe I will." His hand shook at Ani's throat. Geric halted.

"Ungolad," said Geric, "this is the time for negotiations, not for fighting. If you start fighting, you all die. If you kill her, you all die. Let her go and I guarantee none of you will be executed."

"We take her with us," said Selia. "That will be our guarantee."

"We can discuss that," said the king.

Ani's eyes widened in panic. She was certain that if the Kildenreans used her life to make their escape, they would kill her once they had. Geric saw Ani's reaction and seemed to understand its meaning.

"No," he said. "No, that's not possible. Settle this now, in this room."

"If we can't leave with her as our assurance of safety," said Selia, "then there will be nothing to settle."

There were soldiers in the chamber and soldiers in the corridor. Ani blinked hard and swallowed against the knife. Soldiers in the corridor. She knew that because something had told her, something had touched her and carried the image of those men in perfect lines, javelins in hand, waiting for entrance, their muscles tight and anxious. A breeze from the open door.

"Tell them to back away, Crown Princess. Tell them to let us pass, and once we're on our way we will send you back." Selia's voice quavered with too many tones, confusing the roles she played—commanding, regal, humble, coercive, friendly, and under it all the hate and jealousy that shook her bones when she spoke Ani's title. Ani concentrated on turning the voice, her words that had always struck like javelins and pinned down her mind with their commands, turning those shooting words into feathers, floating away. Her eyes were closed. She was listening for any breeze, any movement of air on her skin. *Please*, she prayed, *please come*.

"Tell them," said Selia.

A trickle of air, a cool corridor draft, brushed her brow. Selia tapped Ungolad, and he loosened the fingers on Ani's mouth so she could tell them to back away.

"No," said Ani.

The breeze pulled with it more breezes, and they circled her ankles. The air stirred around her legs, and the breeze pulled that movement into itself. She felt a draft from the high walls and beckoned it near, and a new breeze from the door that pulled in a wind from the out-of-doors on its tail, and they all merged at her feet and rustled her hem.

The room was still as they watched her gather wind. Geric watched her face, his lips parted in awe.

Quickly the wind climbed, circling her hips and waist, pushing itself between her body and Ungolad's arms and attempting to press his blade away from her throat. His hold on her tightened, and the blade slid just a little across her skin.

"Stop it! Stop it!" he said, his voice edged with terror.

That new source of wind touched the back of her head. Ani beckoned it, and it came, the very breath out of Ungolad's mouth, one long string of wind unhooked from his lungs and throat, drawn out like a snail from its shell. Breathless, he choked and stumbled, and his hold slackened. The circling wind fattened and, rising, pressed itself between his hand and her throat. As he gasped for air, Ani punched hard backward with her elbow and stepped out of his reach.

She turned to face her countrymen. The wind raised her

arms at her sides and spun through her hair, beating it against the air, lifting high her locks like bright yellow flames. The Kildenreans stared at her, and some backed against the wall. She did not want to release it, the coolness on her skin, the soft touch, the shield it gave her, and the feeling at last of safety, at last that they could not touch her.

"Your war's done," said Ani.

Her hair whipped above her head. Her skirts beat around her legs with a sound like hands clapping. No one moved. They were all staring at her.

"Undone," said Selia, as if the word were a mournful song.

It all happened in a moment. Ungolad growled, his voice touching every corner of the chamber. He raised his sword and ran to Ani, hacking down at her neck. The blade was caught and slowed by Ani's twisting, invisible armor, and she had a moment to turn away from his stroke. His sword came down hard on the stone floor. Ani swung around to face him again. She held the winds circling her body and searched the room for more, but his blow had disrupted and loosed some. The Bayern soldiers stood as if bewitched, watching the strange wind, their sword tips resting on the ground. She saw Ungolad's eyes. He would strike again.

"Geric," she said, and turned to see him already advancing, shouting a warrior's cry as he ran. But he was too far away. Ungolad ignored him and raised his sword again.

"Ungolad!"

Ungolad stopped his stroke at the familiar voice. He turned and looked. Talone stood in the doorway, the swords of soldiers pointed at his chest and the soldiers looking to the king for sign of what to do.

Talone, red faced and sweating, shouted as though over a great din, though the hall was quiet, the soldiers confused. He banged his sword on his shield and shouted, desperate to keep Ungolad's attention. "Come on, you mercenary, you coward, you slayer of cook-men and women without weapon. Fight me! Fight me!"

Ungolad's snarl changed to a smile, and his eyes betrayed a loss and a madness that Ani had never before seen. He rushed to his former captain, and the guards released Talone to meet Ungolad's strike with his own sword. Behind them, struggling through the crowded corridor came the workers, lifting crooks and staffs and shouting, "For her! For the yellow lady! For the princess!"

The shout broke the silence. The soldiers raised weapons and the Kildenreans charged, hacking their blades at any who stood near them, hoping to cut down others before they were cut down themselves. Instantly battle was engaged. Every Kildenrean fought, and for every Bayern two more soldiers stood at his back. Terne killed his soldier and met Ani's eyes. He advanced, his anger and desperation pushed before him like a hot breath. He knocked aside one soldier with his shield arm, and he pointed his sword at Ani. Her skirts were still now. Her wind had dissipated into a coolness on her face. She backed away and stumbled against the dais steps. She looked around her for a weapon and found none. And then Geric was there.

"I will have you, little prince," said Terne.

Geric raised his sword against Terne's attack. Terne leapt forward and then stopped, his eyes suddenly like a fish's, dim and shallow. He fell forward from the impact of the javelin in his back. Ani blinked. Razo stood several paces behind him, his arm still outstretched with the throw, a look of wonder and horror heavy on his young face.

Geric pulled Ani to her feet and put his shield arm around her protectively. They were in the midst of battle. On all sides sounded the deadly rings of sword on sword, the dull thuds as javelins met flesh, the eerie echoes of groans, and the grim noise a weapon makes when it breaks skin and cracks bones. A Kildenrean rushed toward them with sword flashing. Geric parried his blows and kicked him away, backing Ani toward the wall.

"Are you all right?" he said.

"Yes."

He held her closer and pressed his cheek against her head. She closed her eyes briefly at the comfort of his touch, her heart warming at the feel of his exhale on her brow.

Reluctantly, she opened her eyes again to look over the scene. Everywhere, Kildenreans sprawled motionless on the floor. Hul lay in a heap, his head bowed over his death wound. Redmon and Uril were lifeless bodies at the feet of the king's soldiers. But several combats still raged, and the sight of one of these dried the exclamation on Ani's tongue. She pressed Geric's arm and pointed.

In the center of the room, Talone barely met Ungolad's onslaught. He was on his knees, defending with shield and sword, being pushed down to the ground. He grabbed Ungolad and held him close, their swords locked. Talone's sword gave a little, and Ungolad's blade entered his shoulder. Ungolad withdrew it, bright with Talone's blood, and shouted a laugh.

"Here!" said Geric. The prince ran to Ungolad, hoping to distract him with a new enemy before he could finish the job of death. "Here, I will fight you."

Ungolad nodded. "Yes, you. You would have touched Selia. You would have shared her bed." Ungolad's face became serious. Without seeming to move, he swept his blade before him. Geric was there with his own blade, and the two met with a clash like a bell to battle. The prince was taller than Ungolad and nearly as broad, but Ani thought it likely that Geric's swordplay had never left the training fields, while Ungolad was an experienced killer.

Ani looked to make certain that Talone was out of danger. Two soldiers near him had taken hold of his shoulders and legs and carried him from the room. None stepped forward to aid the prince in his fight against Ungolad, so Ani grabbed a javelin from a fallen guard and prepared to join the fray. Two pairs of hands grabbed her shoulders and stopped her short. She protested and turned to see two of the king's guards. They pulled her back against the wall.

"Princess Anidori," said one, "you'll stay with us. The king wants you safe."

"But, Geric. Why do you all stand still and let that traitor fight him?"

The older of the two shook his head. "It's the prince's battle and his first. It's his honor, and I won't interfere."

The cacophony of many battles died out, leaving only one. The bodies of Kildenreans were scattered across the floor. The soldiers of Bayern stepped back toward the walls, creating an open circle in the center of the room like a stage. Ungolad did not look around to see his fallen comrades. His eyes never left Geric's, and he swung his sword with strength and confidence, pushing Geric back and down, down, the broad man standing over him and striking again, again, again. They locked swords, and Ungolad curled back his lips in an animal grin and spat in the prince's face.

"I fight a boy," said Ungolad. "She would never love a boy." Spittle dripped off his lip.

The soldier holding Ani groaned. The room was breathless. The king, his brow wet and his sword tip dripping blood, took one step forward and hesitated. Ungolad pressed, and Geric was pushed to his knees, their arms shaking, their faces sweating with exhaustion and pain. Ungolad raised his shield arm and struck Geric in the head. He fell back.

Ungolad pulled back his sword for a deathblow.

"Honor," whispered Ani.

Wrapped around her hand and wrist were every breeze and draft, every movement of air that had touched her since Geric had left her side, and she begged of it now a new course, quick and sure. A bolt of wind like a dull arrow thumped Ungolad in his chest. He stumbled backward and, shifting his eyes, saw Ani and cursed. Geric had time to stand and shake his vision straight before Ungolad was on him again. He blocked with his sword and pushed Ungolad back. The next time, his sword was too slow and he blocked a strike with his shield. Ungolad's shield hand suddenly held a dagger, and he stuck it in Geric's side. Geric cried out and kicked Ungolad away, and the dagger pulled free from Ungolad's grasp and fell clanging across the floor. Geric grimaced and advanced again.

There was power behind Geric's strike now, as though the wound gave him strength, and the fight became as real as the pain. He was on the attack, pushing Ungolad onto the dais. Ungolad defended with his shield, and when his shield dented, Geric's sword slipped down it to bloody his fist. They locked swords, and Geric kneed Ungolad in the belly. Ungolad lost his balace and stumbled backward against the dais steps, falling against the seat of the throne. Their swords locked again. With a shove Geric sent Ungolad's sword slipping down his own with a painful peal of metal. Geric shook off Ungolad's sword, found an opening, and then pierced

Ungolad's leather jerkin clean through.

Ungolad sat heavily in the throne. His sword dropped to the ground with a cry that echoed in the corners of stone. He looked around wildly.

"Selia," said Ungolad.

His hand found the wound in his middle. He held it there, and the blood slipped through the cracks between his fingers. He looked up as if he saw Selia standing there before him, and he held up his red hand, showing her the death blood, showing her the color of his heart, a final pledge. He slumped and died.

eric sat on the dais steps and let his sword and shield drop. The echo was dimmer than Ungolad's had been, the noise finding not bare walls but snuffed out by a room full of people. The king put a hand on his shoulder.

"Stand up, son."

The king picked up a misshot javelin that lay on the floor, brought it down hard on his knee with a loud snap and once again to break it clean through. He dropped the pieces at Geric's feet.

"Sword," said the king.

Geric held out his sword, the tip murky with blood. A soldier at the king's right cleaned it on his own tunic and handed it to the king.

"I give it back to you to wear in defense of your people and your land and your sovereign. May it be quick and thick with the blood of your foes."

Enna came to Ani's side. "Are you all right?"

"Yes," she said. "What does it mean?"

"It was his first kill," said Enna. "A javelin bonds a boy to a community. A sword makes him a man."

"I think he was already a man," said Ani, rubbing her tired eyes.

The other workers stood near Enna. When the fighting ceased, they had gathered behind Ani. She looked at them now. Razo was stunned and tired, his thoughts seemingly caught in that moment when he had fired a javelin at Terne's back. Ratger had a scratch on one cheek, and Offo held a hand to his arm where there was a little blood. They had all chosen to not merely make an entrance, but throw themselves into the fight.

"This's a grim sight." Enna looked about the room, bodies slumped and crumpled, their bleeding stopped by stones and carpets.

"Where's Selia?" said Ani.

The king heard her and looked around. Geric sheathed his sword at his side and stood ready, a hand at his bleeding side. Razo grumbled, "Oh, that's just perfect."

"How did you let that murderess escape?" The king's voice trembled with anger.

"Through the secret door," said Ani. She remembered now, the draft that she had used as an arrow against Ungolad. It had carried images of cool stone and musty cloth and anger and a girl in yellow.

"First body," said the soldier at the king's side, "search the estate. Second body, secure the wall. Third body, inform the gate guards and then report to me. Go."

Soldiers in ordered groups ran from the room, and the sounds of their boots running in the corridors bled through the stone walls.

"Sly little cat," said the king. "She knows the punishment for treason. She named it herself."

"She'll be found, sire," said a soldier. He paced to the chamber door and stood waiting for the first report.

"Get that thing out of my chair," said the king. Two soldiers removed Ungolad's body from the throne and wiped off the blood with a tunic torn from one of the fallen. The king sat down, his elbows on the rests, his head in his hands.

"Sire," said Geric.

The king waved him toward the door. "Go on, son, you're not doing me any good by bleeding."

A gray-haired soldier held a white handkerchief swiftly turning red to Geric's side. He bade him lean upon him, and together they walked across the chamber. Ani watched him, wondering, *Will he come to me now? Should I go to him?* She hesitated, and Geric left the room, his eyes on the ground. *Later*, she thought. She hoped.

Servants were gathering fallen swords and javelins in their arms like wood for a bonfire. Ani took a breath and approached the king and tried to avoid looking again at the bodies that lay at her feet and made her eyes itch and the room tip unpleasantly. Already estate workers were dragging away the bodies and rolling up blood-spotted carpets. Ani was feeling rolled up and blood spotted herself, but her friends stood at her back.

"Sire." She spoke again in the Bayern accent, having found that it felt most natural. "I've a bold request."

The king looked at her without raising his head. "It would seem, my dear, that you're in a good position for making bold requests."

"There're men in my company who'd like to receive their javelin and shield. I ask for them, and also mercy for Ratger, who left his post at your gates to come with us on this errand."

"All those boys?" said the king.

"Yes, Razo here slew Terne before he could slay me, and Offo and Beier and Conrad . . . Where's Conrad?"

"Conrad?" said Enna.

The workers looked from one to another, bewildered. "He was with us," said Razo.

With dread they looked through the bodies for sight of Conrad's orange cap, freckled face, and boyish hands. Among the Kildenreans there were three Bayern soldiers, but not Conrad.

Someone screamed. Ani looked behind the throne. The tapestry thumped, and a high voice shouted curses.

"Lift it aside," said the king. Two soldiers jumped to the task, unveiling Conrad standing in the portal, his hands full of pale hair. Behind him, prostrate on the ground, he dragged Selia. His hands were bleeding from her fingernails and his face was red from exertion, but his eyes met those of his friends and suggested a glimmer of humor.

"Look what I found," he said. "The pretender yellow girl, though she's not so yellow as ours now that I get a look at her. But she scratches like a cat."

The soldiers were upon her and in moments had her standing with her arms pinned behind her back. Conrad released her hair and put his hands to his mouth, nursing the scratches. Ungolad's body was one of the few still in the room. It lay near Selia's feet, partially covered by a stained rug. She glanced at it, then returned her gaze to the king, no recognition registering on her face.

"Let me loose," said Selia. Her voice sounded falsely sweet and tight with anger. "Let me loose, sire, I promise I will leave. You don't want to kill a lady. I'm a lady."

The king wrinkled his brow and sighed. "You may save your breath, lady. The crime of treason has been named, and the punishment you yourself have specified."

Selia looked at the king, panic alive in her eyes, and she stomped and screamed as though even then the barrel-held nails pierced her skin. Her face contorted red and purple, and she thrashed against the soldiers' holds.

"Enough," said the king, his hands covering his ears. "We'll talk of this later. I want this child out of my hearing." The king gestured, and the soldiers carried her from the room, spitting and swearing vengeance. She did not meet Ani's eyes.

Selia's howl faded down the corridor and all were quiet, listening, until Enna snorted and said, "And a meow to you, too."

"Did you see that I caught her, Enna?" said Conrad. He dabbed a bleeding scratch against his tunic and smiled with pride. "By her hair and all. I saw her sneaking away, and I thought, That's the one what tried to kill our goose girl, and there'll be no more of that. So I ran after her and found her trying to get through a window."

"Sire," said Ani, "this is the goose boy, Conrad."

Conrad stuck out his hand to shake, then dropped it and bowed gawkily.

"She's the real yellow lady," he said, pointing at Ani, "and I'm sorry I ever thought otherwise."

A draft left Ani's hand and nudged Conrad's cap off his head. He looked at her with mild panic, and she grinned. "Nicely done, Conrad."

They were each escorted to a room with, to Ani's delight, a real mattress and enough pillows to make her body forget the cruel slats of her hard little bed in the west settlement.

When morning declared its fullness in Ani's east window, she rose and bathed and sat in a much too comfortable chair with her back to the light, letting its heat dry her just washed hair and sipping from an endless pitcher of iced grape juice.

She was just thinking about skulking down the corridor in search of the others when her door was rapped and opened by Enna.

"May I enter?" she said.

"Enna, you're not going to get formal on me now. Last night Ratger bowed to me, and Razo asked my leave to depart to his room."

"At least Conrad'll never bow," said Enna, sitting beside Ani. "I've never seen him so content as he was last night, bleeding hands and all. He almost looked smug."

Ani smiled. "Keeping geese was too dull for him. He'd make a fine peace-keeper."

"Yes, I think he'd stay in the city, unlike Finn and some of the others whose faces seem full of the Forest."

"Oh, Finn'll never leave the Forest, especially not if he could accompany a certain lady there."

Enna smiled and stretched her feet to reach a spot where a sunbeam warmed the floor. She cleared her throat before speaking. "Isi, you've spoken to the prince? To Geric?"

"He . . . I . . . no." Ani sighed. "He's stashed in a sickroom somewhere, getting that dagger wound tended, and I was afraid to ask to see him in case, you know, in case he didn't really want me to."

"Of course he does," said Enna.

"Well, I don't know, we were friends, but there were lies between us, and what if he was happy he was going to marry Selia?"

"Not likely," said Enna.

That was just the response Ani had hoped for, though she was uncertain if it was true. She poured grape juice for Enna into a white cup. The juice sliding against the sides of the cup looked like thick blood against pale skin. Ani shivered.

"What a day it was," she said.

"Yes," said Enna. "Do you think they'll really stick that Selia into a barrel studded with nails?"

"I do. I think they will. We've seen them hang traitors and murderers up on the walls, and she's both. I don't know what to think of it, Enna. I don't know how to feel. Sometimes I catch myself thinking, But she's a friend. And then I remember, no, no she's not, she never was. She really did kill. She really would've started a war so that she could wear rubies on her brow."

"Have you seen Talone?"

"I tried. They won't let me go to him, saying that he's fine and resting and doesn't need overconcerned friends bothering him out of his sleep."

"But you worry still," said Enna.

"I want to see him well. I can't get certain images to rest easy in my mind, and one of those is Talone, and Ungolad's sword is in him, and he's on the ground." Ani shook her head.

"It was a horrible day," said Enna. "I've never seen such things and don't care to. Maybe I never should've come inside, but all I could think of was getting to you. I was horror-struck just thinking that you were alone again, and after all I'd promised."

"Thank you," said Ani. She fingered Enna's thick locks. They were as smooth as wet clay between her fingers. "I always wanted black hair. I thought it was exotic."

Enna laughed. "Now you're the exotic one, with your hair longer than a horse's tail and yellow, even."

A knock sounded, and Ani jumped up to admit a prim little man in shiny boots who called her to the king.

"I'd hoped to see my friend," she said. "Talone, who's wounded. Last night the physician sent me away to let him rest."

"I hear your friend's in no danger. The king's call'll be heeded first."

Ani shot Enna a look of lighthearted terror and followed the man out.

He introduced her into the conference room, a small but brightly lit space. The air was tense. Several men sitting at a great wood table covered with maps and letters rose as she entered. Geric's face was flushed, as though he had been shouting before her arrival, but she was relieved to see him sitting up and looking well. The prime minister's face barely buried a glower. The king motioned for her to be seated.

"Good morning, my dear," said the king. "We're sorry to have neglected you so long and to greet you now with the grim details of a war meeting in place of a banquet and pro-cession. All in its course." He cleared his throat, and his expression seemed unsure, but when he spoke again the words bore all the power of the throne. "We beg you to give us reason to believe there's no war preparing in Kildenree."

Ani's head bent back slightly, as though pushed by the king's words.

"I don't understand, sire." Ani swallowed a laugh. "You're still contemplating war?"

"Unless you can give us evidence."

"Evidence? Of what? Of peace? Teach me how to give evidence of peace and I will." She paused to check her anger. The men still stared. "You must know that Kildenree will not attack Bayern."

The prime minister rose, exuding authority with one exact gesture of his hand. "This, my dear, is evidence." He picked up several papers before him. "Letters given to us by the Princess Anidori-Kiladra, or this Selia, if you will. They're written and signed by the queen of Kildenree and detail inimical intentions, with dates, numbers, places, all stamped with the royal insignia."

Ani grabbed a parchment and had to absorb its aspect for only a moment before understanding. "This isn't my mother's hand. Forgery. Selia's mother is the key-mistress of the palace, a woman with access. She might have found a way to steal my mother's crest ring to make the seals."

The prime minister glanced at the king's thoughtful face and turned back to Ani with new ardor. "Evidence. Show evidence and we'll believe. It's another ploy, Your Highness, to keep us unwitting and unprepared while our enemies move to crush us in our sleep."

"Oh, stop it." Ani covered her face in her hands and breathed in the momentary darkness. She dropped them and stood up, anger prickling her fingertips. "This is ridiculous. You want evidence? History will show you that Kildenree hasn't warred with any of its neighbors in over three hundred years. Numbers will prove that Kildenree is far too small to attack a kingdom like Bayern. And the girl who gave you the only evidence you have to the contrary is a fraud, a deceiver, and a murderer. You should already know these facts.

"But in a country where you hang your dead up on walls and pride whether or not a man bears a javelin more than his character, how am I to persuade you out of a war? It would be suicide for Kildenree to war on Bayern and butchery for Bayern to attack Kildenree. If you don't believe me, then send me back. Or if you don't trust me to leave, I'll return to my little room on the west wall and tend your geese, and you can be sure that on my watch no thieves will touch my flock."

Ani walked to the door but stopped and turned around. "Did you know that there're workers in your city who aren't allowed into shops and taverns because they're from the Forest and therefore don't hold a javelin? And men who call themselves peace-keepers, obeying their own code of law and not the king's, sworn to keep the streets safe because the king's soldiers do not or will not? And areas so crowded that children live on the refuse of others?"

While the prime minister's look remained indignant, Geric's eyebrows raised and the king looked up from his study of his hands.

"I see from your faces that you don't think much about these things. Maybe I know more about your city than you do, and I certainly know more of Kildenree. Believe me, there is no war. If you want evidence, explain why a mother would send her first daughter into her enemy's camp. I'll be your evidence." She shut the door behind her.

An hour later, Geric found her sitting on the steps to the kitchen in the shade of the tallest chimney. Her anger had worn down into a righteous indignation that was fraying into embarrassment when she saw his approach. She knew it was Geric from a distance, and she felt spots of heat on her cheeks. She covered her face with her fingers. He smiled at her, and there was real humor in the lines of his smile. He sat beside her and after a moment released a short laugh.

"That was something," he said. "I've never seen anyone make the king and his entire council feel like utter fools."

"They listened?" she said.

"Oh, yes, thoroughly. You, my lady, have just stopped an unnecessary war." He looked down and swallowed. "May I beg your pardon? I've behaved so badly to you, and I've been aching to explain."

"Is this about the 'I can't love you as a man loves a woman' bit?"

Geric grimaced. "Ah-ha, yes, that's the very line. I, you see, I noticed that last day in the goose pasture that I'd begun to—feel—something about you that I shouldn't, as I was betrothed and all, and I thought it best if I just stopped seeing you altogether. I was feeling rather terrible for betraying your sentiments, besides having lied to you about who I was. But then when I saw you yesterday, well, maybe you can imagine that I haven't had a steady heartbeat since you walked into the throne room."

Just then, Ani could feel her own heartbeat pounding against her ribs.

"I wish I had known somehow who you were and set things right," said Geric, "and spared you the horrors of yesterday. When I walked in and saw that man holding you with a knife to your throat . . ."

He shut his eyes as though against the image. Ani had an impulse to kiss his eyelids but quickly spoke instead.

"How's your . . ." She pointed to his side.

Geric opened his eyes, looked to see what Ani was indicating, and put a hand over his side. "Bandaged. Pulsing with my heart like the wound is a living thing, but certainly healing. Thank you."

"I want to thank you for stepping in to save Talone," said Ani.

"He seems to be a noble man and a fine soldier."

"Yes, he's been more than good to me. It was a relief for us to find each other after the massacre and not feel alone."

"You spoke with fire about him there before my father, and he risked a lot to see you safe." He looked at her, and the clarity of his dark eyes struck her heart with a sensation of a wound touched. "Does he care for you?"

"I'm sure of it," she said. "He's been more than good to me."

A wrinkle formed between his eyes. "Is it possible that Talone might ask your hand, and that you might want to give it?"

"Oh, no, he won't, I mean, I don't. He's as dear as a father, and I'm the child he protects, that's all."

"Oh," said Geric with a soft exhale. He examined the hilt of his sword, and his lips appeared to fight a smile. "We've been friends, Isi, and I feel I know you, but I don't want to presume anything anymore. This marriage was arranged without your consent, and if you have any hesitation about me, I will understand."

She took his hand. "When Ungolad fought you, it was horrible, Geric, and I thought, if he won, I wouldn't be able to bear it. I've missed you these months."

Geric breathed out as though he had been holding his breath, and he grinned with relief. Ani could not help grinning back, and they laughed lightly at nothing. He looked down at her hand and turned it palm up, running his fingers

over the creases and merging his fingers with hers. She leaned
her head against his shoulder with a familiarity that surprised her.

"You were amazing in there," said Geric. "You were—I
can scarcely believe how lucky I am. Growing up, I tried to
imagine what my mysterious betrothed princess would be
like, and I'd think, I hope she's clever, and I hope we have
things to say to each other, and I wouldn't cry if she was a
beauty as well. But I never imagined that I could marry a girl
who was all those things and knew Bayern's needs better than
I, who would truly be a partner on the throne. What this
kingdom sorely misses is a queen, and you are exactly what
they, and I, what we all need."

Her stomach tingled pleasantly. "Am I really?"

"You are everything and more, Isi."

"I'd like to be."

"Then," said Geric, his brow wrinkling, his voice anxious
and tender, "will you have me?"

"Yes." She smiled and laughed. "Yes, of course, yes."

He smiled slowly and broadly. "I say good. Good and
good. I was afraid I'd lost you forever after I wrote you that
note, and when I saw you at wintermoon, well, you know I
felt as though I'd had a dart thrown into my heart. I think
that Selia could tell, and she didn't like it one bit."

"Nor did I."

"So much has happened since we last spoke, what with
secret identities and a horde of animal-keepers shouting

your name, and what about that, that wind? You've a story I want to hear, goose girl."

"And you have things to tell me, Sir Guard."

"Well then, the first thing I would like to tell you, my lady, and I'd better tell it quickly because my heart is likely to break through my rib cage any moment, the first thing is that I love you. And the second thing is that, as much as I honor your former profession, I don't think your geese care much for your betrothed, and I hope they hadn't any plans on sharing our bed."

"Oh, but think what use they'd be," said Ani. "They'd encourage snooping maids to stay away from our bedroom, and on particularly busy days we could stick hats on them and let them receive some of our supplicants."

"Ah, yes, excellent point."

He smiled, and all signs of worry disappeared from his face. With happy enthusiasm, he stood up, his hand on his sword hilt, and shouted, "I, Geric-Sinath of Gerhard, declare right now that you're beautiful and you're perfect and I'll slay any man who tries to take you from my side. Goose girl, may I kiss you?"

She answered by standing and kissing him first and held his cheeks and closed her eyes and felt sure as bones and deep as blood that she had found her place.

Their embrace was interrupted by a young page clearing his throat. Ani looked down, but Geric did not seem embarrassed at all.

"Are they ready?" he said as though he had been expecting the interruption.

The pageboy nodded and bade them follow, taking two steps for their every one like a short-legged dog. He stopped before the door to the dining hall, his hand gesturing that they should enter. Geric was grinning madly.

"What is it?" said Ani.

"You'll see."

The doors opened.

"Welcome, daughter," said the king.

There was a kind of silence in the room because no one spoke, but a silence that betrayed the truth of one hundred hearts beating, one hundred mouths breathing, one hundred hands that held themselves, fisted, before their chests. The king's guard and the captains of the royal army and of every hundred-band stood at attention, their fists showing loyalty, their heads inclined respectfully.

"Captains," said Geric, "Princess Anidori-Kiladra Talianna Isilee, first daughter of Kildenree, she who ended our war before the javelin was thrown."

The captains banged their javelins against the ground.

"Oh, my," said Ani.

"We're supposed to walk among them," said Geric.

She placed her hand on his forearm and they walked past the lines, and Ani noticed with relief that there were mostly the signs of gratitude in their eyes and not the bitterness she had feared for this girl who had stopped their war.

In the center of the room, between two groups of worn and experienced captains of hundred-bands, stood a strange group of soldiers. They held javelins firmly in right hands, and on their arms hung freshly painted shields bearing the images of two trees—one green and one yellow.

They looked forward with proud and stoic expressions, but Finn smiled so broadly that his lips slid tight to show his teeth, and he looked at Ani and grinned wider. Razo stared ahead, his eyes unblinking, and cried freely. Offo was solemn, but his javelin trembled in his hand. Ratger stood by also, his palace guard tunic worn openly, and Conrad's calmness was betrayed by a slim smile. Enna and the other girls stood at their far end, each holding a larger shield in both hands.

"We're debating between calling ourselves the Forest-band or the yellow-band," said Enna. "What do you think?"

Geric and Ani spoke over each other. "The yellow-band, definitely," he said.

"Oh, the Forest-band, for pity's sake," she said.

They strolled through the rows of captains and bade them relax, and the presentation became a supper. Talone left his sickbed to sit at Ani's right for a while, and they drank to his health. After a drink he showed some vigor and related the story of when he had first met Ani, a child asleep on the shore of the swan pond who had tried to run away.

The captains ate and laughed and traded stories with Geric, so content as to never leave. One taught Razo how to throw a javelin straight and far, one taught Enna the song of a tale she had never heard. Ani tried to teach them all how to greet several different species of birds in their own tongue, and they clicked and trumpeted and moaned in their throats until they thought they could never stop laughing. The hours stretched out and the kitchen-hands brought new trays of hot food and then, at Geric's insistence, the kitchen-hands stayed and ate as well. The light from the windows faded to the pulsing blue of evening, and no one left.

There was no hurry. There would be time for the captains to announce to their troops the end of the unfought war and bid them all home with their wives. There would be time to return to the workers' settlements in the city and see them all with javelins and shields, and to see Talone, healed and well, commanding a hundred-band of the king's own. And a wedding in the market-square in the Thumbprint of the Gods where the javelin dancers came at festivals and where all could witness, noble and city-dweller and Forest dweller alike, the marriage of their future king and queen. Gilsa, too, there and at last rewarded.

There would be time to take down the white horse head from the west gate and have a burial, belated and quiet, Falada laid to rest under the beech tree by the goose pond, and over that spot a monument laid, a carving in white stone of a colt and a girl seemingly too young for such adventures so far from home.

And there would be time to spend in the stables in late

spring, befriending the loose-gaited stable-master and aiding a mare to foal. And when the colt, nothing but a bundle of legs and wet fur as black as Enna's hair, fell into her arms, Ani might hear a name.

The End